ACKNOWLEDGMENTS

I consider myself very lucky that I have pretty much the same group of people to thank every time out. It means my support structure is sound and doing a terrific job. So, once again, here goes:

A huge, sincere thank you for everything you've done and continue to do to Larry Mirkin, Beverley Slopen, Tracy Fisher, Elizabeth Reed, Emily Bestler, Sarah Branham, Judith Curr, Laura Stern, Louise Burke, David Brown, Carole Schwindeller, Brad Martin, Maya Mavjee, Kristin Cochrane, Val Gow, Adria Iwasutiak, and all the other wonderful people at the William Morris Agency, Atria Books in the United States, and Doubleday in Canada who work so hard to make my books a success. Thank you to all my foreign publishers and translators and also to the best website designer and operator in the world, Corinne Assayag.

A special thank you to software developer and personal trainer Michael Raphael for not only whipping me into shape twice a week but for providing me with the killer workout routine described in this book.

On the home front, thanks to Aurora Mendoza for keeping me well fed and looked after. I also want to thank my husband, Warren, for his continuing encouragement and support, and for not getting his nose out of joint when I name the bad guy after him. Thank you to my daughter, Shannon, for (a) being the beautiful, talented daughter she is, and (b) for managing my Twitter and Facebook sites. Thank you to my other beautiful and talented daughter, Annie, and her husband, Courtney, who will have made me a first-time grandmother by the time you read this. I'm so excited and grateful.

And lastly, as always, to you, the readers, who make everything worthwhile.

JOY FIELDING

THE WILD ZONE

POCKET BOOKS
LONDON • SYDNEY • NEW YORK • TORONTO

First published in the USA by Atria Books, 2010
A division of Simon and Schuster, Inc.
First published in Great Britain by Simon & Schuster UK Ltd, 2010
This edition published by Pocket Books, 2010
An imprint of Simon & Schuster UK Ltd
A CBS COMPANY

1 3 5 7 9 10 8 6 4 2

Simon & Schuster UK Ltd
1st Floor
222 Gray's Inn Road
London
WC1X 8HB

www.simonandschuster.co.uk

Simon & Schuster Australia
Sydney

A CIP catalogue record for this book
is available from the British Library

ISBN 978-1-84739-363-0

Printed in the UK by Cox & Wyman, Reading, Berkshire RG1 8EX

To Rod and Bessie

THE WILD ZONE

ONE

THIS IS HOW IT starts.

With a joke.

"So, a man walks into a bar," Jeff began, already chuckling. "He sees another man sitting there, nursing a drink and a glum expression. On the bar in front of him is a bottle of whiskey and a tiny little man, no more than a foot high, playing an equally tiny little piano. 'What's going on?' the first man asks. 'Have a drink,' offers the second. The first man grabs the bottle and is about to pour himself a drink when suddenly there is a large puff of smoke and a genie emerges from the bottle. 'Make a wish,' the genie instructs him. 'Anything you desire, you shall have.' 'That's easy,' the man says. 'I want ten million bucks.' The genie nods and disappears in another cloud of smoke. Instantly, the bar is filled with millions and millions of loud, quacking ducks.

'What the hell is this?' the man demands angrily. 'Are you deaf? I said *bucks,* you idiot. Not *ducks.*' He looks imploringly at the man beside him. The man shrugs, nodding sadly toward the tiny piano player on the bar. 'What? You think I wished for a twelve-inch pianist?'"

A slight pause followed by an explosion of laughter punctuated the joke's conclusion, the laughter neatly summing up the personalities of the three men relaxing at the crowded bar. Jeff, at thirty-two, the oldest of the three, laughed the loudest. The laugh, like the man himself, was almost too big for the small room, dwarfing the loud rock music emanating from the old-fashioned jukebox near the front door and reverberating across the shiny black marble surface of the long bar, where it threatened to overturn delicate glasses and crack the large, bottle-lined mirror behind it. His friend Tom's laugh was almost as loud, and although it lacked Jeff's resonance and easy command, it made up for these shortcomings by lasting longer and containing an assortment of decorative trills. "Good one," Tom managed to croak out between a succession of dying snorts and chuckles. "That was a good one."

The third man's laughter was more restrained, although no less genuine, his admiring smile stretching from the natural, almost girlish, pout of his lips into his large brown eyes. Will had heard the joke before, maybe five years ago, in fact, when he was still a nervous undergraduate at Princeton, but he would never tell that to Jeff. Besides, Jeff had told it better. His brother did most things better than other people, Will was thinking as he signaled Kristin for another round of drinks. Kristin smiled and tossed her long, straight blond hair from one shoulder to the other, the way he'd noted the sun-kissed women of South Beach always seemed to be doing. Will wondered idly if this habit was particular to Miami or endemic to southern climes in general. He didn't remember the young women of New Jersey tossing their hair with such frequency and authority. But then, maybe he'd just been too busy, or too shy, to notice.

Will watched as Kristin poured Miller draft into three tall glasses and expertly slid them in single file along the bar's smooth surface, bending forward just enough to let the other men gathered around have a quick peek down her V-neck, leopard-print blouse. They always tipped more when you gave them a flash of flesh, she'd confided the other night, claiming to make as much as three hundred dollars a night in tips. Not bad for a bar as small as the Wild Zone, which comfortably seated only forty people and had room for maybe another thirty at the always busy bar.

YOU HAVE ENTERED THE WILD ZONE, an orange neon sign flashed provocatively above the mirror. PROCEED AT YOUR OWN RISK.

The bar's owner had seen a similar sign along the side of a Florida highway and decided the Wild Zone would be the perfect name for the upscale bar he was planning to open on Ocean Drive. His instincts had proved correct. The Wild Zone had opened its heavy steel doors in October, just in time for Miami's busy winter season, and it was still going strong eight months later, despite the oppressive heat and the departure of most tourists. Will loved the name, with its accompanying echoes of danger and irresponsibility. It made him feel vaguely reckless just being here. He smiled at his brother, silently thanking him for letting him tag along.

If Jeff saw his brother's smile, he didn't acknowledge it. Instead he reached behind him and grabbed his fresh beer. "So what would you clowns wish for if a genie offered to grant you one wish? And it can't be anything sucky, like world peace or an end to hunger," he added. "It has to be personal. Selfish."

"Like wishing for a twelve-inch penis," Tom said, louder than Will thought necessary. Several of the men standing in their immediate vicinity swiveled in their direction, although they pretended not to be listening.

"Already got one of those," Jeff said, downing half his beer in one long gulp and smiling at a redhead at the far end of the bar.

"It's true," Tom acknowledged with a laugh. "I've seen him in the shower."

"I might ask for a few extra inches for you though," Jeff said, and Tom laughed again, although not quite so loud. "How about you, little brother? You in need of any magical intervention?"

"I'm doing just fine, thank you." Despite the frigid air-conditioning, Will was beginning to sweat beneath his blue button-down shirt, and he focused on a large green neon alligator on the far brick wall to keep from blushing.

"Aw, I'm not embarrassing you, am I?" Jeff teased. "Shit, man. The kid's got a PhD in philosophy from Harvard, and he blushes like a little girl."

"It's Princeton," Will corrected. "And I still haven't finished my dissertation." He felt the blush creep from his cheeks toward his forehead and was glad the room was as dimly lit as it was. I should have finished that stupid dissertation by now, he was thinking.

"Knock it off, Jeff," Kristin advised him from behind the bar. "Don't pay any attention to him, Will. He's just being his usual obnoxious self."

"You trying to tell me that size doesn't matter?" Jeff asked.

"I'm telling you that penises are way overrated," Kristin answered.

A nearby woman laughed. "Ain't that the truth," she said into her glass.

"Well, you ought to know," Jeff said to Kristin. "Hey, Will. Did I tell you about the time Kristin and I had a three-way?"

Will looked away, his eyes skirting the dark oak planks of the floor and sweeping across the far wall without focusing, eventually settling on a large color photograph of a lion attacking a gazelle. He'd never been comfortable with the sort of sex-charged banter Jeff and his friends seemed to excel at. He had to try harder to fit in, he decided. He had to relax. Wasn't that the reason he'd come to South Beach in the first place—to get away from the stress of academic life, to get out in the real world, to reconnect with the older brother he hadn't seen in years? "Don't think you ever mentioned it," he said, forcing a laugh from his throat and wishing he didn't feel as titillated as he did.

"She was a real looker, wasn't she, Krissie?" Jeff asked. "What was her name again? Do you remember?"

"I think it was Heather," Kristin answered easily, hands on the sides of her short, tight black skirt. If she was embarrassed, she gave no sign of it. "You ready for another beer?"

"I'll take whatever you're willing to dish out."

Kristin smiled, a knowing little half grin that played with the corners of her bow-shaped mouth, and tossed her hair from her right shoulder to her left. "Another round of Miller draft coming right up."

"That's my girl." Once again Jeff's muscular laugh filled the room.

A young woman pushed her way through the men and women standing three-deep at the bar. She was in her late twenties, of average height, a little on the thin side, with shoulder-length dark hair that fell across her face, making it difficult to discern her features. She wore black pants and an expensive-looking white shirt. Will thought it was probably silk. "Can I get a pomegranate martini?"

"Coming right up," Kristin said.

"Take your time." The young woman tucked a strand of hair behind her left ear, revealing a delicate pearl earring and a profile that was soft and pleasing. "I'm sitting over there." She pointed toward an empty table in the corner, underneath a watercolor of a herd of charging elephants.

"What the hell's a pomegranate martini?" Tom asked.

"Sounds revolting," Jeff said.

"They're actually quite good." Kristin removed Jeff's empty beer glass and replaced it with a full one.

"That so? Okay, then, let's give 'em a try." Jeff made a circle in the air with his fingers, indicating his request included Tom and Will. "Ten bucks each to whoever finishes his pomegranate martini first. No gagging allowed."

"You're on," Tom agreed quickly.

"You're crazy," Will said.

In response, Jeff slapped a ten-dollar bill on the bar. It was joined seconds later by a matching one from Tom. Both men turned expectantly toward Will.

"Fine," he said, reaching into the side pocket of his gray slacks and extricating a couple of fives.

Kristin watched them out of the corner of her eye as she carried the pomegranate martini to the woman sitting at the small table in the far corner. Of the three men, Jeff, dressed from head to toe in his signature black, was easily the best looking, with his finely honed features and wavy blond hair, hair she suspected he secretly highlighted, although she'd never ask. Jeff had a quick temper, and you never knew what was going to set him off. Unlike Tom, she thought, shifting her gaze to the skinny, dark-haired man wearing blue jeans and a checkered shirt who stood to Jeff's immediate right. *Everything* set him off. Six feet, two inches of barely contained fury, she thought, wondering how his wife stood it. "It's Afghanistan," Lainey had confided just the other week, as Jeff was regaling the bar's patrons with the story of how Tom, enraged by an umpire's bad call, had pulled a gun from the waistband of his jeans and put a bullet through his brand-new plasma TV, a TV he couldn't afford and still hadn't fully paid for. "Ever since he got back . . . ," she'd whispered under the waves of laughter that accompanied the story, leaving the thought unfinished. It didn't seem to matter that Tom had been home for the better part of five years.

Jeff and Tom had been best friends since high school, the two men enlisting in the army together, serving several tours of duty in Afghanistan. Jeff had come home a hero; Tom had come back disgraced, having been dishonorably discharged for an unprovoked assault on an innocent civilian. That was all she really knew about their time over there, Kristin realized. Neither Jeff nor Tom would talk about it.

She deposited the rose-pink martini on the round wooden table in front of the dark-haired young woman, casually studying her flawless, if pale, complexion. Was that a bruise on her chin?

The woman handed her a rumpled twenty-dollar bill. "Keep the change," she said quietly, turning away before Kristin could thank her.

Kristin quickly pocketed the money and returned to the bar, the ankle straps of her high-heeled silver sandals chafing against her bare skin. The men were now placing bets on who could balance a peanut on his nose the longest. Tom should win that one, hands down, she thought. His nose boasted a natural ridge at its tip that the others lacked. Jeff's nose was narrow and straight, as handsomely chiseled as the rest of him, while Will's was wider and slightly crooked, which only added to his air of wounded vulnerability. Why so wounded? she wondered, deciding he probably took after his mother.

Jeff, on the other hand, looked exactly like his father. She knew that because she'd stumbled across an old photograph of the two of them when she was cleaning out a bedroom drawer, just after she'd moved in, about a year ago. "Who's this?" she'd asked, hearing Jeff come up behind her and pointing at the picture of a rugged-looking man with wavy hair and a cocky grin, his large forearm resting heavily on the shoulder of a solemn-faced young boy.

Jeff had snatched it from her hand and returned it to the drawer. "What are you doing?"

"Just trying to make room for some of my things," she'd said, purposely ignoring the tone in his voice that warned her to back off. "Is that you and your dad?"

"Yeah."

"Thought so. You look just like him."

"That's what my mother always said." With that, he'd slammed the drawer closed and left the room.

"Ha, ha–I win!" shouted Tom now, raising his fist in the air in triumph as the peanut Jeff had been balancing on his nose dribbled past his mouth and chin and dropped to the floor.

"Hey, Kristin," Jeff said, his voice just tight enough to reveal how much he hated losing, even at something as insignificant as this. "What's happening with those grenade martinis?"

"Pomegranate," Will corrected, then immediately wished he hadn't. A bolt of anger, like lightning, flashed through Jeff's eyes.

"What the hell is a pomegranate anyway?" Tom asked.

"It's a red fruit, hard shell, tons of seeds, lots of antioxidants," Kristin answered. "Supposedly very good for you." She deposited the first of the pale rose-colored martinis on the bar in front of them.

Jeff lifted the glass to his nose and sniffed at it suspiciously.

"What's an antioxidant?" Tom asked Will.

"Why are you asking him?" Jeff snapped. "He's a philosopher, not a scientist."

"Enjoy," Kristin said, placing the other two martinis on the counter.

Jeff held up his glass, waited for Tom and Will to do the same. "To the winner," he said. All three men promptly threw back their heads, gulping at the liquid as if gasping for air.

"Done," Jeff whooped, lowering his glass to the bar in triumph.

"Christ, that's awful stuff," said Tom with a grimace half a second later. "How do people drink this shit?"

"What'd you think, little brother?" Jeff asked as Will swallowed the last of his drink.

"Not half-bad," Will said. He liked it when Jeff referred to him as his little brother, even though, strictly speaking, they were only half brothers. Same father, different mothers.

"Not half-good either," Jeff was saying now, with a wink at no one in particular.

"*She* seems to be enjoying it." Tom nodded toward the brunette in the corner.

"Makes you wonder what else she enjoys," Jeff said.

Will found himself staring at the woman's sad eyes. He knew they were sad, even from this distance and in this light, because of the way she was leaning her head against the wall and looking off into space, her gaze aimless and unfocused. He realized that she was prettier than he'd first suspected, albeit in a conventional sort of way. Not strikingly beautiful like Kristin, with her emerald green eyes, a model's high cheekbones, and voluptuous figure. No, this woman's looks tilted more toward the ordinary. Pretty, for sure, but lacking sharpness. Her eyes were her only truly distinguishing feature. They were big and dark, probably a deep-water blue. She looks as if she has profound thoughts, Will was thinking as he watched a man approach her, experiencing an unexpected wave of relief when he saw her shake her head and turn him away. "What do you think her story is?" he heard himself ask out loud.

"Maybe she's the jilted lover of a British prince," posited Jeff, downing what was left of his beer. "Or maybe she's a Russian spy."

Tom laughed. "Or maybe she's just a bored housewife looking for a little action on the side. Why? You interested?"

Was he? Will wondered. It had been a long time since he'd had any kind of girlfriend. Since Amy, he thought, shuddering at the memory of the way that had turned out. "Just curious," he heard himself say.

"Hey, Krissie," Jeff called out, leaning his elbows on the bar and beckoning Kristin toward him. "What can you tell me about the pomegranate lady?" He pointed with his square jaw toward the table in the corner.

"Not much. First time I saw her was a few days ago. She comes in, sits in the corner, orders pomegranate martinis, tips very well."

"Is she always alone?"

"Never noticed anyone with her. Why?"

Jeff shrugged playfully. "I was thinking maybe the three of us could get better acquainted. What do you say?"

Will found himself holding his breath.

"Sorry," he heard Kristin answer, and only then was he able to release the tight ball of air trapped in his lungs. "She's not really my type. But, hey, you go for it."

Jeff smiled, exposing the two glistening rows of perfect teeth that not even the dust of Afghanistan had been able to dull. "Is it any wonder I love this girl?" he asked his companions, both of whom nodded in wonderment, Tom wishing Lainey could be more like Kristin in that regard–hell, in every regard, if he was being honest–and Will pondering, not for the first time since his arrival ten days earlier, what was really going on in Kristin's head.

Not to mention his own.

Maybe Kristin was simply wise beyond her years, accepting Jeff for who he was, without trying to change him or pretend things were otherwise. Clearly, they had an arrangement they were comfortable with, even if he wasn't.

"I have an idea," Jeff was saying. "Let's have a bet."

"On what?" Tom asked.

"On who can be the first to get into Miss Pomegranate's panties."

"What?" Tom's guffaw shook the room.

"What are you talking about?" asked Will impatiently.

"A hundred bucks," Jeff said, laying two fifties on the countertop.

"What are you talking about?" Will asked again.

"It's simple. There's an attractive young woman sitting all by herself in the corner, just waiting for Prince Charming to hit on her."

"I think that might be a contradiction in terms," Kristin said.

"Maybe all she wants is to be left alone," Will offered.

"What woman comes to a place like the Wild Zone by herself hoping to be left alone?"

Will had to admit Jeff's question made sense.

"So, we go over there, we chat her up, we see which one of us she lets take her home. A hundred bucks says it's me."

"You're on." Tom fished inside his pocket, eventually coming up with two twenties and a pile of ones. "I'm good for the rest," he said sheepishly.

"Speaking of home," Kristin interrupted, looking directly at Tom, "shouldn't you be heading back there? You don't want a repeat of last time, do you?"

In truth, Kristin was the one who didn't want a repeat of last time. Lainey was as formidable a force as her husband when she was angry, and she wasn't too proud to wake up half the city when it came to ferreting out her errant husband's whereabouts.

"Lainey's got nothing to worry about tonight," Jeff said confidently. "Miss Pomegranate's not going to be interested in his bony ass." He turned toward Will. "You in?"

"I don't think so."

"Oh, come on. Don't be a spoilsport. What's the matter? Afraid you'll lose?"

Will glanced back at the woman, who was still staring off into space, although he noticed she'd finished her drink. Why hadn't he just told his brother he was interested? *Was* he interested? And was Jeff right? Was he afraid of losing? "Do you accept credit cards?"

Jeff laughed and slapped him on the shoulder. "Spoken like a true Rydell. Daddy would be very proud."

"How are we going to do this exactly?" Tom asked, bristling at all this newfound brotherly camaraderie. During the almost two decades he and Jeff had been friends, Will had been nothing but a thorn in his brother's side. He wasn't even a real brother, for shit's sake, just a half brother who was as unwanted as he was unloved. Jeff had had nothing to do with him, hadn't spoken to or about him in years. And then, ten days ago, Will showed up on his doorstep out of the blue, and all of a sudden it's "little brother" this and "little brother" that, and it was enough to make you puke. Tom gave Will his broadest smile, wishing "little brother" would pack his bags and go back to Princeton. "I mean, we don't want it to look like we're ambushing her."

"Who said anything about an ambush? We just go over there, thank her for introducing us to the pleasures of vodka-laced antioxidants, and offer to buy her another."

"I have a better idea," offered Kristin. "Why don't I go over, chat her up for a few minutes, and try to feel her out, see if she's interested."

"Find out her name anyway," Will said, trying to think of a way to extricate himself from the situation without embarrassing himself or alienating his brother.

"How much do you want to bet her name starts with a J?" Tom asked.

"Five dollars says it doesn't," Jeff said.

"More names start with J than any other letter."

"There are still twenty-five more letters in the alphabet," Will said. "I'm with Jeff on this one."

"Of course you are," Tom said curtly.

"Okay, guys, I'm on my way," Kristin announced, returning to their side of the bar. "Anything you want me to say to the lady on your behalf?"

"Maybe we shouldn't bother her," Will said. "She looks like she has a lot on her mind."

"Tell her I'll give her something to think about," Jeff said, giving Kristin's backside a playful tap to send her on her way. All three men followed her exaggerated wiggle with their eyes as she sashayed between tables toward the far corner of the room.

Will watched Kristin retrieve the empty glass from the woman's table, the two women falling into conversation as easily and casually as if they were lifelong friends. He watched Miss Pomegranate suddenly swivel in their direction, her head tilting provocatively to one side, a slow smile spreading across her face as Kristin spoke. "You see those three guys at the end of the bar?" he imagined Kristin telling her. "The good-looking one in black, the skinny, angry-looking one beside him, the sensitive-looking one in the blue button-down shirt? Pick one. Any one. He's yours for the asking."

"She's coming back," Jeff said as, moments later, Kristin left the woman's side and began her slow walk back to the bar, the three men swaying forward in unison to greet her.

"Her name's Suzy," she announced without stopping.

"That's another five you owe me," Jeff told Tom.

"That's it?" Tom asked Kristin. "You were over there all that time, and that's all you got?"

"She moved here from Fort Myers a couple of months ago." Kristin returned to her side of the bar. "Oh, yeah. I almost forgot," she said with a big smile in Will's direction. "She picked you."

TWO

"WHAT?" WILL WAS SURE he'd misunderstood. Kristin wasn't really looking at him. Her smile was clearly meant for Jeff. It was simply a case of wishful thinking on his part.

"You're kidding me, right?" Jeff said, equally incredulous.

"Well, well," Tom snickered. "Looks like 'little brother' is the night's big winner."

"You're sure she picked Will?" Jeff said, as if needing verbal confirmation.

Kristin shrugged. "Apparently she's always had a soft spot for men in button-down shirts."

Tom laughed, enjoying the evening's unexpected turn of events. Not that he liked losing any more than Jeff did. Especially to a smug little twerp like Will. "The Chosen One," Jeff used to call him. Well, he'd been chosen all right.

"What are you laughing about?" Jeff snapped. "You just lost a hundred bucks, you moron."

"So did you. Besides, it's not your wallet that's wounded. It's your ego." Tom laughed again. "Don't worry. It happens to the best of us." It would do Jeff good to get a taste of the rejection he'd been dealing with for most of his life, Tom was thinking. A little humility never hurt anyone.

Jeff said nothing, letting his scowl speak for him.

"Anyway," Tom continued, finishing off his beer, "we haven't lost a cent until he seals the deal."

Jeff's shoulders instantly relaxed, shaking off his rejection as if it were an unwanted coat. His smile returned. "That's right, little brother," he said, patting Will's shoulder with perhaps a touch too much vigor. "The night is young. A lot remains to be done. Your test is just beginning."

Will felt his mouth go dry and his palms grow moist. He'd always hated tests. And this time it wasn't some stuffy old professor judging his worth. It was his beloved older brother. A brother he'd spent years trying–and failing–to impress. "What am I supposed to do?" he whispered, not sure whether it would be better to pass this particular test or to fail.

"Can't help you there, little brother. You're on your own."

"You could fuck her on the table right in front of us," Tom offered with a smirk.

"Why don't you just take her this," Kristin said, a freshly mixed pomegranate martini materializing in her hand.

Will took the drink from her fingers, sheer willpower steadying his hand. It was bad enough that Jeff and Tom would be watching his every move. He wouldn't give them the satisfaction of seeing his hands tremble. He took a deep breath, forced a smile onto his face, then swiveled around on his heels, pushing one foot in front of the other, like a toddler learning to walk.

"Be gentle," Tom called after him.

What's the matter with you? Will was thinking, feeling every eye in the place trailing after him as he crossed the room. It wasn't as if he'd never done this before. He'd dated lots of girls, was hardly a virgin, although truthfully, there hadn't been that many girls, he was forced to admit. And none at all since Amy. Shit, why was he thinking of her now? He pushed her out of his head, his right hand shooting forward involuntarily, pink fluid spilling out over the top of the glass and trickling down his fingers.

Suzy watched his approach from her seat at the table, her eyes sparkling playfully as he drew nearer. Even now Will was convinced there'd been a mistake. It was Jeff she'd meant for Kristin to send over. "What are you doing here?" he could almost hear her say.

"Smile, sucker," she said instead. "Pull up a chair."

Will hesitated, although only for an instant, before doing as he'd been told—pulling up the nearest chair and grinning like an idiot as he sank into it. He deposited her drink on the table, pushed it toward her. "For you."

"Thank you. You're not having anything?"

Will realized he'd left his beer at the bar. No way he was going back there to get it. "I'm Will Rydell," he said. Not exactly clever, he knew. No doubt Jeff would have come up with something more provocative. Hell, even Tom would have managed something snappier than his name.

"Suzy Bigelow." She leaned forward, as if she had something important to impart, and so he did the same. "Shall we cut right to the chase?"

"Okay," Will said, but inside he was thinking, What chase? What is she talking about? He was beginning to feel as if he'd walked into a movie ten minutes after it started, and already he was missing a vital piece of information.

"What's the wager?" she asked.

"What?"

"I understand you guys have some kind of bet going on," she said, luminous blue eyes widening, waiting for him to confirm what she obviously already knew.

"What exactly did Kristin tell you?"

"The waitress? Not much."

"Actually, she's the bartender." Will bit down on his tongue. What was the matter with him? Why bother to correct her? He was going to blow this if he wasn't careful. He knew it. "What did she say?"

"That the three of you had some kind of bet going, and that I could make your night if I picked you."

Will felt a sinking sensation in the pit of his stomach. What was she saying—that Kristin had set this whole thing up? That he hadn't actually won anything?

"How much do you collect if we walk out of here together?"

"Two hundred bucks," Will admitted sheepishly.

She looked impressed. "Wow. Not half-bad."

"I'm sorry. We weren't trying to insult you."

"Who said I was insulted? That's a lot of money."

"I can leave if you'd like."

"I wouldn't have asked you to come over if I wanted you to leave."

Now Will was more confused than ever. What is it with women? he wondered. Are they genetically incapable of carrying on a straightforward conversation?

"I just want to set the record straight right off the top," she continued. "I'm not going to sleep with you, if that's what you were thinking, so you can get that particular thought right out of your head."

"Consider it gone," he said, an unexpected jolt of disappointment shooting through his body.

"However, I'm more than happy to sit here and have a few drinks with you. Then we walk out of here together, maybe go for a stroll along the beach, and go our separate ways. How's that sound to you?"

"Sounds fair enough," Will said. What he thought was, Sounds like crap. But what the hell, a few drinks were better than nothing. Maybe she'd change her mind.

"I'm not going to change my mind," she said, as if reading his. "But feel free to tell your buddies anything you like."

"I'm not one to kiss and tell. Or *not* kiss and tell," he added, and she laughed, for which he felt inordinately grateful.

"You *are* kind of cute," she said. "Maybe I *will* sleep with you. Just kidding," she added quickly. "So, what's the story? You don't drink?"

"No, I do. Of course I do. A Miller draft," he said to the passing waitress. He motioned toward Suzy's martini. "I understand pomegranates are supposed to be good for you."

"Especially when you combine them with vodka," Suzy said, laughing as she raised the glass to her lips.

Will decided he liked the sound of her laugh–it was surprisingly full and throaty.

"I think good health is a combination of good luck and good genes, more than anything else," she said.

"Biology is destiny," Will concurred.

"What?"

"I agree," Will amended quickly.

Suzy smiled. "So, what do you do?"

"Nothing."

Her smile widened, a pair of deep dimples bracketing her small mouth. Blue eyes crinkled with amusement. "Nothing?"

"Well, no, not nothing exactly."

"Not nothing exactly or exactly nothing?" she teased.

"I'm sounding like a complete jerk, aren't I?" Will asked, voicing his thoughts out loud. What the hell–she'd already told him she wasn't going to sleep with him. What did he have to lose?

"Why don't you take a few deep breaths," she told him. "You've already won your bet. You know nothing's going to happen between us, so you don't have to work so hard to impress me. You can just relax and have a good time."

Again, Will did as he was told, taking a few deep breaths and leaning back in his chair. Relaxing was another matter entirely. When was the last time he'd been able to relax, as far as women were concerned? In fact, it seemed to him that the words "relax" and "women" didn't belong in the same sentence together.

"So, I'll ask the question again. What do you do–when you're not doing nothing, that is?"

He could make up anything, Will realized. Tell her he was an airline pilot or a financial adviser, something either so straightforward he wouldn't have to explain it, or something so complicated she wouldn't want him to. "I'm a student," he said, opting for the truth. *I'm Will Rydell. I'm a student.* No doubt about it–he was on a roll.

"Really? What are you studying?"

"Philosophy."

"Which I guess explains the 'biology is destiny' observation," she remarked.

His turn to smile. So, she'd understood him after all. "Actually, I'm working on my PhD."

"Now I really *am* impressed. Where? The University of Miami?"

"Princeton."

"Wow."

"Does that mean you'll reconsider sleeping with me?" he asked.

"Not a chance."

"Didn't think so."

Again, she laughed. Again the lovely dimples that creased her pale skin. "But that was cute. You get points for that."

"Thank you."

"So seriously, you're a student?"

"Seriously, I'm a very serious student," he said. "Or I *was*. I'm taking a bit of a break."

"For the summer, you mean?"

"I'm not sure how long."

"Sounds like that's not all you're not sure of."

Will tried to make his mind a blank. The woman sitting across from him had an uncanny knack for being able to read his thoughts. He glanced toward the bar, saw Jeff staring back at him through hooded eyes as Tom leaned over to whisper something in his ear.

"Sorry. I didn't mean to be presumptuous," Suzy said.

"You weren't."

"You're a bit of a conundrum, aren't you?"

"A conundrum, no less." Will laughed, flattered in spite of himself. "My mother always said I was an open book." The waitress approached with his beer.

"Mothers don't always know their children very well."

Will lifted his glass. Clicked it against hers. "I'll drink to that."

They each took a sip, her knuckles accidentally brushing against his as they lowered their glasses to the table. A sudden surge of electricity charged through Will's fingers, and his hands shook. He lowered them to his lap to keep her from noticing.

"So, what brings you down to Miami?" she asked.

"I'm visiting my brother."

"That's nice. Is he here tonight?" She glanced toward the bar.

Will nodded.

"Was he part of the bet?"

"The instigator," Will allowed.

Suzy studied the crowd milling around the bar. "Let me guess. The good-looking one in the black shirt?"

"That's him." Of course she'd notice Jeff, Will thought, trying not to feel jealous. Of course she'd think he was handsome. How could she not? Without Kristin's prompting, she'd no doubt have selected him. "Actually, we're only half brothers. That's why we don't look very much alike."

"Oh, I think I see a family resemblance," she said, her eyes lingering on Jeff's profile perhaps a beat too long.

"I don't have his muscles," Will said, acknowledging the obvious.

"And I'm betting he doesn't have your brains," she countered.

Will felt a flush of pride.

"What does he do, your brother?"

Will closed his eyes, his pride collapsing around him like a broken umbrella. What was it they said—pride goeth before a fall? "Regretting your choice already?" he asked, then immediately wished he hadn't. "Sorry, that must have sounded incredibly petulant."

" 'Incredibly petulant'?" she repeated. "That's quite a mouthful."

"I'm sorry," Will said again.

"I was just trying to make conversation, Will. You seemed a little uncomfortable talking about yourself."

"My brother's a personal trainer," Will said, answering her earlier question.

Suzy nodded, her eyes slowly drifting back toward Jeff, as if pulled there by a magnet.

"He lives with the bartender," Will added.

"I assume we're talking about the gorgeous blond and not the fat guy with the gold chains."

Will laughed. "Actually, that's the owner."

"They make a very attractive couple," Suzy said. "Your brother and the bartender."

"Yeah, they do."

"She seems very nice."

"She is."

The conversation came to a halt. Suzy returned her attention to the drink in her hand.

"Kristin said you just moved here from Fort Myers," Will said after several uncomfortable seconds.

"Kristin?"

"Jeff's girlfriend."

"Jeff?"

"My brother," Will qualified. What was the matter with him? Had he always been so totally inept with women? No wonder Amy had dumped him.

"The bartender and the bodybuilder," Suzy stated.

"Personal trainer," Will said, then almost kicked himself. Was he a *complete* idiot? "So what prompted the move from Fort Myers?" he asked.

"Have you ever been there?" she asked, as if this was answer enough.

"No."

"I guess it's not a bad place. The people are certainly nice enough. It was just time for a change." She shrugged, took another sip of her martini.

"A change from what?"

"Everything."

"What did you do in Fort Myers?"

"Worked in a bank. I was an assistant manager."

"Sounds interesting."

"Let's say it was *exactly* as interesting as it sounds."

Will laughed, felt his body genuinely beginning to relax, as if he'd released his belt a notch. "Did you get transferred here?"

"No. Believe me, the last thing I ever want to see is the inside of another bank. Unless, of course, I'm depositing money."

"So, where are you working now?" Will asked.

"I'm not. I'm kind of like you, I guess. Taking the summer off."

"And then what?"

"Haven't decided. You?"

"Me?"

"What happens when the summer's over?" she asked. "Must be a little crowded at your brother's."

All roads lead back to Jeff, Will thought. "A little. I don't know. Maybe I'll go back to school. Maybe I'll go to Europe. I've always wanted to see Germany."

"Why Germany?"

"My thesis–it's about this German philosopher. . . . Martin Heidegger."

"Don't think I've ever heard of him."

"Not too many people have. He writes about death and dying."

"Yeah, they kind of go together." She smiled. "Sounds a little depressing."

"People always say that. But it isn't really. I mean, death is a fact of life. We're all going to die sooner or later."

"They teach you that at Princeton? Because if they do, I'm sure as hell not going there."

Will laughed. "There's nothing to be afraid of."

"Are we talking about death now or Princeton?"

"Do you believe in God?" he asked, thinking of all the earnest undergraduate discussions he'd had on the subject, the arguments he'd had with Amy. . . .

Suzy shook her head. "No."

"You sound very sure."

"You seem surprised."

"I guess I am. Most people are more circumspect."

"Circumspect?"

"Cautious," he said, although he sensed she knew exactly what he meant. "Guarded. They hedge their bets, say they don't know, that they'd *like* to believe, or that they believe in some sort of a higher power, whether you want to call it God or a life force. . . ."

"I guess I've never been very good at circumspect." Her eyes drifted toward the large ceiling fan whirring overhead.

"You look like you have very deep thoughts," Will ventured.

Suzy laughed, her focus restored. "First time I've ever been accused of that."

"It was meant as a compliment."

"Then that's how I'll take it. You ever been married, Will?"

"No. You?"

"Yes. But let's not talk about that, okay?"

"Fine by me."

"Good." She took another sip of her drink. "What do you say I finish this, then we get out of here?"

"Whatever you want."

"My three favorite words."

"You're really very beautiful," he told her, surprising them both. Until this moment, he hadn't actually thought she was.

"No. I'm too skinny," she said. "I know it's all the rage, but I've always wanted curves. Like, what did you say her name was—Kristin?"

"Yeah, she's pretty hot."

"She doesn't mind about your brother . . . ?"

"What about him?" Hadn't he just told her she was beautiful? Why was she asking about Jeff again?

"Well, you said he instigated the bet. What if I'd picked him? She'd really have been okay with that?"

"I think they have a pretty open arrangement."

"Really." It was more statement than question.

"You finished that drink yet?" he asked, aware Suzy's eyes had drifted back toward Jeff and standing up to block her line of sight.

Suzy took one last gulp, then lowered her now-empty glass to the table. "All gone. Lead the way, Dr. Rydell."

Will tried not to enjoy the sound of that as he tucked a twenty-dollar bill beneath his beer glass and followed after Suzy as she zig-zagged her way through the tables toward the front door. He saw her acknowledge Jeff and Tom with a sly nod, then wave good-bye to Kristin as she walked past.

"Shit," he heard Tom mutter. "Can you believe that?"

Will waited for Jeff to say something, but there was only silence. When he reached the exit, he looked back, hoping for a thumbs-up from his brother. Instead Jeff stared right through him, as if he weren't there. He was still staring when Will turned and followed Suzy into the night.

THREE

"SHIT," TOM SAID AGAIN. "Did you see that stupid grin on his face? Like he just swallowed a goddamn canary. I'd like to bust that grin wide open, man." He banged his fist against the marble countertop.

"Leave it be," Jeff advised.

"You need something over there?" Kristin asked from the other end of the bar.

Jeff shook his head no.

"I mean, it's one thing to win the bet, man," Tom continued. "But you gotta be gracious about it. You can't go walking around like you're the Second Coming, for shit's sake. The goddamn cock of the walk."

Jeff almost laughed. What did Tom know about graciousness?

Although he was strangely grateful for Tom's anger. It spared him from feeling more of his own. "I think you're mixing too many metaphors there, Tommy boy."

"What the hell are you talking about? You trying to tell me you're not pissed?"

"Hey, what's done is done."

"Well, we don't exactly know that, do we?"

"What do you mean?"

"I mean, we don't know where they're going or what they're gonna do when they get there," Tom explained. "Assuming they do anything. Suzy Pomegranate could be giving little brother the kiss-off right now, and how are we gonna prove otherwise? We're just supposed to take his word that he scored?"

"You think he'd lie about it?"

"Wouldn't you?"

"Wouldn't have to," Jeff said.

"Yeah? Well, she didn't pick you, did she? So, I guess it's a mute point."

"I think you mean 'moot,'" Jeff corrected him.

"Whatever," Tom said, pushing himself away from the bar.

"Where are you going?"

"I'm gonna follow them."

"What? No. Get back here. Sit down. You're drunk."

"So what?"

"So, they'll see you, that's what."

"No, they won't. You don't think I learned anything in Afghanistan?"

Jeff said nothing. The truth was he didn't think Tom had learned a damn thing in Afghanistan.

"You coming?" Tom asked, shifting impatiently from one foot to the other.

Jeff shook his head. There was no way he was going to go chasing after his brother. No way he'd give the kid that kind of satisfaction. It was bad enough he'd been upstaged and humiliated by Will all through their formative years. But to have to relive it all over again now, here, on his own turf . . . I should never have let him back into my life, Jeff was thinking, signaling Kristin for another drink. He should have told Will to get lost when he'd first shown up on his doorstep ten days earlier. He should have slammed the door in his smiling, eager face.

Jeff recalled the joke he'd told earlier. "Make a wish," the genie said. "Anything you want, you shall have."

I want him gone, Jeff thought.

"Last chance," Tom said, backing toward the exit.

"Go for it," Jeff said quietly as Tom pushed open the door and vanished in an imaginary cloud of smoke.

THE WARM, HUMID air immediately wrapped itself around Tom's body, clinging to his skin like Saran Wrap, as his eyes searched the busy sidewalk for signs of Will and Suzy. Where were they? How could they have disappeared so quickly? He looked across the street toward the ocean he could hear but not see in the dark, except for the occasional crest of moonlit wave careening restlessly toward the shore. Where the hell could they have gone so fast?

It was several seconds before he spotted them. They were standing on the corner of Ocean Drive and Tenth Street, in the middle of a group of Friday-night revelers, waiting for the traffic light to change. He propelled himself toward them, his gait unsteady, his footing unsure. Maybe Jeff was right, he was thinking, stumbling over his own feet and almost falling into a group of giggling teenage girls in thigh-high skirts and five-inch heels. Maybe he *was* too drunk to go after them. Where the hell were they going anyway?

He watched Suzy suddenly grab hold of Will's sleeve to steady herself as she flipped off her sexy, black sling-back sandals. He saw Will's hand reach for hers as she let go, saw her ignore it and dart from his side, running across the street toward the ocean, seemingly oblivious to the steady stream of moving cars around her. When she got to the other side of the road, she stopped and turned around, waiting for Will as he waited for a break in the traffic. The ocean breeze whipped several strands of long brown hair into her face, and as she brushed them aside, her eyes penetrated the darkness, stopping directly on Tom. Had she recognized him? Tom wondered, ducking behind a middle-aged couple, both wearing long shorts and flip-flops, who were walking arm in arm. He felt the ground suddenly lurch beneath him, as if he'd been dropped on a moving sidewalk, and lifted both arms out to waist height to steady himself.

When he looked back again, Will and Suzy were gone.

"Shit," Tom swore, loud enough to draw a look of displeasure from several passersby, all of whom promptly picked up their pace, as if to put as much distance between them and Tom as they could. "Where the hell did you go now?" he demanded, stepping off the curb into the path of an approaching car.

The driver of the black Nissan screeched to a halt, honked his horn, and swore loudly as he lowered his front window to give Tom the finger.

Normally Tom would have sworn right back, maybe even jumped into the front seat beside the driver, given the asshole more than just his middle finger. But tonight he was on a mission, and he couldn't allow himself to be distracted. Distraction could be deadly. Tom knew that all it took was one second when you weren't paying attention. That's when you stepped on a buried land mine, and *bam!*—your legs went flying through the air, no longer attached to your body.

This was a stupid idea, he decided now as his shoes sank into the dry sand. Ever since he'd come back from that godforsaken country, he'd hated sand. Lainey was always after him to take the kids to the beach. But he never would. He'd seen enough sand to last a lifetime.

And now, look at him. Not only was he up to his ankles in the goddamn stuff, he was going to ruin his brand-new high-topped black sneakers that cost almost three hundred bucks, or *would* have, had he actually paid for them instead of just walking out of the store wearing them. Tom executed a slow 360-degree turn, trying to locate Will and Suzy in the dark. Where were they? Had Suzy seen him, then confided her suspicion that he was tailing them to Will? Were they watching him right now from behind one of the giant palms that lined the beach like sentries, laughing at his ineptitude and waiting to see what he'd do next?

Should he give them something to see?

Tom chuckled as he reached for the small handgun tucked behind the silver buckle of his heavy, black leather belt and concealed by his checkered shirt. Jeff would have freaked if he knew he was carrying, but what the hell? Contrary to public opinion, he didn't always do what Jeff told him to.

Tom had acquired four guns since returning from Afghanistan, none of them registered–two .44 Magnums, an H&R nine-shot .22, and an old Glock .23, which he rotated on a regular basis. His favorite was the .22, more a girl's weapon really, because it was small, easy to hide, and relatively lightweight, although it never ceased to amaze him how heavy the damn thing actually was. He'd given it to Lainey on their first anniversary. Of course, she'd refused to touch it. Guns were a disaster waiting to happen, she'd lectured. He hadn't argued. What was the point? Wasn't Lainey convinced she was right about everything?

Tom left the weapon tucked into his belt, raised an invisible gun into the air instead, pulled its imaginary trigger.

That was when he saw them again.

They were skipping along the water's edge about thirty yards down the beach, their bare toes playing hide-and-seek with the incoming waves. Tom quickly slipped off his sneakers, groaning as he felt the warm granules of sand worm their way between his toes.

"I can't believe it's still so warm out," he heard Will say, the wind effortlessly transporting his voice along the shore.

"Can't ever be too hot for me," came Suzy's reply.

Are they really talking about the weather? Tom wondered. What kind of morons do they admit to Princeton?

"It's kind of weird to think that there's a whole other world going on under there," Suzy remarked, stopping to peer out at the ocean, seemingly unaware of Tom lurking nearby.

"Kind of neat, too," Will said.

Jesus, Tom thought. This was pathetic.

Maybe Suzy thought so, too, Tom realized. Because she suddenly picked up her pace, her thin calves wobbling on the uneven ground. Will ran after her, forcing Tom to follow suit. Which was when Will abruptly stopped and turned around.

"Shit," Tom said, dropping his sneakers to the sand and reaching for his gun as Will walked briskly back toward him.

"Dropped my sock," Will called back to Suzy, falling to his knees and ferreting through the sand until he found it.

Suzy was laughing as Will returned to her side, holding the limp, sand-covered sock out in front of him as if it were a dead fish. "My hero," she said, still laughing.

I could have been her hero, Tom thought, deciding to go to Brooks Brothers the next morning and help himself to one of those preppy button-down shirts. He quickly retrieved his sneakers from the ground, slapping them against his sides to rid them of sand, and followed after them.

Will and Suzy continued along the beach for several more miles, mostly in silence, the waves chattering along beside them as they walked, Tom staying a discreet distance behind. Luckily, there were quite a few other people on the beach enjoying the warm night air, so his presence aroused no undue suspicion.

"Let's go to a movie," Suzy announced suddenly.

"Now?" Will asked.

A movie? At this hour? Were they crazy?

"Why not? It'll be fun. There's a theater just around the corner that's open all night."

You gotta be kidding me, Tom moaned silently. Instead of going to a motel, they were going to the movies? Lainey was going to be furious.

"Sure. I'm game," Will said.

"Shit," Tom muttered, trailing after them. Lainey would kill him for sure.

They stopped briefly at the road to put on their shoes, and Tom did the same. "Shit," he said again as fresh sand from inside his sneakers attached itself to the underside of his toes, piercing his skin like hundreds of tiny daggers. God, he hated sand.

He followed them for several blocks, relishing the feel of the hard concrete beneath his rubber soles. Minutes later, he watched from the doorway of an ancient haberdashery store as they approached the box office of an old-fashioned neighborhood theater. Five minutes later, he bought his own ticket and went inside.

The previews were already under way, and the theater was surprisingly full, considering it was almost midnight. Tom stood at the back, waiting until his eyes adjusted to the darkness. After a few minutes, he located Suzy and Will three rows from the front. Only then did he settle into a free seat on the aisle in the very last row. He wondered what movie they were going to see and hoped it wasn't a love story. He hated those.

Happily, the movie turned out to be a violent action flick starring Angelina Jolie. Could she be any hotter? he wondered as she flew across the screen, effortlessly emptying a round of submachine-gun fire at anything that moved. Tom patted the gun tucked inside his waistband in a gesture of solidarity, enjoying the movie so much, he almost forgot about Will and Suzy until he saw them heading up the aisle approximately an hour later. Where were they going? He hunkered down in his seat, hiding his face with his hand. Surely they weren't leaving. Not before the movie was over.

Reluctantly, he edged himself out of his seat and slipped into the lobby, hoping to see them at the refreshment counter, loading up on popcorn. But no, they were actually leaving. "Too violent for me," he heard Suzy say to the ticket taker on their way out the door.

"Shit," Tom said, following after them, so pissed off he almost didn't care whether or not they saw him. Where the hell were they going now?

"My car's back at Ninth and Pennsylvania," he heard Suzy say.

He considered turning around and admitting defeat, going back into the theater, enjoying the rest of the film before heading home. "Nah," he said out loud. He couldn't very well go back to Jeff with nothing. "Can't do that." He waited until they turned the corner before resuming his pursuit.

Twenty minutes later, they were back in the heart of South Beach.

"That's my car," Suzy said, pointing to a small, silver BMW parked on the other side of the road. The distinctive chirp of a car's remote control echoed down the street, accompanied by the flash of headlights.

So, she's got money, Tom thought as she and Will crossed the street on the diagonal. Suzy's high heels clicked against the pavement, her hand outstretched, already reaching for the car door.

Two men in matching skintight white jeans strolled by, holding hands, and Tom used the opportunity to sneak across the street, then duck behind a black Mercedes.

"Well, I guess that's it," he heard Suzy say. "The end of the line."

The end of the line? Tom repeated, having to restrain himself from shouting with glee. He knew it! No way was "little brother" going to score tonight.

"It doesn't have to be," Will protested weakly.

"Yeah, I'm afraid it does." Suzy angled her face toward Will's, held his gaze with her own, parting her lips in seeming anticipation. "I'm getting a stiff neck here," she said after several more seconds.

And suddenly they were kissing. Shit. What did that mean? Couldn't she have simply climbed into her car and driven off into the midnight sun?

"Okay, whoa," Suzy said, pulling back.

Good girl, Tom thought. Now, get into your car.

"I'm sorry," Will apologized immediately.

Pussy, Tom sneered.

"For what? Being such a great kisser? Trust me, no apologies necessary."

You call that a great kiss? You picked the wrong guy, sweetheart. I'm the guy you should have picked.

"Stop grinning," she told Will. "That still doesn't mean I'm going to sleep with you."

"Ever?"

She laughed, opening her car door and climbing inside.

Finally, Tom thought.

"Am I going to see you again?" Will asked.

Shit, how lame could you get?

Her response was to start the engine. Only as she was pulling away from the curb did she lower her window. "You know where to find me," she called out, leaving Will standing in a shifting cloud of exhaust.

"Jerk-off," Tom muttered, watching her car race down the street, then turn north on Ocean Drive. You don't even have a car, do you, little brother? You couldn't go after her if you tried.

But *I* can, he realized, impulsively chasing after her, careful to keep his body low and hidden behind the cars parked along the route, smiling as her car became mired in the traffic that was as constant along this strip of roadway as the ocean, even at this late hour. His own car was parked just a couple of blocks away. It was possible he could get to it before she was able to advance much farther, that he might actually be able to pick up her trail, at least find out where she lived. Maybe even persuade her to give him a chance. Some women just needed a little extra persuasion, he thought, remembering that stupid girl in Afghanistan, the one who'd gotten him in all that trouble, resulting in his dishonorable discharge, as if he were the only American soldier to ever get a little carried away. Hell, he'd risked his life every day for those goddamn ingrates. Was it too much to expect a little reward?

A few minutes later, he was behind the wheel of his ancient mustard-colored Impala, Suzy's BMW barely half a block ahead, signaling her intention to turn left. He could follow her or he could turn around, he was thinking. Will was probably still wandering the streets of South Beach on foot. He could pull up beside him, offer him a lift back to Jeff's apartment, let him know the jig was up.

Or he could keep following Suzy Pomegranate, see where she went, find out where she lived. Who knows? She might even be expecting him. He'd caught her smile as she exited the bar. He'd seen her eyes searching through the darkness, as if she knew he was there. Had she? Had she known all along? Was she even now checking her rearview mirror to make sure he was still behind her?

Hell, he thought, turning left when he reached the intersection, her car firmly in his sights. He'd come this far. Lainey was going to be furious with him no matter what. No point in giving up now. "Ready or not," he whispered, winking at his own reflection, "Suzy Pomegranate, here I come."

FOUR

JEFF'S CELL PHONE WAS ringing as Kristin drove her secondhand green and tan Volvo into the parking garage of the canary-yellow, three-story apartment building on Brimley Avenue, a twenty-minute drive from the Wild Zone. She didn't have to guess who would be calling at this hour. There were only two people who thought nothing of calling at almost three o'clock in the morning, she noted wearily, glancing over at Jeff, who was snoring drunkenly in the seat beside her, oblivious to the opening bars of "The Star-Spangled Banner" playing repeatedly in his pocket. One was Tom, no doubt phoning to report on the night's developments; the other was Lainey, calling to find out where the hell Tom was. Kristin had no desire to speak to either of them.

She pulled the car into the first available space and turned off the engine, then sat there, staring at the gray concrete wall in front of her, the national anthem playing beside her, and wishing, not for the first time, that the building had an elevator. Or that they didn't live on the third floor. Or that they lived in a newer building. In another part of town. A nicer part of town. That's what she'd ask for, she decided, if a magic genie ever materialized to offer her one wish.

No point in setting her sights any higher than that, she decided. What was the point in dreaming big when such dreams invariably turned into nightmares? She'd already had more than her share of those.

It wasn't as if they couldn't afford a better apartment, or maybe even a small house. Between bartending and the occasional modeling assignment, she made pretty good money, and Jeff was doing well as a personal trainer. Assuming he didn't quit this gym as abruptly as he'd left the last two. Oh, well, she thought, as she thought whenever she found herself wishing things were other than the way they were. At least this place was preferable to where she'd grown up.

Hell, anything was better than that.

"Hell" being the operative word.

"Jeff," she said, poking at him gently. "Jeff, honey, come on. Wake up."

Jeff made the kind of sound—a kind of half grunt, half groan—that begged to be left alone.

"Does that mean you're awake?" Kristin pressed.

This time the groan was longer, more purposeful. Go away, it said.

"Sorry, but if you don't wake up, I'm going to have to leave you here." Kristin didn't want to do that. Jeff always insisted on carrying a lot of cash. Someone could stumble upon him and rob him, maybe even beat him up, or worse. Just for kicks. Like those teenage boys she'd read about in the *Miami Herald* a few weeks back. They'd come across a homeless man huddled in the underground garage of their parents' condo during a recent storm, and when the poor man had explained that he was just trying to stay dry, they'd responded by setting him on fire. "Just wanted to keep him warm," one of the boys had been quoted as saying to the arresting officer. So, no, she couldn't very well just leave him there.

Kristin climbed out of the car, marched to the passenger door, opened it, and began pulling on Jeff's arm. "Come on, Jeff. Time to wake up and go to bed." Now that makes a lot of sense, she thought, pulling harder.

"What's happening?"

"We're home. You need to get up."

"Where's Will?"

"I have no idea." Kristin felt movement at her breasts and looked down to see Jeff's head buried between them, his eyes still closed, his mouth reflexively searching for the nipples beneath her leopard-print blouse. "I don't believe you. You're unconscious, and you're still at it." She pulled out of his reach, watching his head roll back against the seat, a silly smile on his handsome face that somehow managed to be simultaneously smug and endearing. "Come on, Jeff," she urged. "It's late. I'm tired. I've been on my feet all night."

It took Kristin another five minutes to coax Jeff out of the car, another ten for them to reach the top of the stairwell, another two for Kristin to half carry, half drag Jeff along the exterior hallway to their apartment door. "If you're going to throw up, please do it before we get inside," she said, glancing toward the ledge that ran along the side of the building. Like many low-rise complexes in Florida, the building looked more like a motel, its thirty units—ten per floor—overlooking a small in-ground pool, each apartment accessible only from an outside corridor. Still holding on to Jeff, Kristin fished in her purse for her keys, ignoring the three-quarter moon winking at her from between a nearby cluster of palm trees. The majestic old palms made everything look better, she was thinking as she opened the door and pushed Jeff inside. They hid a multitude of sins.

Would that they could do the same for the interior of the apartment, she thought as they entered the rectangular living room, notable primarily for its lack of anything notable. There were no picturesque nooks or crannies, no crown molding to interrupt the plain white walls, no pot lights or decorative details in the low ceiling. Even the large picture window that took up most of the west wall was uninviting, looking out, as it did, at a similar building across the way.

The furniture was only slightly more interesting, consisting of a blue and green print sofa that currently doubled as Will's bed, a navy leather ottoman, a few mismatched standing lamps, a couple of plastic, white stacking tables, and an oversize beige leather chair, all decidedly more functional than fashionable.

A surprisingly large eat-in kitchen stood at a right angle to the living room, while a small hallway led from the living area to the bedroom at the back of the apartment. There was one bathroom.

"The Star-Spangled Banner" began playing as soon as Kristin closed the door, as if heralding their arrival. Kristin watched Jeff's shoulders straighten instinctively. "Don't answer that," she said as he began fumbling for the phone in his pocket.

A second later, Lainey's voice was running along the dark blue, sixties-style shag carpeting and climbing up the walls, like toxic fumes. "Where is he?" Kristin heard her demand as Jeff held the phone an arm's length away from his ear.

"Told you not to answer it," Kristin couldn't help but whisper.

"Don't lie to me, Jeff," Lainey continued. "If Tom's with you, you better tell me."

"Who is this?" Jeff asked, smiling playfully at Kristin and letting the phone slide from his hands.

Kristin caught it before it hit the floor. "Tom's not here," she told Lainey.

"I've had as much crap as I'm going to take from that man," Lainey cried. "I mean it, Kristin. I've had it."

"Why don't you try to get some sleep?"

Her response was the phone going dead in her ear.

"Always a pleasure talking to you." Kristin tossed the phone onto the sofa.

"Hey!" came a startled cry. "What the hell . . . ?"

Kristin gasped as a figure bolted upright on the couch, rubbing the side of his head and looking thoroughly confused.

"Will?" Kristin asked, flipping on the overhead light.

"Shit," Jeff said. "What are you doing home?"

"Trying to sleep?" Will asked, shielding his eyes from the sudden intrusion of light.

"Anybody else under those covers?" Jeff lunged toward him, pulled the blanket off the makeshift bed, threw it to the floor.

"What are you doing?"

"Where is she?"

The veil of sleep slid abruptly from Will's pale face. He took a deep breath, released it slowly. "If you're referring to Suzy, obviously she's not here."

"Where is she?" Jeff repeated.

"I assume she went home."

"You assume? You didn't go with her?"

"No," Will said. "She had her car. I grabbed a cab. . . ."

"What are you saying?"

"What are you asking?"

"Did you fuck her or didn't you?" Jeff demanded, suddenly very sober and alert.

Will looked to Kristin, hoping she'd intervene. She didn't. In fact, her eyes told Will she was as interested as Jeff in the answer. "No," he said finally.

"What *did* you do?"

"Walked on the beach, went to a movie."

"You're shitting me," Jeff said incredulously.

Will shook his head, releasing another deep breath as he fell back against the sofa's soft cushions. "Sorry to disappoint you."

"You walked the beach, went to a movie, she went home, you didn't fuck her," Jeff reiterated, as if trying to force the words to make sense. "What the hell happened?"

"Nothing happened."

"Yeah, I get that. What I don't get is why. It was a done deal, little brother. How could you blow it?"

"I didn't blow it."

"You didn't fuck her."

"You think you could stop saying that?"

"Did you or didn't you fuck her?"

Again Will's eyes traveled toward Kristin. "I didn't."

"Okay, Jeff," Kristin said, responding to Will's silent plea. "Why don't you go to bed? You can find out all the gory details in the morning."

Jeff shook his head and laughed. "Doesn't sound like there were any." He turned around and walked toward the bedroom down the hall, still shaking his head and chuckling. "You coming?" he called to Kristin.

"Be right there." Kristin waited until Jeff turned the corner to their bedroom before sitting down next to Will and covering his hand with hers. "You okay?"

"I'm fine."

"You want to talk about it?"

"I think you pretty much know everything," he told her, his voice low and conspiratorial. "Considering you set it up."

Kristin's lips formed a sad little half smile. "You mad at me?"

"Why would I be mad? It was the best night I've had in a long time."

"I'm glad. She seemed very nice."

"She is."

"Think you'll see her again?"

Will shrugged. "Who knows?"

"It's been a rough year, huh?"

"I admire your capacity for understatement."

"Nice to be admired. In any capacity," Kristin said with a laugh. "Anyway, there's no place like Miami for smoothing over rough patches. I'd say you came to the right place."

"And what does my brother say?"

"He doesn't say much about anything. You know Jeff."

"That's just the point. I don't know him."

"Give him a chance, Will," Kristin urged. Hadn't she been saying the same thing to Jeff ever since Will's unexpected arrival?

"My mother didn't want me to come, you know. She said I was just asking for trouble."

"Why would she say that?"

"The Star-Spangled Banner" suddenly started to play. Will patted the sofa around him, locating Jeff's phone and looking at Kristin expectantly.

Her response was to take the phone from Will's hand and flip it to mute. "Enough of that nonsense. It's time for everybody to get some sleep."

Will needed no further encouragement. He lay back down and closed his eyes, curling into a tight, fetal ball. Kristin reached down and retrieved the blanket from the floor, laying it across him and stroking his back. "If you ever want to talk," she began. "About anything . . ."

"Thanks," Will said, the word sliding out from between barely parted lips.

Kristin pushed herself off the sofa, laying Jeff's phone on the ottoman. "Sweet dreams," she whispered before turning off the overhead light and returning the room to soft, welcoming darkness.

SHE DREAMED ABOUT Norman.

Kristin was five years old when her mother's new boyfriend offered to babysit while her mother auditioned for a local TV commercial. He'd made himself comfortable on the secondhand brown velvet sofa in the living room of the run-down apartment, opened a can of beer, and put his feet up on the stained coffee table, all the while restlessly fiddling with the TV's remote control. Kristin was on the floor, playing with the two battered Barbies she'd rescued from a neighbor's garbage bin the previous week. Their tangled hair still smelled of rotting potato peel, even after several washings with dishwasher detergent. "Hey, kid," Norman said, patting the cushion beside him. "You want to see something interesting?"

Kristin had joined him on the sofa, her eyes opening wide at the sight of a man and woman kissing deeply.

"You know what they're doing, don't you?" Norman asked. "They're tasting each other's tongues."

Kristin giggled. "Do they taste good?"

"Very good. Do you want to try it?" He leaned forward, so that his face was very close to hers, and she could feel his beery breath warm against her nose. "Open wide," he instructed before she could say no.

Kristin did as she was told–hadn't her mother told her she was to listen to Norman and do exactly what he said?–and Norman promptly thrust his tongue deep inside her small mouth. Saliva filled her throat, and for a moment, she felt as if she couldn't breathe. She pulled back, stifling the impulse to gag.

"Did you like that?" he asked, seemingly oblivious to her discomfort.

Kristin shook her head, afraid to speak, as if his tongue had robbed her of her voice.

Norman laughed and pulled a package of Life Savers out of the back pocket of his jeans, peeling a red one off the top and handing it to her. "Think you'll like this better?"

Kristin nodded, popping the Life Saver quickly into her mouth. Red Life Savers were her favorite.

"Don't say anything to your mother about what you did," he cautioned her as the taste of cherry died on her tongue.

What *you* did, Kristin could hear him repeat now, the words jolting her awake as, once again, she stifled the impulse to gag. She checked the clock on the nightstand beside the double bed. It was a little past four, which meant she'd been asleep less than an hour. She tried to lie back down, but Jeff's body had already shifted in his sleep, and both his right arm and leg were now stretched out onto her side of the bed.

"What are you doing?" said the sleepy voice beside her.

"Just trying to get comfortable."

Kristin felt his hand curl around her left breast. You've got to be kidding, she thought. "What are you doing?"

"What do you think I'm doing?" His fingers began circling her nipple as he inched himself up on his elbows, drawing her body back down.

"I thought you were sleeping."

"I was. Now I'm up. As you can see." He grabbed her hand, positioned it on his groin.

"Very impressive," Kristin deadpanned as he maneuvered himself on top of her. He pushed his way inside her without further preamble, beginning a series of slow, deliberate thrusts that knocked the brass headboard repeatedly against the back wall of the bedroom.

Kristin went where she usually went during such moments. To her safe place, a sunny field of high grass and beautiful red flowers. She'd seen such a place once in a book of impressionist paintings that her fourth-grade teacher had been kind enough to allow her to take home one night. Kristin had been leafing through the book when Ron had come home early. Ron was her mother's new husband, a good-looking out-of-work actor with a big voice and an easy sneer, so when he'd called her into the bedroom, when he'd told her to shut the door, when he'd ordered her to come here, she did. And when he was on top of her, when he was poking at her with his fingers, when he was tearing at her and making her bleed, she'd numbed the pain by focusing all her energy on that sun-filled field and the woman in her long, flowing dress who was standing at the top of the hill, delicate white parasol in hand, watching her young daughter romp happily among the magical red flowers. And because the artist had rendered their faces so purposely hazy, it was almost possible to pretend that she was the little girl running merrily through the grass and that the woman with the parasol was her mother, watching to make sure no harm would befall her.

It was a place Kristin returned to often.

And then one day her mother had come home early from her shift at the International House of Pancakes, where she'd been employed for the better part of six months, and she'd found Ron on top of her now almost fifteen-year-old daughter, and she'd started screaming, except she hadn't been screaming at Ron. "What are you doing, you little slut?" she'd cried as a hairbrush flew toward the wall, so close to Kristin's head she actually felt a breeze disturb the tiny hairs on the back of her neck. "Get out of here. I never want to see your miserable face again."

Kristin hadn't bothered trying to defend herself. What was the point? She knew her mother was right. It was her fault. She was the one responsible. If she hadn't been so flirtatious, so seductive, as Ron never tired of telling her, he might have been able to control himself.

Don't say anything to your mother about what you did, she heard Norman say.

What *you* did.

First Norman. Then Ron. So clearly it was her fault and not her mother's bad choices.

Her fault.

Kristin felt Jeff begin to pick up the pace of his thrusts, pushing her out of her field of red flowers. This was her cue, she understood, contributing the appropriate soundtrack of squeals and sighs, nothing too loud, nothing that would draw Will's attention to what they were doing or arouse Jeff's suspicion that she might be faking it. Not that he'd care one way or the other. Strangely enough, that was one of the things she liked best about him—this minimum of pretense. She grabbed his buttocks to push him even deeper inside her, feeling him shudder and release as her hands moved to his torso, absorbing the last of his energy.

"How was that?" he asked, his proud smile looming above her.

"Terrific," Kristin told him. "Suzy has no idea what she missed out on tonight."

Jeff's smile grew even wider as he flipped over onto his side, pulling Kristin's arms across his waist. "She will," Kristin thought she heard him say just before he drifted off to sleep.

FIVE

"WHERE THE HELL ARE you taking me?" Tom wondered aloud, following Suzy's car across the Venetian Causeway, suspended high over picturesque Biscayne Bay, into mainland Miami. Once across, the cars slowed to a virtual standstill at the intersection of Biscayne Boulevard and Northeast Fourteenth Street. "Shit. What now?" Where was everyone going? "Doesn't anybody stay home anymore?" he shouted out his open window at no one in particular. It was after two in the morning, for shit's sake. He was hot; he was tired; he was very drunk and more than a little queasy. So what was he doing running after some twat who'd rejected him once tonight already?

A white Lexus SUV suddenly appeared from out of nowhere to cut in front of him. "Goddamn motherfucking son of a bitch," Tom swore as the traffic began inching forward. "I'll blow your motherfucking head off." He reached for his gun, then quickly thought better of it, counting to ten, and then twenty, in a concerted effort to calm himself down. Much as the bastard deserved a bullet in the back of his big, fat, ugly head, Tom thought, the last thing he wanted was to create an unnecessary scene. Even honking his horn would be risky, he realized, forcing his hands into his lap. He didn't want Suzy craning her neck around, straining to see what all the commotion was about. Besides, there were police everywhere. All he needed was for some inquisitive young cop to pull him over, smell his breath, and discover he was carrying. They'd haul his ass off to jail so fast his head would spin. Although it was already spinning pretty good, he thought, and laughed. He pictured Lainey having to come down to the station in her pajamas to bail him out, a screaming kid in each arm, her outraged parents following close behind, and the laugh quickly died in his throat.

"What's the matter with you?" he could hear her cry. "What are you doing chasing after some woman you saw in a bar when you have a wife and children and a houseful of responsibilities waiting for you at home?"

Which is precisely the point, Tom thought now, and laughed again.

"You think this is funny?" Lainey continued to berate him. "Are you insane? When are you going to grow up?"

"When I damn well feel like it," Tom shot back, banishing her to a far corner of his mind and shifting in his seat, trying to see over the top of the white SUV. Stupid car, he thought, imagining it taking the next corner at too high a speed, then flipping over and bursting into flames, its snot-nosed driver trapped inside, clawing at the windows as he struggled—frantically, and in vain—to escape the blaze. That'd be great, Tom thought.

Suzy's silver BMW turned left at the Museum of Science and the Space Transit Planetarium—whatever the hell that was—then continued southwest along the wide boulevard, before turning right onto Douglas Road. After that, Tom stopped paying attention to the signs. What difference did it make what street they were on? What was important was what happened when they got there.

Ten minutes later, they were driving through the twisting labyrinth of streets that made up the upscale suburb of Coral Gables. "Coral Gables, shit," Tom groaned. He hated Coral Gables.

Lainey was always going on about moving there when they could afford it. Like that was ever going to happen. He worked at the Gap, for shit's sake. He earned minimum wage. If it weren't for her parents, who'd paid the down payment on their tiny house in the decidedly ungentrified section of Morningside and continued to make the monthly mortgage payments, they'd probably have been living in some crummy, cramped apartment like Jeff and Kristin. Although if he were living with Kristin, he doubted he'd mind being cramped.

As Suzy's car disappeared around the next corner, Tom was surprised to realize that most of the other cars, including the white Lexus SUV, had vanished somewhere along the route without his noticing. Lainey's fault, he decided. As most things were. She was always getting in his way, distracting him from the task at hand. He had to pay attention, he understood, turning onto Granada Boulevard and spotting Suzy's car at a stop sign several blocks ahead.

He watched the silver BMW turn right on Alava Avenue and followed after it. Suzy quickly turned left, then right, then right again, picking up speed. What was she doing? Had she realized he was tailing her? Was she trying to lose him? And hadn't they already driven down this same street just minutes ago? He was sure he recognized that pink stucco house on the corner. Hadn't they just passed it? Was this some sort of joke? Had she recognized him and decided to lead him on a wild-goose chase? Had she known from the very beginning he was following her? "Stupid bitch," he cursed under his breath, fighting a sudden surge of nausea.

Just turn around and go home, he told himself. Yes, Lainey would be waiting up for him. Yes, she'd yell and carry on. But what the hell? He was used to her histrionics. Eventually she'd wear herself out, cry herself back to sleep. She'd forgive him in the morning, the way she always did. And if she didn't, if she continued to give him a hard time, he'd just go over to Jeff's place, or to the gym where Jeff worked, or to the Wild Zone. Wherever Jeff was. Wherever Lainey wasn't.

Damn her anyway. It was Lainey who was responsible for all his problems, Lainey who'd gotten herself pregnant, who'd pushed him into a marriage she knew he wasn't ready for, who was so bloody fertile she'd found herself pregnant again barely a year later, saddling him with not one but two children, both of whom looked exactly like him, so there was absolutely no question as to their paternity. It was her fault he had to work at a job he hated, her fault he couldn't just go off gallivanting with Jeff whenever he felt like it, even if Kristin let Jeff do whatever the hell he wanted. "What's the matter with Kristin anyway?" Tom could hear Lainey shout.

There is absolutely nothing wrong with Kristin, Tom thought silently. She was the perfect woman. She didn't whine about responsibilities and complain if Jeff blew a few hundred bucks on a leather jacket. She never gave him grief for how late he came home, or how much he drank, or how stoned he got. Hell, she even turned a blind eye to his playing around. In fact, according to tonight's exchange, Kristin wasn't averse to even joining in herself on occasion.

Sex with two women had always been a favorite fantasy of Tom's. A big-busted blond like Kristin on one side, a willowy brunette like Suzy on the other, Tom sandwiched happily in between. He'd take turns with them, doing one from the front, the other from the back, and then flip them over, repeat the whole process again in reverse, do stuff Lainey wouldn't even let him talk about.

Not that he'd even want to do them with Lainey, who was short and a little on the stocky side. Unlike Kristin, who was statuesque and, in a word, stacked. Of course, Lainey always insisted Kristin's boobs were fake, but what difference did it make what they were made of? She'd paid for them, so that made them hers, as far as he was concerned. Besides, they looked good, so who cared if they were made of plastic? When he'd suggested to Lainey (delicately, he'd thought) that she might want to ask Kristin for the name of her cosmetic surgeon—hell, he'd even offered to pay for her boob job himself—she'd responded by bursting into a flood of angry tears and stomping from the room, yelling something about how Kristin had never had to nurse two babies and he could just go to hell.

"Already there," Tom said now, taking a deep breath and releasing it, watching it tremble toward the car's front window. He pulled a cigarette out of the pocket of his shirt and lit it, inhaling deeply and pretending it was a joint. He'd read somewhere that marijuana was supposed to be good for fighting nausea. "Hah!" he laughed. He'd have to remember to tell that to Lainey. She hated it when he got stoned. "It's illegal, and it's irresponsible," she'd say. "Irresponsible"—her favorite word. "What happens if you're stoned and one of the kids wakes up and wants their daddy?"

As if that's even in the realm of possibility, he thought. When was the last time either of his children had ever asked for their daddy? His three-year-old daughter, Candy, cried whenever he approached, and Cody, his two-year-old son, who everyone said was his spitting image, would recoil in genuine horror whenever Tom tried to pick him up, as if Tom was just some stranger who'd wandered into the house by mistake. Which was pretty close to the truth, Tom thought now, idling at a stop sign for several seconds before pursuing Suzy down another residential street.

Where was she taking him?

Despite looking like his father, Cody was actually just like his mother, Tom thought. No matter what he did, no matter how hard he tried, nothing was ever good enough. His son would cry and carry on, his wiry little body rigid in his father's awkward embrace, his arms extended into the air, straining for his mother's softer, more familiar touch, his round little face getting redder and redder with each successive sob, until he looked like a ripe tomato on the verge of exploding.

Tom shuddered. He'd actually seen a man's head explode once when he was in Afghanistan. A girl had been lying along the side of the road. She appeared to be injured. As a young American soldier climbed out of his jeep to come to her aid, the girl had reached inside her dirt-encrusted robe. Next thing you knew, severed limbs were flying through the smoke-filled air in all directions, and the helpful young soldier was minus his head.

Tom felt the bile rise in his throat and swallowed several times, trying to force it back down. Where the hell had that memory come from? he wondered, tossing his cigarette out the side window and trying to drag some fresh oxygen into his lungs. It didn't help. The air was sticky and sat like an expanding clump of cellophane in his throat, threatening to cut off his air supply altogether. He had to stop the car. He needed to get out, walk around, get his circulation going, stop his head from spinning. He needed to get away from this stupid, un-air-conditioned car before he threw up all over himself.

He angled the old Impala toward the curb and was about to open his door when he saw Suzy's BMW come to a halt halfway down the street, as if she were waiting for him. What was she doing? Was she going to back up? Was she planning to confront him? Just get out of here, he told himself. Get out now.

Except she wasn't backing up. She was turning into the driveway of a tan-colored bungalow with a white slate roof and a vine-covered double garage. Tom's eyes shot to the street sign on the corner. Tallahassee Drive, the sign announced. "She's my Tallahassee lassie," he grunted tunelessly, forgetting about his nausea as he inched his car down the street.

Her garage door opened, her car hesitating in the driveway. What's she waiting for? Tom wondered, noting the presence of a second car—a shiny red Corvette, no less—in the garage. Two luxury automobiles. A house in the suburbs. Everything but a white picket fence. "What does that tell you?" he asked, watching Suzy emerge from the garage and cut across the front lawn.

Could she move any slower? Tom thought, holding his breath as the front door opened and a man—tall, imposing, wearing a jacket and tie despite the lateness of the hour—appeared in the doorway. What's this all about? Tom wondered as the man grabbed Suzy's elbow and ushered her inside, shutting the door after her.

Tom switched off the engine and stepped out of the car. Time for a little reconnoitering, he decided, running on a diagonal across the street toward her house, staying close to the myriad of palm trees lining the way.

Which was when it hit him. A sudden wave of nausea, followed quickly by another, and then another, each one stronger than the one before, each accompanied by sharp, stabbing pains. He grabbed his stomach and doubled over, his body wracked by a succession of violent heaves as he spilled his guts into a clump of flowering bushes. He gasped for breath, his eyes stinging with tears as he tried to straighten up. When was the last time he'd been sick like that? He pushed back the urge to throw up again, his knees wobbling as he sank to the grass, burying his head in his hands. He had to go home. He had to lie down. He had to let Lainey take care of him.

As soon as Tom felt his legs were strong enough to hold him, he returned to his car. "One twenty-one Tallahassee Drive," he noted as he drove past the neat, tan-colored bungalow with the white slate roof, repeating the address several times out loud in order to ensure he'd remember it.

"You haven't seen the last of me, Suzy Pomegranate," he said as he rounded the corner and headed for home.

"WELL, LOOK AT you," Suzy said, smiling at the man in the doorway, actually managing to sound pleased to see him, as she fought to steady the erratic beating of her heart. It was never a good idea to show fear. What was Dave doing here? He wasn't supposed to be back until tomorrow night. "I wasn't expecting you back until—"

"Get inside." He grabbed her elbow, pushed her inside the front foyer, slammed the door shut after them.

"Did something happen? Is everything all right? Your mother . . . ?" Had the nursing home called to inform him she'd finally succumbed to the cancer that had been ravaging her insides for the better part of two years?

"Where the hell have you been?" Long, angry fingers dug into her flesh. The same spot Will had touched so tenderly not more than thirty minutes before.

"I went to the movies."

"What theater is open at this hour?"

"The Rialto, over in South Beach."

"You expect me to believe you went all the way over to South Beach to go to a movie?"

"It's the truth."

"What movie?"

"That new one with Angelina Jolie, the one you didn't want to see."

"Who'd you go with?"

"A girlfriend."

"What girlfriend?"

"Kristin," Suzy said, the first name that sprang to mind.

"Kristin," he repeated, shaking his head as if trying to dislodge the unfamiliar name and rubbing the five o'clock shadow along his chin with the fingers of his right hand. "Who the hell is Kristin?"

"She's just this girl I met."

"When?"

"A few days ago."

"Where'd you meet her?"

"What difference does it make?"

Her answer was the back of his hand as it came crashing against the side of her cheek. Suzy fell back against the cream-colored wall, then tumbled to her knees.

"Get up," Dave directed, looming above her. At almost six feet tall and a hundred and eighty pounds, he had five inches and nearly seventy pounds on her. A man of substance, she'd thought when they were first introduced five years earlier. The handsome prince, come to rescue her. A man who'd take care of her. A man she could look up to.

Which is exactly what I'm doing now, she thought from her position on the floor, and strangled a laugh in her throat.

"What? This is funny to you?"

"No. Of course not."

"You're laughing?"

"I'm not. I didn't mean–"

"Get up," he said again.

She struggled to her feet. "Please don't hit me again."

"Then don't lie to me again."

"I'm not lying."

"Tell me where you met her." Ice-blue eyes stared at Suzy, radiating fury.

To think she'd once found those blue eyes kind. "She works in this place in South Beach."

"What place?"

"It's called the Wild Zone," she whispered.

"What? Speak up."

"I said it's called the Wild Zone," Suzy repeated, her body bracing for another blow.

"The Wild Zone?" Dave repeated incredulously. "What the hell kind of place is that?"

"It's just a bar."

"A bar called the Wild Zone," Dave said, his fingers forming impatient fists at his sides. "And just what were you doing in said Wild Zone?"

"Nothing. Honestly. I'd been at the beach. I got thirsty—"

"So, naturally, you popped into the nearest bar." Another disbelieving shake of his head, another tightening of his fists.

"I was only there a few minutes."

"Long enough to hook up with the local 'wildlife.'"

"She works there."

"She's a waitress?"

"A bartender."

"You made friends with the bartender," he repeated incredulously.

"We just talked for a few minutes. She seemed nice."

"What'd you talk about?"

"What?"

"I asked you what you talked about."

"I don't remember."

"Sure you do, Suzy. Unless you need me to remind you." He raised his right hand into the air.

"No!"

"Tell me what you talked about, Suzy."

"I asked her for a pomegranate martini. She said she'd heard they were good for you."

"You were drinking martinis in the middle of the afternoon?"

"It was after five o'clock."

"What else did the two of you talk about?"

"We talked about the weather," Suzy said, trying to recall the exact words of her conversation with Will.

"The weather?"

"She asked me if it was still so hot outside, and I said it could never be too hot as far as I was concerned, and she asked where I was from, and I told her I'd just moved here from Fort Myers."

"You told her *you'd* just moved here?"

"I meant 'we.'"

"But you didn't say that, did you?"

"I don't know. I probably did. I'm sure I must have."

"Tell me what you said."

"I said we'd just moved here from Fort Myers."

"You talked about me?"

"What? No."

"What did you tell her?"

"Nothing. I didn't say anything about you."

"You didn't say a word about the hardworking husband you swore to love and obey? About my recent appointment to the staff of Miami General? That I was attending a radiology conference in

Tampa and wouldn't be back until Saturday night? You didn't mention any of that?"

"No."

"Why didn't you?"

"What?"

"Didn't she ask?"

"No."

"She just asked about the weather," he stated.

"Yes. And where I was from."

"And then what? She just happened to mention she was free to go to a midnight movie with you on Friday night, one of the busiest nights of the week, I would imagine, for a place called the Wild Zone?"

"I don't remember what she said."

Suzy didn't see Dave's fist until it collided with her cheek. She staggered back into the dark living room, grabbing at the end table by the sofa in order to keep from falling, and knocking over the lamp.

"Pick it up," he commanded, advancing toward her.

Suzy struggled to return the lamp to its former position on the small, cloverleaf-shaped table.

"What—do you really think I'm that stupid? You think I can't tell when you're lying?" he demanded, knocking the lamp back to the floor, its delicate, pleated, ivory-colored shade coming dislodged. "Pick it up."

Again, Suzy returned the lamp to the table. Again, he knocked it to the floor.

"Fix the goddamn shade."

Suzy's shaking fingers wrestled with the now severely dented shade, eventually succeeding in securing it in place.

"Now pick it up," he directed again.

Suzy hurried to replace the lamp, but his arm was already descending. The lamp went shooting out of her hand, its shade coming loose and flying toward the ceiling, its coral-colored, oval-shaped base missing the end of the beige and green needlepoint carpet and shattering against the cold marble floor. "Oh, God," Suzy cried as he lunged for her, dragging her to her feet and throwing her against the far wall. Beside her head, a famous black and white photograph of a sailor embracing a woman in the middle of Times Square at the end of World War II wobbled precariously for several seconds before dropping to the floor.

There was no stopping him now, Suzy knew, so she closed her eyes, gave herself over to his fists, and waited for it to be over.

SIX

FORTY MINUTES LATER, TOM finally turned into his driveway on Northwest Fifty-sixth Street, in the so-run-down-it-was-almost-fashionable neighborhood of Morningside. Damn that Coral Gables anyway, he cursed silently. Finding your way out of there was almost as impossible as trying to navigate those damn caves in Afghanistan. Roads twisting this way and that without any rhyme or reason, dead ends popping up out of nowhere like snipers, streets doubling back on themselves like snakes. It was a miracle anyone ever got out of there. Three times he'd thought he'd escaped, only to find himself back on the same damn road. He'd been almost embarrassingly grateful when the massive, blocks-long concrete skeleton of the condo-and-shopping complex known as Midtown Miami suddenly loomed into view.

He turned off the car's headlights and tossed a stick of Juicy Fruit into his mouth, on the slight chance Lainey was still up and he could persuade her to make him some tea, then proceeded slowly into the carport, shutting off the ignition and feeling the car shudder to a complete halt. Was Lainey watching him from an upstairs window? he wondered, opening the car door, his eyes scanning the exterior of the plain white, two-story house. Ostensibly, Lainey's parents had bought them the house as a wedding gift, but it was registered only in Lainey's name. Tom understood that, in the event of a divorce, he'd be out on his ear.

It wouldn't be the first time he was out on the streets, he thought, remembering when his parents had kicked him out of the house after he'd been caught cheating on his final exams and was told he wouldn't be graduating high school with Jeff and the rest of his friends. Jeff had immediately headed south to the University of Miami, while Tom had been stuck in dreary old Buffalo.

Without Jeff at his side, everything changed. Pretty girls no longer hovered; they didn't tell him he had soulful brown eyes and a cute butt; their hands didn't accidentally brush against his when they walked by; they no longer giggled and deserted their girlfriends when he beckoned. If anything, they avoided him entirely, unless it was to ask about Jeff. What was he doing these days? Was it true he'd dropped out of college, that he was thinking of settling permanently in Miami? Was he planning to come back for a visit any time soon, and did Tom happen to know when that might be?

Tom got a job at McDonald's, then quit as soon as he'd saved up enough money to join Jeff in South Florida. He'd met Lainey within days of his arrival, and she'd glommed on to his side, like gum to the bottom of a shoe. Several months later, still reeling after a night of boozing and whoring, with Jeff egging him on, betting him a hundred bucks he didn't have the guts, Tom had walked into an army recruitment office and enlisted, then turned around and bet Jeff that same hundred bucks he lacked the cojones to do the same. What the hell? they'd reasoned, signing on the dotted line. It was an adventure, an opportunity to see the world, a chance to shoot the big guns. Besides, the war was only going to last a few months, right?

"Right this way, gentlemen," the recruiting officer had said with a smile.

"Next stop, purgatory," Tom said now, pushing his way through the humidity to his front door, painted a noxious shade of purple. His mind returned to the tasteful, tan-colored bungalow in Coral Gables as he fumbled in his pocket for his keys. Who paints a front door purple? he wondered, listening to the key twist in the lock.

"Purple's supposed to be good luck," he heard Lainey say, bracing himself as he stepped over the threshold. Lainey wasn't above jumping out at him in the dark, accusations, like bullets, raining down on his head as she pursued him from room to room, her voice like the whine of a guided missile, mercilessly honing in on its target.

But there was no one lurking when he stepped into the tiny front foyer, no one waiting to chop off his head when he peeked, turtle-like, into the dark living room. He sank into the nearest chair, staring at the empty space where the plasma TV used to sit. After several minutes of trying—and failing—to get comfortable in the too-small flower-patterned chair, he got up. He'd never liked this room, never adjusted to Lainey's parents' castoffs.

He headed up the stairs, wincing with each creak in the wood.

Something was wrong, he realized when he reached the top of the landing, and he stood there for several seconds, not moving, barely breathing, his muscles on full alert, trying to figure out what it was. And then he knew—it was too quiet.

His eyes shot to the ceiling, as if he half expected a bomb to drop suddenly out of the sky. He reached for his gun, pulling it from his belt and holding it out in front of him as he proceeded down the narrow hallway, sidestepping invisible land mines as rockets exploded silently behind him.

The doors to the kids' bedrooms were open, which was unusual. Didn't Lainey prefer them to be closed? He tiptoed into Cody's room, approaching his crib slowly, listening for the soothing sound of his son's breathing.

He heard nothing.

Saw nothing.

Even in the dark, he could see his son wasn't there.

What's going on? Tom thought, rushing into the next room, his eyes immediately absorbing his daughter's empty bed, the imprint of her little body clearly visible on the pink-striped sheets, as if someone had awakened her in the night and spirited her off.

Racing down the hall into his bedroom, Tom reached up and flipped on the overhead light, his breath freezing in his lungs at the sight of the neatly made bed. He slammed his fist against the pale purple wall, finally forced to admit what instinctively he'd known all along.

Lainey had taken the kids and left him. She was gone.

And if he hadn't spent the better part of two hours trailing after that stupid bitch from the bar, he might have been home in time to stop his wife from leaving. Damn that Suzy anyway, he thought, watching her in his mind's eye as she slowly approached the man waiting ominously at her front door.

This was all her fault.

"COME HERE," DAVE said tenderly, smiling at Suzy and patting the space beside him in their king-size bed as he drew back the crisp, white sheets to allow her entry. He was naked from the waist up, his tanned chest lifting up and down with the regularity of his breathing.

Suzy swayed in the doorway, damp hair falling on the shoulders of her pale pink terry-cloth bathrobe, her toes gripping the thick, white broadloom, reluctant to let go.

"Come on," he said, his voice soft and reassuring, full of forgiveness, as if she were the one who'd done something wrong.

She took several tentative steps forward.

"Did you bring the ice?" he asked.

Suzy held up her bruised right hand, displaying the Baggie full of ice cubes he'd instructed her to get from the freezer.

"Good. Now get into bed. Let's have a look at what we've got here."

As if he doesn't know, Suzy thought, crawling in beside him. As if he isn't responsible. She winced as he reached for her chin, manipulating it up and down and from side to side as he examined his handiwork.

"Not too bad," he commented dispassionately. "A little ice should take down the swelling. Some makeup will take care of the rest. Not that I'd recommend you go anywhere for a few days."

She nodded.

"In fact, I was thinking of taking the next couple of days off, staying home to look after my girl."

"Can you do that?" Suzy asked meekly.

His answer chilled her more than the ice in her hand. "I can do anything," he said.

"I just meant, you're new at Miami General. . . ."

"They think I'm at that stupid conference," he reminded her. "Besides, I ask you, what's more important, my job or my wife?"

Suzy said nothing.

"I asked you a question."

"I'm sorry. I didn't think–"

"You didn't think my question was worthy of a response?"

"I thought it was . . . rhetorical."

"Rhetorical," he repeated with a raise of his eyebrows. "Good word, Suzy. I'm impressed. The next time people ask me what a successful, good-looking doctor is doing married to a skinny high school dropout, I'll just ask them if that's a rhetorical question. That ought to shut them up. Here, hold the ice against your cheek. That's a good girl." He leaned his head against hers, burying his mouth in her hair. "Mmmn. You smell so good."

"Thank you."

"Nice and clean. What is that? Ivory Soap?"

She nodded.

"How was your bath?"

"Good."

"Not too hot?"

"No."

"Good. You shouldn't make your baths too hot. It's not healthy."

"It wasn't too hot."

"I cleaned up the mess in the living room."

The mess in the living room, Suzy thought. As if it got there on its own. As if he'd had nothing to do with it. "Thank you."

"We'll have to get a new lamp."

She nodded.

"I'll have to take it out of your allowance."

"Of course."

"Sounds like I'm giving you too much anyway. If you can afford to waste it on midnight movies and places like the Wild Zone."

Suzy felt her body stiffen. The last place she wanted him to revisit was the Wild Zone. She swiveled around in his arms, tilting her head up toward him and lifting her lips toward his, hoping to distract him.

She thought of Will, the sweet tentativeness of his kiss, as her husband's mouth pressed down hard on hers. Of course, Dave's kisses had started out just as sweet, just as tender, she remembered. Just as soft. As soft and as soothing as his voice the first time they'd met.

"This is Dr. Bigelow," the nurse had said. "He's been studying your mother's X-rays. He'd like to talk to you, if you have a minute."

"Alone," Dr. Bigelow added with quiet authority. "Before your father gets here."

"Is something wrong?" she'd asked, thinking he was handsome in a bookish sort of way. Dark, curly hair. High forehead. Strong nose. Nice mouth. Wondrously long lashes guarding pale blue eyes. Kind eyes, she'd thought.

He took her elbow, led her gently from her mother's hospital room into the corridor. "Suppose you tell me."

"I don't understand," she said, although she understood all too well.

"How did your mother receive her injuries?"

"I already told the other doctors. She was walking the dog. Her feet got tangled up in the leash. She fell face-first into the road, hit her head on the curb."

"You saw her fall?"

"No. She told us what happened when she got home."

"Us?"

"My father and I."

"My father and *me*," he corrected, then smiled sheepishly. "Sorry. A little bugaboo of mine. You wouldn't say 'She told *I* when she got home.' You'd say 'She told *me*.' That doesn't change just because you add another name. I thought your father was at work," he continued in the same breath.

"What?"

"You told the admitting doctors your father was at work at the time of your mother's accident, that he didn't know anything about it."

"That's right. He was. He didn't. He didn't have anything to do with this."

"I didn't say he did. Is that what you're saying?"

"What? No. You're confusing me."

"I'm sorry . . . Miss Carson, is it?" he asked, checking her mother's chart. "Suzy?" he asked tenderly, her name as soft as a wisp of cotton candy. "Why don't you tell me what really happened?"

She shook her head. "I can't."

"Tell me, Suzy. You can trust me."

"Nothing happened. Her feet got tangled up in the dog's leash. She fell."

"Her injuries are inconsistent with the type of fall you describe."

"Well, maybe I got it wrong. I told you I wasn't there. I didn't see what happened."

"I think you did."

"I didn't," Suzy protested. "I wasn't there."

"How'd you get those bruises on your arms, Suzy? Another accident with the dog?"

"These are nothing. I don't even remember how I got them."

"What about this one?" He pointed to a red mark on her cheek. "It looks pretty fresh."

"I don't know what you're talking about."

"Your father did this, didn't he? He caused your mother's injuries. And yours," he added softly.

"No, he didn't. You don't know what you're talking about. Am I through here?"

"You don't have to protect him, Suzy. You can tell me what really happened. We'll go to the police together. They'll arrest him."

"And then what?" Suzy demanded. "Do you want me to tell you

what happens next, Dr. Bigelow? Because I can tell you exactly what happens next. My mother gets better, her bruises heal, she comes home from the hospital, she drops all charges against my father, the way she always does. And then we move to another city, and everything's all right for a few weeks, or maybe even a couple of months, and then bingo–surprise! It starts all over again."

"It doesn't have to be that way, Suzy."

"I'm twenty-two, Dr. Bigelow. This has been going on ever since I can remember, probably since before I was born. You think you can just come along and wave your magic stethoscope and make everything better?"

"I'd like to try," he said.

She'd believed him.

She'd let him talk her into going to the police, let him persuade her to testify against her father, despite her mother's wishes and fervent denials. He'd been by her side when her father was convicted and sentenced to six months in jail. Of course, he'd ended up serving less than four before being released and sent home to the welcoming arms of his wife. Three weeks later, those same arms had been broken in half a dozen places, along with her collarbone, and she was back in the hospital. Two weeks after the doctors signed her release, her father decided to move the family to Memphis, their eighth move in almost as many years. This time Suzy hadn't gone with them. She'd stayed in Fort Myers, to be near her protector, the kindly Dr. Bigelow.

She and Dave were married ten months later. Nine weeks after that, he hit her for the first time. She'd misused "I" and "me." Of course he apologized profusely, and Suzy blamed herself. He was less apologetic the following month, when he slapped her over another egregious grammatical error. A full-scale beating wasn't long in coming. Over the last five years, there'd been many such beatings: She took too long getting ready for bed; the pasta she'd prepared wasn't al dente enough; she'd been "flirting" with the clerk in the bookstore. Too many beatings to keep track of, Suzy thought now, not bothering to resist as Dave's hands pushed her head down toward his groin.

She thought of biting down, then quickly banished the thought from her mind. He'd kill her for sure.

Besides, it wasn't enough to maim him. Not anymore.

Now she wanted him dead.

She thought she might have found the man to help her.

SEVEN

THE FIRST TIME JEFF tried to kill his brother, he was eight years old.

Not that he had anything against Will personally. Not that he wished him any particular harm. Just that he wanted him gone. Will was always there, always the center of attention, his every cry heeded, his every wish attended to. The Chosen One. He took up all the space of every room he entered, guzzling up all the oxygen, leaving Jeff abandoned on the fringe, gasping for air.

He was a colicky baby, and he cried often. Jeff used to lie in his bed at night listening to Will's howls and feeling strangely comforted by the fact that, despite all the attention lavished on him, his brother seemed as miserable as he was.

Except for one crucial difference: When Will cried, everybody listened, whereas when he cried, he was told to stop acting like a baby. He was told to be quiet, to lie still, and not to get up, even if he had to go to the bathroom in the middle of the night, because he might disturb the baby. And so he would lie there in the dark, his stomach cramping, surrounded by his stepmother's meticulously hand-woven quilts that loomed up at him, like hostile ghosts, from every corner of the room. And then, one night he hadn't been able to hold it any longer, and he'd wet the bed, and the next morning, his stepmother, the squalling baby wriggling in her arms, had discovered the still damp sheets and berated him, and Will had suddenly stopped crying and started gurgling, almost as if he understood what was happening and he was glad.

It was at that moment that Jeff decided to kill him.

He'd waited until everyone had gone to bed, then he'd crept into the nursery. Will's hand-painted wooden crib stood against one pale blue wall, a mobile of delicate, brightly colored cloth airplanes lazily circling his head. Toys of all shapes and sizes filled the shelves on the opposite wall. Stuffed animals–giant pandas and proud ponies, plush puppies and furry fishes–sat everywhere along the soft blue broadloom. It was a *real* room, Jeff understood even then. Not just some makeshift space in a room originally intended for another purpose. Like *his* room, with its small cot pushed up against the plain, white wall. His stepmother's former sewing room. Of course he was only supposed to be staying there temporarily. Until his own mother got her act together and came back to get him. Which couldn't have been soon enough. At least that's what he'd heard his stepmother confiding to a friend one afternoon, as they cooed happily over Will.

Jeff had stood over his brother's crib, watching him sleep, then grabbed the largest of the stuffed animals–a smiling, moss-green alligator–and covered Will's face with its fuzzy, lemon-yellow underbelly. Will's little feet had kicked frantically at the air for several seconds, then stopped, his lithe little body going suddenly, completely still, whereupon Jeff had fled the room. He spent the night cowering under his cot, terrified the quilted ghosts would come after him and smother him as he slept.

The next morning, when Jeff walked into the kitchen, there was Will, sitting proudly in his high chair, banging on its tray with his spoon, and crying for his cereal. Jeff had stared at him in awed silence, wondering whether he dreamed the whole episode.

He still wondered.

Even now, more than two decades later, lying in the double bed he shared with Kristin, poised between sleep and consciousness, Jeff wondered. Not whether he was capable of killing. He knew the answer to that. He'd killed at least half a dozen men in Afghanistan, including one man dispatched at point-blank range. But that was different. That was war. Different rules applied. You had to act quickly. You couldn't afford to second-guess yourself. Everyone was a potential suicide bomber. And Jeff was convinced the man had been reaching for a weapon, not lifting his arms in surrender, as his distraught wife later claimed.

Even now Jeff felt the sand in his eyes and the weight of the rifle in his hands. He heard the click of a trigger, followed by a woman's hysterical screams, and saw the look of disbelief in the man's dark eyes as an explosion of red circles suddenly splattered across the front of his white robe, like a pattern on one of his stepmother's quilts.

Yes, he was capable of killing.

But deliberate, cold-blooded murder?

Had he really tried to smother Will?

And later, when Will was three years old and Jeff was pushing him so high on the backyard swing set that his stepmother had come running out of the house and snatched him off, screaming, "What are you trying to do? Kill him?" Had that been his intent?

Or had he merely been trying to get her attention?

Whatever his goal, it hadn't worked. Will continued to thrive, no matter how nasty Jeff was to him. His father continued to ignore him, no matter how hard Jeff tried to please him. His mother never did get her act together or come back to claim him. His stepmother continued to shoo him out of her way.

And then, when he was fourteen, he'd met a tall, lanky bundle of angry energy by the name of Tom Whitman, a natural follower looking for someone to show him the way, and a lifelong friendship was born.

By the time Jeff was eighteen, rigorous daily workouts had added twenty pounds of well-sculpted muscle to his almost six-foot frame. The handsome face he'd inherited from his dad ensured that girls were as constant as they were easy. It seemed that all Jeff had to do was smile lazily in their general direction, and they came running.

Jeff grinned at the memory of those early conquests, opening his eyes to the warm sun pushing through the heavy blue drapes of his bedroom window. "Krissie?" he asked, feeling the empty space next to him in bed and glancing at the clock on the bedside table. *Two o'clock? In the afternoon?* Could that possibly be right? "Krissie?" he called again, louder this time.

The bedroom door opened. A man appeared in silhouette. "She went out," Will said.

Jeff pushed himself into a sitting position, flicked a wayward lock of blond hair away from his eyes. "Where'd she go?"

"Publix. Apparently we're out of toilet paper."

"No shit," Jeff said, laughing at his own joke.

Will laughed as well, although in truth, he didn't find the joke that funny. "You feeling okay?" he asked.

"Why wouldn't I be?"

"I don't know. You were pretty drunk last night. And it *is* the middle of the afternoon."

"It's Saturday," Jeff reminded him testily. "I get to sleep in."

"People don't need personal trainers on Saturday?" Will tried to keep his voice light. He hadn't meant to sound judgmental.

"I don't need *them*." Jeff climbed out of bed, not bothering to cover his nakedness as he headed for the bathroom, chuckling as Will averted his eyes. He relieved himself, washed his hands, threw some water over his face, and was back a minute later. "I don't suppose there's any coffee," he said, standing at the side of the bed and arching his back, stretching well-cut arms above his head. If Will was uncomfortable with this seemingly casual display of nudity, too bad, Jeff thought. It never hurt to let the competition know what they were dealing with. A little subtle intimidation could go a long way. Jeff grabbed his jeans from the edge of the bed and pulled them up over his bare hips.

"I think Kristin made a fresh pot before she went out," Will said, his eyes resolutely on the floor as he answered the question. He didn't want Jeff to think he was staring.

Jeff walked past Will through the living room and into the kitchen. He poured some coffee into a flamingo-shaped mug, added a bit of milk, then sipped at it gingerly. "When did she leave?"

"About twenty minutes ago. Said she'd be back in an hour."

"She makes a good pot of coffee."

"She does everything well."

"That she does," Jeff said, thinking of last night.

"You're really lucky."

"Yes, I am." Jeff caught a look of hesitation on his brother's face. "What?" he asked warily.

"What?" Will repeated.

"You look like you have something you want to say."

"No. Not really."

"Yes, really," Jeff insisted.

Will looked away, cleared his throat, looked back again. "It's just that . . ."

"Spit it out, little brother."

"Well . . . it's just that . . . last night . . ."

"Last night?"

"She doesn't mind?"

"Doesn't mind what?"

"You know," Will said. "About Suzy." Her name felt like a prayer on his lips. It made him feel good just saying it.

"Nothing happened with me and Suzy."

"She doesn't mind that you *wanted* something to happen, that something might have happened if . . ." What the hell was he doing? Will wondered. Was he just curious, or was he purposely trying to antagonize his brother?

" . . . if she'd chosen me?" Jeff said, finishing Will's sentence for him. "Trust me, something definitely would have happened. But she didn't choose me, did she? She chose you." The Chosen One, Jeff thought, taking another sip of coffee, tasting it suddenly bitter on the tip of his tongue.

"That's kind of beside the point."

"Exactly what *is* the point?" Jeff asked impatiently. God, was it any wonder his brother had struck out last night? Was he always this damn tentative? "What are you trying to say, Will?"

"I just have a hard time accepting Kristin's really okay with this."

"She's an amazing woman."

"Then why cheat on her?" The question popped from Will's mouth before he could stop it.

"It's hardly cheating when the other person says it's okay, now, is it?" Jeff said.

"I guess not. Just that . . ."

"What?"

"I don't understand why you'd want to."

"Hey, man. You know what they say. 'Nothing smells like fresh pussy.'" Jeff laughed. "And speaking of which, what exactly happened last night?" He pulled up a kitchen chair and straddled it, enjoying his brother's obvious discomfort.

Will remained standing. "You know what happened."

"I know what *didn't* happen. You didn't–"

"Can we not have this conversation again?" Will asked.

"Did you at least cop a feel? Please tell me you got something out of last night besides a hangover."

"We kissed," Will admitted after a lengthy pause. He didn't want to cheapen the memory by talking about it.

"You kissed? That's it?"

Will said nothing.

"Did you at least get a little tongue action going?"

"It was a good kiss," Will said, turning away and heading back into the living room.

Jeff was right behind him. "Aw, come on, little brother. You gotta give me more than that."

"'Fraid that's all there is." Will sank down on the sofa. "Sorry to disappoint you."

"Who says I'm disappointed? I saved a hundred bucks."

Will shrugged. "Contest isn't over yet," he said quietly.

Jeff's laugh filled the room. "Now that's more like it. Looks like you might have a little of Daddy's blood in you after all."

There was a moment's silence before Will spoke. "You speak to him lately?"

"Who?"

"You know who. Our father."

"Our father who art in Buffalo? Why would I?" Jeff asked, wandering back into the kitchen to top up his coffee.

"Just to check in, I guess. Say hello. See how he's doing."

"He's alive, isn't he?"

"Yeah. Of course he is."

"So, what's left to say? I assume someone will notify me when he croaks." Jeff returned to the living room in time to see his brother wince. "Not that I'm expecting to be named in the will or anything like that."

"Trust me, there isn't much of anything to inherit," Will said.

Jeff nodded understanding. "I guess all those years at Princeton pretty much depleted the family savings."

"That money came from my grandparents," Will said defensively. "On my mother's side," he added unnecessarily.

"Lucky you."

"I was really sorry to hear about your mom," Will said after another moment's pause.

"Don't be."

"Ellie says the cancer's very aggressive, that she only has a few months left at best."

"Yeah, well. These things happen. Not much you can do."

"You could go home," Will pressed, "see her before she dies."

"No. I can't do that."

"Ellie says she's been asking for you."

"My sister's quite the chatterbox. I didn't realize you two were so close."

"She's *my* sister, too," Will said.

"Half sister," Jeff corrected sharply. "She ask you to say something to me about this? Is that what you're doing here?"

"She asked me to mention it, yes. But no, that's not why I'm here."

"Just why *are* you here?"

"I missed you," Will replied simply. "You're my brother."

"Half brother," Jeff corrected a second time. This time his voice was flat, like a dull blade.

"I'd been going through a difficult time," Will said, deciding to throw caution to the wind. Maybe if he took him into his confidence, Jeff would be more inclined to take him into his. "There was this girl I was tutoring at Princeton. Amy . . ."

"Amy?" Jeff made himself comfortable in the oversize beige leather chair, leaning forward, his elbows resting on his thighs, steam rising from the coffee mug in his hands, only partly obscuring the smile on his lips.

"She was in first year. I was tutoring her in logic. We hit it off. One thing led to another. . . ."

"You fucked her," Jeff said.

"Jesus, Jeff. Is that all you ever think about?"

"Pretty much."

"There's more to a relationship than that."

"You didn't fuck her."

"I didn't say that."

"Did you or didn't you?"

"Yes, I . . . I did."

"Well, thank God for that. So, what was the problem?"

"There wasn't one. Not that I knew of anyway. We were pretty solid for most of the year, and then suddenly, she broke it off. She wouldn't give me a reason. I kept calling her, trying to talk to her, you know, to find out what I'd done wrong."

"What was his name?" Jeff asked.

"What?"

"The guy she dumped you for. What was his name?"

"How'd you know she dumped me for another guy?"

"It's not exactly rocket science, little brother. When did you finally figure it out?"

"I came out of a tutorial one morning and saw her kissing this guy in the hall, and I just lost it. I threw myself at him, like some deranged superhero. Next thing I knew, there was blood everywhere."

"Way to go, little brother."

"Way to get kicked out of Princeton."

"They kicked you out?"

"The guy's parents threatened to sue. Apparently I broke his nose and a couple of his teeth. So they suspended me for the rest of the semester. It's no big deal, really. I'm almost finished with my thesis anyway."

"Well, well," Jeff said, laughing. "I had no idea you philosophers were such a feisty bunch."

"We have our moments."

"I'm proud of you, little brother."

Will felt a surge of unexpected pride. His brother was proud of him.

A sudden, loud banging on the door shattered the moment.

"Guess Krissie forgot her key," Jeff said, not moving from his chair.

Will crossed to the door and opened it. Tom immediately burst through.

"What the hell's going on here?" he demanded, striding into the center of the room. "You don't answer your damn phone anymore?"

Jeff began searching through the pockets of his jeans.

"Is this it?" Will asked, retrieving Jeff's cell phone from the navy ottoman and tossing it at Jeff, who caught it with his left hand.

"Shit. I must have called you fifty times," Tom said angrily, pacing back and forth in front of Jeff's chair.

Will noted Tom was still wearing the same clothes from last night and that his breath reeked of beer and lack of sleep.

"Sorry, man," Jeff said. "I was pretty out of it."

"Can I get you a cup of coffee?" Will offered.

"Do I look like I want a cup of coffee?" Tom asked angrily.

"You look like you could use one," Jeff told him. "Double cream, double sugar," he instructed Will. "Is there a problem?" he asked Tom as Will left the room.

"Lainey's gone," Tom said. "She took the kids and left me."

"She'll be back."

"No. Not this time."

"You talked to her?"

"I tried to. She's over at her parents' house. I went there this morning, but she wouldn't see me. She's really pissed."

"Give her a few days to cool off. She'll change her mind."

"Her parents said I had until next Saturday to clear my things out of the house. Does that sound like she's going to change her mind?"

"Sounds like you need a good lawyer," Will said, venturing back into the living room with Tom's coffee.

"Sounds like you should mind your own damn business," Tom snapped.

"He might be right," Jeff said.

"Yeah? Like he knows jack shit about anything."

"Why don't I clear out of here for a while?" Will offered, depositing Tom's coffee on the ottoman in front of the sofa and walking toward the front door. He had no desire to get into an altercation with Tom, who was clearly spoiling for a fight.

"Why don't you go visit your girlfriend in Coral Gables?" Tom called after him. "She's married, by the way. Did you know that, Mr. Know-It-All?"

"What?" What was Tom talking about?

"What are you talking about?" Jeff asked in Will's stead.

"I'm talking about the fact that Suzy Pomegranate is a married woman."

"You're crazy," Will said.

"She forget to mention that during your romantic stroll along the beach?"

"You followed us?"

"To the beach, to the movies, back to her car. A silver BMW, in case you're wondering," he said to Jeff before turning his attention back to Will. "Saw you drop a sock in the sand, saw you drop the ball at the side of her car." Tom laughed. "That was some kiss-off, by the way. He tell you he struck out?" he asked Jeff.

"He did."

"I don't believe you," Will said, although the sinking feeling in the pit of his stomach told him he did.

"How much do you want to wager? A hundred bucks? How about a thousand?"

"You sound awfully sure of yourself," Jeff said.

"I should be. I followed the lady all the way to Coral Gables. One twenty-one Tallahassee Drive. Nice house. Two-car garage. Hubby waiting in the doorway. I can show you, if you want proof."

Jeff was instantly out of his seat and at the door. "Lead the way," he told Tom, motioning back toward Will. "You coming, little brother?"

What? No way. Absolutely not, Will thought. "After you," was what he said.

EIGHT

"THIS IS RIDICULOUS," WILL said twenty minutes later, still trying to find a comfortable position in the cramped backseat of Tom's rusty Impala. But the car was old and smelled worse than Tom did, even with all the windows open. Plus, Tom was a terrible driver, his foot moving restlessly back and forth between the accelerator and the brake for no obvious reason, so that the car was constantly jerking back and forth, as if it had the hiccups. If they didn't stop soon, Will was afraid he was going to be sick. "Where the hell is this place?"

"Patience, my man, patience," Tom said. The laugh in his voice indicated he was enjoying himself immensely.

Bastard, Will thought, realizing in that instant how much he disliked Tom, how much he'd always disliked him. You're loving this, aren't you? Loving the feeling of control you have over us, the unfamiliar rush of power.

"You sure you know where you're going?" Jeff asked from the front passenger seat.

"Relax, man. I was just here last night."

"Didn't we pass this corner five minutes ago?" Jeff pressed.

"All these streets look alike. Trust me. I know where I'm going."

"How you doing back there, little brother?" Jeff called over his shoulder.

"Not quite sure what the hell we're doing," Will replied honestly.

"We're going house hunting," Tom said, chuckling.

"And when we get there?" Will asked.

"Guess that'll be up to you, little brother," Tom said.

Will bristled at Tom's casual usurpation of the term. "I'm not your brother," he said, louder than he'd intended.

"You got that right," Tom agreed, followed by another sly cackle.

"How are they anyway?" Jeff asked.

"Who?"

"Alan and Vic. How are they doing?"

"How the hell should I know?" Tom asked defensively, the cackle dying in his throat.

Will sat up straighter in his seat, his interest suddenly sparked. "Isn't Alan some big-shot computer genius in California?"

"I don't know. Is he?"

"I'm pretty sure that's what my mother told me. She said she heard both your brothers have done extremely well for themselves."

"Screw you," Tom sneered.

"Well, somebody should," Jeff said. "Since it doesn't look like Suzy Pomegranate's going to be screwing him any time soon." He laughed, and Tom laughed with him, his annoying cackle reasserting itself, ripping through the dark green vinyl upholstery like a serrated-edged knife. Jeff swiveled around in his seat to wink at his brother. The wink said, "Relax. We're all in this together." Although clearly, Will thought, it was every man for himself.

Tom's car lurched to a sudden stop. "Ta-dah!" he announced triumphantly, both hands motioning across the street. "Here we are, boys. I give you one twenty-one Tallahassee Drive."

The three men stared at the modest, tan-colored bungalow with the white slate roof.

"Nice house," Jeff said. "You're sure this is where she lives?"

"Absolutely."

"Why should we believe you?" Will asked.

"Hey, man. I don't give a flying fuck whether you believe me or not. I'm telling you this is her place. She pulled into that driveway, drove into that garage, walked up that pathway to that door, where some guy was waiting. And not looking too happy either."

"Maybe it was her father," Will said, thinking it was possible Suzy still lived at home. Maybe she'd moved back in with her parents after her marriage fell apart. Although she hadn't actually said her marriage had fallen apart, he thought, straining to remember.

"Have you ever been married, Will?" she'd asked.

"No. You?"

"Yes. But let's not talk about that, okay?"

So, she'd never actually said her marriage was over. Which meant that technically, at least, she hadn't lied.

"Her father?" Tom scoffed. "Are you shitting me?"

"What did this guy look like?" Jeff asked.

"About six feet tall, one eighty, one ninety. Late thirties, maybe forty. Not bad looking. Well dressed. Wearing a jacket and tie at two in the morning, if you can believe it."

"Sounds more like a visitor than a husband," Will said, trying to make himself believe it.

"Sure, buddy. Dream on."

"What difference does it make who the guy is?" Jeff asked after a pause. "Does anybody here really care if she's married? I mean, as far as I'm concerned, it just makes things that much simpler. No worries about her getting too attached, no promises to break, nobody getting hurt. The girl's just out for a little fun. Same as we are. Sounds like the perfect fit to me."

"But if that's all she was after, why didn't . . . ?"

"Why didn't you score?" Tom interrupted, happily finishing Will's sentence for him.

"Maybe you just didn't turn her on, little brother."

"Maybe she realized she'd picked the wrong guy," Tom added.

"I say we confront her," Jeff said.

"What?"

"A hundred dollars to whoever knocks on her door and asks her husband whether little Suzy can come out and play."

"You're on," Tom said, pushing open his car door.

"Wait. No." Will reached over the front seat and grabbed Tom's shoulder, holding him back. "This is ridiculous. Please, can we just get out of here?"

"Let go of me, man."

"I won't let you do this."

"You think you can stop me?"

"Now, now, boys," Jeff said. "Behave yourselves." He laughed. "We're just playing with you, little brother. Tom's not going anywhere, are you, Tom?"

Tom was chortling as he closed the car door. "Really had you going there, didn't we? Shit, you sounded just like a little girl. 'Please, can we just get out of here?'" he mimicked.

"Hey," Jeff said, catching sight of curtains moving in the front window of 121 Tallahassee Drive. "Did you see that?"

"See what?"

"Somebody's watching us."

"What?" Tom immediately ducked down in his seat. "Get down. They'll see you."

"Shit," Will swore, doing as he was told.

Only Jeff remained upright. "The front door's opening," he announced as Will closed his eyes and said a silent prayer.

Please let this be all a dream, he wished. Please let me be asleep on the sofa in Jeff's living room, lost in sweet dreams about romantic walks along the ocean and soft kisses on the street. Please let none of this be happening. "Who is it?" he heard himself ask.

"It's Suzy."

"What's she doing?"

"Just standing there, looking around," Jeff said. "Wait. Now she's coming this way."

"What? Shit."

Will peeked out the open side window as Suzy ran down her front walk, crossing the road without looking in either direction and making a beeline for Tom's car. She was wearing long pants and a long-sleeved blue shirt, despite the oppressive heat. Large, dark glasses hid most of her face. But even with the glasses, Will could tell she was frightened.

"What are you doing here?" she asked without preamble, her head moving back and forth between Jeff and Tom in the front seat and Will in the back.

"We might ask you the same thing," Tom replied, sitting up tall.

"You have to leave," Suzy said, staring imploringly at Will. "Now." She glanced back at Jeff. "Please."

"Is there a problem?" Jeff asked.

"Please, before he sees you . . ."

"You're married," Will stated more than asked.

Suzy lowered her head, said nothing.

"Told you," Tom said.

"Please, just go," Suzy said, ignoring him.

"Suzy?" A man's voice floated effortlessly across the street from the doorway of 121 Tallahassee Drive. "What's going on out there?"

Suzy's chin dropped toward her chest and her shoulders slumped.

"He's coming over," Tom said.

"Quick," Suzy said. "Do you have a map?"

"What?"

"A street map. Please tell me you have one in your glove compartment."

Jeff opened the glove compartment, began rifling through the mess inside. His fingers made contact with a torn package of chewing gum, a crumpled ball of old tissues, and something sticky he didn't even want to think about.

"Is there a problem?" the man asked, approaching the car. He was casually dressed in khaki slacks and a blue and gold striped golf shirt, but otherwise he was much as Tom had described, Will thought, taking note of the man's broad shoulders and large hands.

"They're lost," Suzy said, a touch too brightly.

"Just asking the lady for directions." Jeff made a great show of unfolding the large and unwieldy map he'd miraculously managed to locate scrunched at the back of the glove compartment. "Trying to figure out where the hell we are."

The man crouched down, his tanned face filling the driver's-side window as he nudged Suzy aside. She took several steps back, closer to where Will was sitting. It took all Will's resolve not to reach for her hand.

"I'm afraid my wife isn't very good with directions. Are you, sweetheart?"

"I'm afraid not."

You're afraid of something, Will thought.

"Don't I know you?" the man suddenly asked Jeff.

Will found himself holding his breath.

"Don't think so," Jeff said easily.

"I'm pretty sure we've met somewhere. You work around here?"

"Nah. I work in Wynwood. Elite Fitness over on Northwest Fortieth. You know it?"

"Can't say that I do. You're a personal trainer?"

"Jeff Rydell, at your service."

"I might take you up on that one day. What street are you looking for?" he asked, flexing his fingers.

Will thought he detected some bruising at the man's knuckles. His eyes shot to Suzy's face.

"They're trying to find Miracle Mile," Suzy said, avoiding Will's penetrating gaze and staring down at her feet, her sunglasses acting as a shield from his prying eyes.

"Miracle Mile? Everybody knows where to find Miracle Mile."

"Everyone except my friend here," Jeff said, rolling his eyes in Tom's direction.

"You can go inside now, sweetheart," the man said softly, although it was clear it wasn't a request. "I can take care of this."

Suzy backed away from the car. "Good luck," she said directly to Will. Then she turned and hurried up the front walk toward her house without a backward glance.

"Thanks for your help," Jeff called after her.

"The Miracle Mile," the man mused, as if giving the matter serious consideration. "Let's see. What's the best way to get there from here? Probably along Anderson Road."

"Anderson Road?" Tom asked.

"Go to the end of this street, turn left, go straight for two blocks, then turn left again, then right at the next stoplight. That's Anderson. Keep going till you hit the Miracle Mile."

"Sounds simple enough," Jeff said.

"You're sure I don't know you from somewhere?" the man asked pointedly. "I'm sure I've seen you around. The Wild Zone, maybe?"

Will felt his throat go instantly dry. What was going on? You didn't just pull a name like the Wild Zone out of thin air. How much did Suzy's husband know? How much had she told him?

"The Wild Zone?" Jeff repeated, chewing on the words, his face betraying nothing. "Is that a clothing store?"

The man laughed, although the sound was hollow. "It's a bar over in South Beach. You've never been there?"

"Don't think so."

"Me neither," echoed Tom. "What about you, Will? You ever take a trip to the Wild Zone?"

"I'm new in town, remember?" Will said, pushing the words from his mouth.

"Well, enjoy the Miracle Mile," the man told Jeff, as if the others didn't exist. Clearly, if he suspected anything—and just as clearly, he suspected *something*—then his suspicions fell squarely on Jeff. The man straightened up, began backing away.

"Thanks again," Tom said with a wave.

He was turning on the ignition when the man's face suddenly reappeared in the open window. "Oh," the man said, as if it were an afterthought. "Don't let me catch you boys in this neighborhood again." He winked, then turned away, striding purposefully back to his house.

"What the hell?" Tom sputtered as the front door shut behind him. "Who does that asshole think he is?" He reached under his seat, pulled out a small handgun, brandished it in the air. "I've got half a mind to shoot that motherfucking piece of shit."

"Whoa!" Jeff exclaimed, stopping Tom's hand as it began waving the gun back and forth. "You've got half a mind all right. What the hell are you doing with that thing?"

"He's got a gun?" Will cried. "Is he crazy? You want to get us killed?"

"Aw, don't get your panties all in a knot. It's no big deal."

"We're not in Kandahar, jerk-off," Jeff admonished him. "Put the damn thing away."

"Shit," Tom said, returning the gun to its previous location.

"A gun. I don't believe it." Will's breath was short and labored. It stabbed at his windpipe. "Is it loaded?"

"Of course it's loaded. You think I'm some pussy, walking around with an unloaded gun?"

"I think you're a lunatic. That's what I think."

"Okay. Enough." Jeff reached across Tom to start the ignition. "Let's get out of here."

"What the hell just happened?" Tom asked as he pulled away from the curb.

Will said nothing, Tom having taken the words right out of his mouth.

"SO, SUZY, YOU want to tell me what that was all about?" her husband asked gently.

She was sitting on the sofa, Dave standing directly in front of her, looming large above her, like a spitting king cobra.

"I don't understand."

"Tell me about the men in the car, Suzy."

"There's nothing to tell," she started to explain. "I looked outside, saw this strange car sitting there—"

"You just happened to look outside?" he interrupted.

"Yes." She'd looked outside, thoughts of escape swirling around in her head. Could she make it out the door without his noticing? How long before he realized she was gone? How many hours before he tracked her down, came after her, made good on his threat to kill her should she ever try to leave?

"And you saw a strange car with three strange men sitting in it, and so you naturally went outside to say hello?"

She'd recognized the car immediately as the one that had tailed her the night before, the one she'd assumed belonged to a detective hired by her husband. Then she recognized the men from the bar, saw Will in the backseat. "I saw them struggling with a map," she told Dave. "They were obviously lost. I was just trying to be helpful." I was just trying to get away, she thought. She'd run across the street with only that in mind. She couldn't afford to waste any more time. "Take me with you," she'd been about to cry. Instead, what emerged was, "What are you doing here? You have to leave. Now."

Dave smiled, sat down beside her, took her hand in his. "Your hands are ice cold," he noted.

"Are they?"

"Are you cold, sweetheart?" He put his arm around her, pulled her tight against him.

"A little."

He started rubbing the side of her arm. She winced as he pressed down, hard, on one of her sore spots. "Oh, I'm sorry, darling. Did I hurt you?"

"No. It's fine."

"Because you know how much I hate hurting you. Don't you?"

"Yes."

"Yes, what?"

"I know how much you hate hurting me."

"Almost as much as I hate being lied to. You're not lying to me, are you, darling?"

"No."

"You've really never seen any of those men before?"

"No. Of course not."

"Not even at the Wild Zone?"

"The Wild Zone?" Dear God, what had they told him?

"The good-looking one with the blond hair? The personal trainer," Dave clarified. "You haven't been hooking up with him?"

"What? No."

"Don't tell me it's that stupid-looking one in the driver's seat. Please tell me you have better taste than that."

"I don't know what you're talking about. I haven't seen any of those men before."

"So, they just happened to be driving through Coral Gables and stopped in front of our house, looking for the Miracle Mile."

"That's what they said."

"Which any idiot could find blindfolded."

Suzy said nothing. It sounded lame even to her ears.

Dave's arm snaked its way around her neck, his hand massaging the top of her spine. "You know one of the best things about being a doctor, Suzy?" he asked. "People respect you. They think that because you're a doctor, it follows you're an honorable man. So they tend to believe whatever you tell them."

Suzy nodded, although his arm wasn't allowing her much room to maneuver.

"For example, if I were to tell people, the police for instance, that my wife had been moody and depressed of late, they probably wouldn't be too surprised to learn she'd taken her own life. Which is one of the other nice things about being a doctor," he continued, almost cheerily. "I know how the body works. And what it takes to make it stop working. Do you understand what I'm saying, sweetheart?"

"Dave, please—"

"Do you understand? A simple yes or no is all that's required."

"Yes."

"Good." He relaxed his grip. "Because it would truly break my heart if something were to happen to you. You know that, don't you? Again, a simple yes or no will suffice."

Suzy closed her eyes, pushed the word from her mouth. "Yes."

"Good. Now, why don't you slip into something sexy? Seems your husband's feeling a little amorous."

Suzy pushed herself off the sofa, walked silently toward the bedroom.

"Hurry back," she heard him say.

NINE

"JEFF, PHONE FOR YOU," Melissa called from behind the reception desk that was tucked near the entrance to the small boutique gym.

"If you'll excuse me," Jeff said to the middle-aged woman in the black leotard and turquoise jersey. "Why don't you do a couple of minutes on the treadmill? I'll be right back."

"I told him you were with a client," Melissa apologized, "but he says it's an emergency."

The old-fashioned black rotary phone was barely out of Melissa's hand before Tom's voice was bellowing in Jeff's ear. "She's with a goddamn lawyer," he was shouting.

Jeff looked anxiously over his shoulder to check on whether his boss was hovering. But Larry was busy with a ponytailed young woman on the elliptical machine. Still, he'd have to be careful. You weren't supposed to take personal calls at work. Larry might have been only a couple of years older than he was, and he was pretty laid-back, as far as bosses went, but he was still Jeff's superior, and Jeff didn't want to lose this job. Elite Fitness, located above a bakery, wasn't too far from his apartment, and the clientele was nice. Not half as snooty as the last place he'd worked. "Who's with a lawyer?" he asked, his voice low, barely audible over the loud rap music blasting from the nearby speakers.

"Who do you think? Lainey, that's who. Who the hell else would I be talking about?"

Jeff decided not to remind Tom about the weekend. "Please tell me you're not following her," he whispered, holding one hand over the mouthpiece, his eyes darting between the large machines at one end of the room and the benches and free weights at the other. He shifted his position, trying to avoid both the direct noontime sun pouring in through the large front window and the mirrors that were pretty much everywhere. Despite the air-conditioning, it was pretty warm in the long, rectangular room, although the pleasing aroma of freshly baked bread wafting up from the vents did a nice job of masking the smell of sweat that permeated the wood floors.

"Of course I'm following her," Tom said impatiently. "How else would I know where she is? First thing Monday morning, and already she's talking to a goddamn attorney."

"Tell me you don't have a gun."

"I don't have a gun."

Jeff knew immediately Tom was lying. "Jesus, Tom, you can't keep doing this. You're gonna get yourself killed."

"Anybody gets killed around here, it's not gonna be me."

"What about your job?" Jeff asked, deciding to try a different tack.

"Not to worry. I called in sick."

Jeff felt the dull thud of an incipient headache at the base of his neck. He didn't have the patience for Tom right now. "Look, I can't talk now. I'm with a client."

"I go over to her parents' house around nine o'clock this morning," Tom continued, as if Jeff hadn't spoken. "I figured I'm being polite, you know, not getting there too early. Lainey's just leaving the house, she's dressed all nice, so I know something's up. I mean, why is she all dressed up so early on a Monday morning? Where's she going? So, I decide to follow her, find out what's going on. She drives over to West Flagler, goes into this bright pink building that looks like a giant bottle of Pepto-Bismol. I check the directory. All lawyers, man."

"Okay, so she's talking to a lawyer. That doesn't mean—"

"It means she's gonna file for divorce. It means she's gonna try to take my kids away from me. Those kids mean everything to me, man. You know that."

Jeff decided this probably wasn't the best time to point out that Tom rarely spent much time with his children. "Look, why don't you take a few deep breaths and try to calm down. Then call your boss, tell him you're feeling better, and go in to work. It'll take your mind off Lainey."

"I won't let that bitch take my kids away from me."

"Just hold tight. Don't do anything stupid. Wait and see what happens in a few days."

"I know what's going to happen in a few days. I'm gonna get served with divorce papers, that's what's going to happen."

"Maybe not. Maybe if you don't go flying off the handle, if you stay calm . . ." Jeff stopped. This was Tom he was talking to, he reminded himself.

"Maybe you could talk to her," Tom said.

"What? No way."

"Please, Jeff. You gotta help me. It's your fault I'm in this mess."

"What?" What is Tom talking about now? Jeff wondered as he watched Caroline Hogan reduce the speed of her treadmill, thinking that for a woman of almost sixty, she was in remarkably good shape. "How the hell do you figure that?"

"If it hadn't been for you and that stupid bet at the bar . . ."

"Hey, it was *your* idea to go chasing after Suzy."

The receptionist cleared her throat, her eyes motioning to her right.

"So what time works best for you?" Jeff asked loudly as Larry walked by, his young client trailing after him, her ponytail swaying from side to side.

"Hi, Jeff," the girl, whose name was Kelly, said, a big smile on her pretty, heart-shaped face.

Jeff returned her smile as Tom's voice boomed against his ear. "What are you talking about?" he asked.

"Certainly. Why don't you check your schedule again and get back to me? I'm sure we can work something out."

"What the hell's going on there?"

"I'm afraid I don't have any openings until seven o'clock."

"Are you shitting me or what?"

"Look," Jeff whispered when Larry and the girl were comfortably out of earshot. "I told you I can't talk. My boss is watching."

"Who gives a shit? You don't think this is more important?"

"I'll call you later. In the meantime, go home, calm down, stop following her. You hear me, Tom? Are you listening to me?"

"I won't follow her."

"Okay, good. I'll talk to you later." Jeff hung up the phone, finding it fascinating that someone who lied as often as Tom did was still so bad at it. He handed the receiver back to Melissa. "Thanks for the heads-up."

"Anytime. Oh, your eleven o'clock canceled."

"Everything all right?" Caroline Hogan asked, stepping off her treadmill and walking toward him, the front of her turquoise T-shirt sprinkled with coin-sized beads of perspiration, manicured red fingernails dabbing at her moist upper lip.

"My eleven o'clock canceled," Jeff said dryly. "And a friend of mine's wife just left him."

She arched one carefully plucked eyebrow, her forehead wrinkling ever so slightly.

A spot the Botox missed, Jeff thought, guiding her toward a nearby exercise bench and directing her to lie on her back.

Caroline Hogan lay down and arranged her chin-length, curly blond hair on the white towel beneath her head, her still-shapely legs dangling over the end of the narrow bench, her Adidas runners resting on the light hardwood floor.

"How fast did you go on the treadmill?"

"Six-point-five."

"Not half bad for an old broad." The words were out of Jeff's mouth before he had time to edit them, and he was grateful when he heard Caroline laugh. She had such a nice laugh. Not too harsh, not too girlish. Substantial. Genuine. Not like Kristin, whose laugh was surprisingly tentative, or Lainey, whose laugh always sounded forced, both women laughing almost in spite of themselves. "He's better off without her," Jeff said, placing a twelve-pound weight in Caroline's outstretched hands.

"I assume you're talking about your friend whose wife left," Caroline stated, bending her elbows to lower the weight to the middle of her forehead and then bringing it up into the air again, without needing to be told. She'd been coming in twice a week for the last three years, warming up on the treadmill and then working out for an hour with a trainer. Her previous trainer had left for New York two months ago, and Jeff had been hired to take his place. Caroline knew exactly what was expected of her, a quality Jeff liked in a woman.

A quality sadly lacking in Lainey Whitman.

Although surely she'd known what she was getting into when she married Tom.

"Arms straight," he reminded Caroline. "Bring them up a little higher. That's good, Caroline. Do another eight."

"Why'd she leave?" Caroline asked.

"Who knows?" Jeff shrugged. "Why'd you leave *your* husband?"

"Which one?"

"How many have there been?"

"Just two. I left the first one when I caught him in bed with the nanny–trite, but true; the second one died of cancer four years ago, so technically, I guess, *he* left *me*."

"Think you'll ever get married again?"

"Oh, I hope so," Caroline said, sounding like a teenager, as Jeff took the weight from her hands. "I always liked being married. What about you?"

"I've never had the pleasure." The word "pleasure" stuck in Jeff's throat. Sometimes, often when he least expected it, he could still hear his mother and father screaming at each other behind the closed door of their bedroom. Not much pleasure in that. He pointed to the floor. "A set of push-ups."

"It's so easy for you men," Caroline said, getting down on the floor and extending her legs straight out behind her, pushing up and down with the palms of her hands.

"Slower," Jeff cautioned. "You think it's easy for us?"

"Isn't it?"

"In what way?"

"With women," Caroline grunted.

Jeff looked toward Melissa, whose slightly embarrassed smile revealed she'd been watching him, and then over at Kelly, who gave him a discreet little wave with the fingers of her left hand as she prepared to hoist two ten-pound barbells to her chest. "I guess," he said, imagining his mother reflected in the large mirror behind her.

"Who were you with this time?" his mother demanded, her voice an accusation.

"I wasn't with anyone," came his father's testy reply. "I was at the office."

"Yeah, sure. Like you were at the office last Thursday night, and the Thursday night before that."

"If you say so."

"I say you're a no-good son of a bitch, that's what I say."

"Takes one to know one."

"Okay, come down a little farther, Caroline," Jeff said loudly, using his own voice to block out the sound of his parents' fighting, the way he used to when he was a little boy. "That's better. Do another ten."

"Why are you shouting?" Caroline asked.

"Sorry. Didn't realize I was."

"Everything all right?" Larry asked, walking past, muscular arms bulging from beneath his sleeveless white T-shirt, Kelly following dutifully after him, although her eyes followed Jeff.

"Music's a little loud," Jeff said.

"It is, isn't it?" Larry agreed. He walked over to the far wall and turned it down. "How's that?"

"Much better," Jeff lied. In truth, he loved loud music. Especially rap and hip-hop, the kind of music that got not only inside your head but underneath your fingernails and in between your toes. The kind of music that usually obliterated all conscious thought.

When he was a little boy trying not to listen to his parents screaming at one another in the next room, he'd turn his radio up as loud as he could, singing along with Aerosmith or Richard Marx, and if he didn't know the words, making them up. Hell, he even sang along with Abba. *You are the dancing queen.*

Ellie had loved that one. His sister was three years older than he was, and sometimes, when their parents were going at it, he'd run into her room, and they'd put on the radio and he'd sing, and she'd dance, sometimes grabbing him and twirling him around and around in circles until, exhausted and dizzy, they'd collapse in a heap on the floor, the room continuing to spin happily about their heads.

You are the dancing queen.

That was before their mother had pulled them out of their warm beds one wintry night, throwing their coats on over their pajamas, then bundling them into the car in the bitter cold and driving down the highway, without even making sure their seat belts were fastened, crying and sputtering words he didn't understand but knew were bad just from the way she was spitting them at the windshield. And then driving for such a long time before pulling into the parking lot of a motel on the outskirts of town and dragging them out of the car, making them trudge through the snow without their boots, the bottoms of their pajamas trailing through icy, cold puddles, everybody crying by the time they reached door 17.

"Do seventeen more," Jeff said now.

"What?" Caroline pushed herself up onto her knees. "Seventeen more? Are you kidding me?"

"Sorry. Just wanted to see if you were keeping track."

"Oh, I'm keeping track all right."

"Have a seat at the edge of the bench." Jeff reached for a twenty-five-pound bar as Caroline held up both hands. He lowered the bar into her open palms, her long, red fingernails curling around it. "Hands out a little wider. That's good. Okay, exhale on the way up. Try to keep the arms straight."

The child Jeff took a deep breath as he watched his mother's hands pummel the motel room door. "Let me in, you bastard," she yelled into the cold night air. "I know you're in there."

And then the door to room 17 opening slowly, and his father standing there, wearing only his boxer shorts and a loopy grin, a woman sitting up in the bed behind him, a sheet gathered up under her chin. But before he had time to wonder what his father was doing with this strange woman in this strange place in the middle of the night, his mother was already pushing him and his sister out of the way, screaming that the woman was a filthy whore, and snatching the sheet away from her, so that her naked breasts were fully exposed, and then lunging at her, scratching at the side of her face with her long, red fingernails.

Just like Caroline's, he realized, watching the bar in Caroline's hands go up and down, up and down. Was that what had triggered these unwanted memories of his mother? Or maybe it was the conversation he'd had on Saturday with Will.

Did his mother really have only a few months left to live?

"Stupid bitches," he heard his father mutter, a look of bemused indifference on his face as he watched the two women wrestling on the motel bed.

"That's very good, Caroline," Jeff said now, careful to keep his voice steady and low. "You're very strong."

"Well, they do say women are the stronger sex."

"You think it's true?" He handed her a skipping rope. "Do one minute."

"I think in some ways we are," Caroline said.

"What ways?"

"Emotionally." She began to skip in place. "You men are a lot more fragile than you realize."

"Didn't you just finish saying it was so easy for us?"

"Having things easy doesn't make you any less fragile," Caroline said cryptically.

What the hell is she talking about? Jeff wondered, growing irritated with the conversation. He didn't like it when women made him feel stupid. "Why don't you grab some water?" he suggested when she was through skipping.

"Stupid bitches," he heard his father repeat.

"You're going to go live with your father for a while," his mother was saying in the next breath.

The child Jeff stood ramrod straight, trying desperately to contain the tears he felt forming behind his eyes as he watched his mother throwing his clothes into a small brown suitcase on the bed. "But I don't want to live with him." He was all of seven years old. Ten-year-old Ellie stood in the bedroom doorway, eyes wide as saucers, watching.

"I'm afraid you don't have a choice. Your father doesn't give me enough money to take care of both of you, and I'm tired of fighting with him over every last dime. So, let him look after you for a while. That should take some of the bloom off the rose with Miss Clarabelle."

Miss Clarabelle was the name his mother had christened his father's new wife, although her name was actually just Claire. Jeff had never really liked her. She was thin and bony and always upset about something. And now that she had a new baby, whenever he visited, he always seemed to be in the way.

"I just need some time to myself," his mother continued, snapping his suitcase shut. "To figure out what's best for me. For all of us," she added, an afterthought at best, Jeff realized even then.

"What about Ellie? Is she going to Daddy's?"

"No. Ellie stays with me."

"Why can't I stay, too?" Jeff cried. "I promise I won't be any trouble. I promise I'll be a good boy."

"It's just that he reminds me so much of his father," he heard his mother say on the phone later, making no effort to soften her voice, as he sat sniffling on the stairs, waiting for his dad to pick him up. "I swear they have the same damn face. And I can't help it, but every time I look at him, I just want to strangle him. I know it's irrational. I know it's not his fault. But I just can't stand looking at him."

"This is just temporary," his father said later, leading Jeff into his stepmother's quilt-filled sewing room and depositing his suitcase on the narrow cot that had been hastily pushed against the far wall. "Soon as your mother gets her act together, she'll be back for you."

She never did come back. Except for the occasional strained visit, during which she always seemed to focus on a spot just past his head. Eventually, even those visits stopped, although Ellie had been vigilant about maintaining contact with both her father and her brother over the ensuing years.

"Ellie says she's been asking for you," Jeff heard Will say.

"Jeff? Jeff?" Caroline was saying now. "Earth to Jeff. Are you there?"

Jeff returned abruptly to the present, the image of his younger self disappearing in a streak of reflected sunlight. "Sorry."

"I think there's somebody here to see you." Caroline pointed toward the reception desk. Jeff's head snapped toward it, for one crazy second expecting to see his sister, or maybe even his mother, standing in the doorway. Instead he saw a frail-looking young woman with dark hair and large sunglasses.

"Excuse me a minute," Jeff said, walking quickly toward her. What the hell was she doing here?

Suzy removed her sunglasses as he approached, revealing a cheek that was bruised and swollen. "I need to talk to you," she said.

TEN

THIRTY MINUTES LATER, JEFF slipped into an uncomfortable wooden chair at the back of the bakery located directly beneath Elite Fitness. The bakery boasted a long, exotic coffee bar, and half a dozen tiny round tables for two were crowded into the rear of the small, sweet-smelling space. "Glad you could wait," he said, wondering exactly what he was doing here, what *she* was doing here.

"Thanks for squeezing me in," Suzy said, stirring the cinnamon-laced cappuccino she'd ordered while waiting for Jeff to finish up with his client.

"My eleven o'clock canceled."

"Lucky for me," Suzy said.

"You don't look very lucky." Jeff glanced out the long side window, watching his boss accompany Caroline Hogan across the street to the chocolate-brown Mercedes parked in front of a hydrant. She'd commented more than once during their session that his mind seemed to be elsewhere—especially after Suzy's unexpected appearance—and he hoped she wasn't complaining to Larry about it.

Suzy adjusted the sunglasses she was wearing despite the dimness of the room's interior and took a sip of her coffee. When she looked back up, foam was clinging to her upper lip. She pressed her lips together, swiped delicately at the foam with the back of her fingers, as if even the slightest pressure would be too painful.

"Your husband do that?" Jeff asked, motioning toward her face.

"What? No. Of course not."

"You gonna tell me you walked into a door?"

Suzy laughed self-consciously. "Actually, I was walking a neighbor's dog." The familiar lie escaped her mouth with surprising ease. "Fluffy. She's this really cute little Pomeranian. All white and . . . fluffy. Anyway, she has one of those leashes, the kind you can click when you want the dog to stop. You know the kind I mean?"

"Can't say that I do."

"Well, anyway, Fluffy started running, and I tried clicking, but I obviously wasn't doing it right, and I guess I wasn't paying attention either, and my feet got caught up in the leash, and I went flying, ass over teakettle, as they say."

"Who says that?" Jeff rubbed his forehead. He was getting tired of people lying to him.

"Well . . . my husband's mother, for one," Suzy replied. "Or at least she used to. She's been pretty sick lately. Cancer."

"My mother has cancer," Jeff said, then shook his head. Why had he told her that?

"I'm sorry to hear that."

"Don't be." Jeff fidgeted in the too-small chair, inhaling the smell of freshly baked bread. "What are you doing here?" he asked.

"I was going to ask you the same thing," Suzy said. "About Saturday," she clarified.

Jeff shrugged. Two could play this game, he was thinking, although truthfully, he wasn't sure exactly what game they were playing. "What can I say? We were just three guys out for an afternoon drive."

"Who just happened to find themselves in front of my house?"

"You trip over dog leashes," Jeff said pointedly. "We go for afternoon drives."

Suzy nodded, looked down at her cappuccino. "Your friend followed me the other night. I recognized his car."

Jeff laughed. "Tom was never very good at reconnaissance work."

"Why did he follow me?"

"Why don't you ask him?"

"I'd rather ask you."

"Why is that?"

"I'm not sure. Maybe because you have a kind face," she said, then paused. "And your friend doesn't."

"And my brother? What kind of face does he have?"

Another pause, another glance at her coffee. "What is it you want me to say?"

"Why did you choose Will?" Jeff asked, unable to stop himself. Why had she come to see him? What was she really doing here?

Suzy smiled, although the corners of her mouth turned down instead of up. "I thought he looked nice."

"Nice?"

"Harmless."

"Nice and harmless," Jeff observed. "Clearly a winning combination."

Suzy fidgeted in her chair, looked toward the counter on her left. "They have such wonderful-looking pastries here."

"Thinking of taking some bagels home for hubby?"

"Do you think we could dispense with the sarcasm?"

"Do you think we could dispense with the lies?" Jeff countered.

"I'm sorry. It's just that my life's a little complicated at the moment."

"Lives tend to get that way when married women go to places like the Wild Zone, trolling for men."

"I didn't go there to pick up men."

"You just couldn't resist nice and harmless."

"I don't know what I was thinking. I really don't. The bartender brought me my drink, told me about the bet you guys had going. Suddenly, the whole thing took on a life of its own. I acted on impulse, and, obviously, I made a mistake."

"Your mistake was that you picked the wrong guy."

"Did I?"

"I think you know that."

Suzy shook her head, revealing a panoply of bruises. "I don't know what I know anymore."

"I think you do. I think that's why you're here." What am I doing? Jeff wondered. Was he really coming on to this woman? Why? Because he was genuinely interested in her? Or because his brother was?

Suzy slowly removed her glasses, revealing a yellowing half moon beneath her right eye. "You think I'm here because of you?"

"Aren't you?" Back off, Jeff was thinking. Don't do this. Not only was her husband a lunatic, the man was a wife beater as well. Who knew what else he might be capable of? Although men who beat up women were generally cowards, he thought, afraid to pick on somebody their own size. Jeff was definitely his size.

"I thought you had a girlfriend," Suzy said, sidestepping his question. "Kristin. Right?"

"Right," Jeff agreed. "Kristin."

"She's very beautiful."

"Yes, she is." Not only was she beautiful, she was everything he'd ever wanted in a woman—adventurous, understanding, nonjudgmental, great in bed. In truth, Jeff had never felt any real desire to cheat on her and did so far less often than he let on. Still, appearances had to be maintained, and it was never a good idea to let a woman get too comfortable. Besides, in this case, there were several hundred dollars at stake. And, even more important than money, bragging rights.

"So, what's this all about?" Suzy was asking.

"You tell me. This was your idea, remember?" Jeff sank back in his chair, throwing one arm over its high back, exaggerating the already exaggerated swell of his bicep.

"Contrary to what you think," she began slowly, "I came here today because I didn't know how else to get in touch with Will, and I remembered your telling my husband where you worked."

Jeff felt his entire body tense. "We're in the phone book. You could have called." Had she really come all this way to talk about Will?

"I have a message I'd like you to give him," she said, ignoring his remark.

"I'm not a messenger boy," Jeff said, bristling.

"He's your brother."

"Which doesn't make me his keeper."

"Please. I just want to apologize. I know I've hurt him. I could see it in his face."

"I think you're giving yourself way too much credit."

"Maybe. I'd just really appreciate it if you'd tell him I'm sorry."

"Tell him yourself."

"I can't."

"Sure you can."

"Clearly I won't be going back to the Wild Zone any time soon."

Jeff stood up. "You won't have to. Come on. You have your car? I'll take you to him."

"Now? You really think that's wise?"

"I don't know. I've never been very good with 'wise.'"

"Me neither."

"You coming?"

Suzy pushed herself to her feet, pausing for an instant to draw the pleasing aroma of newly melted chocolate into her lungs, then reluctantly following Jeff out of the bakery into the blistering heat of the fast-approaching noontime sun.

"YOU WANT TO talk about it?" Kristin was asking. She was standing at the open fridge door, wearing a low-cut, lime-green T-shirt and short, tight Daisy Dukes. Her long blond hair was pulled into a loose bun at the top of her head. A series of wispy tendrils spiraled down toward her ears. Bare toes, their toenails painted a bright coral, tapped against the cheap linoleum floor.

Will stared over at her from his seat at the kitchen table. He was wearing jeans and a white T-shirt. His feet were also bare. "What do you mean?"

"You've been staring at that bowl of soggy cereal for the past hour. That tells me you have something on your mind."

"So she's not only gorgeous, she's perceptive as well."

Kristin pulled a quart of fresh orange juice from the fridge and poured herself a glass. "I love it when you talk dirty," she said, holding out the carton. "You want some?"

"Sure."

Kristin poured him a glass and deposited it on the table, pulling up the chair beside him. "So, are you going to tell me?"

"She's married," Will said simply.

Kristin didn't have to ask whom he was referring to. "Yeah, I know. Jeff told me about your little trip to Coral Gables."

"Why am I such an idiot?"

"How can you be an idiot? You have a PhD from Princeton."

"I haven't finished my dissertation," he reminded her. "And trust me, when it comes to women, I'm an idiot."

"Well, don't sweat it. It's part of your charm."

"You think I'm charming?"

Kristen laughed. "I don't think you're an idiot." She lifted her glass into the air, clicked it against his. "To better days."

"I'll drink to that." They downed the contents of their glasses. "What time do you start work?" he asked.

"Not till five. What about you? You have any plans?"

"Haven't decided."

"We could hang out, maybe go to a movie," she offered.

"I think I've seen enough movies for a while."

"Oh, that's right. I guess that means the beach is out, too, huh?"

Will laughed. "God, I'm pathetic."

"Just a little. You liked her; what can you do?"

"How can you like somebody you don't even know?" Will asked.

"I think sometimes it's actually easier that way," Kristin said. "Sometimes the more you know about someone, the harder it gets to like them. The less you know, the better."

"I think you're the one who should be going for her doctorate."

"There you go, talking dirty again." She sighed. "I'm sorry. This is all my fault, isn't it?"

"How could anything be your fault?"

"I'm the one who told Suzy about the bet you guys had going, asked her to pick you."

"You didn't know she was married."

Kristin shrugged. "I understand her husband was pretty creepy."

"Creepy's an understatement. Guy's a psychopath."

"Worse than Tom?"

"Smarter than Tom," Will said. "I'm not sure which is worse. Can I ask you something?"

"Sure."

"It's kind of personal."

"What kind?"

Will smiled. "What would you have done if she'd picked Jeff?"

Kristin shrugged again, said nothing.

"Would you really have been okay with it?"

A third shrug. "It's no big deal."

"It isn't?"

"Look. Before I started bartending, I was working every seedy strip club in Miami Beach. Occasionally, I got a job modeling swimsuits or lingerie. More often, I supplemented my income by appearing at stag parties. Which is where I met Jeff. It was a pretty rough group of guys, they'd all been drinking, and for a few minutes, it looked as if things might get a little out of hand. But your brother stepped in, calmed everybody down, got me out of there. Even made sure I got paid. He asked for my phone number. We ended up at his place. Of course, I found out later the whole thing was a setup, that he'd bet the guys a hundred bucks he could get into my pants. But by then, it didn't matter. We were already living together. I quit stripping, took a course in bartending, the Wild Zone opened, and I got a job. And that's the story. It's easy with Jeff. There's no drama, no fuss, no mess, no unrealistic expectations. He lets me do my thing; I let him do his."

"Which includes other women," Will stated.

"If that's what he wants . . ."

"What about what you want?"

"Sometimes he asks me to join in."

"That's not what I meant, and you know it."

"What are you really asking me?"

"Do the same rules apply?" Will asked after a pause. "Do you ever . . . ?"

"Ever what?" she said, goading him, a sly little half smile tugging on her lips.

"Well, they say what's good for the goose is good for the gander."

"Really? Do they say that at Princeton?"

"I believe it was Nietzsche who said it first."

Kristin laughed, a sweet, surprisingly delicate sound that Will found very appealing.

He cleared his throat in an effort to clear his head. "What's it like–making love to another woman?"

"It's all right."

"Just all right?"

"It's different," Kristin said, remembering the first time she'd been with a woman. A *girl,* really. They'd both been so young.

It was just after her mother had kicked her out of the house. She'd dropped out of school, been picked up a few weeks later as a truant, and was put in the care of Child Services, then sent to a group home, where she'd stayed the better part of three years. It was there, in those drab, indifferent surroundings, eight girls to a room, that she'd met someone as damaged, in her way, as Kristin was. For months, they'd circled each other warily, rarely speaking, carefully sizing each other up. Eventually, Kristin had broken the silence: "I can't find my wallet. You have something to do with that?"

Despite that provocative beginning, or perhaps *because* of it, the two girls soon became inseparable, their friendship only gradually developing into something more, something neither one had expected. It happened naturally, effortlessly. One night, the girl had simply climbed down from her top bunk and slipped into Kristin's narrow bed below. Kristin had slid over to make room, holding the young woman in the dark, marveling at her softness and the exquisite tenderness of her touch. For the next eighteen months, they'd spent every minute they could together. The love of her life, Kristin understood, even then.

And suddenly, one day, without warning, she was gone. The semi-official explanation was that her parents had taken her home. Later came the news that the family had moved to Wyoming, that she wasn't coming back.

She didn't. Nor did she visit. Or write. Or phone.

Two months later, on Kristin's eighteenth birthday, Kristin had walked out of the group home and disappeared into the humid, mean streets of Miami.

"Do you think Jeff would be upset if you slept with another guy?" Will was asking now, returning Kristin abruptly to the present.

"Only if he didn't get to watch." This time Kristin's laugh was harsher, more forced. "God, Will. You should see your face." She suddenly stopped laughing, her face growing dark and serious. "Did you just proposition me?"

"What? No. I just meant—"

"Relax. I know what you meant." She leaned forward so that their knees were touching. "There are no other guys, Will."

"Do you love him?"

"Do I love him?" Kristin repeated. "Now that's a loaded question."

"I would have thought it was pretty simple."

"Nothing's simple."

"You either love him or you don't."

"I haven't really thought about it. I guess I do. In my own way."

"What way is that?"

"The only way I know how." She stood up. "Anyway, enough soul-searching for one day."

"I'm sorry," Will apologized immediately. "I didn't mean to upset you."

"You didn't." She reached over, stroked his cheek. "God, you're sweet. I'm really sorry you're hurting, Will. I wish I could kiss you and make everything all better."

"Be careful what you wish for," Will said with a laugh. He pushed himself to his feet, so that they were standing no more than a foot apart.

For several seconds they remained that way, neither moving, their eyes locked as their bodies swayed slowly toward one another.

Is she going to kiss me? Will wondered. Could he do that to Jeff?

Is he going to kiss me? wondered Kristin. Can I let that happen?

From the other room came the sound of a key turning in the front door.

"Hello?" Jeff called out. "Anybody home?"

Kristin quickly pulled back and away. "Jeff?" She marched out of the kitchen, taking several deep breaths along the way. "Is everything all right? I thought you had clients all day."

"My eleven o'clock canceled. I only have a few minutes. Is my brother here?"

Will stepped into the doorway between the kitchen and living room. Jeff was standing just inside the front door. "Is there a problem?" he asked.

"Somebody wants to talk to you."

In the next instant, Suzy was standing in the doorway, a genie freshly freed from her bottle, backlit by the sun. Her soft voice emerged from the shadows. "Hello, Will," she said.

ELEVEN

TOM STOOD IN THE glass-enclosed foyer of the pink three-story building on West Flagler Street, scanning the office directory for at least the fiftieth time. He'd read it so many times in the last sixty minutes, he knew it by heart. First floor: Lash, Carter, and Kroft, Attorneys-at-Law, Suite 100; Blake, Felder & Sons, Attorneys-at-Law, Suite 101; Lang, Cunningham, Attorneys-at-Law, Suite 102; Torres, Saldana, and Mendoza, Attorneys-at-Law, Suite 103. Second floor: Williams, Seyffert, and Keller, Attorneys-at-Law, Suite 200; Marcus, Brenner, Scott, and Lokash, Attorneys-at-Law, Suite 201; Levy, Argeris, Kettleworth, Attorneys-at-Law, Suite 202; Sam Bryson, Attorney, Suite 203. Third floor: Tyson, Rodriguez, Attorneys-at-Law, Suite 300; Michaud, Brunton, Birnbaum, Attorneys-at-Law, Suite 301; Abramowitz, Levy, and Carmichael, Attorneys-at-Law, Suite 302; and finally Pollack, Spitzer, Walton, Tepperman, and Rowe, Attorneys-at-Law, Suite 303.

"What do you call a hundred lawyers at the bottom of the ocean?" Tom asked out loud, pacing back and forth across the small space. "A start!" he shouted, laughing at his own joke and wondering whether anyone had heard him. The place seemed deserted. There was an elevator to his left and a stairwell right behind it, but nobody had used either since he'd arrived. "Business is obviously booming," he muttered, thinking he could start at the top floor and work his way down. "Hello, Misters Pollack, Spitzer, Walton, Tepperman, and Rowe. Greetings, Misses Lash, Carter, and Kroft. Any of you legal beagles seen my future former wife?" He laughed again, wondering how long it would take to locate her. Certainly not any longer than the hour he'd already wasted waiting for her down here.

Why didn't any of these big-shot attorneys list their specialties, for shit's sake? Surely they had them. Was it too much to ask for a little clarification? How about Lang, Cunningham, *Family Law*? Or Sam Bryson, *Specialist in Divorce*? Something—anything—to give him a clue, point him in the right direction. No, that would be too easy.

And Lainey wasn't about to make this easy for him.

Not that she ever had.

"Never should have gotten mixed up with her to begin with," Tom muttered. Jeff had warned him about her, said she was a leech and that he deserved better. Except "better" usually consisted of Jeff's discards, and he was tired of the hand-me-downs he'd been getting all his life, first from his brothers' closets, then from his best friend's bed. He wanted a woman that didn't come with Jeff's prior-rated seal of approval, and one of the things he liked best about Lainey was that she'd always been relatively impervious to Jeff's charm. "I just don't get what all the fuss is about," she'd said one night, not long after they'd started seeing each other, and Tom had fallen instantly in love.

Of course, he'd fallen out of love even faster. Just seeing Lainey through Jeff's eyes—"Christ, man, she's not even pretty. She's got these little beady eyes and her nose is way too big for her face. Plus, man, her legs are like bowling pins. You can do better than that"—had been enough to completely quench his already cooling ardor. Except by then it was too late. Lainey was already pregnant, and she was pressuring him to get married. He'd let her talk him into believing that, after Afghanistan, what he needed was a little stability. Let me take care of you, she'd urged. And why not? he'd decided. He deserved a little looking after. He could always get a divorce later on.

So why was he so upset now that it actually seemed to be happening?

Because nobody walks out on Tom Whitman, he thought. "I decide who leaves when," he announced to the directory of lawyers. He thought of Coral Gables. That asshole husband of Suzy's. *Don't let me catch you boys in this neighborhood again,* he'd warned them. Who the hell did he think he was talking to? "I decide who does what," Tom said now. "I decide how. *I* decide when." Just ask that little cunt in Afghanistan.

Of course, the bitch had almost gotten him thrown in jail. Tom remembered the accusations, the weeks of investigation, the very real threat of incarceration. Ultimately, the army had decided against bringing the matter to trial, choosing instead to ship him home. After having laid his life on the line for almost two years, two years spent eating sand and watching friends die, his prayers reduced to a single wish—*Please let me come home with my legs*—he'd been unceremoniously tossed out on his ass. Dishonorably discharged. That was the thanks he got.

Just like with Lainey.

Another dishonorable discharge.

He'd done the right thing by her, and now she was trying to screw him out of what was rightfully his—his kids, his house, his way of life. Was that what she wanted? After almost five years together, did she really expect him to just walk away? So what if her parents owned the house? That was just a technicality. It was still the matrimonial home. *His* home. And Candy and Cody were *his* children. Did Lainey really think she could just walk away from him, that he would give up without a fight? Hell, if a fight was what she wanted, he'd give her the battle of her life.

The elevator doors suddenly opened, and a woman got out. She was blond and middle-aged, and was wearing a suit jacket, despite the heat of the day. She had a cigarette in one hand and a lighter in the other, ready to light up as soon as she stepped outside.

"Excuse me, ma'am," Tom said, propelling himself forward so abruptly the woman almost dropped her cigarette. "Are you a lawyer?"

The woman looked wary. "Yes. Can I help you?"

"I'm looking for Lainey Whitman."

"Lainey . . . ?"

"Whitman."

"I don't think I recognize the name. Which firm is she with?"

"She's not with anyone. She's here seeing somebody."

Now the woman looked confused. "I'm sorry. I wouldn't know—"

"Can you tell me which firms specialize in divorce?" Tom asked as the woman backed toward the door.

"I believe Alex Torres deals with divorce, and Michaud, Brunton, Birnbaum has a family law department. Maybe Stuart Lokash handles divorce cases. I'm really not sure." She pushed open the door, backed into the street, was swallowed by a flash of sunlight.

A wave of hot air blew across Tom's face. "Alex Torres, of Torres, Saldana, and Mendoza, I presume. Suite 103." He could start there, he decided, taking the stairs two at a time, pushing open the door to the first floor seconds later.

The hallway that greeted him was wide and lined with blue and silver carpeting. He walked down the corridor, passing the offices of Lash, Carter, and Kroft; Blake, Felder & Sons; and Lang, Cunningham, before stopping in front of the closed double doors to suite 103. Probably should have worn a tie, he thought, tucking his shirt into his jeans and patting the gun tucked inside his belt buckle, making sure it was well concealed. Then he grabbed the brass knob of the heavy, wooden right-hand door and pulled it open.

He wasn't sure what he'd been expecting, but whatever it was, it wasn't this. Weren't lawyers supposed to be rich? Weren't they supposed to inhabit spacious rooms with spectacular views? Weren't they supposed to have beautiful furniture and well-dressed secretaries and a drop-dead gorgeous receptionist waiting to offer him a cup of much-needed coffee? Instead, what Tom saw was an elderly Hispanic woman behind a strictly utilitarian desk in front of a dreary beige wall, a line of closed office doors stretching out behind her.

"Can I help you?" she asked pleasantly.

"I'm here to see Alex Torres." She's probably his mother, Tom thought.

"I'm afraid Mr. Torres isn't in today. Do you have an appointment?"

"No." Tom didn't move.

"Oh. Well, then, perhaps I can find someone else to assist you."

"Perhaps," Tom repeated, with exaggerated politeness. Where'd she learn to speak that way? "I'm looking for Lainey Whitman."

"Lane Whitman?"

"Lainey. Elaine," Tom corrected. It would be just like Lainey to go all formal on him.

"I'm afraid we don't have anyone here by that name."

"She doesn't work here," Tom corrected sharply. "She's here seeing someone about a divorce."

"Are you sure you're in the right place?"

"I saw her come into this building an hour ago."

The woman grew flustered. She reached up, patted her gray-streaked, black hair, which was pulled into a high bun. "You realize there are many law firms in this building."

"Twelve, to be exact," Tom said. "Four per floor. You want me to name them?"

The receptionist reached for her phone. "If you'd like to sit down, I'll see if I can find someone to help you."

Dumb bitch, Tom thought, tempted to blow her head off, just for the fun of it. Instead he mumbled, "Don't bother," and walked out of the office. "Where are you, Lainey?" he muttered, deciding to return to the lobby, rather than risk another confrontation with some lawyer's snooty grandmother, and wait for her there. Surely, wherever she was, she wouldn't be there much longer.

But another half hour passed, and still she wasn't back. What was she doing up there? What was she telling those legal dickheads? "He drinks; he plays around; he has a terrible temper; the children are afraid of him," he could almost hear her recite.

"Wouldn't mind a drink right about now," he said out loud, staring at the greasy spoon across the street. He wondered if they served alcohol, then checked his watch. Just past eleven o'clock. A little early to be drinking, even for him. What the hell, he thought. Like the song said, it's five o'clock somewhere.

"You got any beer?" he asked the young girl behind the counter minutes later, his eyes focused on the pink building across the street as he plopped down on a stool at the front of the old-fashioned diner.

"Just root beer," the girl said. The name tag on her orange uniform identified her as Vicki Lynn. She was maybe eighteen, with chin-length, curly brown hair and bad skin she tried to cover up with too much makeup. She smiled, and Tom wondered if she was coming on to him.

"I'll have a Coke," he said.

"We just have Pepsi."

"Then I'll have Pepsi."

"Diet or regular?"

"Diet's not good for you. It's got something in it that alters your brain waves," Tom said. Lainey had told him that.

Vicki Lynn stared at him blankly.

"Regular," Tom said.

"Small, medium, or large?"

"Are you shitting me?"

Vicki Lynn blinked once, twice, three times. "You want small, medium, or large?" she repeated, a blink for each option.

"Large."

"Will that be everything?"

"I believe it will." Tom glanced over his shoulder at the sparsely populated room. Vinyl-upholstered booths–only one of them occupied–lined the sides of both walls, a small jukebox sitting atop each Formica-topped table. The walls were decorated with old rock 'n' roll memorabilia: music sheets and concert announcements, ancient photos of the Beatles and Janis and the Grateful Dead. Two posters of Elvis stared each other down from opposite sides of the room. In one, he was young, beautiful, and dressed from head to toe in black leather. In the other, he was older, bloated, and wearing a rhinestone-covered white jumpsuit, complete with matching cape.

Dead at forty-two, Tom thought. "Long live the King," he toasted when Vicki Lynn returned with his drink.

Tom was just about to take a sip when he saw Lainey emerge from the pink building. He jumped off his stool, knocking over his drink, the sugary brown liquid splashing across the counter and dripping toward the floor. "Shit," he said, vaulting toward the door.

"Hey, wait," Vicki Lynn called after him. "That's four dollars you owe me."

"Four dollars for a Coke I didn't even drink?"

"Pepsi," Vicki Lynn corrected him.

"Four dollars," Tom mumbled angrily, fishing around in his side pocket for some loose bills. "For a goddamn Pepsi."

"You asked for large."

"Shit," he said, unable to find anything smaller than a ten-dollar bill. He pushed it at Vicki Lynn as he watched Lainey walk toward the parking lot at the end of the street, head high, a definite bounce to her step. What the hell was she looking so damn cheery about? He tapped his fingers impatiently on the counter, wondering if she'd notice his car, parked two rows behind hers. "Can you hurry up with that change?"

Vicki Lynn proceeded to the cash register as if she were wading through molasses.

"Look. I'm in a hurry." He thought of shooting at her feet, the way they did in those old westerns he sometimes watched on TV. That would make her dance. Make her *move,* he thought, watching as she opened the register and meticulously began counting out the change. "Forget it," he yelled in exasperation, exiting the diner and running down the street toward the parking lot, pushing his way through the heat as if it were a solid steel door. Lainey was probably halfway across the state by now.

Leave it to Lainey, he was thinking. He'd waited for her for how long? A goddamn hour and a half? And then, just when he decides to relax for a few minutes, have a Coke—a *Pepsi*—she decides to show her face. As if she knew he was there. As if she'd timed the whole damn thing.

He reached the parking lot, perspiration soaking through the back of his blue-striped shirt. Lainey's white Civic was second in line at the checkout station. A woman in a red Mercedes was fishing around in her purse, gesticulating as if she'd lost her ticket. Whatever the reason for the holdup, Tom was grateful. It gave him a chance to sneak around to his car while keeping Lainey in his sights. Minutes later, he was on her tail, careful to stay several cars behind her. He was getting pretty good at this, he thought.

His stomach rumbled, reminding him it was almost lunchtime and he hadn't eaten since early that morning. Maybe he could persuade Lainey to let him take her out to lunch, somewhere nice, maybe even expensive. Somewhere like the Purple Dolphin. Lainey loved seafood, and even if it wasn't his favorite, they probably served hamburgers. And Kristin said they served the best piña coladas in town, although he didn't think he'd tell Lainey that. She'd never been a big fan of Kristin. "There's just something about her I don't trust," she'd said.

There was something about her, that was for sure, Tom thought now, pushing thoughts of Kristin from his mind. This was no time to be thinking about other women, he reminded himself. He had to focus on Lainey.

Maybe the next time she had to stop at a red light, he'd pull up beside her and suggest lunch. She was always complaining that they never went anywhere, that he never took her to nice places. Now was his chance to show her otherwise, to prove to her he could be as romantic, as caring, as the next guy.

Except the lights wouldn't cooperate, turning green at each intersection just as she approached, almost as if they were doing it on purpose. Twenty minutes of green lights, he thought, shaking his head in disbelief. When did that ever happen? He had to stop her before she got home. Otherwise it would be too late. Her parents wouldn't even let him talk to her on the phone. They certainly weren't about to invite him in for lunch.

They were driving west along Southwest Eighth Street when Lainey suddenly stopped in the middle of the road, then backed expertly into an available space between two cars. "Not bad," Tom noted, wondering what she was up to now. He continued on to the next corner, then pulled over to the curb and stopped, watching as Lainey got out of her car, fed the nearby meter, and disappeared inside a store. Which one? He was too far away to tell.

He left his car in a no-stopping zone and crossed the street, peeking into each storefront as he walked by. He passed several restaurants, a dry cleaner, and a shoe store. Was Lainey buying another pair of shoes? She only had, what–thirty pairs? All of them with flat heels. Old-lady shoes, he called them, urging her–how many times?–to get something sexy, something with stiletto heels and flirty ankle straps. The kind Kristin wore. Or Suzy, he thought, feeling a renewed surge of anger as he pictured her husband's smug face leaning into his car window. "Dickhead," he said, pulling open the door and entering the air-conditioned shoe store.

"Can I help you?" a salesgirl asked immediately. She smiled, and Tom wondered if she was flirting with him.

"Just looking," he said, sensing immediately that Lainey wasn't there but walking to the back of the store anyway, in case she was on her knees, looking through boxes.

He hated to leave the soothing arctic air of the store for the stifling tropics of the street, but he couldn't afford to waste any more time. There was a nice-looking restaurant across the street. Was it possible Lainey had gone in there, that she was meeting someone for lunch? Who? Another man? Had she been seeing someone else all along? Was that the reason for this sudden desire to end their marriage? Damn it, he'd kill her before he let another man move into his house, be a father to his kids.

And then he saw it: Donatello's Hair Salon.

Lainey went there every six weeks to have her hair cut and styled. She was always jabbering on about the guy who did her hair, calling him a genius and a miracle worker. So how come your hair always looks like crap? he'd been tempted to ask on more than one occasion.

He approached the front window, peeking through the black, cursive swirls of Donatello's name into the interior of the salon, surprised to find the small place bustling. Lots of women looking for miracles, he was thinking as he pulled open the front door.

"Can I help you?" a young, spiky-haired brunette asked from behind the high reception counter. She gave him a wide smile that told Tom she wanted to sleep with him.

"Is Lainey Whitman here?" he asked, his voice low, his eyes skirting the perimeter of the salon. He didn't have time to deal with her right now.

"She's in the back, having her hair washed." The girl pointed around a curved, aquamarine wall toward the back of the salon.

Tom followed the curve into the main room. There, half a dozen women wrapped in blue plastic capes sat in adjustable chairs in front of mirrored walls, being tended to by men with sharp objects in their hands and gun-shaped blowers at their clients' heads.

"I don't know what to do about her anymore," a middle-aged woman was confiding to her hairdresser, a rotund young man with pink streaks in his short, dark hair. "All she eats is peanut butter and sushi. How healthy can that be?"

Do women really tell their hairdressers everything? Tom wondered, continuing to the very back of the salon. Did Lainey confide everything to Donatello? What exactly had she told him?

He almost didn't see her. Instead he saw a row of aquamarine-colored sinks and a bored young man, his hands full of lather, his eyes glazed and staring at the far wall, as if in a trance, massaging the head of a woman who was reclining in her chair, eyes closed, her neck stretched back across the top of the sink, her jugular fully exposed, as if waiting for an executioner's blade. The woman was Lainey, Tom realized, recognizing the bowling-pin legs protruding from the bottom of the aquamarine-colored cape. He stopped several feet away.

"Can I help you?" the young man asked, eyes opening, a Spanish accent twisting through the English words.

"Lainey," Tom said, the word a command.

Lainey bolted up in the chair, her long, wet hair falling into her eyes and dripping lather onto the shoulders of the plastic cape. "What are you doing here?" She glanced warily from side to side, her eyes full of fear.

The look suited her, Tom thought. "We need to talk."

"Not here. Not now."

"Yes," Tom said, widening his stance, making it clear he wasn't going anywhere. "Right here. Right now."

TWELVE

WILL STOOD IN THE doorway between the kitchen and the living room, his eyes darting between Suzy and his brother.

"What's going on?" Kristin asked, standing midway between the two.

Jeff shrugged, not moving from his position by the front door. "Apparently the lady has something she'd like to say to Will."

"I owe you an apology," Suzy began.

"You don't owe me anything," Will countered quickly.

"I think I do."

"Never argue when a woman is apologizing," Jeff instructed him. "That day may never come again."

"Smart-ass," Kristin said.

"Which I believe is my cue to get back to work," Jeff said. "Come on, Krissie. You can give me a ride."

"Let me get my shoes." Kristin disappeared into the bedroom, her ear on the room she'd just left. What was Suzy planning to say to Will? And more important, what was she doing with Jeff? She rifled around the bottom of her closet for her sandals, sliding her feet into them without bothering to undo their buckles, then grabbed her purse from the top of the dresser and returned to the living room. Everyone was frozen to the spot, staring at each other nervously, expectantly, like participants in a duel. "Okay, I'm ready." She looked from Jeff to Suzy, and then to Will. "Okay, you guys. Don't worry. Take your time. I won't be back for a few hours."

"I'm sorry. I don't mean to kick you out of your apartment—"

"You aren't. Honestly. I have a whole bunch of errands to run." Kristin walked to the door. "Coming?" she asked Jeff as she stepped into the outside corridor.

"Right behind you, babe."

"Jeff," Suzy called out suddenly, stopping him.

Jeff turned around.

"Thank you," she said.

"Anything to help a lady in distress." Jeff's eyes lingered on hers, penetrating right through her dark glasses. You know where to find me, his eyes told hers. Then he left the apartment, closing the door behind him.

"Distress?" Will asked.

"Figure of speech," Suzy said after a moment's pause. "How are you?"

"Me? I'm fine." I'm shitty, he corrected himself silently. Not to mention confused as hell. "You?"

"I'm okay."

"Just okay?"

She nodded. "It's really hot out there today."

"It's Florida."

"I guess."

"Can I get you something cold to drink?" Will wished she'd take off her sunglasses. He found it disconcerting trying to carry on a conversation when he couldn't see her eyes. What was she doing here? Had she really come to offer an apology? What had she been doing with Jeff? "Water? Juice? Soda?"

"Nothing. Thank you."

"You're sure?"

"Maybe some water."

Will proceeded to the kitchen sink, his heart racing. What did she want from him? What was she expecting? Was she expecting anything? *What had she been doing with Jeff?*

He poured her a glass of cold water from the tap, waiting until his hands stopped trembling before returning to the main room. Suzy hadn't moved from her original position, her sunglasses still firmly in place, her oversize canvas purse dangling from her left hand, as if at any moment she might bolt from the premises. Will walked over, held out the glass of water for her to take.

"Thank you."

"Have a seat." He motioned toward the sofa.

"Thank you," she said again, balancing on the sofa's edge, as if afraid to get too comfortable, and sipping gently from her glass. "Water's nice and cold."

"Made it myself," he joked. Then, "You caught me off guard. I didn't think I'd ever see you again."

"I wasn't sure you'd want to," she admitted, her head tilting up toward him. "Aren't you going to sit down?"

Will sank down on the opposite end of the sofa, waited for her to continue.

"I'm sure you have all sorts of questions."

"No," he said. What were you doing with Jeff? he thought.

"Your brother mentioned where he worked the other day," she offered, as if he'd voiced this thought out loud. "I went there to ask if he'd give you a message."

"You don't have to explain."

"Please. I want to."

"Look, I have as much explaining to do as you do. I'm the one who showed up in front of your house, unexpected and uninvited–"

"Are you married?" Suzy asked, cutting him off.

"What? No."

"Then I'd say the onus is on me."

"For what?"

"I should have told you."

"Why?"

"Because I should have. I owed you at least that much."

"You didn't owe me anything. You were just being nice."

"Nice? How do you figure that?"

"By playing along with Kristin, by going along with the bet."

"It sounded like fun." Suzy smiled, her lips turning down at the corners instead of up. "We had a good time, didn't we?"

"We did," Will agreed.

"Did you know your friend was going to follow me home?"

"What? No," Will said quickly. "And he's not my friend."

"I'm glad."

"He's an idiot," Will told her. "A real loose cannon. Apparently he'd been following us around all night."

"Too bad we didn't give him more of a show."

Will's eyes shot to hers, although he couldn't see past the dark glasses. What was she saying? That she was sorry she'd pulled away after only one kiss, that she was interested in more, that that was the real reason she was here: not to apologize for not telling him she was married, but because she was sorry for not following through? If only I could see her eyes, he thought, wishing he understood women better. If a magic genie had suddenly appeared to offer him one wish, that's what it would be, he was thinking, remembering the joke Jeff had told at the bar. "Why don't you take those things off," he said finally, reaching for her glasses.

She pulled back. "It's probably better if I keep them on."

"Why?" Will pulled them gently from her face. "Oh, God," he said, the glasses dropping into his lap as his eyes swept across the myriad of bruises dotting Suzy's otherwise pale complexion. They pulsed at him like strobe lights, a flash of fading purple here, a hint of dull yellow there. "He did this to you," he said without needing to be told.

"No. I fell."

"You didn't fall."

"It was an accident with a neighbor's dog. My feet got tangled up in the leash."

"Is that what you told Jeff?"

She lowered her head. "He didn't believe me either."

Will's fingers were shaking as he reached out to touch her cheek. "How could anyone do this?"

"It's all right. I'm all right."

"This is my fault," he said.

"This has nothing to do with you."

"If we hadn't shown up on your doorstep, like a bunch of stupid teenagers . . ."

"It wouldn't have mattered."

"What are you saying?"

"Nothing."

"Are you saying he's done this to you before?"

"This was *my* doing," Suzy insisted.

"How do you figure that?"

"I goad him."

"You goad him," Will repeated incredulously.

"I should never have gone to the Wild Zone. I knew how risky it was."

"What do you mean 'risky'?"

"Bars are strictly off-limits when Dave's away."

"What?"

"Normally I go with Dave when he has to attend a conference out of town," she explained, talking more to herself now than to Will, as if trying to understand what had happened. "But this time he said he was going to be so busy all week with meetings and lectures–he's a doctor–and there was no point in my being cooped up in a hotel room all week by myself, that I might as well stay home, get a few things looked after around the house. And I'm usually so bored at those medical conventions. I was really looking forward to having time to myself, going for a walk on the beach, going into some of those cute little shops along the ocean. I never should have gone into the Wild Zone. For sure, I never should have gone back more than once. I don't know what I was thinking. I guess I thought Dave wouldn't find out. He wasn't supposed to be back until Saturday. But he left right after his last meeting on Friday night, drove all the way from Tampa without stopping, just to be with me. Only I wasn't there."

"You were with me," Will stated, feeling sick to his stomach. When he'd left her, he'd all but floated home. He'd been asleep on this very sofa, dreaming of long, soft, tender kisses while she was being beaten to a bloody pulp.

"It was the most fun I've had in I don't know how long."

"I don't understand. Why do you stay with him? You don't have kids. Do you?" Will asked sheepishly, suddenly realizing how little he actually knew about her.

She smiled. The smile accentuated the small scratch at the corner of her upper lip, a scratch he hadn't even noticed before. "No, I don't have any children. I also don't have a choice."

"Of course you have a choice," Will argued. "You can leave him, you can report him to the police, you can—"

"I can't," she said simply.

"Why not?"

"He'll kill me," she said, simpler still.

"No, he won't. He's just a bully, a—"

"He'll kill me," she said again. "Please. I can't stay much longer. Can we please talk about something else?"

"You want to talk about something else?" Will asked helplessly, his head spinning.

"What do you think of Miami?" she asked brightly, as if this was the most natural of questions.

"What?"

"Please, Will. Can we just pretend to be a normal couple? Boy meets girl. That kind of thing. For a few minutes, before I have to go?"

Tears filled her eyes, and Will felt his own eyes moistening. He looked away. Why do things always have to be so complicated? he was thinking. Maybe Kristin and Jeff had the right idea after all. Keep things as simple as possible. No expectations, no recriminations. "I think Miami's great," he said. "A little hot, but . . ."

"It's Florida," she said, completing the thought, with a shy chuckle. "I guess it's a lot different than New Jersey."

"Actually I'm from Buffalo. I just went to school in New Jersey."

"I've never been to either."

"Buffalo's okay," he said, continuing the pretense. "I mean, I know it's popular to badmouth the city, but I always liked it there. It was a pretty cool place to grow up."

"You had a happy childhood," she stated more than asked.

"You didn't?"

"We were always moving, so I never really settled in anywhere. It was hard to make friends. I was always the new girl. Just when I'd start to get comfortable, we'd take off again." She raised her glass of water to her lips, then returned it to her lap without taking a sip. "So, what did you want to be when you were a little boy?" she asked, suddenly shifting gears. "Don't tell me you wanted to be a philosopher."

He laughed. "No. I wanted to be a fireman. Don't all little boys want to be firemen when they grow up?"

"I don't know. Do they?"

"I did. Jeff did," Will added, remembering Jeff pleading for a fireman's costume one Halloween, a request that was denied.

"And you wanted to be Jeff," Suzy said.

"I guess I did." Still do, he thought. "What about you?"

"I never wanted to be Jeff."

Will smiled. "What *did* you want to be?"

"When I was little, I wanted to be a ballerina."

"Of course."

"When I was a little older, I changed my mind, decided I was going to be a fashion designer."

"What changed your mind?"

My father's fist, Suzy thought. "No talent," she said out loud.

"When I was a teenager, I wanted to be a rock star," Will confessed.

"Singer or lead guitar?"

"Drummer."

Suzy laughed. "Get out."

"Seriously. I was very gung-ho, as I was about everything in those days. Very, *very* intense. I actually talked my parents into buying me this incredibly expensive set of drums, and I used to bang on those damn things morning, noon, and night, drive everybody crazy . . ."

"And?"

"And then one day someone took my drumsticks and punched holes through the tops of all my drums. They were completely ruined."

"Jeff?"

"No," Will said. "Although that's what everyone thought. But it wasn't Jeff."

"Who was it?"

Will took a deep breath, released it slowly. It scraped painfully along the side of his windpipe. "It was me," he admitted.

"You ruined your own drum set?"

"I couldn't stand it anymore. Talk about having no talent!" He laughed. "And I was sick of taking lessons, sick of practicing, sick of never getting any better, of pretending to enjoy it. But my parents had spent all this money, right? I couldn't just give it up. And then one afternoon, I come home from school, my parents are out, and there's Jeff sitting in my bedroom, beating on my drums. And he was great. Perfect. It was effortless for him. Just like everything was. And I don't know. I just snapped. I yelled at him to get out of my room, not to touch my things ever again, standard little-brother shit, and next thing you know, I'm slashing at those drums like some monster in a horror flick. Of course, my parents blamed Jeff. And I was too much of a chickenshit to tell them otherwise."

"Jeff never said anything?"

"What for? He knew they'd never believe him."

"So you just let him take the fall?"

Will hung his head. He was suddenly twelve years old again, crying in the privacy of his room. Why had he told her that story? He'd never confessed his shame to anyone before. "They never gave him anything, you know. Not like me. 'The Chosen One,' Jeff used to call me. And he was right. I was my parents' golden boy. My mother's pride and joy. Whatever I wanted, she made sure I got. Drum sets, basketballs, private schools, money for Princeton." He rubbed his forehead.

"Jeff was like Cinderella, the kid nobody wanted. He had to beg for every scrap. And he had too much pride for that. He wasn't going to put up with it any longer than he had to."

"What happened?"

"He took off for Miami, dropped out of college after a couple of semesters, joined the army, became a personal trainer. He keeps in touch with his sister, Ellie," Will explained, answering the question on Suzy's face. "She's how I knew where to find him."

"Is that why you came here? To make amends?"

"I'm not sure why I came."

"Have you talked to Jeff about this?"

"What's there to say he doesn't already know?"

"That you're sorry," Suzy said.

"I used to worship him, you know?" Will continued, as if a valve had been turned on in his memory and he was powerless to turn it off. "He was like this god to me. He was everything I wanted to be. Everything I wasn't. Handsome, charismatic, athletic, talented. The girls couldn't keep their hands off him. He'd cock his little finger and they'd come running. Me too. I used to run after him when I was little, which drove him absolutely crazy. He'd yell at me to get lost, call me a dork and a loser, and I'd just bask in all that fury. I finally had his attention. As much as he hated me, that's how much I loved him. Except I hated him, too, hated him for being everything I knew I could never be, hated him for not loving me back. Shit," Will said, feeling his eyes fill with unexpected tears.

Suzy reached for his hand. "I think you should tell him."

Her touch sent shivers up his arm. "I think you should leave your husband."

She smiled. Again, the corners of her lips turned down instead of up.

Smile, sucker, he heard her say as strains of Beethoven's "Ode to Joy" began emanating from deep inside her purse.

"Oh, God. That's Dave." She quickly extricated her cell phone from her canvas bag. "I have to take this."

"Do you want me to wait in the kitchen?"

She shook her head, lowered the phone to her lap. "I want you to kiss me," she said. "Like you did the other night."

In the next second she was in his arms, his lips brushing tenderly against hers, afraid to apply any pressure to her bruised mouth.

"Don't worry," she whispered. "I won't break."

Will kissed her again, this time harder, deeper. Once again, the opening bars of Beethoven's "Ode to Joy" pushed their way between them.

Reluctantly, Suzy pulled out of Will's arms, although he continued to hold on tight. She smiled her sad smile and flipped open the phone. "Hi," she said.

"Where are you?" Will heard Dave demand. "What took you so long to answer your cell?"

"I'm just heading into Publix," Suzy lied. "It took me a minute to find the phone."

"You're sure that's where you are?"

Suzy's eyes shot to the window, as if Dave might be standing there, staring inside. Will jumped to his feet, walked to the door, opened it, took several steps into the outside corridor, and returned shaking his head, assuring her no one was there.

"Of course I'm sure. I was thinking of making some chicken with Cumberland sauce for dinner, and we didn't have any red currant jelly, so I—"

"I might be a little late coming home today," he interrupted.

"Is there a problem?"

"Have dinner ready for seven o'clock."

The phone went dead in her hands.

Suzy returned the phone to her purse. She sat very still for several seconds, her head down, her breath seemingly frozen in her lungs. When she looked up again, her eyes were clear, hinting at defiance. She looked at Will. "I have until seven o'clock," she said.

THIRTEEN

"PLEASE, TOM," LAINEY WAS saying, her hands in front of her chest as if she was trying to keep him at bay. "Don't make a scene."

"Who's making a scene?" Tom asked, eyes sweeping the back of the salon as if there might be someone else present who was creating a disturbance. He glanced at the young man, whose hands were still full of lather. His black eyes were open so wide, they were threatening to overtake his forehead. "You must be Donatello. I'm Tom, Lainey's husband." He extended his hand.

The young man shook it warily, said nothing.

"This is Carlos," Lainey explained. "He does shampoos. He doesn't speak much English."

"In that case, *vamanos,* Carlos," Tom said dismissively.

Carlos looked to Lainey. "It's okay," she told him, nodding.

"What–I need his permission to talk to my wife?"

"What do you want, Tom?" Lainey asked, her voice low and radiating disdain, as Carlos disappeared around the curved wall to the front of the salon.

Her dark eyes were losing some of their fear, Tom realized, his fists clenching with disappointment. Who the hell did she think she was? He noted the wet hair plastered against her scalp like a bathing cap, accentuating the width of her nose. She was hardly a beauty, he thought, watching her push the hair away from her face and swipe at the soapy water running down her cheeks with the palm of her hand, as if aware of his silent assessment. What gave her the right, the *nerve,* to be acting so high and mighty, to think she was so much better than he was? "You know what I want," he said.

"No, I don't. I never have."

"What's that supposed to mean?"

"It means I don't know what you want, and I'm tired of trying to figure it out."

"You're tired of trying to figure *what* out?"

"What you want," Lainey snapped, obviously louder than she'd intended, her voice ricocheting off the walls and echoing throughout the shop. She lowered her chin, stared down at the narrow walnut planks of the floor. "Look, let's not do this. I'm too tired to keep going around in circles."

"You're saying you're tired of being married?"

"I'm tired of your attitude."

"What's my attitude?" Tom demanded.

"You use our home like it's a hotel, somewhere you can visit whenever you don't have somewhere better to go or something better to do. You have no respect for my time or my feelings. You don't give a damn about what *I* want."

"That's bullshit."

"It's not bullshit."

"I'm telling you it's bullshit," Tom said angrily.

"Okay. Call it whatever you want. I'm sick and tired of it."

"So . . . what? You just leave?"

"I didn't just leave."

"I come home the other night, you're not there, the kids aren't there. What would you call it?"

"You're missing the point."

"What *is* the fucking point?"

"Please, Tom, can you keep your voice down?" Lainey looked anxiously toward the front of the salon. "Not everyone has to know our business."

"Just the lawyers," he said.

"What?"

"I know you've been talking to a lawyer, Lainey."

"How do you know that?"

Tom noted the fear was back in her eyes. He couldn't help but smile.

"Have you been following me?" she asked.

"You think I'm going to just let you take my kids away from me?"

"Nobody's trying to take your kids away from you. Once things settle down, once you've moved into your own apartment—"

"My own apartment? What the hell are you talking about? I have a house. I'm not moving anywhere."

"—and a settlement has been worked out," she continued as if he hadn't spoken, "you'll be able to see the kids."

"I just told you I'm not going anywhere."

"You don't have a choice, Tom. You signed away your legal rights when my parents agreed to take on our mortgage."

Tom shook his head. "I didn't know what I was signing."

"Then you might want to consult a lawyer of your own."

"Oh, I might want to consult a lawyer of my own," he mimicked. "Where am I supposed to get the money for that? Tell me that, bitch, since you seem to have an answer for everything."

"Okay, Tom. That's enough. I think you should leave."

"Oh, you do, do you?"

"It's obvious we aren't going to settle anything here."

"You think you're entitled to a settlement?" he demanded, deliberately misinterpreting her remarks. "You think I'm gonna just hand you money for kicking me out of my own house?"

"I'm not asking for alimony," Lainey said, a slight tremor rippling through her words.

"Well, aren't you the generous one," Tom sneered.

"Only child support."

"Child support?" What the hell was she talking about? He barely made enough money to cover his own damn expenses. "With what?"

"A portion of your earnings. The courts will decide what's fair."

"None of this is fair, and you know it. I don't care what the courts decide. You're not getting a goddamn dime."

"It's not for me, Tom. It's for your children, who you claim to love."

"You're saying I don't?"

"I'm saying they have certain needs—"

"I'll tell you what they need. They need their father," he shouted.

"Maybe you should have thought of that before."

A man peeked his way around the curved wall. His black hair was shaped into a high pompadour, and he was wearing a white T-shirt tucked inside tight black leather pants. "Is everything all right back here?" he asked.

"Who the fuck are you?"

"I'm Donatello. This is my salon," the man said politely. Then less politely, "Who the fuck are *you*?"

"I'm the lady's husband. We'd appreciate a little privacy."

"Then perhaps you might consider lowering your voice."

"Sorry about that, Donny boy," Tom said. "We'll try to keep it down."

"I don't think your wife wants to talk to you anymore," Donatello said, looking to Lainey for confirmation.

She nodded.

"I'm afraid I'm going to have to ask you to leave the premises," Donatello said.

"And I'm afraid I'm going to have to knock you on your fat little ass."

With that, Donatello spun around on the heels of his black leather boots and returned to the front of the shop.

"Stupid faggot," Tom muttered, turning back to Lainey, watching fresh resolve harden in her eyes.

"I want you to leave," she said.

"And I want you to come home."

"That's not going to happen."

"Look. I'm sorry. Okay?" Tom said, hating the whine in his voice. "I didn't mean to create a scene. It's just that you have no idea how frustrating this whole thing is for me."

"Trust me. I understand exactly how frustrating it is."

"You don't understand a goddamn thing," Tom snapped.

"Fine," Lainey said.

"Fine," he repeated. "You think you know everything, don't you? You think you're in the driver's seat. That you can just order me around. That you can say, 'Jump,' and I'm gonna say, 'How high?'"

"I think we haven't been happy in a very long time."

"Who hasn't been happy? *I've* been happy."

"Well, then, I guess that's all that matters, isn't it?"

"You're telling me you haven't been happy?"

Lainey looked at him as if he'd suddenly sprouted a second head. "Where have you been the last couple of years, Tom?"

"What the hell are you talking about?"

"I've been telling you I'm not happy till I'm blue in the face. It's like talking to a brick wall."

"All you ever fucking do is talk," Tom said. "That, and complain. Nothing's ever right. Nothing I do is ever good enough."

"That's because you never do anything!" Lainey shot back.

"And you're so fucking perfect?"

"I never said I was perfect."

"Oh, you're a long way from perfect, sweetheart. I can tell you that. Take a look in the mirror if you want to see exactly how far from perfect you are." He grabbed her elbow, spun her around, forced her face toward the wall of mirrors across from the sinks. "You think you're some sort of prize catch? You think once you dump me, they're gonna start lining up for you? In case you haven't noticed, you look like shit. You still haven't lost the baby weight, and Cody's two fucking years old. And I'm supposed to want to come home? I'm supposed to want to spend time with you or take you out, show you off to my friends? Lose a few pounds, get your nose fixed and your boobs done, and maybe I'll feel like spending more time at home."

Tears filled Lainey's eyes. Her cheeks reddened, as if she'd been slapped. "You know, I think I always knew you didn't love me," she said quietly.

"You got that right," Tom said.

"But I don't think I realized until right now how much you actually hate me."

"Right again, sweetheart."

Lainey took a deep breath, her shoulders slumping with the effort as she turned away from her reflection. "Then what are you doing here, Tom?"

"I want you and the kids to come home," he said, as if this was the logical explanation.

"I'm sorry. We can't do that."

"So I don't get any say at all?"

"I think you've said more than enough."

"Oh, I'm just getting started."

"I'd say you're pretty much finished," Donatello announced, returning to the back of the salon, although he maintained a comfortable distance between himself and Tom.

"Get lost, jerk-off."

"I've notified the police. They'll be here momentarily."

Tom groaned. "Shit. You gotta be kidding me."

"I recommend you leave before they get here."

Tom spun toward Lainey. "I'm warning you, bitch. You're not kicking me out of my own house. You're not taking my kids away."

Lainey said nothing.

"This isn't over," he said. Then he pushed past Donatello, knocking him against the curved wall as he fled the salon.

THEY'D BEEN LOCKED in each other's arms for the better part of an hour, talking, giggling, exchanging soft kisses and tentative caresses, like nervous teenagers afraid to proceed too quickly, when they heard footsteps running along the outside corridor. The footsteps came to an abrupt halt in front of their door. A loud banging followed immediately.

"Oh, no," Suzy whispered, pulling out of Will's arms and staring at the door in horror.

"Open up in there," a voice demanded, followed by more banging.

"Tom?" Will said, jumping to his feet.

"Open the goddamn door!" More pounding. "Will, is that you? For shit's sake, open the fucking door!"

Goddamn it, Will thought, signaling Suzy to hide in the bedroom. "I'll get rid of him as fast as I can," he said quietly, grabbing her as she was about to leave and kissing her again.

"Could you just kiss me for a while?" she'd asked, and he'd been happy to oblige. Hell, I could spend all day kissing her, he thought now, watching her disappear around the corner. What the hell was Tom doing here?

"Do you always come busting in here?" he asked, opening the door.

Tom's arms were flailing about wildly in all directions at once. "Where's Jeff?"

"He's at the gym."

"Shit. Of course he's at the gym. Where else would he be? Shit," he said again.

"Is there a problem?" Will asked reluctantly.

"Is Kristin home?" Tom looked toward the bedroom.

"She had some errands to run," Will said quickly, prepared to throw himself between Tom and the bedroom should Tom take even one step in that direction.

"So, it's just you. That's what you're trying to tell me."

"I'm not trying to tell you anything."

"Oh, man. Not you, too," Tom said, groaning audibly. "I had enough of that bullshit today from Lainey."

"I don't know what you're talking about."

"Lainey went to see a lawyer this morning."

"I'm sorry," Will said, although he couldn't have cared less. He just wanted Tom out of the apartment so he could go back to kissing Suzy.

Tom plopped into the leather chair across from the sofa, stretched his long legs out in front of him as if he wasn't going anywhere. He pointed toward the glass on the floor. "What are you drinking?"

"Water."

"You got something stronger?"

"It's a little early, isn't it?"

"Who are you–my mother?"

"I think there's some beer in the fridge."

"Sounds good," Tom said, without moving.

Will walked into the kitchen, thinking of Suzy in the bedroom. How long would she wait? How long before she lost her nerve and ran home to Dr. Dave? He opened the fridge door, found a bottle of Miller Light, opened it, and carried it back to the living room.

"What? No glass?" Tom said.

"Help yourself."

Tom raised the bottle to his lips. "This'll do." He threw his head back, took a long sip. "That's better. It's been quite the morning."

"Look, I've got things to do."

"So who's stopping you?"

Will sank down on the sofa, said nothing. Just finish your beer and get the hell out, his eyes told Tom's.

"You know what that bitch said to me?" Tom asked. "She said I have to pay child support. She gets the kids, but I gotta pay to support them."

"They're your kids," Will reminded him.

"I'll rot in jail for the rest of my life before I pay her one fucking dime."

You do that, Will said silently. "Shouldn't you be at work?" he asked out loud.

"I'm quitting that motherfucking job. If Lainey thinks she's gonna take half my paycheck, she's got another think coming."

"That's kind of like cutting off your nose to spite your face, isn't it?" Will said, then immediately wished he hadn't.

"What?"

"Nothing."

"What are you talking about–cutting off my nose to . . . what?"

"Cutting off your nose to spite your face," Will repeated. "It's something my mother used to say."

"Yeah? Sounds like the Wicked Witch all right. That's what Jeff and I used to call her, you know. The Wicked Witch of West Buffalo."

"I know she was never your biggest fan."

Tom shrugged, took another sip of beer. "Like I care. When are you going back anyway? I'm sure the Wicked Witch misses her golden boy."

"I haven't decided yet."

"Shouldn't overstay your welcome, little brother. You know what they say about houseguests, don't you?" When Will failed to respond, Tom continued. "They're like fish. After three days, they go bad."

Again Will said nothing. He wondered what Suzy was doing, if she was listening to the conversation. He thought of the softness of her skin, the clean, fruity scent of her hair, the vaguely peppermint taste of her lips.

"You should have seen her, man," Tom said, laughing now. "There she was, her head in the sink, her hair dripping wet. . . ."

"What are you talking about?" Will asked impatiently.

"I'm talking about Lainey. At the hairdresser's. This morning," Tom answered in exasperation, as if Will should know this already.

"I thought she was at the lawyer's."

"*First* she was at the lawyer's, *then* she was at the hairdresser's." Tom bristled visibly. "She didn't like me showing up there, I tell you. She got all nervous, warned me not to cause a scene, like it's my fault this is all happening, like she's not the one who took the kids and left. So we got into it a bit, and suddenly Donny Osmond's there, telling me I've got to leave."

"Donny Osmond?"

"Yeah, dickhead. Like Donny Osmond goes to Lainey's hairdresser. What are you, retarded? It was a figure of speech."

A figure of speech, Will thought, straining to make sense of the conversation. "Okay, so it didn't go well."

"Stupid faggot called the cops."

"And you naturally came here," Will said.

"I drove around for a while first, trying to calm down. Miami, man. Might as well be in downtown Havana. I'm telling you, the foreigners are taking over. I mean, I grant you the Cuban women wear miniskirts instead of burkas, and paella sure beats the hell out of whatever the crap it is they eat in Afghanistan, but it all amounts to the same thing. Pretty soon this country's going to be nothing but a sea of brown faces. Lainey once told me she'd read how by the end of the next decade, white people are gonna be in the minority. Shit," he said, finishing the rest of his beer. "I should have just shot her, man. I should have popped her one right between her beady little eyes. Blown her stupid brains all over those ugly blue sinks and reclining leather chairs." He was laughing as he drew his gun out from underneath his shirt.

"What the hell?" Will exclaimed, jumping to his feet.

"You think old Donny boy is doing her?"

"Put that damn thing away."

"Should have plugged him, too. Just in case."

"Put the gun away, Tom."

"You gonna make me?"

"Put the gun away, Tom," a voice said from several feet away.

Tom spun toward the sound as Will held his breath.

Suzy advanced into the center of the room. "Put the gun away," she said.

FOURTEEN

TOM TOOK A STEP back. "What are you doing here?" He glanced from Will to Suzy, then back to Will, his voice an accusation. "Shit, man. You scored?"

"Looks like you're out a hundred bucks," Suzy said.

"Shit. I should shoot you just for that."

"Relax," Will told him. "Your money's safe."

"You didn't score?"

"He did," Suzy said.

"I didn't," Will countered.

Tom lowered his gun to his side, although he made no move to put it away. "Don't tell me I interrupted something."

"Your timing is as impeccable as ever."

"Actually I was just leaving," Suzy said.

"No," Will said quickly. "Stay awhile. Tom's the one who's leaving. Aren't you, Tom?"

Tom immediately assumed his former position in the beige leather chair. "Doesn't look like I'm going anywhere."

"I really should get going," Suzy said.

"She has a husband, remember?" Tom asked.

Suzy walked toward the door.

"Your husband do that to your face?"

"What?" Suzy's hand shot to her cheek, hovered above the bruise at her chin. "No, of course not. He's a doctor. He'd never . . . I tripped. . . ."

"Uh-huh. You buying that shit, little brother?"

"Please don't go," Will whispered as Suzy reached for the doorknob.

"Don't beg," Tom said. "It's pathetic."

"Go to hell."

"Why don't we all go?" Tom raised the gun, aimed it directly at Suzy.

"For Christ's sake, Tom . . ."

"I can shoot her in the foot, if you'd like. That'll stop her."

Will took a step toward Tom, wondering if he was strong enough—brave enough, *foolhardy* enough—to try wresting the gun from Tom's hands, when the sound of Suzy's voice stopped him.

"Or you could shoot my husband instead," she said.

"What?" Will spun back toward Suzy.

Suzy's eyes filled with panic. "I'm so sorry," she apologized. "I can't believe I said that. I didn't mean it. You know I didn't mean it."

"I know," Will said.

"It sounded like you meant it to me," Tom argued.

"It was a stupid thing to say."

"I don't know about that," Tom said, chuckling. "I mean, if

that's what you really want, I'm sure we could work out some sort of deal. . . ."

"Please, just forget I said anything." Suzy opened the door, stepped into the hall, Will close on her heels.

Tom waved. "Say hi to the good doctor."

Suzy stopped. "Please tell me you know I didn't mean it," she whispered to Will.

"It's okay. I understand."

"I know you do." She leaned forward to kiss Will on the side of his mouth as her eyes locked on his. Don't let me leave, they said. "Don't follow me," was what emerged. And then, in the next second, she was running along the outside corridor and down the stairs.

"You blew it, buddy," Tom said as Will reentered the apartment, closing the door behind him.

"You're a real piece of work," Will muttered.

"A real piece of work with a gun," Tom reminded him, waving it back and forth as if it were a small flag. "A real gun. With real bullets." He pointed the gun at Will's chest.

"You want to shoot me?" Will took two giant steps into the center of the room. His heart was pounding. His head was spinning. "Go ahead. Shoot me."

Tom was smiling as he tucked the gun into his belt, although it remained clearly visible. "I just might take you up on that one day," he said.

SUZY HEARD FOOTSTEPS behind her as she neared the visitors' parking area. She glanced quickly over her shoulder, saw no one. But seconds later, the footsteps resumed, falling in step with her own, mimicking her gait, getting closer. Was it possible Dave had followed her to the gym, watched her having coffee with Jeff, then followed the two of them here? Had he been puzzled to see Jeff and Kristin emerge without her soon after? And had he been patiently waiting ever since, his eyes trained on their apartment, eagerly anticipating her next move?

Had he witnessed Tom's sudden appearance, followed by her hasty exit? Had his hands formed murderous fists at his sides as he watched her lean in to plant a delicate kiss on the side of Will's mouth? Were those fists waiting for her now?

Suzy reached into her purse and grabbed her car keys, holding them in front of her as she continued briskly toward her car, her breathing ragged, her eyes darting nervously from side to side, on the lookout for Dave's red Corvette. She didn't see it, but that didn't mean it wasn't there. Damn it, why had she parked so far away?

She heard the footsteps behind her suddenly picking up speed. Suzy's shoulders stiffened, automatically bracing themselves for the impact of Dave's angry blows against her back. Would he be so bold as to attack her here, in the middle of the day, in such a public place? Or would he simply grab her arm, smile, and mutter, "Hello, darling," as he pushed her toward her car, then wait until they were safely back inside their home before beating her to a bloody pulp?

She almost laughed. When had her home ever been safe? she wondered, feeling a slight breeze at her back, a faint tremor in the surrounding air, as if it were being brushed aside, and then the weight of a hand on her shoulder.

"No, please," she cried, her eyes already filling with tears as she turned around.

"I'm sorry," a woman quickly apologized. "I didn't mean to startle you. I think you dropped this."

"What?" Suzy had to blink several times before she could dislodge Dave's features from the face of the short, elderly woman standing in front of her.

"You wouldn't want to lose this," the woman said, pushing something into Suzy's palm. "Not with all this identity theft going on. It *is* yours, isn't it? I'm sure I saw it fall out of your purse."

Suzy found herself staring at the small photograph of herself on her Florida driver's license. The license must have tumbled from her purse when she was getting her keys. "It's me," she acknowledged, although she barely recognized the bruise-free, confident-looking woman in the picture. "Thank you."

"Have a nice day," the woman said, walking toward a black Accord parked several spaces away and climbing awkwardly inside it.

"You too," Suzy said quietly, returning her license to her purse. Her eyes skipped across the concrete floor of the parking lot, in search of any more of herself she might have lost along the way.

"Who are you anyway?" she asked her reflection in the car's rearview mirror moments later. "Are you sure you know what you're doing?" She started the car, checking in all directions as she backed out of the narrow space, looking for any sign of Dave, seeing none.

Which meant nothing, she understood as she turned onto the street. She would only see Dave if and when he wanted her to see him. Unlike Tom, Suzy knew that if Dave were following her, she wouldn't know it until it was too late.

She checked her watch. Almost two o'clock. What was Dave up to that he wouldn't be home until seven? Was he planning a surprise? Something to make up for the ferocity of his more recent attacks, something to reassure her of his love? Back when they first got married, when she was still naive enough to think that his apologies meant something, when he was still making an effort to disguise the enjoyment his tormenting her brought, he would often bring home little gifts—a piece of antique jewelry she'd admired in a store window; a chocolate Easter egg, the kind with the rich vanilla cream filling and the sticky lemon cream center that she loved; the latest Nora

Roberts novel. "I'm so sorry," he used to say, promising it would never happen again. "You know I never meant to hurt you."

He never said he was sorry anymore. Instead, she was the one who was always apologizing. How had that happened? *When* had that happened? When had she begun accepting the blame for what he did to her? When had his temper become her responsibility?

How could she have let this happen? She, who had all the answers, who'd openly disdained and disparaged her mother for permitting all-too-similar abuse, she who'd sworn it would never happen to her, who thought she was so smart, so tough, so in control, when she was nothing but a pale carbon copy of her mother, the carbon evident in the black-and-blue smudges on her face.

She'd read somewhere that people choose what is familiar to them, that they seek out patterns, however heinous and ill advised, repeating them, often to their detriment, because they are unconsciously comfortable with them. They know what to expect.

The devil you know, she thought.

Had her subconscious known exactly the kind of man Dave Bigelow was all along? Had she married him understanding who he was, *what* he was, but pretending not to, pretending that if she was good enough, kind enough, diligent enough, woman enough, *not her mother* enough, she could change him, she could rewrite her sad history, effect a happy ending? Was that what she'd fooled herself into believing? Was that why she was so busy apologizing now?

Except she was through apologizing.

The light at the next corner turned yellow, and she pressed down on the accelerator, speeding through the intersection and almost colliding with a car that was making a left-hand turn. She gasped, swerved to her left, pulled her foot off the gas pedal.

I can shoot her in the foot, if you'd like, she heard Tom say.

Or you could shoot my husband instead, had been her quick response.

Had she really said that?

Had she meant it?

Could she go through with it?

"What's the matter with me?" she asked out loud, realizing she'd been driving for the last ten minutes with no clear idea where she'd been going. Rather like the last ten years of my life, she thought, turning east toward Biscayne Bay.

She soon found herself in the section of downtown Miami known as Brickell. Brickell was famous for its futuristic-looking condos and towering glass office buildings that made South Beach look downright quaint. Constructed in the eighties, financed by what was rumored to be laundered cocaine money, and pulsating to a distinctive Latin American beat, it was a paean to all that might be considered excessive anywhere else. Here, extravagance was the norm.

Everything was oversize, from restaurants like Bongos Cuban Cafe, which comfortably accommodated 2,500 people and whose bar stools were shaped liked giant bongos, to Duo, an American bistro with a wine list of more than 600 bottles. Then there were the nightclubs. At least a dozen at last count, all competing for the title of Biggest, Loudest, Most Happening.

Suzy drove by the warehouse that was Bricks Nightclub and Sunset Lounge, a recent addition to the Brickell nightlife scene. She'd come here with Dave just after they moved to Miami, but they'd never bothered going back. The promoters liked to trumpet its "kinetic color lighting system," under which club-goers danced to a mixture of house music, Latin, and hip-hop, but Dave said he preferred the clubs on the other side of the river, north maybe a dozen blocks. There was Metropolis Downtown, 55,000 square feet of young, intoxicated, drugged-out space cadets swaying to the deafening blare of electronic music under a circling succession of colored beams and flashing strobe lights; and Nocturnal, 22,000 square feet over three floors and a terrace that had cost roughly twelve million dollars to build. There was also Space, a cavernous, multilevel labyrinth of ear-splitting energy, where dancers indulged in high-end drugs and big-name DJs spun vinyl into gold. They'd gone there a couple of times, even though the action didn't really start until the wee hours of the morning. But then Dave had accused her of staring too long at a passing waiter and dragged her out of the club by the scruff of her neck, like a puppy that had misbehaved. A smattering of applause had followed their exit. Outrageousness was to be encouraged after all. No one had chased after them to see if she was all right.

Would anyone notice if I just disappeared off the face of the earth? she'd wondered over the years. *Would anyone care?*

Will, she thought, seeing his sweet face flash across her front window. Will would notice. Will would care. She touched her mouth, relived the softness of his kisses, the tenderness of his touch.

Which was exactly the problem, she realized, pulling the car to the side of the curb in front of the Pawn Shop Lounge and stopping, staring at the original WE BUY GOLD sign that graced the nightclub's slummy-looking exterior. Will was too sweet, too tender. His soft, patient kisses told her he was incapable of deliberate cruelty, that he would never be able to kill another human being.

Tom was a different story altogether. Cruelty fit him like a second skin. It flowed effortlessly through his veins, accompanied by equal doses of anger and entitlement. He was itching for a fight. And he had a gun.

But while Suzy knew Tom would have no trouble taking a life, she also recognized he was, in Will's words, a loose cannon and that she could never depend on him to do what needed to be done without messing up or demanding too much in return.

And she wasn't about to exchange one psychopath for another.

Which left Jeff.

Tough-talking, cynical, and not quite as smart as he liked to think he was, Jeff was exactly the man Suzy had been wishing for. Almost painfully proud of his sexual prowess, he was also full of wounded pride. Desperate to prove himself—to women, to men, but mostly to himself—he was full of the kind of false bravado that barely masked the scared little boy inside. And scared little boys were easy to manipulate.

Could she do it? Suzy wondered, watching a dark-haired couple weave by in each other's arms. The man was at least a head taller than the woman and maybe two decades younger. She saw them stop at the corner, the young man's right arm reaching down to cup the woman's buttocks, which pressed against her brightly patterned jersey dress. She watched the woman's head tilt back between her shoulder blades and laugh as the man covered her newly exposed throat with kisses. Who's using who? she wondered.

Who's using *whom*? she heard Dave correct.

Suzy groaned, long and loud.

Yes, she could do it, she decided in that instant, opening the car window and breathing in the rush of warm, humid air. She could use Jeff, use Tom, use Will—hell, she'd use all three, if necessary—to help rid her of Dave. She pulled away from the curb, speeding down the street in the direction of I-95.

Only two questions remained: when, and how?

"OKAY, NORA. ONE leg in front of the other, not so far apart, that's right. Keep your back straight. Good. Now, squat. Ten each side."

"I hate squats."

"I know," Jeff said, looking toward the clock on the wall opposite the mirrors. It was almost four o'clock. Was Suzy still with Will in his apartment? Had anything happened between them?

"They don't do any good," Nora Stuart whined.

Another five minutes and she'll be out of my hair, Jeff thought, praying for patience. Nora was one of his least favorite clients, a pear-shaped harridan, always complaining about something: the room was too warm, the music too vulgar, the exercises too tough.

"Trust me, squats are the best thing for your glutes," he said, picturing Suzy standing beside the reception desk, remembering the way she'd looked at him in the bakery.

You think I'm here because of you? she'd asked.

Damn right he did. He knew enough about women to know when they were interested. Suzy was definitely interested. And no matter what she said, or how much she protested otherwise, it wasn't in Will.

Nora Stuart rolled her heavily shadowed brown eyes toward the ceiling, her large, red lips stretching toward her chin in a pronounced frown. Her unnaturally black hair hung limply past her rounded shoulders, making her look every one of her forty-three years. "If squats are so damn good for you, how come my ass is still two feet off the ground?"

"That's a foot higher than it used to be," Jeff said, hoping for a laugh.

"Is that supposed to be funny?" Nora asked instead, hands on her wide hips. "Larry, I think I've just been insulted." Her tone made it difficult to determine whether or not she was joking. Kidding on the square, his sister used to call that.

Larry glanced over from his position on the other side of the room, where he was loading four twenty-pound steel plates onto a hundred-pound bar. He pulled his iPod out of his ear. "Sorry. Is there a problem?"

"I don't know," Nora said, looking at Jeff. "Is there?"

"What say we skip the squats for today?" Jeff said.

"Good idea. Squats don't do squat." Nora laughed at her own joke.

She was still chuckling as Jeff threw a mat across the floor and instructed her to lie on her back.

"What? That's it? You're going to stretch me out already?" Nora asked. "We're done?"

"It's four o'clock."

"So? We didn't start till ten after three."

"That's because you were ten minutes late."

"I told you—that couldn't be helped."

"I understand, but I have another client waiting." Jeff nodded toward Jonathan Kessler, already warming up on the treadmill.

"I pay a lot of money for these sessions."

"I appreciate that."

"I don't think you do."

"Is there a problem?" Larry asked again, ambling toward them.

"I'd like to make a change," Nora told him. "Starting next week, I'd prefer if you were my trainer."

Larry looked from Nora to Jeff and then back to Nora. "Did something happen?"

"Just not a good fit," Nora said.

Larry nodded, as if he understood, and smiled. "Talk to Melissa. She has my schedule. I'm sure we can work something out." When he looked back at Jeff, his smile was gone. "We'll talk later," he said.

FIFTEEN

"YOU WANT TO TALK about it?" Kristin asked, leaning across the bar, her impressive cleavage on full display. A bountiful bosom, a sympathetic ear—normally a winning combination, guaranteed to produce a generous tip. Yet the middle-aged man sitting on the stool at the far end of the bar, nursing his glass of single-malt, seemed curiously unimpressed.

"Hmm?" he replied without looking up. He was pasty skinned, balding, and perspiring into his pale blue shirt. He'd been sitting at the bar for the better part of an hour, his pale jowls sinking despondently into the palms of his nervous hands.

"Thought you might like that drink freshened," Kristin said.

"Good idea." He handed over his glass without lifting his head.

"Any particular preference?"

"Whatever," the man said.

Kristin retrieved a bottle of Canadian Club from its glass shelf and poured the man another drink, giving him a slightly more generous serving than required. Poor guy, she was thinking. He looks like he could use it. She filled a bowl with peanuts and pushed it toward him. "Everything okay?"

The man looked from the bowl of peanuts to the fake Rolex on his wrist. "What time do you have?"

Kristin checked her watch, an old Bulova she'd been wearing for more than a decade. "Five after six."

"That's what I've got."

"Somebody's late?"

"Somebody's been stood up," he said, his eyes reaching toward hers.

Kristin gave the man her most sympathetic frown. "What time were you supposed to meet her?"

"Five thirty."

"Well, she's not that late. Maybe she got stuck in traffic. Or maybe she's having trouble finding a place to park."

"Or maybe she's not coming," the man said.

"Have you tried calling her?"

"I've left three messages."

The front door opened and a gorgeous woman with long red hair walked inside. She was about thirty, tall and willowy, wearing black satin shorts and thigh-high, black leather boots. "Is that her?" Kristin whispered, trying not to sound too surprised.

"God, I hope so," the man said, sucking in his stomach and preparing to stand up when the front door opened again, and a curly-haired man with slim hips and a sly smirk ambled inside, slid his arm around the redhead's waist, and kissed her full on the mouth. They were laughing as they walked—seemingly joined at the hip—to a table near the back of the room. "Guess that wasn't her," the man said, sitting back down, letting his stomach relax over the top of his gray slacks.

"You don't know what she looks like?"

"We met on the Internet," the man admitted. "Her name's Janet. We've been exchanging e-mails for months. This was supposed to be our first date."

"She might still show up."

"Nah. She's not coming. I'm an idiot."

"You're not an idiot," Kristin said. Yeah, you are, she thought. "What's your name?"

"Mike." He tried to smile. "She calls me Mikey."

Kristin looked toward the entrance, willing the front door to open and Janet to walk through, looking for her Mikey. But the door stayed resolutely closed. "I'm sorry," she said after another minute had passed.

Mike shrugged, as if to say, What are you gonna do?

Half an hour later, the bar was filling up, and Janet still wasn't there. Kristin poured Mike another glass of whiskey. "On me," she was about to tell him when the front door opened, and a stylishly dressed, middle-aged woman with frosted hair and tortoise-shell-rimmed glasses walked up to the bar. "Could I have a gin and tonic, please?"

"Your name wouldn't be Janet by any chance, would it?" Kristin asked hopefully.

"No," the woman said. "It's Brenda. Why–do I look like a Janet?"

"Just a little game I sometimes play with myself," Kristin told her, trying to signal to Mike with her eyes. "One gin and tonic coming up."

"I'll be over there." Brenda pointed to a nearby table.

"So, what do you think?" Kristin asked Mike as soon as Brenda was gone.

"What do I think about what?"

"Brenda," Kristin stated, pouring several ounces of Beefeater gin into a glass.

"What do you mean?"

Kristin lifted her eyes toward the ceiling. Were men really this dense? "You're alone. She's alone. She looks very nice." She added the appropriate amount of tonic to the clear fluid. "You could take this over to her. . . ."

The man glanced in Brenda's direction without lifting his head. "Not interested."

"Why not?"

"Not my type."

"Why not?" Kristin said again.

"Too old for me."

"Too old? What are you talking about? How old are you?"

"Forty-six."

"So? She can't be more than forty."

"Too old for me," he repeated. "Thirty-five's my limit. Besides, she's hardly a beauty." He reached for his glass of whiskey.

Are you kidding me? Kristin demanded silently. Have you looked in the mirror lately? What is it with men? she wondered. Were they innately programmed to see only what they wanted to see? "That's twelve dollars," she said, bristling.

Mike pushed a twenty-dollar bill across the counter. "Give me six back," he told her.

Figures, Kristin thought, counting out six one-dollar bills. And to think I felt sorry for the weasel. She handed Brenda's gin and tonic to a passing waitress. "Table three."

"So," Mike said, raising his glass. "What time do you finish up here?"

"We close at two o'clock."

"That's a little late for me. Think you could beg off early?"

"What?"

"I asked if you could leave early."

"Why would I do that?" Is he coming on to me? Kristin wondered, a sinking feeling in the pit of her stomach. This is what comes from being nice to people, she thought.

"I thought maybe we could grab a late bite somewhere."

"Sorry. I can't do that."

"Another time, maybe?"

"I don't think my boyfriend would be too happy about that."

Mike downed his scotch in two quick gulps, then pushed himself away from the bar and stood up. "Yeah, well. Can't blame a man for trying, can you?"

"Wouldn't dream of it," Kristin said. "Take care."

She watched Mike weave his way toward the exit and hoped he had enough brains to take a cab home. She glanced over at Brenda, sipping gingerly on her gin and tonic and staring wistfully at the empty seat on the other side of the table. Nah, she thought. Mike's brains were all in his pants. Why were men smart enough to rule the world yet too stupid to know what was good for them?

"You handled that very well," a man's voice said, breaking into her reveries.

Kristin snapped to attention.

"I guess you get hit on a lot," the man continued. He was in his late thirties, maybe forty, bookishly handsome in his seersucker suit and navy blue tie. She hadn't seen him come in, wondered how long he'd been sitting there.

Kristin ignored the remark, which was generally a come-on of its own. "What can I get you?"

"Vodka, rocks."

"Vodka, rocks, it is."

"You didn't answer my question."

"I didn't hear one."

He laughed. "You're right. It was a guess."

She handed him his drink. "Then you guessed right. Twelve dollars," she said. "Unless you want to run a tab."

He handed her a fifty-dollar bill. "Keep the change," he said.

Kristin pocketed the money before he could realize he'd made a mistake or change his mind. Her expression betrayed no sign of surprise or undue gratitude.

"These clowns really think they have a chance with someone like you?" the man asked.

"Can't blame a man for trying," Kristin said, echoing Mike's words. "Or so I've been told."

The man laughed. "Must get pretty old though."

"I guess there are worse things."

"I'm sure there are."

"Hey, Kristin," a man at the other end of the bar called out. "Can we get a couple more beers down here?"

"Coming right up. Excuse me," Kristin said to the man in front of her.

"Take your time. I'll be right here."

It was almost ten minutes before she returned. "Rowdy bunch," she said, laughing over the increasing din from the far end of the bar. "How are you doing with that drink?"

The man held up his glass. "Just about ready for another one."

"Another vodka, rocks, on the way."

"Your name's Kristin?" he asked.

"It is."

"Pretty name."

"Thank you."

"So, tell me, Kristin," the man said, the name settling comfortably on his tongue. "What do you want to be when you grow up?"

Kristin groaned silently, although her smile remained steady. She'd been expecting a much better caliber of line than that. "In case you hadn't noticed, I'm pretty much grown."

"Oh, I noticed. You're very beautiful."

"Thank you."

"Too beautiful to be tending bar."

"Is this where you hand me your card and tell me you're a photographer or a modeling scout?"

He laughed. "I'm not a photographer or a modeling scout."

"Movie producer? Talent agent? TV director?"

"You've met them all?"

"Every last one."

"You meet any doctors?"

"What kind of doctor?"

"Radiologist. Over at Miami General." He extended his hand. Kristin noted the bruises around his knuckles. "Dave Bigelow," he said. "Pleased to meet you."

JEFF WAS JUST getting out of the shower when the phone rang. Probably Will, he was thinking as he wrapped a flimsy white towel around his waist and raced toward the phone in the bedroom. Will hadn't been there when he'd returned home at just past six o'clock. There'd been no note. Probably off somewhere with Suzy, Jeff had thought, deciding he'd been a fool for delivering her right to his brother's doorstep. *My* doorstep, he thought now, grabbing the phone from the nightstand beside the bed and raising the receiver to his ear. "Hello?"

"Jeff? It's Ellie. Please don't hang up."

Jeff's chin fell toward his chest. "How are you, Ellie?" He pictured his sister swaying from one foot to the other, her top teeth biting down on her narrow bottom lip, her long slim fingers twisting the cord of the phone's extension wire, her gray-green eyes already filling with tears. All he'd asked was how she was, and already she was crying.

Ellie swallowed the catch in her voice. "I'm fine. You?"

"Never better."

"How's Kirsten?"

"Kristin," Jeff corrected her.

"Sorry. Of course. Kristin. I'll have to meet her one of these days."

Jeff said nothing, his wet hair dripping down his forehead onto his cheeks. He glanced at himself in the mirror over the dresser, thinking it was probably time for a touch-up.

"Will says she's terrific," Ellie said.

"Then terrific she must be," said Jeff sardonically.

"Jeff . . ."

"How are Bob and the kids?"

"They're good. Taylor's going to be two in August. I can't believe you haven't seen her yet," she continued when he failed to respond.

"Look, Ellie. You caught me at a really bad time. . . ."

"You have to come home, Jeff," Ellie pleaded.

"I can't do that."

"Our mother is dying," Ellie told him. "She took a turn for the worse last night. The doctor says she has maybe another week, two at the most."

"What do you want me to say, Ellie? That I'm sorry? I can't say that."

"I want you to say that you'll come home, that you'll see her before she dies."

"I can't say that either."

"Why not? Would it be so hard to hear her out?"

"Yes," Jeff acknowledged. "It would be so hard."

"She knows what she did was wrong. She just wants to apologize."

"No. What she wants is forgiveness," Jeff said. "That's not the same thing at all."

"Please, Jeff. She cries all the time. She's so sorry for everything."

"It's easy to be sorry when it's too late to do anything about it," Jeff said.

"It doesn't have to be too late," Ellie insisted. "Not for you."

"It was too late a long time ago." Jeff lowered the phone to the nightstand.

"Jeff, please–" he heard his sister say before he disconnected the call.

He stared at his reflection. "It's way too late," he said.

"NICE TO MEET you, Dr. Dave Bigelow," Kristin said, shaking the man's hand.

"You can call me Dr. Bigelow," he joked, and Kristin obliged him with a smile.

"So what exactly does a radiologist do at Miami General?" she asked.

"He reads X-rays, makes diagnoses, heals the sick, cures the afflicted, performs miracles on a regular basis."

"Sort of like what I do here."

"More or less," Dave said, and laughed. "Have you worked here long?"

"Since it opened. About a year, I guess. This your first time in the Wild Zone?"

"It is. I just moved here a few months ago. Just starting to feel my way around."

"Where are you from?" Kristin asked.

"Phoenix, originally. More recently, Fort Myers."

"Really? I just met someone from Fort Myers. Suzy somebody. You know her?" She laughed.

"I might. I actually used to know a Suzy. And Fort Myers isn't that big a place. You know her last name?"

Kristin shook her head. "I don't think she told me."

"What's she look like?"

Kristin pictured the door to her apartment opening and Jeff ushering the young woman inside. "Pretty, dark hair, pale complexion," she rattled off. "Very thin."

"Doesn't sound familiar. She come in a lot?"

"No. Just a few times." She wondered what, if anything, had happened between Suzy and Will. By the time she'd returned to the apartment to get ready for work, no one was there.

"You ever go to a movie together?" Dave was asking.

"What?"

"The Suzy I knew in Fort Myers loved movies."

Kristin nodded. "I love movies, too. Not that I get to see too many of them, what with the hours I work."

"Somebody told me there's a movie theater nearby that's open all night."

"Oh, yeah. The Rivoli. It's great. One of those really old-fashioned movie houses. One screen, actual curtains, no stadium seating, great popcorn. You should go."

"Are you asking me out?"

Kristin smiled. "Afraid I can't do that."

"Against house rules?"

"Against *my* rules."

"So it's true you have a boyfriend? It's not just something you tell guys to keep them at bay?"

"I have a boyfriend," Kristin said.

"And I actually do have a friend who's a photographer." Dave winked.

Kristin laughed.

"Scout's honor. His name's Peter Layton. I understand he's pretty famous."

Kristin shook her head. "Can't say I've ever heard of him."

"He does a lot of fashion and magazine work. You should meet him."

"I probably should."

"I could set something up, if you'd like."

"I don't think so."

"Hey, Kristin," the man at the end of the bar called out again. "We're feeling a bit neglected down at this end."

"I'm coming," she called back.

"I'm not bullshitting you," Dave said, reaching out to cover her hand with his. "I'm a doctor, remember? And doctors never lie."

Kristin felt an unwanted jolt of electricity pass from his fingers through hers. She made no attempt to dislodge her hand. "You really have a friend who's a fashion photographer?"

"I swear."

"Don't. Your mother wouldn't like it."

"She'd like you though. She'd say, 'Dave, that girl's a spitfire. Don't let her get away.'"

"I have a boyfriend," Kristin said again.

Dave smiled. "Here's my card. Call me if circumstances change."

SIXTEEN

"I'M TELLING YOU, MAN. He didn't score." Tom took a deep drag off his cigarette, then laughed, long and loud, into his cell phone.

"You're crazy," came Jeff's immediate reply. "How could he not score? I hand-delivered her, gift-wrapped, for Christ's sake. I did everything but tuck them into bed together."

"He didn't score."

A second's silence. Then, "How do you know?"

Tom repeated the details of his day, including his encounter with Lainey at Donatello's and his subsequent visit to Jeff's apartment. "Looks like I might have gotten there just in the nick of time," he boasted.

"Well, then, kudos to you, Tommy boy. You saved the day."

"Not to mention a hundred bucks."

"You may still lose that hundred," Jeff said. "Looks like big brother's back in the hunt."

Tom forced another laugh from his throat. It was just like Jeff to make it all about him, to turn Tom's moment of glory into a mere anecdote while, in the same breath, dismissing Tom's chances for scoring with Suzy himself. No, not dismissing. Negating. Negating utterly and entirely. As if the possibility of Tom's succeeding with Suzy was too ludicrous to even consider. Worse–as if it had never even crossed Jeff's mind. Big brother was back in the hunt, after all. There was no need for anyone else to bother showing up. "How come it took you so long to answer the phone?" Tom asked, trying to mask his irritation.

"I thought it might be my sister again," Jeff said. "She's trying to get me to come home, see my mother before she dies."

"You gonna do it?"

"I don't know," Jeff admitted after a pause.

"Don't let her lay a guilt trip on you, man," Tom said. "You got nothing to feel guilty about."

"I know that."

"She deserted you, man. Pawned you off on the Wicked Witch of the West."

"Apparently she wants to apologize."

"Bullshit. She only wants to see you so she can feel better about herself before she dies."

"I know that, too."

"She's going to hell, man. Hell in a handbasket. What's that mean anyway?"

Jeff laughed. "Damned if I know."

"Women," Tom sneered, sucking on his cigarette, then blowing out a long puff of smoke and watching it circle his head like an angry cloud. "Hold on a minute. I gotta open the window."

"What window? Where are you?"

"In my car." Tom took a final drag off his cigarette, opened his window, and tossed the still-burning butt onto the road.

"I don't hear any traffic."

"That's because there isn't any."

"Where are you?"

Tom almost laughed at the wariness he heard in Jeff's voice. "Nowhere special."

"Please tell me you're not still following Lainey."

"I'm not still following Lainey," Tom repeated dutifully.

"Good man."

"Don't have to," Tom said.

"Meaning what?"

Tom shrugged. "Meaning I already know where she is. She and the kids are staying with her parents," he continued unbidden. "Bitch came home about an hour ago. Hasn't budged since. They're probably finishing up with dinner right about now."

Another silence. Then, "You're parked in front of their house," Jeff said.

Tom could almost see Jeff shaking his head in dismay. "No." He laughed. "I'm parked three houses down."

"Shit," Jeff exclaimed. "Are you kidding me?"

"It's no big deal. They don't know I'm here."

"You're sure about that?" Jeff's question made it clear he wasn't sure at all.

"Sure as shit. You want to bet on it?"

"I want you to get the hell away from there."

"I'm just looking out for my interests."

Jeff sighed loudly. "Okay, look. Do what you have to do. I'm heading over to the Wild Zone in about an hour. You want to meet me there, fine."

Tom looked out the car's front windshield toward the sprawling, vine-covered bungalow where Lainey's parents lived. All the lights in the place seemed to be on, he noted, even though it was still quite bright outside. He snorted derisively. Lainey was always on his back about conserving energy, trailing after him from room to room, turning off the lights he'd left on, unplugging appliances that weren't in use, quoting various experts on global warming. What a hypocrite, he thought, grabbing another cigarette from the front pocket of his blue plaid shirt and lighting up.

The bungalow's front door suddenly opened, and a man—short, barrel chested, full head of black hair graying at the temples—emerged. He stood motionless in the doorway for several seconds and only moved when he was grabbed around the knees by his young grandson. "Cody," Tom whispered.

"What?" Jeff asked in his ear.

"Grandpa, come on," Cody squealed. "It's your turn to hide."

"Tom," Jeff said, "are you still there? What's going on?"

"Sam, what are you doing out there?" a woman's voice called from inside the house, her voice skipping effortlessly down the street.

"Come on, Grandpa. Let's play."

"Tom?" Jeff asked. "Tom? Talk to me."

"No way I'm letting that bitch take my kids away from me," Tom said as Lainey's father retreated back into the house with Cody, closing the door after him.

"Tom, listen to me. Don't do anything stupid."

"See you in an hour," Tom said, clicking off.

"SO, I SPOKE to Jeff," Ellie was saying.

Will leaned back into the park bench on which he'd been sitting for the better part of an hour trying to calm his nerves after the shocking events of the late afternoon. One minute Suzy was in his arms, the next minute Tom was waving a gun in his face. What the hell had happened? Had he actually dared Tom to shoot him? Will stretched his legs full out in front of him and switched his cell phone from his left ear to his right, realizing his hands were still shaking.

"When did you speak to him?"

"Twenty, maybe thirty minutes ago."

"And?" Will heard small children squabbling in the background. He pictured Ellie in her tiny kitchen, her light brown hair falling past her chin in a succession of loose waves, a faint trace of blush staining her cheeks, her two children running in circles around her.

"He says he won't come."

"And you're surprised because . . . ?"

"I'm not surprised. I'm disappointed."

"Can you really blame him?" Will asked.

"It's not that I blame him. Taylor, stop hitting Max."

Will chuckled, picturing the little firebrand that was his two-year-old niece laying into her more sedate five-year-old brother.

"I just think it's really important for his mental health that he sees our mother before she dies."

"I wouldn't worry too much about Jeff's mental health."

"He has to come to terms with his feelings," Ellie said.

"I think Jeff knows exactly how he feels," Will stated. "He hates his mother's guts."

"Adults don't hate each other's guts," Ellie said.

Will shrugged. Ellie had majored in psychology in college. There was no point arguing with her. Especially when she was right.

"You have to talk to him," Ellie urged.

"I did," Will argued. "He's not buying it."

"You have to convince him."

"Give it up, Ellie. He's not going back."

"What if you talk to Kirsten?"

"Kristin," Will corrected her.

"Whatever," Ellie said impatiently. "Maybe she can persuade him."

"Trust me," Will said. "She knows better than to try."

"It's in her own best interests," Ellie insisted.

"Meaning?" The word was out of Will's mouth before he had time to stop it. The last thing he wanted to do was prolong this conversation any more than he had already.

"Until he resolves things with our mother," Ellie stated emphatically, "he's always going to have issues with women. He'll keep putting her face on theirs, revisiting old wounds. . . ."

"Somebody's been watching too much Oprah," Will said, hearing Tom's sneer in his voice. He softened it immediately. "Listen, I've really gotta go."

"Why? What are you doing?" Ellie asked.

"Getting ready to go out," Will lied, his eyes scanning the park. Across the way, a young father was pushing his child on a swing, and a man was tossing a Frisbee toward a large black Lab.

"Do you have a date?"

Will could hear the hope in her voice. "Ellie," he began, "you're only my half sister. Do you think you could dial down the concern half a notch?"

She laughed. "Not a chance. Where are you off to?"

He sighed. "Nowhere special. Probably just over to the Wild Zone for a drink."

"That's that bar where Kirsten works?"

"Kristin," Will said.

"You're not drinking too much, are you?" Ellie asked, ignoring his correction.

Will laughed, said nothing.

"Your mom called this morning," Ellie said, abruptly shifting gears. "She's worried about you, said she hadn't heard from you in almost a week. You might want to give her a call, reassure her you're still alive and, well, that Jeff hasn't done something terrible to you."

"I'll do that."

"And you'll talk to him again?" she added. "Try to impress on him that there's not a lot of time?"

"I'll try," Will said, understanding there was no point in saying anything else.

"You're a good boy," Ellie told him before hanging up.

"HELLO, MOM?" TOM asked, thinking, Moron, of course it's your mother. Who else would it be?

"Alan," she exclaimed happily. "How are you, darling? Everybody," she called out, "it's Alan."

"It's not Alan. It's Tom."

"Tom?"

"Your son, Tom. The black sheep in the middle," he added bitterly.

"Tom," his mother repeated, as if trying to comprehend a word in a foreign language. "It's Tom," she relayed to whomever else was in the room. Then, back to him, "Is there something wrong? Are you in trouble?"

"Do I have to be in trouble to call home?"

"Are you?" his mother asked again.

"No."

His mother's relief was audible, although she said nothing. Tom pictured her standing in the doorway between the dining room and the kitchen, her sad brown eyes appealing for help from those gathered around the dining room table, her mouth pinched into a worried pout, as if she were sucking on a piece of sour candy.

"Am I interrupting something?" Tom asked.

"We were just sitting down to dinner. Vic and Sara are here with the kids."

Tom tried conjuring up an image of his brother, older by a year and a half, but since he'd seen him less than half a dozen times in twice as many years, it was difficult. When Tom and his brothers were younger, people used to have trouble telling them apart, so similar were they in appearance and stature. But as the years progressed, Tom grew taller, Alan wider, Vic handsomer. By the time they were in their late teens, no one had trouble distinguishing one from the other, especially since they were rarely together. "How is everyone?"

"Great. Lorne and Lisa are growing like weeds."

"Carole, get off the phone," Tom heard his father say. "Your dinner's getting cold."

"What kind of mess has he gotten himself into now?" Vic's wife, Sara, muttered in the background, although her voice was loud enough for Tom to make out every word.

"Is there a reason you're calling?" his mother asked warily.

"Do I need one?" Tom asked in return, lighting a fresh cigarette with the end of the one he was currently smoking, then flicking the butt out the car window to join the growing pile.

"You're not sick, are you?"

"For God's sake, Carole," Tom's father said. "He's fine."

"Let me talk to him," Vic said.

"I don't want to talk to Vic," Tom protested.

"Tom, how are you doing, buddy?" his brother asked, coming on the line, his deep voice radiating confidence and success.

"I'm fine, Vic. You?"

"Fantastic. Sara's terrific, the kids are doing great, I love my work—"

"How can you love crunching numbers all day?"

"—I've got my health," Vic continued, as if Tom hadn't spoken.

"What are you—eighty years old? You sound like an old man with this 'I've got my health' shit."

"You don't have anything if you don't have your health. Trust me on that one."

"Why should I trust you? You're a fucking accountant, for shit's sake. Who trusts an accountant?"

"Ever the smart-ass, I see."

"You don't see a goddamn thing."

"Then you better spell it out," Vic said. "What is it, Tom? You need money? Is that why you're calling?"

"What are you doing?" Sara hissed. "We're not giving your brother any more money. He didn't repay us the last time."

"You lent your brother money?" Tom's father asked incredulously.

"It wasn't much," Vic said dismissively. "Just a few thousand . . ."

"Hey, if you're offering," Tom said.

"How much do you need?"

"Vic, for God's sake," Sara said, closer to the phone now than before.

"A few thousand sounds pretty good."

"I can't do that," Vic said quietly.

"Damn right you can't," Sara said.

"You're the one who offered."

"I can maybe spare a couple hundred. That's it."

"What are you doing?" Sara demanded angrily. "You're not giving your brother another dime."

"Mommy, what's wrong? Why are you yelling at Daddy?" a child asked in the background.

"What's going on, Tom? Is there something you're not telling us?"

"Lainey and I split up," Tom admitted after a pause.

"You're kidding! Lainey left him," Vic shouted to the others.

"What?" His mother.

"Big surprise." His father.

"What took her so long?" Sara.

"She's threatening to take my kids away," Tom said.

"Sounds like you need a lawyer."

"I need *money* for a lawyer," Tom barked. "And a few hundred bucks isn't going to do it."

"Sorry, Tom. I really am. I'd help you if I could."

"You are not giving your brother any more money," Sara said.

"Tell that stupid cunt to shut the fuck up," Tom yelled.

"Hey," Vic warned him, "watch it."

"What's the matter with you? Where are your balls, for Christ's sake? You let that bitch boss you around like that?"

"That's enough, Tom."

"Enough? I'm just getting started where that twat is concerned."

"No, Tom. Trust me. You're finished."

The line went dead in his hands.

"Shit!" Tom yelled, holding on to the word until he ran out of breath. His hands slammed down on the steering wheel, inadvertently triggering the horn. The noise blasted its way into the thick, warm air, like dynamite. "Shit, fuck, fucking shit!" He lowered his head, tears of frustration stinging his eyes. Damn that smug bastard of a brother of his, with his terrific wife and great kids and a job that he loved. Not to mention his fucking health. "Trust me, you don't have anything if you don't have your health!" Tom mimicked, his head snapping up, a loud cackle escaping his mouth to bounce off the car's interior and echo down the street. "Trust me!" he shouted. "Like I'm gonna fucking trust you, you miserable piece of shit!"

Which was when he saw the cop car in his rearview mirror and a uniformed officer walking cautiously toward him, his hand hovering above the gun in his holster as he approached.

"Everything all right here?" the officer asked.

"Everything's just fine," Tom said, not looking at him.

"Could I see your license and registration?" A command in the shape of a question.

"What for? I'm not doing anything. I'm not even driving."

"License and registration," the officer repeated, signaling to another officer waiting in the police car, as if he expected trouble.

Tom fished into the side pocket of his jeans to retrieve his driver's license, then reached across the front seat into his glove compartment for his registration. The officer, a young Hispanic with a scar that ran the length of his upper lip, glanced at both before handing them to his older partner. "We've had a complaint of a car matching this description loitering in the area," he explained.

Tom glanced toward his father-in-law's bungalow. So the bastard had seen him and called the police. Fucking moron. "I haven't been here all that long."

"Long enough to smoke half a pack of cigarettes." The officer glanced at the discarded butts beside his black leather boots.

"What–is it a crime now to smoke in this country?"

"Mind stepping out of the car?" the officer said.

"Yeah, I mind," Tom told him. "I haven't done anything."

"Come on, Tom," the officer said, having noted the name on his license. "Don't make me haul your ass off to jail."

"For what, jerk-off?" Tom snapped, seeing a flash of alarm light up the officer's dark complexion.

The next thing he saw was the barrel of a gun pointing directly at his face.

SEVENTEEN

"HEY, GOOD-LOOKIN'," JEFF SAID, taking a seat at the bar and smiling at Kristin. "Tom been in yet?"

"Haven't seen him. You heard anything from Will?"

Jeff shook his head. "He's probably too embarrassed to show his face."

"Why would he be embarrassed?"

Jeff leaned in, lowered his voice to a whisper. "'Cause nothing happened between him and Suzy Pomegranate, that's why." He laughed. "Can you believe that? Strike two!"

"How do you know nothing happened?"

"Because Tom walked in on them."

"He interrupted them?"

"Apparently there was nothing to interrupt. Can you believe

that?" he said again, his eyes sweeping across the lightly populated room. "Not too busy tonight," he commented.

"It's Monday," Kristin said. "Although it was pretty busy earlier." She touched the business card in the side pocket of her tight black skirt, wondering if she should show it to Jeff. *Dr. Dave Bigelow, Radiologist, Miami General Hospital.* How would Jeff react? she wondered. Would he be indifferent, or would it shake him up a little bit? And was that what she wanted—to shake him up? And if so, how much?

He already knew that other guys found her attractive. He loved hearing her stories about the men who came on to her, the men she turned down on an almost nightly basis, whose hopeful business cards she quickly tossed into the trash.

Except she hadn't tossed this one.

Why hadn't she?

Was she actually considering calling him?

How would Jeff react to that?

"What are you drinking?" she asked.

"Gimme a Miller draft." Jeff laughed. "I can't believe he struck out again."

He was still chuckling when Will walked through the door some ten minutes later. "Well, well. The unconquering hero finally resurfaces," Jeff said, hoisting his glass into the air. "Give the man a drink, Krissie. He looks like he could use hydrating."

"Miller draft," Will told Kristin.

"Atta boy. Okay. So, out with it. Details, details."

"You know what happened," Will said testily. "I'm sure Tom couldn't wait to tell you."

"I know what *didn't* happen. *Again,*" Jeff said. "What I don't know is why."

"We're not all like you, Jeff," Will told his brother. "Some of us like to take things slow."

"Slow is one thing. Stupid is another."

"You all right?" Kristin asked, handing Will his beer.

"I'm fine. Honestly. It was a lovely afternoon."

"A lovely afternoon?" Jeff repeated incredulously. "What are you talking about? Who the hell says things like 'It was a lovely afternoon'?"

"People like me," Will said. "Call me crazy, but is there anything wrong with getting to know someone first?"

"You're crazy," said Jeff.

"I think it's sweet," Kristin offered.

"Suzy's very vulnerable right now," Will explained. "It wouldn't be fair to take advantage—"

"Who cares about being fair?" Jeff demanded. "What's the matter with you? Christ, no wonder Amy dumped you."

Will raised his glass to his lips, drank half his beer in one gulp.

"Jeff," Kristin cautioned. "Go easy."

"It's okay," Will said. "It's nothing I haven't said to myself a million times."

"You gotta seize the moment, little brother. How many chances do you think you get at the brass ring?"

"I guess we'll just have to wait and see."

"Guess we will," Jeff agreed, looking toward the front entrance. "You haven't seen Tom around, have you?"

"Not since this afternoon." Will thought that if he never saw Tom again, it would be too soon for him. "Did that lunatic tell you he pulled a gun on me?"

"He what?" Kristin gasped. "Jeff, you really have to do something about him."

"And what is it you'd have me do exactly?" Jeff snapped.

Kristin shrugged, raised her palms into the air in defeat.

"Ellie called." Will broached the subject cautiously. "She said she spoke to you about going home. . . ."

"Don't start," Jeff warned.

"I'm not. I just—"

"Don't," Jeff said again.

Will downed the rest of his beer, signaled to Kristin for another. "I'm sorry," he said to Jeff. "I should mind my own business."

"I shouldn't have made that crack about Amy."

Will nodded, although he was thinking that Jeff had been right about Amy. Maybe if he hadn't been so sweet with her, so damn respectful, if he'd been more of a man, if he'd seized the moment, been more forceful, *more like Jeff,* she might not have left him for someone else.

"Hey. Go easy with that beer," Kristin cautioned him.

A muffled "Star-Spangled Banner" began to play. Jeff reached into the back pocket of his jeans, pulled out his cell, checked the caller ID. It was a number he didn't recognize, so he returned it to his pocket unanswered. A few seconds later, it started up again.

"You better answer it," Kristin said. "Or we'll be jumping to attention all night."

Jeff was chuckling as he flipped open his phone. "Hello? Tom, where the hell are you? I almost didn't answer, for Christ's sake. I didn't recognize the number. What? You gotta be kidding me."

"What's going on?" Will asked, curious in spite of himself.

"All right. Hold on. We'll be there as fast as we can."

"Where are you going?" Kristin asked.

Jeff downed the rest of his beer. "Drink up, little brother. We're going to jail."

"WHAT THE FUCK took you so long to get here?" Tom jumped to his feet, almost knocking over the metal folding chair he'd been sitting on, as Jeff marched into the small, windowless room, Will close on his heels. Tom tossed the wildlife magazine he'd been leafing through onto the wooden table in front of him. "Shit, man. What's he doing here?"

"More to the point, what are *you* doing here?" Jeff asked. He hated police stations. Even walking by one made him feel as if he was guilty of something.

"That cunt's father called the cops, reported a suspicious-looking automobile lurking in the area. They hauled my ass down here."

Jeff looked toward the door. "I told you to get the hell out of there, didn't I?"

"What–I'm not allowed to park my car on a public street anymore? I wasn't doing anything wrong. This country's turning into a fucking fascist state, when a man can't even sit in his goddamn car and smoke a few cigarettes. . . ."

"Maybe you should keep it down," Will urged, raising his fingers to his lips.

"Maybe you should get it up," Tom shot back.

"Okay, okay," Jeff said, trying not to laugh. "Will's right. You don't want to end up spending the night in a holding cell."

"What are they gonna hold me on? I didn't do anything, for shit's sake. They can't arrest me."

"They already have," Will said.

"What the fuck do you know? I'm not under arrest, dickhead."

"Then what are we doing here?"

"I don't know what *you're* doing here. I sure as hell didn't ask you to come. What'd you bring him for anyway?" Tom asked Jeff.

"Be glad I did," Jeff told him. "The cops are only releasing you on condition someone else drives you home. They think you're too emotionally precarious–their words, not mine," Jeff qualified, "to be behind the wheel right now. Frankly, I'm inclined to agree with them."

"Emotionally pre . . . *what*? What the fuck are they talking about? Fucking fascists," Tom muttered.

"Listen," Jeff said. "You're lucky they're letting you out of here with just a warning."

A uniformed officer stuck his head in the door. "How are things going in here? He cooled off any?"

"You got no right to keep me here," Tom shouted.

"Still hot," the officer noted wryly.

"He'll be okay," Jeff said. "Give us another couple of minutes. What is it with you?" he asked Tom as soon as the policeman was out of sight. "Do you want them to arrest you?"

"For what?"

"For being an obnoxious prick," Will said, not quite under his breath.

"What'd you say?"

"He said, for stalking," Jeff improvised.

"Stalking? I wasn't stalking anybody."

"You followed Lainey all day; you confronted her at the hairdresser's; you were parked in front of her parents' house for more than an hour. . . ."

"I parked down the street."

"It's still considered stalking. Just how much ammunition do you want to give Lainey?"

"I'm not giving that bitch a damn thing."

"Then you've got to calm down. Be smart. Be contrite. No more of this shit, Tom, or you'll lose everything."

"I've already lost everything," Tom moaned, sinking back down into the metal folding chair and burying his head in his hands.

For an instant, Will thought Tom was about to cry, and he actually felt himself feeling sorry for him.

It was at that moment that Tom lifted up his head and smiled. "Contrite enough for you?" he asked with a wink.

"Much better," Jeff said, laughing.

"Shit," said Will.

"Okay. Think you're ready to get out of here?"

"He's not driving my car," Tom said, pointing an accusing finger at Will.

"Fine. I'll drive your car," Jeff said. "Will, you can drive mine."

"Good by me."

"Okay, so what are you gonna tell the cops?" Jeff asked Tom.

"That I'm sorry, and that I promise to be a good little boy," he answered.

"You'll stay away from your wife?" the police officer who'd brought him in was asking moments later.

"I wouldn't touch her with a ten-foot pole."

"Good," the officer said. "Because it's my understanding she'll be filing a restraining order against you first thing in the morning."

"What the fuck . . ."

"Tom," Jeff warned.

"Her parents, too. And once they do that, our hands are tied. We'll have to arrest you if you go anywhere near them."

"Sons of bitches . . ."

"Look," the policeman said. "I understand your frustration. I really do. My ex pulled the same shit with me. But there's nothing you can do except make matters worse. Trust me."

"'Trust me,'" Tom repeated. "Why do people always say that?"

"You ready?" Jeff asked.

Tom reached for the magazine he'd been perusing prior to Jeff's entrance. "Mind if I take this with?" he asked. "There's this article I was reading. . . ."

"Be my guest."

"Thanks."

"Stay out of trouble," the officer called as they walked past the high counter of the reception desk in the main lobby toward the exit. A woman officer smiled at Jeff as they were leaving.

As soon as they were in the parking lot, Tom tossed the magazine into a nearby garbage bin.

"What'd you do that for?" Will asked.

"It's a magazine about fucking wildlife," Tom sneered. "Speaking of which, did you know that armadillos are running amok in the state of Florida?"

Jeff laughed. "Get in the car, bozo, before I turn you in again myself." He tossed his car keys toward Will. "You know how to get home?"

"No idea," Will said.

"He's clueless," Tom said, sliding into the passenger seat of his car.

"Okay, follow me." Jeff climbed behind the wheel of Tom's Impala, turned on the ignition. "Shit. Do you know you're almost out of gas?"

"It wasn't my idea to drive all the way down here." Tom started to laugh, was still laughing as Jeff backed out of the tight parking space and turned onto the dark street.

"You think this is funny, do you?" Jeff asked, almost choking on the stale odor of cigarette smoke. He rolled down the window.

"You'd think it was funny too, man, if you knew what I do."

"Which is?"

"Stop the car a minute and I'll show you."

"What?"

"I'm telling you–stop the car."

Jeff pulled Tom's Impala to a halt a block from the station house. Immediately, Will pulled to a halt behind them.

"What's wrong?" Will asked, approaching quickly on foot.

"Check under the seat, man," Tom instructed Jeff.

"What?"

"Check under the seat."

Jeff lowered his arm beneath the driver's seat and began rummaging around until he felt something hard and cold. When he brought his hand up seconds later, his fingers were curled around the barrel of a gun.

"Shit," Will exclaimed, feeling as if he was about to be sick.

"What a hoot!" Tom shouted. "Dumb cops drive my car all the way down here. They don't even do a search. Don't have a warrant, I guess. Can you beat that? Stupid fascists."

"I don't believe you," Will said, his legs starting to shake with a combination of fear and relief. "You're going to get us all thrown in jail, you stupid son of a bitch."

"Get back in the car, Will," Jeff told him. "We'll meet you at the apartment." He dropped the gun to his lap.

"Give me that," Tom said, reaching for it.

Jeff knocked his hand aside. "Finders, keepers," he said.

KRISTIN WAS WAITING for them at the front door of their apartment.

"What are you doing home?" Jeff asked her as the three men walked inside. He checked his watch. It wasn't even eleven o'clock.

Kristin followed the movement of Jeff's arm. "It wasn't busy. Joe said I could go home early. Is that a gun?" she asked, all in one breath.

Jeff handed it to her. "Put it somewhere safe," he said without explanation.

"Hey," Tom protested. "That's mine."

"Not till you learn a little self-control."

Tom plopped down into the beige leather chair he'd occupied earlier in the day. "No biggie. You can keep it. I got others."

Will marched into the kitchen and poured a glass of water, which he drank down in one gulp.

"Is somebody going to tell me what happened?" Kristin asked, her gaze shifting from the gun in her hand to Jeff.

"Allow me," Tom said, quickly detailing the events of the past twelve hours. "Did you know that there is actually such a thing as a flying squirrel, although they don't really fly so much as glide, by way of a skin flap that balloons out from their bodies?" He smiled.

"What the hell is he talking about?" Kristin asked Will as he reentered the room.

Will shrugged, feeling faint as he sank down on the sofa.

"It's true," Tom said. "I read about it in *Wildlife Digest.* Anyone for a beer?"

"Bar's closed," Kristin said. "Look, Tom, you've had a very full day. I think you should go home and get a good night's sleep."

Tom reluctantly pushed himself to his feet. "You really not gonna give me back my gun?" He extended his hand toward Kristin.

"Not a chance," Jeff said, stepping between them.

"Aah," Tom moaned. "And I really felt like killing someone tonight."

"Just stay away from Lainey," Jeff warned him.

"How about we kill the good doctor instead?"

"What?" asked Jeff and Will simultaneously.

"What?" Kristin asked, half a beat behind.

"The Pomegranate's husband. Apparently he's some big-shot doctor at Miami General."

"His name wouldn't be Dave Bigelow, would it?" Kristin asked, as all three men's heads swiveled in her direction. She was holding her breath as she reached into the side pocket of her short black skirt, extracted Dave's card, held it out.

"Where'd you get this?" Jeff asked, taking it from her and perusing it quickly.

"He was at the bar tonight," Kristin explained, feeling her pulse quicken. "He hit on me."

"Smug bastard," Jeff said, crumpling Dave's business card in his tight fist. "Do you believe this guy?"

"But how would he know . . . ?" Kristin began.

"He mentioned the Wild Zone at the car the other day. Suzy must have told him about it," Jeff said.

"He probably beat it out of her," Will added.

"Piece of shit," Tom said. "We should go over there right now, kill the bastard dead. Just like Suzy asked us to."

"What?" Jeff and Kristin asked in the same breath.

"She wasn't serious," Will said quickly.

"I beg to differ," Tom said. "I think she was serious as shit. Come on. We could bet on it. Whoever fires the first shot wins the damsel in distress. What do you say?"

"I say, go home, Tom," Jeff said.

"It's perfect. We go over there, we shoot the bastard, Suzy's so grateful, she fucks all three of us. You, too, if you're interested," he offered Kristin.

"Go home, Tom," Kristin said.

"Will you at least think about it?"

Jeff walked Tom to the door. The nerve of that guy, he was thinking. What was that smug bastard trying to prove? That he was top dog? That you didn't mess with him without consequences? Well, if consequences were what the good doctor wanted, consequences were what he would get. Jeff draped one arm across Tom's shoulder. "I'll think about it," he said.

EIGHTEEN

JEFF WAS ASLEEP AND dreaming about Afghanistan when the phone rang. At first his subconscious interpreted the ring as the sound of a bullet whizzing past his ear, and he groaned and ducked down lower in his bed, dragging his pillow over his head. A rocket exploded nearby, and he heard Tom's voice give the order to attack. Behind closed eyes, he watched himself grab his rifle and rush toward the enemy, although who the hell knew where they were. They could be anywhere, for God's sake, there were so many damn caves, and the land was so barren, so rocky, so damn *foreign,* they might as well have been on the moon. The bullets kept flying by, and rockets kept exploding all around him, and soldiers were screaming, some in pain, some in the throes of a pure adrenaline rush, and all hell was breaking loose, and suddenly someone was running directly at him, and Jeff was firing his weapon, as many shots as he could manage as fast as he could manage, and still the man kept advancing, even though the front of his white jacket was soaked through with blood, still he kept coming, and Jeff kept shooting, until the man staggered backward and collapsed, falling to the ground, arms and legs splayed out in all directions, and Jeff walked over to him, kicking at the stethoscope that was wrapped around his neck like a snake, ignoring the eyes that were staring up at him, begging silently for mercy, and shot Dr. Dave Bigelow straight through the heart.

"Jeff," a voice called from somewhere beside him.

Jeff raised his rifle, spun around, released another round of ammunition, the bullets slapping against the early morning sky. He peered through the darkness. There was no one there.

"Jeff," the voice said again.

He felt something sharp pierce his side. A bayonet, he thought, grabbing at it and twisting hard.

"Hey," the voice cried. "That hurts. What are you doing? Let go."

Jeff opened his palm.

Kristin was rubbing her sore fingers as Jeff opened his eyes. "Aren't you going to answer the phone?"

In a daze, Jeff reached for the phone next to the bed, his mind only beginning to wrap itself around what was happening. He wasn't in Afghanistan; he was in his apartment; he wasn't running across unfamiliar, treacherous terrain; he was lying in his comfortable warm bed. No one was shooting at him; he hadn't shot anyone. It was only the persistent ring of the damn telephone. What time is it? he wondered, checking the clock on the nightstand as he picked up the receiver. Six thirty in the morning, for God's sake. Who calls anybody at six thirty in the morning unless it's to relay bad news?

Ellie, he thought, lifting the phone to his ear. Calling to tell him their mother had died.

"Hello," he said warily, feeling an unexpected surge of sadness, the threat of tears stinging his eyes. He should have gone to see her, he was thinking. He should have gone to say good-bye. She was his mother, after all. No matter what. "Hello," he said again, the stony silence that greeted his ear as sharp as any sword.

Kristin pushed herself onto her elbows, stared at him through half-parted lids. "Who is it?"

"Hello?" Jeff said again.

"Hang up," Kristin advised him, flopping back down and letting her eyes close, trying to will herself back to sleep. "It's probably just some kid playing around."

"What?" she heard Jeff ask, and was about to repeat herself when she realized he wasn't speaking to her. "Oh. Okay. Sure," he was saying. "Yeah, I guess I can do that. Sure. Okay." He hung up the phone, pushed his legs out of bed.

"What's happening?" she asked.

"I have to get going."

"What do you mean, you have to get going? It's six thirty in the morning." Her eyes followed him as he walked toward the bedroom door and opened it. "Who was that on the phone?"

"Larry. He's a bit hungover. He asked me if I'd take his seven o'clock client."

"I didn't think Larry drank," Kristin said.

"Guess he doesn't very often. Anyway, I said I'd go in." Jeff crossed the narrow hall into the bathroom, closed the door after him.

Seconds later, Kristin heard the shower running. She debated getting up, pouring Jeff a glass of orange juice, maybe even making him some breakfast, then quickly decided against it. Jeff would have to hurry to be at the gym by seven o'clock, and besides, who had any kind of appetite this early in the morning? Minutes later, she heard him at the sink brushing his teeth, followed by the soft hum of his electric shaver. A few minutes after that, he was back in the bedroom, the comforting scent of his freshly scrubbed body filling the air like a gentle mist. She felt him tiptoeing around the bed and opened her eyes just wide enough to watch him slithering into the jeans he'd been wearing for the last several days, only to quickly pull them off again, leaving them in a crumpled heap on the floor as he opened the closet and pulled out another pair. He put them on, dragged a clean black T-shirt over his head, tucked his cell phone into his back pocket, and walked to the side of the bed, where he crouched down beside her. Kristin thought he was about to kiss her good-bye and she angled her body subtly toward him, but his focus was on the nightstand beside the bed. She watched him pull open the top drawer, his fingers disappearing inside it. "What are you doing?" she mumbled sleepily, picturing Tom's gun at the back of the drawer where she'd hidden it. Was that what he was looking for?

"Nothing. It's okay," he whispered, his breath smelling of toothpaste and mouthwash. He closed the drawer and stood up. "Sorry if I disturbed you."

"You didn't."

"Go back to sleep."

"You'll call me later?"

"Sure thing." Jeff walked toward the hall. "Have a good day."

"You, too." Kristin watched Jeff disappear around the corner before sitting up in bed and fighting the impulse to check the contents of the nightstand. Did she really want to know if Tom's gun was still secreted inside? The less she knew, the better for everyone, she decided, listening to Jeff talking to his brother in the other room.

"Who called so damn early?" Will was asking, his voice hoarse with sleep. She pictured him sitting up on the sofa, his chest bare, his hair twisting attractively this way and that, his blanket bunched around his waist.

"My boss has a hangover," Jeff explained. "Asked me to come in early."

"Nice of you to oblige."

"That's me. Mr. Nice Guy."

"See you later."

The sound of the apartment door opening and closing.

Kristin glanced at the phone, wondering who had really called at six thirty this morning. She knew it wasn't Larry. Jeff's boss was a dedicated health nut who never touched alcohol. And when had Jeff ever told her to "have a good day"? Ignoring the little voice in her head warning her to keep her distance, she reached for the phone, pressed in *69.

"The last number that called your line was . . . ," a recorded voice informed her in the next instant, rattling off a series of digits.

Kristin held the phone against her bare breasts for several seconds before returning it to its cradle. Trying to control the rapid beating of her heart, she lay down, curled into a tight fetal ball, and willed herself back to sleep.

JEFF WALKED BRISKLY along the outside corridor and down the three flights of steps to the parking garage where his burgundy Hyundai was parked next to Kristin's Volvo. What would my brother think if he knew where I'm really going? he thought, wondering when he'd started caring how his brother felt about anything. And why had he lied to Kristin? One of the nice things about their relationship was that he'd never felt he had to lie to her about anything. What had changed? What was different now? And was it for her benefit he'd been less than forthcoming, or his own? He unlocked his car door and climbed behind the wheel. "Hey, this wasn't my idea," he said to his reflection in the rearview mirror. Still, he felt the uncomfortable and unexpected sensation of guilt gnawing at his gut. Probably just hunger pangs, he told himself. A cup of coffee and some bacon and eggs would take care of that.

He extricated his cell from his pocket and called the gym. It didn't open until seven, and it was only five minutes to, so he was hoping for the answering machine. Instead Melissa answered on the third ring.

"Elite Fitness," she announced, an annoying chirp to her voice.

"It's Jeff," he told her. "Listen, I'm not feeling very well. I spent the night throwing up," he added for good measure.

"Oh, yuck."

"I'm hoping it's just something I ate and I'll be feeling better in a few hours."

"I hope you're right. You've got clients booked all day."

"See if you can reschedule, and tell Larry I'm gonna try my best to get there by noon." That should be more than enough time, Jeff thought.

"Have lots of tea."

"What?"

"Have lots of tea," Melissa repeated. "And toast with jam. No butter."

"Thanks for the advice."

"Feel better," Melissa said before hanging up.

Jeff returned the phone to his side pocket as he pulled out of his parking space onto the street. Minutes later, he was on the road, heading toward Federal Highway and Northeast Fifty-fourth. He'd get there early, but so what? He'd have some breakfast, calm his jitters, prepare himself for whatever lay ahead. Why was he so damn nervous anyway? "Absolutely nothing to be nervous about," he assured himself out loud. "You're the one who's in control here." But even as he was saying the words, he knew they weren't true. "Shit," he said, shaking his head. He was turning into as bad a liar as Tom.

THE SMELL OF freshly brewed coffee roused Kristin from her sleep about an hour later. She'd been dreaming about Suzy, she realized, opening her eyes and then quickly closing them again, trying to hang on to the fleeting image of the sad-eyed young woman. Kristin pushed herself out of bed, wrapped herself in a pink silk robe, and padded toward the kitchen in her bare feet.

"Aren't you the sweetest thing in the whole world," she said to Will, who was already at the table, wearing a blue shirt and brown pants, and nibbling on a piece of toast. "How did you know this is exactly what I needed?" She poured herself a mug of coffee, inhaled its rich aroma.

"I can make you some scrambled eggs, if you'd like," he offered.

"Are you kidding? I would love that," Kristin said, laughing. "It's been forever since anybody's made me scrambled eggs."

"Well, they just happen to be my specialty."

They exchanged positions, Kristin sitting down at the table, Will walking to the counter, smiling as their shoulders touched briefly in passing.

"Don't look at me." She brought her hand to her face in an effort to hide it. "I look like crap."

"You look gorgeous."

"I didn't sleep well, and I don't have any makeup on." She sipped on her coffee, her large mug effectively blocking most of her face.

"You look better without it," Will said. "Why didn't you sleep?"

"I don't know. I guess I kept worrying about what Tom said about killing Suzy's husband. You don't think he meant it, do you?" Again she pictured the gun in the back of the drawer in the nightstand and wondered if it was still there.

"Nah," Will said, although truthfully he wasn't certain. Tom's behavior was growing ever more erratic. Surely it was only a matter of time before all that big talk exploded into something far more ominous. "Guess that early-morning phone call didn't help your sleep any," Will said, trying to erase thoughts of Tom from his conscious mind. "Nice of Jeff to go in early." He walked to the fridge, reached for the eggs. "Two or three?" he asked.

"Two."

Will removed two jumbo-size brown-shelled eggs from their carton. "You like them made with milk or water?"

"Your choice," Kristin told him.

"I prefer water. It makes them fluffier."

"Fluff away." She watched Will crack the two eggs into a bowl, then add water, salt, and pepper. "I bet you did this for Amy all the time, didn't you?"

"Sometimes," Will answered, feeling her name sting his skin, like the sharp bite of a wasp.

"And she let you get away? What was the matter with that girl?"

"Maybe she preferred French toast."

Kristin smiled, took another sip of coffee. "The more I hear about that girl, the less I like."

"What have you heard?"

"Just what you told Jeff."

"Which Jeff promptly told you." It was more statement than question.

"Is that a problem?"

"He always tell you everything?"

"Jeff isn't exactly Mr. Discreet."

"He doesn't tell me anything," Will said.

"Men like Jeff don't talk to other men," Kristin said knowingly. "Not about personal stuff. They talk to women." She lowered her mug to the table, then lifted up her right leg so that the bottom of her foot rested on the seat of her chair, exposing a flash of inner thigh as she rested her chin against her knee.

Will quickly looked away, turned on the stove, and extricated a pan from the cupboard directly beneath it. Then he returned to the fridge and located the butter at the back of the second shelf. He scooped some into the pan, stood there listening for the sizzle. "What else has Jeff said about me?" he asked, trying to sound nonchalant.

"What do you mean?"

"Is he glad I came? Is he anxious for me to leave?"

"He's glad you came, Will," Kristin said, lowering her leg back to the floor.

"He said that?"

"He didn't have to."

"So how do you know?"

"Because I know Jeff. Trust me. He's glad you're here."

Trust me. Why do people always say that? Will heard Tom sneer as he poured the contents of the bowl into the pan, watching the eggs quickly bubble and congeal. *Did you know that armadillos are running amok in the state of Florida?* he heard Tom ask.

"He scares me," Will said.

"Jeff?" Kristin asked, clearly surprised.

"Tom," Will corrected her, turning down the heat as he poked at the eggs with a rubber spatula. "Sorry. I was thinking about last night."

Kristin watched Will continue scrambling the eggs as he reached into a nearby cupboard for a plate. "You know who scares *me*?"

"Who?"

"Dr. Bigelow."

"Suzy's husband," Will said, although there was no need for clarification. "Yeah, he's a pretty scary guy." He transferred the eggs from the pan to the plate and placed it in front of Kristin.

"Mmmn. This looks fabulous. Aren't you having any?"

"I might have some of yours."

"Not a chance," Kristin joked, pulling the plate closer to her and lifting a forkful of eggs to her mouth. "These are the best scrambled eggs ever."

"Glad you like them."

"Somebody *should* shoot the bastard," Kristin said, swallowing another mouthful.

"What?"

"Sorry. Just thinking out loud. I mean, the guy's obviously a psycho. Threatening you guys the other day, coming into the club last night, hitting on me." She speared another forkful of eggs. "I guess I should be grateful he was hitting *on* me, not actually hitting me. He saves that for Suzy. Guy deserves to be shot," she added between swallows. "I can't believe I actually found him charming."

"You found him charming?"

"He offered to introduce me to this famous photographer who just happens to be a close personal friend. The oldest line in the book, and I almost fell for it."

"You found him charming?" Will asked again.

"Well, he's not a complete Neanderthal. I mean, there has to be a reason Suzy married him. No?"

"I guess."

"First comes the charm, then come the fists. Poor Suzy."

Will lowered his head, tried not to see the bruises marring Suzy's beautiful complexion.

"I really don't understand how a man his size," Kristin continued, clearly on a roll, "not to mention a doctor, a man who's taken an oath to do no harm, how somebody like that can justify hitting a woman, especially someone as delicate looking as Suzy. She's skin and bones, for God's sake. What satisfaction can he get from slapping her around? You wait—he's going to kill her one day. And when he does, it'll be partly our fault because we knew about him, and we didn't do anything."

"What are we supposed to do? Call the authorities?"

"Yeah, like that's going to do any good. They'll ask for proof, we'll tell them we don't have any, and they'll tell us to mind our own business. Maybe they'll question Suzy. But if she's like most battered women, she'll just deny everything and we'll end up looking like idiots. Later on, she'll get the crap kicked out of her even worse." Kristin finished the last of her eggs, pushed her plate aside. "No, there's nothing we can do. Which is why I feel so damn . . ."

" . . . impotent?"

"Exactly."

Will nodded, understanding the feeling well. He felt that way most of the time.

"Oh. I didn't save you any eggs," Kristin said, looking at her empty plate.

"No problem. I can always make more."

"Promise?" Kristin pushed herself off her chair, leaned over, and kissed Will on the cheek. "You really are the sweetest thing." In the next second she was gone, sweeping from the room in a flash of pink silk.

The unmade bed beckoned as she returned to the bedroom, and for a brief moment Kristin toyed with the idea of crawling back inside it, drawing the covers up over her head, and trying for a few more hours of sleep. But it was too late for that, she decided, walking to the window and opening the curtains, almost tripping over Jeff's discarded jeans in the middle of the floor. She smiled. Interesting that Jeff would bother to change into a fresh pair of jeans when he was supposedly so pressed for time, she thought, bending down to pick them up, about to toss them in the hamper when she felt something in their back pocket. "Getting more interesting all the time," she muttered, returning to the kitchen, object in hand. "Jeff forgot his wallet," she announced, waving it at Will.

The doorbell rang.

"Probably him." Kristin ran to the door. "Forget something?" she asked, opening the door, then taking a quick step back.

Lainey Whitman strode into the center of the room. She was wearing a white T-shirt, blue jeans, and a deep scowl. "Kristin," she acknowledged, her gaze quickly shifting to Will. "And you must be the famous little brother."

"Lainey, this is Will. Will, meet Lainey, Tom's wife," Kristin said, introducing the two and wondering what other surprises the day had in store.

"Nice to meet you." Will thought that Lainey wasn't nearly as unattractive as Tom had made her out to be. A little unconventional looking, perhaps, her features maybe a touch too imposing for her face, but pleasing nonetheless.

"Is Jeff here?" Lainey asked. "I need to talk to him about Tom."

"He's at work."

Lainey suddenly looked as if she was about to burst into tears. She stood motionless in the middle of the living room, saying nothing.

"Why don't I walk over there and deliver this?" Will offered, taking Jeff's wallet from Kristin's hand. "Give you two ladies a chance to talk."

"No, that's all right," Kristin began.

"I'll check in later," Will told her, ignoring the look in her eyes imploring him to stay. The last thing he wanted to do was talk about Tom.

"Nice meeting you, Will," Lainey said.

"You, too." He reached the door, gratefully pocketing Jeff's wallet. My brother came to my rescue without even knowing it, he was thinking as he closed the door behind him. He'd have to find a way to thank him.

NINETEEN

"WOULD YOU LIKE A cup of coffee?" Kristin asked, gathering her robe around her and tightening the silk belt at her waist. "Will made a large pot. I think there's some left."

"Will made coffee?"

"And scrambled eggs."

"Tom never makes anything," Lainey said. "Except trouble," she added unnecessarily.

"Can I get you a cup?" Kristin asked again.

Lainey shook her head. "No, thanks."

"Would you like to sit down?" Kristin motioned toward the sofa, where Will's blanket lay neatly folded at one end. She hoped Lainey would say no, as she had with the coffee, and mumble apologies for having disturbed her first thing in the morning, but Lainey seemed grateful for the offer, sinking down into the soft cushions and taking several deep breaths. "Are you all right?" Kristin asked, sitting down beside her.

"Not really. You heard about Tom's latest stunt?"

Kristin nodded, tugging at the bottom of her robe so that it covered her knees.

"We didn't want to call the police. We really didn't," Lainey said. "But what choice did he leave us? What else could we do?" She lifted her hands into the air, palms facing the ceiling, fingers opening and closing, as if grasping for answers. Kristin noted she was still wearing her wedding ring. "He'd been following me around all day, first to the lawyer's office, then to my hairdresser's, where he made the most terrible scene, screaming at me in front of everyone, saying such awful things, you really couldn't believe it. And then later, at dinnertime, he parked himself down the street from my parents' house, just sat there for more than an hour, staring at the house. My mother was so upset, she couldn't eat a thing. My father was so angry he wanted to go out and confront him himself, but we begged him not to, so he called the police instead, and they came and took Tom to the station. But they couldn't hold him—technically he hadn't done anything illegal—which is why we have to go down there this morning to take out a restraining order against him. Not that I think it's going to do any good. I think it's only going to make him angrier. But what choice do I have? I tried reasoning with him, but that didn't work. He doesn't listen. He never has. And I can't have him following me day and night. I can't have him upsetting my parents and scaring the kids. And I'm really frightened, Kristin. What if he does something crazy? What if he tries to kidnap the children?"

"I don't think he'd do anything like that."

"That's what I used to think. I used to think that no matter how crazy he got, he'd never do anything to hurt me or the kids. Now I'm not so sure."

"He's just upset. Your leaving took him by surprise."

"How could he be surprised? I've been warning him for months that this would happen."

"He didn't think you'd actually go through with it."

"What else could I do?" Lainey demanded. "What choice did he give me?"

"No choice," Kristin said quickly. "Believe me, Lainey, I understand. Frankly, I'm amazed you hung around as long as you did."

"He's my husband, the father of my children. I tried to be patient and understanding." She began nervously tugging at her wedding band.

"I know you did."

"He hasn't been the same since he came back from Afghanistan. He doesn't sleep; he barely eats; he has nightmares every night. God only knows what he saw over there, what he did. . . ." Her voice trailed off.

"He needs help," Kristin offered.

"Of course he needs help," Lainey shot back. "But he won't even consider counseling. He says that if Jeff doesn't need therapy, *he* doesn't need therapy. There's no way he'll go."

"Then you've done everything you can," Kristin told her. "You have to look after yourself and your children."

"I told him this would happen. How many times did I tell him?" Lainey asked. "I said that if he didn't stop drinking, if he didn't stop staying out half the night, I wasn't going to stick around."

"You gave him plenty of warning," Kristin agreed.

"As far as he was concerned, I was just a convenience, someone to cook his dinners and keep the bed warm. I tried talking to him, but you can't tell him anything. He doesn't listen. Why should he? He knows everything."

"Nobody blames you for leaving him."

"I did everything in my power to make him happy. I never pressured him to get a better job, I never complained about money, I let him go out with Jeff whenever he wanted. All I asked was that he be home at a reasonable hour. But some nights he wouldn't come back until three, four in the morning. And maybe you don't care what time Jeff comes home . . ."

Kristin was about to interrupt, but Lainey wasn't finished.

" . . . but we have two kids, two kids who don't need to wake up crying in the middle of the night because their father's too drunk to keep his voice down."

"It can't have been easy for you," Kristin offered.

"Easy?" Lainey repeated. "Are you kidding me? Try impossible."

"You gave it your best shot. You have nothing to feel guilty for."

"Who says I feel guilty?" Lainey snapped. "I don't feel guilty. I feel angry. I feel frustrated. I feel frightened. The man's lost his mind. He said the most hurtful things to me yesterday. You can't imagine."

Kristin nodded, conjuring up the string of invectives her mother had hurled at her after finding Ron on top of her more than a decade ago, the words as lethal as if they'd been shot from a gun, as immediate as if they'd been uttered yesterday. Lainey was right: She couldn't imagine; she didn't have to.

"And now he's all upset about the kids? Bullshit! He never cared about them," Lainey said. "Not from day one. How many times did he tell me he never wanted them, that I'd used them to trap him into getting married, that I'd gotten pregnant on purpose, even though he was the one who refused to wear a damn condom? But that was Tom. Nothing was ever his fault. Nothing was ever his responsibility. He blamed me for everything. Hell, he'd blame me for Afghanistan if he could." She swiped at the tears rolling down her cheeks. "He even said he didn't think the kids were really his. And now he suddenly sees himself as father of the year? He's screaming that I can't take his kids away from him? He's telling me he'll quit his job before he'll pay a dime in child support, that we can starve to death for all he cares? Does that sound like a man who loves his children to you?"

"He's just angry and upset. Once he calms down—"

"He's not going to calm down. He's not going to be reasonable," Lainey said, releasing a deep, tremulous breath. "He's going to be Tom."

"What would you like us to do?" Kristin asked after a long pause.

"I need Jeff to talk to him. He's the only one Tom listens to, the only one who stands a chance of getting through to him."

"I think he's tried."

"He needs to try again. He needs to try harder."

Kristin nodded.

"My father wants him out of the house by the end of the week," Lainey said, "or he says he'll have him charged with trespassing."

"Maybe that's not such a good idea," Kristin cautioned. "Maybe you should give him a little more time to get used to what's happening."

Lainey shook her head vehemently. "My lawyer says that prolonging things will only strengthen Tom's resolve, not to mention his legal standing. Something about establishing a precedent. I didn't quite understand. . . ." She folded her hands in her lap, nodded once and then again, as if trying to convince herself. "No, Tom has to leave. Jeff has to persuade him to find his own apartment."

"Can Tom afford one?" Kristin asked gingerly. "Does he even have enough money for first and last months' rent?"

"He has enough money to go out drinking every night, doesn't he?" Lainey burst into tears, buried her face in her hands.

Kristin edged closer, put her arms around Lainey, half expecting to be rebuffed or pushed aside. Instead Lainey grabbed her tight around the waist and burrowed her head into the pillow of Kristin's chest, sobbing without restraint.

"It's okay. It'll be all right," Kristin said soothingly. "I'll talk to Jeff."

"IS JEFF HERE?" Will asked the pretty, young receptionist behind the desk at the entrance to Elite Fitness. He was winded from having run up the steep flight of stairs, and he smiled self-consciously as he looked around the gym for his brother. I should probably sign up for a few sessions, increase my stamina, he was thinking, watching several people working out with weights and a trainer in a sleeveless gray T-shirt instructing two women doing a series of push-ups. Where was Jeff?

"I'm afraid he's not in this morning," Melissa said.

"What do you mean he's not in?"

Melissa stared at him blankly.

"He has to be here," Will persisted. "His boss called first thing this morning and asked him to get here early. He rushed out so fast he forgot his wallet." Will held out the wallet for her to see, as if this was proof she was mistaken.

"I don't know what to say," Melissa said, looking toward the man in the sleeveless gray T-shirt. "Jeff called in sick this morning. Believe me, Larry wasn't very happy about it."

"Jeff called in sick?"

"I took the call myself."

"But that doesn't make any sense."

"Maybe you should lower your voice," Melissa urged. "I'm sure you don't want to get Jeff in trouble."

"Is there a problem?" Larry called from between the two women now doing bicycle kicks on the floor.

"What? No. No problem," Will said, still trying to get his head around his brother's absence. "I was just hoping to see Jeff."

"So were we all. He should be back by this afternoon."

Will handed Jeff's wallet to the receptionist. "In that case, if you wouldn't mind giving him this when he gets in . . ."

"Of course."

What the hell is going on? Will wondered, barely noticing the scent of freshly baked bread as he hurried down the flight of stairs to the sidewalk. Where was Jeff and why had he lied?

He knew three things for certain: Someone had phoned the apartment at six thirty this morning; Jeff had rushed out soon after; he hadn't gone to work.

So where was he?

There was only one logical explanation, Will concluded, walking quickly down the street: Tom.

It had obviously been Tom who'd phoned, talking the same crazy talk as last night, and Jeff had raced over to his house in an effort to calm him down. He hadn't told Kristin or Will where he was really going because he hadn't wanted to worry them. Or maybe Tom had specifically asked him not to say anything because he didn't want Will tagging along. He wanted only Jeff.

Just as Lainey had come over several hours later, also wanting Jeff.

Everybody always wanting Jeff.

The image of a lovely young woman with deep-water blue eyes, fading bruises marring her otherwise lustrous complexion, suddenly filled his head. He smiled, tried to get her attention, but she was looking just past him. Seconds later, Will watched as Jeff emerged from the shadows of his mind to surround her with his muscular arms. In the next second, he watched her willingly disappear inside his brother's embrace.

Will shook his head, trying to dismiss the image.

Was it possible that Jeff, in a stupid, ill-advised effort to win Suzy's favor, was at this very minute meeting with Tom, that the two of them could actually be on their way to murder Dr. Bigelow?

No, it wasn't possible, Will assured himself immediately. His brother was no murderer, no matter how many men he'd killed in Afghanistan. Jeff would never allow himself to be swayed by any of Tom's idiotic ideas. Will checked his watch. Ten minutes after nine. In less than an hour, the stores would be opening, and Tom would be at work. Will decided he'd take a leisurely stroll over to South Beach, visit Tom at the Gap, find out exactly what was going on.

He straightened his shoulders, took a deep breath, and started walking.

BY TWENTY MINUTES after nine o'clock, Jeff had finished his bacon and eggs and was on his fifth cup of coffee. What the hell was he doing here?

He looked toward the entrance to the no-frills coffee shop. No one had come in or out of the wood-framed glass door in the last twenty minutes. He'd been sitting in this oversize booth at the back of Fredo's for almost an hour and a half. He'd finished the morning paper from first page to last. He'd read the daily specials handwritten on the half-dozen chalkboards along the wall so many times he could recite them by heart. His hands were shaking from all the caffeine in his system. It was all he could do to keep from jumping up and fleeing the premises.

For the tenth time in as many minutes, he went over the events of the morning. The phone had roused him from an unpleasant dream, the particulars of which he could no longer recall. He'd answered it in something of a fog, snapping into consciousness only when he heard the familiar voice. Now he was wondering whether it had really happened or if he'd imagined the whole thing. Was it possible he'd still been dreaming?

Except Kristin had heard the phone ring, too. In fact, it was Kristin who'd roused him from his sleep in the first place, he reminded himself, and Kristin who'd sleepily swallowed the series of lies he'd told her. Although she'd been alert enough to question that lame story he'd given her about Larry having a hangover. God, he'd have to be more careful. No, he amended in the next breath. He'd have to tell her the truth.

Whatever that was.

Wasn't that why he was here? To find out?

Again he glanced toward the entrance to the coffee shop. Maybe he'd gotten the name wrong. Maybe it wasn't Fredo's. Maybe it was some other coffee shop with a similar name, or maybe in his semi-comatose state, he'd misheard the address. Maybe there was a competing Fredo's on Federal, and he was sitting in the wrong one.

What the hell was he doing here?

Jeff checked his watch, noting it was less than five minutes since the last time he'd looked. Hell, it wasn't that late. Not even half past nine. He had only himself to blame for getting here so damn early. The least he could do was wait another fifteen minutes. This wasn't the easiest place to find. And Miami's rush-hour traffic was the worst.

He reached into his pocket for his cell, checked his voice mail for messages, but there weren't any, so he returned the phone to his pocket, his hand stopping suddenly in midair. As if possessed of a mind of its own, it disappeared back into first his left pocket, then his right, then quickly into each of them again. "Shit," he said, his eyes closing with the realization that his wallet was missing. He pushed himself out of the booth, searched his pockets a third time and then the red vinyl seat, before getting down on his hands and knees, his eyes scouring the white tile floor.

"Everything okay here, handsome?" the waitress asked as Jeff clambered back to his feet. She was about fifty years old, with ash-blond hair she wore in a high bouffant, making her almost as tall as Jeff.

"I can't find my wallet," he told her sheepishly, trying for his most charming smile.

The waitress, whose name tag identified her as Dorothy, regarded him skeptically. Clearly she'd heard that one before.

"I'm not trying to pull a fast one. Honest," Jeff said, wondering if his wallet had somehow fallen out of his pocket in the car. "Look. Do you mind if I check my car? I'm parked just around the corner."

"You wouldn't be trying to skip out on me, would you, handsome?" Dorothy tilted her head to one side, her hair following suit, threatening to topple over.

"No, I would never do that." He reached into his pocket, laid his cell phone on the table. "How about I leave this with you? That way you know I'll be back."

"Not necessarily. You coulda stole that."

"I didn't. Please. Look. You can come with me if you want."

Dorothy paused as if seriously weighing his offer. "Oh, go on," she said finally. "But if you're not back in three minutes, I don't care how good-looking you are, I'm calling the cops."

"I'll be back in two."

"Leave the phone," she instructed.

Jeff rushed outside, the sun shining in his eyes like a flashlight, blinding him to his surroundings, as the hot, humid air slammed into his face like a well-placed punch. For a second he was disoriented and thought he was back in Afghanistan. A bubble of panic burst inside his chest, ripping through his insides like a bullet. "What the hell is the matter with you?" he asked, breaking into a sweat and forcing himself to take a bunch of long, deep breaths. It was all that damn coffee, he decided, gradually regaining his equilibrium and trying to remember where he'd parked his car. He turned right, proceeding down the first street and picking up his pace as his car came into view.

He quickly searched the front seat, the back, the floor, even the glove compartment, in case he'd put his wallet in there, then forgotten about it. "Shit," he said, spinning around and catching his reflection in the polished side of the car's exterior. He saw himself in his bedroom as he grabbed a pair of jeans from the closet, leaving the original pair—the pair with his wallet in the back pocket!—on the floor. "Shit," he said again, imagining Kristin picking those jeans up off the floor. Had she found his wallet? Had she called the gym? Or worse? Had she tried to deliver it in person? "Shit."

"So what are you gonna do?" Dorothy was asking moments later. "That breakfast isn't going to pay for itself."

Jeff looked around the brightly lit restaurant, still half-full of people, all of them eating, talking, laughing. "I don't know what to do. It doesn't look like my friend is going to show up. . . ."

"Tall girl, dark hair, a little on the skinny side?" Dorothy asked as Jeff's eyes followed hers to the far end of the restaurant.

She was coming out of the ladies' room when she saw him and she smiled tentatively, the corners of her lips turning down instead of up.

"Hello, Jeff," Suzy said.

TWENTY

"SORRY I WAS SO late," she apologized when they were seated. "Dave took forever to leave the house, and then I got stuck in traffic. Were you waiting long?"

"Not really," Jeff lied. "I got here a few minutes early, had some breakfast. You sure you don't want anything to eat? You're paying for it, after all."

She smiled, the smile tugging at the mustard-colored bruise on her chin. "Coffee's fine." She took a sip, as if to prove her point. "When I didn't see you, I assumed you'd gotten tired of waiting and left. Good thing I had to go to the bathroom, or we might have missed each other."

"Good thing."

"I'm glad you waited."

"Why?" Jeff asked.

"What?" Suzy asked in return.

"What are we doing here, Mrs. Bigelow?"

Suzy winced at the sound of her name, as if Jeff had reached over and pinched her cheek. "I don't know."

He studied her as she lifted her coffee cup to her lips and took another long sip. She was wearing a simple white blouse and her hair was pulled back into a low ponytail and secured by a jeweled clasp. Her fingernails were polished a faint pink, although several had been chewed to the quick. Makeup hid most of her bruises. Jeff longed to reach across the table and take her hand, stroke her face. He literally ached to touch her. Why? There was nothing all that special about her. Tall girl, dark hair, a little on the skinny side, to use Dorothy's words. Oh, she was pretty enough, to be sure, but Jeff was used to pretty girls. They threw themselves at him all the time.

What made this one different?

Was it because she *hadn't* thrown herself at him, had in fact chosen his brother over him, not once, but twice, that made her so unbearably attractive to him? That he had no idea where he stood with her, if indeed he stood anywhere at all? That she was equal parts mysterious vixen and vulnerable waif?

"Do you always wear black?" she asked suddenly.

"What?"

"Every time I've seen you, you're always dressed in black."

"Is that why you asked me to meet you? To inquire about my wardrobe?"

"I was just curious."

"There's no big mystery," he told her, his voice purposefully sharp. "I wear black because I look good in it. Why did you call me?"

"How do you know I was calling *you*?"

Jeff sank back in his seat, trying not to look too taken aback. The thought that she might have been calling Will had never occurred to him. "You saying you were calling my brother?"

Suzy returned her cup to its saucer. "No," she acknowledged after a pause. "I was calling you."

"What if Will had answered?"

"I don't know."

"Would he be sitting here now instead of me?"

"No."

"Why did you call?" Jeff asked again.

"Because I wanted to see you."

Jeff nodded, as if now that that fact had been established, there was no need for more questions.

Suzy took a deep breath, released it slowly. "To clear up any misconceptions," she added after a moment's thought.

"Misconceptions?" Jeff leaned forward, putting his elbows on the table and twisting one hand inside the other. He didn't like the sound of that.

"Yesterday, at your apartment. I said some things."

"What things?"

"Things I shouldn't have."

"I don't remember you saying anything particularly regrettable."

"You weren't there," Suzy said. "It was later."

"You said something to Will?"

"And your friend from the bar, I forget his name."

"Tom?"

She nodded. "He came over. He was obviously upset. He had a gun that he kept waving around. I thought I better get out of there. He said something about shooting me in the foot to make me stay." She cleared her throat, looked to the ceiling, then back at Jeff. "Which is when I suggested he shoot my husband instead."

Jeff nodded, not letting on he'd already heard all about this from Will and Tom. "Interesting suggestion."

"That's just the point. I didn't mean it, and I never should have said it."

"I wouldn't worry about it. I don't think anyone took you too seriously."

"I'm not so sure about that. The look on Tom's face when I mentioned it . . ."

"Intense, eager, slightly crazed?" Jeff asked.

"Yes. Exactly."

"Tom's normal expression," Jeff said with a laugh.

Suzy looked unconvinced. "I don't know. He seemed pretty gung-ho."

"Did you offer him anything?"

"What do you mean?"

"Money? Sex? A gift certificate to McDonald's?"

"This isn't a joke, Jeff. I'm really worried."

"Tom wouldn't kill your husband just because you suggested it might be a nice thing to do," Jeff said. On the other hand, he thought, if *I* suggested it . . .

"I don't know. I got the distinct impression he thought it would be fun."

"And fun it might very well be."

"Don't talk like that."

"Are you saying you'd be upset if something *were* to happen to the good doctor?"

Suzy looked away, mumbled something unintelligible beneath her breath.

"What?" Jeff asked.

"No," she admitted, her eyes suddenly welling up with tears. "To be perfectly honest, I'd welcome it. God, that's so awful," she gasped in the next breath. "I can't believe I said that."

"Said what? I didn't hear anything."

"How can you bear to look at me? I'm horrible. I'm a horrible, horrible person."

"You're not horrible."

"I as much as told you that I wish my husband was dead!"

"Which is completely understandable, considering the fact he uses you as a human punching bag."

"I have such terrible thoughts," Suzy continued unprompted. "He'll be sleeping, and I'll think about going into the kitchen and getting one of those big, long knives and stabbing him right through the heart. Or setting fire to the mattress. Or running him over with my car. Sometimes I imagine how wonderful it would be if an intruder were to break into the house and shoot him. Sometimes, if I'm being generous, I just wish he'd have a heart attack and drop dead. I even have his funeral all planned out."

Jeff couldn't help but smile.

Suzy's eyes acquired a distant glaze, as if she were looking into the future. "I'd invite everyone from the hospital, all those doctors who admire and respect him, who treat him like some kind of god, and I'd get up in that chapel and tell them their god was really the devil. I'd tell them the truth about their precious Dr. Bigelow, how he tortures me, and beats me, and rapes me. . . ."

"He rapes you?" Jeff's voice so quiet it was almost inaudible.

"And then I'd have him cremated," Suzy went on, as if he hadn't spoken. "And I'd take his ashes and dump them in the first godforsaken swamp I see."

Jeff reached across the table, took her hand in his. "Bastard deserves to die," he said.

Suzy nodded. "People rarely get what they deserve." She withdrew her hand, wiped the tears from her eyes. "Anyway, I shouldn't be laying this on you. It's my problem, not yours."

"I won't let him hurt you anymore," Jeff said.

Suzy smiled. "How can you stop him?" She paused, looked deep into his eyes. "Do you want to know why I really called you?"

Jeff nodded.

"Because I can't stop thinking about you. Because no matter how hard I try, I can't stop seeing your face. Because I haven't been able to get you out of my mind since the first night I saw you in the Wild Zone, and I knew right away you were going to be trouble. Because we both know you were right when you said I picked the wrong brother. Because I want you so badly I can't think about anything else. And I don't care if I'm just a bet to you–"

"You aren't."

"I don't care if you tell the others–"

"I won't."

"Can we get out of here?" she asked, tucking a twenty-dollar bill underneath her coffee cup and pushing herself to her feet.

"Where are we going?"

"There's a motel around the corner," she said.

TOM HAD BEEN watching the woman ever since the store opened. Up and down, back and forth, into every nook and cranny of the clothing-littered aisles she went, her hands brushing up against the floral-print summer blouses hanging neatly in ascending order of size, her fingers checking for softness in the stacks of multicolored velour hoodies on the various display tables, her eyes on the alert for anything she might have missed, any piece of sale merchandise she might have overlooked.

"Is there a problem, Whitman?" the store manager asked, coming up behind Tom.

Tom spun around, startled by the reedy sound of his supervisor's voice. He hated when people snuck up behind him. "Nothing I can't handle."

"What's to handle?" Carter Sorenson asked. Carter was barely five feet, five inches tall, nearsighted, and twenty-eight years old. Tom hated that he was short, that he wore round, wire-rimmed glasses, and that his voice was pitched like a girl's. He especially hated that he was younger than Tom and in a position of authority over him. He also hated his name. What kind of name was Carter anyway? Carter was a last name, for shit's sake, not a given one. Although Carter seemed to like it, which made Tom hate him all the more.

"Just keeping an eye on that woman over there." Tom indicated the middle-aged woman in question with a nod of his head.

"Really?" Carter asked. "Because it kind of looks like you're just standing around doing nothing."

"Is that what it looks like?" Tom fought to keep his hands from wrapping themselves around Carter's throat and squeezing as hard as he could.

"Has she done anything to arouse your suspicions?" Carter asked.

"Look," Tom answered, his smile not altogether masking the condescension in his voice. "I'm a veteran of a foreign war, and you kind of develop an instinct for this sort of thing."

"You're saying your soldier's instincts are telling you she's a potential shoplifter?"

"Combined with my experience in retail, yes. I consider it a distinct possibility."

At precisely that moment, Angela Kwan, a young Asian salesclerk with long black hair and an irritatingly sunny disposition, approached the woman and asked if she required any assistance.

"Yes, thank you," the woman said gratefully. "I've been waiting for someone to help me, but you were all so busy." She glanced in Tom's direction, as if to say, Except for him. He was just standing there.

"Perhaps you could lay off the surveillance for a while and concentrate on helping the customers," Carter suggested, his thin voice bending with the weight of his sarcasm. "I believe those gentlemen might benefit from your professional expertise." He pointed to two teenage boys who had just entered the store.

"I'm on it," Tom told him. "Jerk-off," he added under his breath as he left Carter's side. "You guys need any help?" he asked the pimply-faced teens. If there was one thing he hated more than middle-aged women, it was teenage boys. Both groups thought they knew everything.

"Just looking," one of the boys said, laughing and cracking his gum. Tom thought he heard the word "loser" as they headed for the back of the store. It was all he could do to keep from running after them and pummeling them into the ground.

Instead he stood there for several minutes, feeling Carter's eyes burning holes in the back of his red and black checkered shirt. What are you staring at? he was tempted to turn around and shout. I asked them if they needed help, didn't I? If you think I'm going to bust my ass chasing after teenagers for less than eight bucks an hour, you're out of your mind. If you think I'm going to suck up to every middle-aged broad who comes in here, like that dumb Asian twat you think is so terrific, then think again. When you pay minimum wage, you get minimum results. Did they forget to teach you that at the Wharton School of Business? Tom demanded silently, spinning around on his heels, preparing to stare Carter down.

Except that Carter was no longer looking at him. In fact, Carter was nowhere in sight. Tom released a deep, audible breath into the air, deciding that despite the fact the store had just opened, it was time for his break. He headed out the front door, grabbing a cigarette from his pocket and lighting it before he was even fully outside.

The wide pedestrian walkway that was Lincoln Road Mall was even busier than usual. Tourists, Tom thought disdainfully, taking a deep drag off his cigarette. Why couldn't they just stay home? They were noisy and demanding and overly enthusiastic about damn near everything. He noted an elderly couple on the corner consulting a map and a couple of gay guys across the street arguing over directions. An attractive woman with ebony skin and silver stiletto heels sauntered by, carrying three bags from Victoria's Secret. One of the bags brushed against Tom's cigarette as she walked by, and she turned around and scowled, as if she thought he'd placed himself deliberately in her path. Bitch, Tom thought. You think I'd try to set fire to a bunch of thongs and push-up bras?

What was it with women anyway? Was he supposed to snap to attention just because he might be in her way? It was almost like they expected you to read their minds, he thought. Like that woman in the store—how was he supposed to figure out she wanted help? Would it have killed her to ask? And this bitch in the stilettos—if she'd wanted him to move, all she had to say was "Excuse me." A little politeness never hurt. And Lainey, for shit's sake. If she'd wanted him to spend more time at home, if she'd wanted him to be a more attentive father, if she'd wanted . . . hell, who knew what she wanted? He wasn't a mind reader, for fuck's sake.

Or that girl in Afghanistan, he thought, her image appearing in a puff of cigarette smoke, undulating seductively in the cloudless blue sky. Hadn't she smiled when he and several other soldiers, including Jeff, had entered her tiny, barely furnished house, searching for signs of the enemy? Hadn't she lowered her eyes—the only part of her he could see under that damn burka—and giggled coquettishly, a sure come-on? How was he to know she was only fourteen years old?

How could he understand that she was saying no when she refused to speak English?

It hadn't even been his idea, for shit's sake. It had been that damn Gary Bekker. "What say we do us some cherry picking?" Gary had said as they were leaving.

"Count me out," Jeff said immediately. "Come on, Tom. We're out of here."

"Is that right, Tommy boy? You need Jeff's permission to have a little fun?" Gary said, taunting him. "What's with you two anyway? You got something going on the rest of us should know about?"

"Come on, Tom," Jeff said again, refusing to be provoked.

"You go if you want to," came Tom's response. "Seems I'm in the mood for a piece of cherry pie."

"Shit," he said now, trying to banish the girl's pain-stricken face with a final exhalation of cigarette smoke from his lungs. He should have listened to Jeff. Then he wouldn't have been shipped home in disgrace. The army would have paid for his schooling. He could have gotten certified, been a personal trainer like Jeff, making good money while being surrounded by a bunch of adoring, scantily dressed women, instead of toiling for minimum wage under jerk-offs like Carter Sorenson at the Gap. Indulging himself with that stupid girl had cost him plenty.

And despite all her wailing, you couldn't tell him she hadn't secretly enjoyed every minute of it.

"Tom?" a familiar voice called out from halfway down the street.

Tom craned his neck around a group of young women walking eastward down the street. Nice ass on the little brunette, he thought as Will's head suddenly bobbed into view. Shit. As if his day wasn't bad enough already. What was he doing here?

"I'm glad to see you," Will said. "I wasn't sure you'd be here."

"Where else would I be?" Tom ground his cigarette into the sidewalk, squinted through the sun at Jeff's little brother. In his white shirt and khaki pants, he was a walking ad for the Gap, Tom thought, sneering.

"Jeff around?"

"What would Jeff be doing around here?"

"You haven't seen him today?" Will asked, ignoring the question.

"Was I supposed to?"

"Somebody phoned the apartment first thing this morning. It wasn't you?"

"Wasn't me," Tom acknowledged, volunteering nothing further.

Will shifted his weight from his right foot to his left. "Jeff said it was his boss, asking him to come in early."

"Then why'd you ask if it was me?"

"Because he didn't go to work. Apparently he called in sick."

Tom shrugged his bony shoulders, although his curiosity was definitely aroused. Still, he wasn't about to let Will know that.

"He left his wallet at home," Will said.

Tom smiled, silently assessing the situation. Someone had phoned Jeff first thing this morning and Jeff had taken off in such a rush he'd forgotten his wallet. He'd also lied about where he was going. Interesting, Tom thought, deciding that one thing was obvious: If Jeff wasn't where he said he'd be, he was where he *wanted* to be. Which could only mean one thing: a woman.

"Did he say anything to you about having to be somewhere this morning?" Will pressed.

"If he had," Tom said coolly, "you think I'd tell you?"

"Look. I'm not trying to pry or butt into something that's none of my business–"

"Really?" Tom interrupted, borrowing Carter's earlier phrase. "Because it kind of looks like that's what you're doing."

"I'm just a little worried. It's not like Jeff–"

"It's *exactly* like Jeff."

"Okay," Will said, conceding defeat. "I guess you know him better than I do."

"Damn right I do."

"So since you know him so damn well," Will said pointedly, "where the hell is he?"

Tom felt his fists clench at his sides. He was thinking he'd like nothing better than to bloody little brother's nose. Instead, he reached for another cigarette. "Think about it," he sneered, lighting it and inhaling deeply. "Jeff lied to both you and his boss about his whereabouts. Why? What does that tell you?"

"It tells me he could be in some sort of trouble."

Tom laughed. "They teach a course in ignoring the obvious at that fancy college you go to?"

"Suppose you enlighten me."

"You're sure you want to know?"

"I'm sure you want to tell me."

"He's with a girl," Tom said.

"A girl," Will repeated.

"And not just any girl either," Tom continued, exhaling directly in Will's face. "How much do you want to bet he's with the Pomegranate?"

"What? You're crazy." Will thought about the afternoon he'd just spent with Suzy, the hours of soft kisses and gentle caresses.

"Think about it," Tom said again. "Who else would have called him first thing in the morning, and why else would he lie?" He paused several seconds to let his questions sink in. "Face it, little brother. He's with your girlfriend. Blood might be thicker than water, but pussy trumps blood every time." He laughed. "Shit, man, you should see your face."

Tom was still laughing as Will turned and ran down the street, swallowed by a horde of approaching tourists.

TWENTY-ONE

JEFF'S HEAD WAS SPINNING as he closed the motel room door behind them. He felt as if he'd been drinking straight whiskey all morning instead of coffee, as if someone had slipped him a mind-altering drug, making everything he was seeing and feeling all the more vibrant and intense, and he raised his hand to the nearest wall to steady himself. Suzy's hand was instantly inside his, her body draped around his own, her breath warm on the side of his neck.

The room was dark, the heavy drapes blocking out all but a few stubborn slivers of morning sun. Jeff could make out the shapes of a round table and two chairs next to the window; a dresser with a TV along one wall; a standing lamp beside it; a king-size bed in the middle of the room, taking up most of it; a bathroom at the far end. He was thinking that it was pretty basic, almost seedy, and that if he hadn't forgotten his wallet they could have checked into one of those charming little boutique hotels in South Beach and spent the day making love between crisp white sheets and lounging in a Jacuzzi full of scented bath oils, maybe even ordering in champagne. He was thinking she deserved better and that he wanted to give it to her. He wanted to kiss her and make everything all right, to prove to her not all men were brutes, that they could be gentle and kind and loving. He was thinking that he had to tread slowly, carefully, that he had to be on guard not to hurt her because she'd been hurt more than enough already, and he didn't want to be the source of any more of her pain.

"Don't worry," he heard her say. "I won't break."

And then her lips were pressing against his with such urgency he felt as if he were fourteen years old again and his stepmother's best friend was initiating him into the wonder of a woman's body, showing him where to put his trembling hands, how best to use his eager mouth. All those afternoons when his stepmother was helping young Will with his school projects, she'd had no idea Jeff had been equally busy, learning some important life lessons of his own.

Or maybe she had. Maybe she just hadn't cared.

When was the last time a woman had really cared about him?

"I don't want to hurt you," Jeff mumbled as Suzy guided his hands toward her breasts.

"You won't."

He felt her small, girlish breast pushing against the inside of his palm, and he groaned out loud, his other arm snaking around her narrow waist as his right leg pushed its way between hers, and they tumbled toward the bed. He proceeded with deliberate care, his lips never leaving hers as he undid the buttons of her blouse and pushed the delicate fabric aside. "You're so beautiful," he whispered, his eyes now comfortable with the dark, seeing her clearly as his fingers flitted delicately across the expensive lace of her bra, effortlessly locating its front clasp and opening it, exposing her breasts to him. Her body arched, her nipples lifting toward his lips.

Soon they were lying naked beside each other, exploring each other's bodies as if it were the first time either of them had ever made love. And later, when he buried his head between her legs, when he probed her gently with his tongue, she cried out and grabbed the back of his head, pushed his tongue harder against her, until her body shook with repeated spasms and she was laughing and crying at the same time.

In the next second, she was rolling him onto his back, tracing a line from the middle of his chest to his groin with a series of soft kisses, and then taking him in her mouth and slowly, expertly, bringing him to the brink of climax. He pulled out of her mouth and entered her quickly, their bodies meshing perfectly as they held tightly on to one another, their every caress pulsating with the heady mix of surprise and familiarity. Jeff felt as if he was making love to a stranger who'd somehow known him all his life.

When it was over, they lay quietly in each other's arms. "Are you all right?" he asked after several minutes. "I didn't hurt you, did I?"

"You didn't hurt me," she replied, kissing his chest. "You're a wonderful lover."

"I wasn't fishing for compliments," Jeff said honestly.

"I know. But *I* am," she said, raising herself on her elbow and giggling like a teenager. "Was I any good?"

Jeff laughed. "Are you kidding me? You were fantastic."

Suzy smiled from ear to ear, her pleasure evident even in the dark. "You know, I'd almost forgotten what it's supposed to be like. Usually I just kind of lie there, let Dave do his thing, wait till it's over."

Jeff said nothing. He didn't want to think about Suzy with anyone else but him.

"Dave doesn't like to, you know . . . with his mouth."

"Then he's an idiot as well as a bastard," Jeff replied.

Suzy sighed, nestled in tighter against Jeff's side. "Are you going to tell anyone what happened?"

"No."

"Not even your brother?"

"No. Not yet."

"What about Kristin?"

"What about her?"

"Will you tell her?"

"No," Jeff said.

"Why not?" Suzy asked. "I thought you had one of those open arrangements."

"This is different," Jeff said, although he wasn't sure how. Or why.

"Tell me about her."

"Kristin? Why?"

"Just curious. What's she like? Aside from being drop-dead gorgeous."

"Aside from being drop-dead gorgeous," Jeff repeated, "I really don't know."

"What do you mean, you don't know? You live with her."

"Kristin's kind of guarded. She doesn't let anyone get too close," Jeff said, knowing he'd never really tried. Even in bed, she kept that air of detachment, he was thinking. Oh, she made all the right moves, said and did all the right things, but there was something missing. And for all her bravado, she rarely took the initiative. In some ways, she was a lot like Suzy's description of being in bed with Dave, just lying there, letting Jeff do his thing, waiting for it to be over.

"How would you feel if you found out she'd been with another guy and hadn't told you?" Suzy asked.

"I don't know." Surprised, more than anything, Jeff thought. Maybe a little hurt. And something else, he realized. He'd be relieved. "Did you know that Dave paid a visit to the Wild Zone yesterday?"

"What?"

"He hit on Kristin, gave her his card, told her to give him a call."

"I don't understand. Why would he . . . ?"

"You know how a dog marks his territory by peeing over another dog's scent? I think your husband was doing essentially the same thing."

"Interesting analogy," Suzy remarked.

"What are we going to do about him?" Jeff asked.

"What do you mean?"

"Are you going to leave him?"

"He'd never let me go."

Jeff nodded understanding, said nothing for several long seconds. "My mother's dying," he said finally.

"I'm sorry."

"According to my sister, it could be any day now. She wants me to come home to Buffalo."

"Will you?"

"No," he said.

"Why not?"

"My mother handed me over to my father when I was eight years old. She said I looked too much like him and that basically looking at me made her sick. I saw her infrequently over the years, and then not at all. She didn't feel any particular need to see me when she was well; I don't feel any particular need to see her now that she's sick. I guess that makes me pretty callous."

"Hey, I'm the one who said she wished her husband was dead," Suzy offered with one of her sad smiles.

"We make a great pair."

"I think we do."

Jeff reached over to brush some hairs away from her cheek. "So do I."

"I think you should see her," Suzy said.

"What? Why?"

"Because I think you should tell her how you feel."

"Tell a dying woman I loathe and despise her?"

"Do you?"

Jeff shook his head. "I don't know."

"I think you should see her," Suzy repeated. "Find out."

"I think you should leave your husband."

Suzy smiled. "How can I do that?"

"I'll think of something," Jeff said.

KRISTIN WAS CHANGING the bedsheets when she heard the door to the apartment open and close. "Will?" she called out. "Is that you?"

"No, it's me," Jeff said, coming into the bedroom, surreptitiously sniffing his fingers to make sure he'd washed away all traces of Suzy. "You see my wallet anywhere around? I thought I left it on the dresser."

"Will has it," Kristin said, a puzzled look filling her face. "He was supposed to take it to you at work. Didn't you see him?" Was it her imagination, Kristin wondered, or had she just seen Jeff flinch? She pushed her hair away from her face and tucked her blue-striped shirt into her cutoff jeans, waiting for his answer.

"I wasn't at work," he admitted after a pause.

"You weren't?"

"No." Another pause. "I lied to you. And to Will. And then to Larry. I told him I was sick."

"Why?" Kristin asked. "Where were you?"

Another pause, longer than either of the previous two. "I was with Tom."

"What? Why?" Kristin asked again, studying Jeff's face. She could almost see the mechanics of his brain working, ticking behind his eyes like the inside of a clock. She listened as he explained his earlier lies with what she recognized immediately were more lies, something about Tom freaking out and having to go over to calm him down, talk him out of doing something crazy. And then more lies about not telling her or Will the truth because he hadn't wanted to worry them. "You don't usually lie to me," Kristin said, her voice soft, betraying nothing. "You're surprisingly good at it."

"I'm really sorry."

Kristin nodded as she absorbed his false apology. Did men really believe women were so gullible or did they just not care? "How is he?" she asked, deciding to play along. "Were you able to calm him down?"

"Yeah." Jeff sighed with what Kristin understood was relief that his story had been so easily accepted. "Took half the morning," he continued, embellishing his account unnecessarily, as liars often did. "He was literally bouncing off the walls when I got there. He's really upset about this shit with Lainey."

"She was here this morning," Kristin told him.

Jeff's body instantly tensed. "Lainey was here? Why?"

"She wants you to talk to him."

"Well, there you go." He forced a laugh from his throat. "Mission already accomplished."

"You really think you got through to him?"

Jeff shrugged. The shrug said, "Who knows?"

"You don't think he'd actually do anything, do you?" Kristin asked, the feel of Lainey crying in her arms still fresh.

"Like what?"

"Hurt Lainey or the kids."

"No. Of course not. Tom's all bluster and bullshit."

"He wasn't all bluster in Afghanistan."

"That was different."

"Tom's the same."

"He'll be okay."

"He has a gun."

"No," Jeff said. "*We* have his gun. Remember?"

Kristin pictured Tom's gun lying in the top drawer of her night-stand. So it's still there, she thought. "He said he has others."

"Tom says a lot of things."

"Most of which scare the shit out of me," Kristin said.

"Which is exactly why I didn't tell you where I was going."

Kristin walked over to Jeff, put her arms around his neck, and raised her lips to his. "You're very sweet."

Jeff kissed her lightly, then backed out of her embrace. "I should get going. I told Larry I'd try to make it in this afternoon."

Oh, no you don't, Kristin thought, catching the faintest whiff of expensive perfume clinging to his skin and batting her eyes seductively as she reached for him again. You're not getting out of this as easily as that. "You sure you don't have a few minutes?"

"I wish I did."

"I just changed the sheets. They're nice and fresh."

"Sounds very tempting, but I can't."

"We could do it standing up," Kristin teased. "Save time. Do it right here against the wall."

"And if Will comes home and finds us?"

Kristin smiled. "Guess we could ask him to join in."

Jeff laughed, backing into the hallway. "Rain check?"

"I don't know," she said, her voice a singsong as she began undoing the buttons on her blouse. "It might not rain for some time."

"Ah, come on, babe. Don't do this to me. I really have to go. You don't want me to lose my job, do you?"

Kristin plopped down on the freshly made bed. "Okay. Be a spoilsport. Go to work. But you owe me."

"I do, indeed." Jeff returned to the bed, planted a delicate kiss on Kristin's forehead. "See you later."

"See you," Kristin called out as Jeff left the room. Seconds later, she heard the front door close.

She remained sitting at the foot of the bed for several minutes, trying to digest what had just happened, to understand exactly what everything meant. Jeff had lied to her, which was unusual in itself. He'd also lied to his brother and his boss and only confessed when confronted. That confession had consisted of even more lies, although kudos to him for coming up with something even vaguely plausible under the circumstances. It wasn't every man who could think on his feet like that when cornered.

Just as it wasn't like Jeff to turn down an offer of sex, no matter what the circumstances, no matter how great the risk to his job. Hadn't he lost his last job because he'd gotten a little too chummy with a client?

Which left only one possible explanation for the deception: He'd been with someone else.

A woman.

And not just some woman he'd picked up at the gym or in a bar, a woman to be used and discarded, like an old tissue. Not just another notch on his belt, another conquest to boast about with the boys. This one was different. This one wore expensive perfume and was worth lying about. Which meant their encounter went beyond mere sex, that Jeff actually felt something for this woman, and *that* was the reason he hadn't told her the truth.

The reason he hadn't told his brother was also easy to deduce, since it only confirmed what Kristin already knew.

The reason's name was Suzy Bigelow.

TWENTY-TWO

JEFF DECIDED TO WALK the dozen or so blocks to work. It was a beautiful day, sunny and hot to be sure, but slightly less humid than in recent weeks. And he was feeling great. Not that he'd enjoyed lying to Kristin. He hadn't. But he was relieved she'd accepted his story about Tom without question, and he rationalized that there was no reason to tell her the truth, not yet anyway, at least until he knew where things stood with Suzy.

"Suzy," he said aloud, enjoying the feel of her name on his lips. When was the last time he'd felt this way about a woman?

Had he ever?

At first he'd assumed his ardor was stoked mainly by rejection, by her seeming indifference to his easy charms, her stated preference for his brother. The fact that she was married had only added to her allure. And yet she'd proved too complicated for simple seduction. As tough as she was vulnerable, she'd wrapped herself around his brain as tightly as an Ace bandage. As late as this morning he'd assumed that by getting into her pants he'd finally get her off his mind. But if anything, the opposite had happened. She was even deeper inside his head than before, etched like hieroglyphics into the side of his skull. Her presence infiltrated his every thought. He couldn't take a breath without feeling the subtle rise and fall of her breasts against his chest.

He was being ridiculous, he knew. He'd known her less than a week, for God's sake. Five days! How could a woman he barely knew have managed to consume him to such a degree? Yes, they were good together in bed, better than good, he amended quickly. Maybe even great. But what was that old saying? Even when sex was bad, it was good?

Except it hadn't been just sex, Jeff realized. He hadn't nailed her, screwed her, fucked her. Whereas the sex act was usually all about him—*his* pleasures, *his* needs, *his* satisfaction—everything he'd done with Suzy had been for *her* pleasure, *her* needs, *her* satisfaction. From the minute they'd entered that motel room, everything he'd done had been done *for* her, not *to* her. They'd actually made love, he realized, stopping dead in his tracks, for the first time beginning to understand the meaning of that phrase.

So what exactly *does* it mean? he wondered, pushing one leg in front of the other, forcing himself to keep walking. Did it mean he was falling in love? "Don't be ridiculous," he told himself, stopping again, catching sight of his reflection in the large front window of a local travel agency. Who are you? he wondered, staring the stranger down. What have you done with Jeff?

How can a man who's never been loved possibly understand what it means to love another human being? his reflection asked.

I don't know, Jeff answered silently. I just know that if loving somebody means thinking about her twenty-four hours a day, then I love her right out of my mind.

"Shit," he said out loud. What was happening?

"Can I help you with something?" a woman mouthed from inside the front window of the travel agency. She stepped into his reflection, her large frame all but obliterating his already tenuous presence as she pointed to a handwritten sign offering a number of trips at a deep discount. He could fly to London for less than seven hundred dollars, Rome for just under nine. There was a seven-day, all-inclusive trip to Cancún for only four hundred and ninety-nine dollars. "A steal," he heard her say through the glass.

Jeff shook his head, waved the woman away, although the thought of spiriting Suzy off to some exotic locale was unbearably tempting. But while he might have been able to persuade Larry to give him some time off work, while he might even have been able to convince Kristin that he needed some time away by himself, he doubted Suzy would be able to come up with any kind of story that would convince her husband to let her take off for a week without him.

Unless Dave Bigelow was no longer in the picture.

Yeah, right, Jeff thought, hurrying away from the window and picking up his pace. What the hell was he thinking now?

I have such terrible thoughts, he heard Suzy say. *He'll be sleeping, and I'll think about going into the kitchen and getting one of those big, long knives and stabbing him right through the heart. Or setting fire to the mattress. Or running him over with my car. Sometimes I imagine how wonderful it would be if an intruder were to break into the house and shoot him.*

Could he do it? Could he burst into the man's house and gun him down in cold blood? Jeff wondered, breaking into a sweat as he turned the corner, the bakery beneath Elite Fitness popping into view. "No way. You're out of your fucking mind," he said out loud, pulling open the door and staring up the steps leading to the gym.

"Hey, you," Caroline Hogan said, appearing at the top of the landing, loud rock music blasting behind the closed gym doors. "Where were you this morning? We missed you."

"Touch of food poisoning."

"Yuck. Well, fortunately Larry was able to find someone to fill in for you," she said, touching his arm as she ran down the steps. "He was actually pretty good. Anyway, feel better. Gotta run."

"Have a good day," Jeff muttered over his shoulder as he headed up the stairs.

Melissa was at his side the minute he entered the gym. "I believe this is yours," she confided, handing Jeff his wallet. "Some guy brought it in this morning, seemed quite upset when I told him you'd called in sick. He might have aroused Larry's suspicions."

"It's okay," Jeff said. "Don't worry."

"Are you all right?"

"Fine. Much better," he amended as Larry approached.

"Perfect timing," Larry said. "Your next client is due any minute. He called about ten minutes ago to make sure you'd be here."

"Sorry about this morning," Jeff apologized, preparing to elaborate. But Larry was already walking away. "Who's the client?" he asked Melissa.

"Somebody new." Melissa was checking her appointment book as heavy footsteps bounded up the stairs. "I think Larry said he's a doctor," she said as the door opened and Dave Bigelow stepped inside.

WILL HAD BEEN walking the streets of South Beach in a fog for the better part of the morning. He'd narrowly escaped being hit by a young man rollerblading down Drexel Avenue, only to walk smack into a woman with a cane coming out of the Espanola Way Art Center. She'd sworn at him in Spanish and raised her cane into the air, as if about to strike him down. A new variation on the old expression "raising Cain," he'd thought, laughing as he'd headed toward beautiful Flamingo Park. There he spent ten minutes absently watching the joggers along the scenic pathways, then another five staring at a bunch of shirtless guys in tight blue shorts playing basketball on the practice courts. When one of the players stopped and asked him if he'd like to join in, Will had demurred and continued on his way, stopping minutes later at the Olympic-size open-air pool to watch a group of giggling adolescent girls butcher an impromptu synchronized swimming routine.

He'd then trailed a bunch of bicyclists to the Art Deco District, its single square mile chockablock full of art deco homes, hotels, and assorted buildings constructed in the 1930s and '40s, most of them repainted a variety of *Miami Vice* pastels during the 1980s. Eventually he'd made his way over to Ocean Drive, where he stood for several minutes outside the Mediterranean-style former mansion of Gianni Versace, staring at its elaborate architectural flourishes and brushing away the dragonflies that buzzed around his head like a bunch of miniature helicopters. A herd of tiny gecko lizards accompanied his every step, racing along the sidewalks and darting between his feet as he continued on his desultory way, ultimately disappearing into the spectacular, if haphazard, display of palms, ferns, and flowers that sprouted along every available surface. South Florida was just a jungle after all, he reminded himself.

You are entering the Wild Zone.

Proceed at your own risk.

Eventually Will found himself back on the corner of Espanola Way and Washington Avenue. He lingered awhile in Kafka's Cyber

Kafe, leafing through a number of obscure international magazines, although he spoke neither French nor Italian nor German. He thought of e-mailing his mother on one of the numerous computers available at the back, then decided against it. What would he say to her, after all?

That she'd been right about Jeff?

Is she? Will wondered, hearing his stomach rumble and realizing he'd missed lunch. "Don't forget to eat," his mother had warned him, practically the last words she'd uttered before he took off for Miami. Not "Say hello to Jeff." Not even "Don't do anything foolish." No. It was "Don't forget to eat." Advice you give a child.

Was that how everyone saw him?

"I'll have a double espresso," he told the young man behind the counter at the Cyber Kafe.

He'd been wrong to come to Miami, he decided. Wrong to seek Jeff out, to think he could reestablish a relationship with the brother he hadn't spoken to in years. Wrong to think he was actually making headway, that he was more than just a mild curiosity, more than a pesky reminder of an unhappy past, that he might actually mean something to Jeff, that they were friends now as well as family. And not just "half brothers" either, with all the unfortunate connotations that "half" contained, as if each brother was somehow lesser, as if both had been cut in two, the two halves never quite equaling a whole.

I was wrong to come to Florida, he thought, trying not to picture Suzy in his brother's arms. Could Tom possibly be right about them being together?

Will shielded his eyes from the relentless sun as he left the cafe, imagining Jeff and Suzy embracing in the corner of every shadow of every tree as he headed north on Washington Avenue with no clear plan for where he was going.

He couldn't very well go back to the apartment. Kristin would take one look at him and know something had happened. Could he lie to her as easily as Jeff had? Could he tell her what Tom had told him?

Was there even the slightest chance Tom was right?

How would Kristin react? Will wondered. Would she care? Would she cry with him over their mutual betrayal and rage at the unfairness of it all, or would she dismiss it as nothing to get upset about and tell him not to take it to heart? "It doesn't mean anything," he could almost hear her rationalize.

Except it did mean something. It meant something to him.

And Jeff knew that.

And he didn't care.

"A bet's a bet, little brother," Jeff would undoubtedly say.

Was that really what this was all about?

"Damn you, Jeff," Will whispered under his breath. Damn you straight to hell.

"YOU HAVE ONE hell of a nerve coming here," Jeff said to the man standing in front of him. His voice was quiet and surprisingly steady considering what was going on inside his body—his nerve endings on fire, his muscles twitching painfully, his throat constricting, his heart thumping against the inside of his chest, threatening to burst.

"I'd say that makes us even." Dave Bigelow was smiling as he crossed his arms over his expansive chest. He was wearing a short-sleeved white T-shirt, navy knee-length nylon shorts, white socks, and expensive Nike runners.

"What do you want?"

"Decided it was time to get back in shape," Dave said. "You mentioned the other day you were a trainer. I did some snooping around, heard some good things about you, thought I'd check it out for myself."

How much does he know? Jeff wondered. Had he been home, seen Suzy, beaten the truth out of her? Had he followed her this morning, seen her and Jeff at the restaurant, then followed them to the motel? "You look to be in pretty decent shape already," Jeff told him, his eyes on Dave's massive hands. Hands he uses to slap a helpless woman around, Jeff thought. Hands he uses to hold her down while he forces his way roughly inside her. You miserable piece of shit, he thought. I should break your fucking neck. What he said was, "I don't think I'm the right trainer for you."

A look of bemusement filled Dave's face. "Really? And why is that?"

"Jeff . . . ," Melissa cautioned him as Larry approached.

"Problems?" Larry asked.

How many times had he asked that lately?

"Dr. Bigelow? I'm Larry Archer," Larry said, extending his hand toward Dave. "We spoke on the phone this morning."

"Nice to meet you." Dave shook Larry's hand vigorously.

"I see you've already met Jeff. Dr. Bigelow specifically asked for you," Larry told him. "Said he'd heard some very good things."

"Unfortunately it seems that Jeff doesn't feel he's the right man for the job," Dave said.

Larry's quick frown was evident, even in profile. It was even more pronounced full-face. "Really? And why is that?"

"I just thought Dr. Bigelow might be happier dealing with the man in charge," Jeff improvised.

Larry's eyes narrowed suspiciously. "I'm sure you'll do a terrific job," he said. "Enjoy your workout, Dr. Bigelow."

"Please call me Dave."

"Enjoy your workout, Dave." Larry walked back to his client at the far end of the room.

"You really want to do this?" Jeff asked Dave after Larry was out of earshot.

"Lead the way," Dave said.

Jeff had to dig the heels of his sneakers into the hardwood floor to keep from flinging himself at Dave. One good kick to the groin, he was thinking, one good snap of his neck; that's all it would take to render him as helpless as Suzy had been. The thought of that bastard's hands on her flesh was making Jeff's skin crawl. What the hell are you really doing here? What kind of game are you playing? Jeff asked him silently, deciding that whatever it was, he could play, too. And win. You want a workout, you bastard? I'll give you a workout. The workout from hell, he thought, and smiled. "Suppose you warm up for a few minutes on the treadmill."

"Suppose I do," Dave agreed, stepping onto the machine.

Asshole, Jeff thought, turning it on and quickly increasing its speed from level one to level four. "I understand you were at the Wild Zone last night," he said, upping the speed to level five, and then six.

"Just thought I'd drop by, check the place out," Dave acknowledged, jogging along easily.

"Did that include checking out my girlfriend?"

Dave looked genuinely surprised. "I'm not sure I know what you're talking about."

"I'm sure you do."

Dave brought his eyebrows together at the bridge of his nose, as if trying to figure things out. "The bartender is your girlfriend? I had no idea."

Jeff increased the treadmill's speed to level seven. "Thought you were a happily married man."

"Oh, I am," Dave said. "Very happy."

"Happily married men don't usually go around hitting on other women."

"Is that what she told you? That I was hitting on her? I'm sorry I gave her that impression. I honestly wasn't," Dave said as Jeff took the speed to level eight. "As I remember the conversation, she told me she did some modeling," he continued, picking up his pace, still breathing with relative ease. "I happen to know this guy who's a big-shot photographer. Shoots all the top fashion models. His pictures are in all the magazines. I offered to put the two of them in touch. That's all."

"Uh-huh. How are you managing at this speed?" Jeff asked.

"Walk in the park," Dave said.

"Think you can handle a little more?"

"Bring it on."

Jeff increased the speed from level eight to level nine and then quickly to level ten, so that Dave was now running a brisk, six-minute mile. After two minutes, Dave was starting to breathe a little harder. That's it, you miserable prick, you can huff and puff until your heart gives out. Jeff let him continue running in place for another two minutes, watching as Dave's face turned from pink to red and perspiration started forming along the line of his scalp. He pushed the Off button only when he saw Larry watching him from the other end of the room. "Twenty push-ups," he said, pointing to the floor.

Dave smiled and instantly obliged, stretching his legs out behind him and bending his arms at the elbows, pushing himself off the floor with the palms of his hands.

"Slower," Jeff said, placing a forty-five-pound weight plate on Dave's back. If Dave wanted him to "bring it on," he'd be more than happy to oblige. What are you doing here, asshole? You think I'm as easy to intimidate as a woman half my size and weight? You think

I'm gonna be impressed because you can do a few push-ups? You can impress me in hell, you conceited piece of crap, he continued silently. "Come down a little lower," he said out loud. "Okay, grab these," he said when Dave had finished his final push-up. The perspiration was dripping from Dave's hairline down his cheeks as Jeff thrust a pair of thirty-pound dumbbells into his hands, then instructed him to do two minutes of walking lunges. "This is great for the heart rate, Doc. Not to mention the thighs," he told him, noting Larry's look of concern as Dave lunged by.

"Okay, on your back," Jeff instructed at the end of the two minutes, grabbing a stability ball and placing it between Dave's feet. "You're gonna do a set of a hundred crunches, transferring the ball from your feet to your hands."

"A hundred?"

"Too much for you?"

"Nah," Dave said, lifting his legs and torso into the air simultaneously and transferring the ball from his feet to his hands. "Piece of cake."

"Good. This'll get that stomach nice and flat. I'm noticing a bit of flab. I'm sure you want to keep middle-age spread at bay for as long as you can."

"I think I'm doing a pretty good job of that."

"Not bad," Jeff said. "And speaking of jobs, how is it a busy doctor like yourself gets to take time off in the middle of the day?"

"I'm skipping lunch."

"Probably not a bad idea. Go slower. Come up a little higher. Keep that chin tucked in." You motherfucker. "That's better."

"What else you got for me?" Dave asked when he was done with the crunches.

"Set of barbell dead lifts, ten reps," Jeff said, adding four plates to an already heavy steel bar, for a total of 225 pounds. "This should work your entire body." If it doesn't kill you first, Jeff thought. "How's that? You okay with this?"

"I can handle anything you dish out," Dave said, grunting with the strain of his exertion, his ruby-red face now bathed in sweat. At the end of the ten repetitions, he grabbed his knees and doubled over, breathing hard.

"Grab some water and follow me," Jeff told him, scooping a twenty-pound medicine ball off the floor. The game's not so much fun now, is it, asshole?

Dave filled a conical paper cup with ice-cold water from the cooler by the side window and gulped it down. "Where are we going?"

"Stairs." Jeff tossed him the medicine ball as they exited the gym. "Up and down. Five minutes."

"Five minutes?"

"Unless that's too much."

Dave smiled, took a deep breath, and began jogging down the stairs. "Something smells good," he said, then laughed. "And I don't think it's me."

"There's a bakery on the ground floor."

"So I noticed. Maybe I'll stop in when I'm done here, pick up some fresh pastries, surprise my wife with breakfast in bed tomorrow morning. Think she'd like that?"

I think she'd like to see you dangling from an alligator's jaws, Jeff thought. "Never been a big fan of pastry myself."

"You don't know what you're missing," Dave said with a wink.

"Three more minutes," Jeff told him. "Is that as fast as you can go?"

"You want faster, you'll get faster," Dave said, although he was almost crawling by the time he reached the top of the landing at the end of the five minutes. "Okay. What next?"

Jeff led him back inside, pointed to a high bar. "A set of twelve chin-ups."

"That's a pretty strenuous workout," Larry commented under his breath to Jeff as Dave began swinging wildly back and forth on the bar after the sixth chin-up. "How are you doing?" he asked Dave. "Jeff's not making you work too hard?"

"I'm fine," Dave spat out, trying to regain control of his legs.

"Maybe you should go a little easy," Larry whispered to Jeff.

"Larry thinks I should take it down a notch," Jeff said, starting to really enjoy himself. "What do you think?"

"Nah, I'm good."

You're a piece of shit, Jeff thought, smiling over at Larry as Dave all but collapsed in a sweaty heap at the conclusion of the exercise. "Okay. Two sets of dumbbell squats. You can manage fifty pounds, can't you?" He thrust one fifty-pound weight in Dave's right hand, joined immediately by a fifty-pound weight in the other. "How's that?"

"It's good."

"Atta boy. Keep that back straight. Come down a little lower."

As soon as Dave finished the thirty squats, Jeff led him over to a nearby bench for two sets of fifty bench dips with two forty-five-pound plates resting on the tops of his legs, then had him ride a stationary bicycle all-out for five minutes at level fifteen.

"I think that's enough," Dave managed to spit out at the conclusion of the exercise, his legs wobbling like Jell-O as Jeff led him to another bench at the far end of the room. "I should probably be getting back to work."

Jeff checked his watch. "We still have time left," he said dismissively. "How about we do some negative presses? We'll start with ten reps at two hundred pounds. Unless you don't think you can manage it. . . ."

Dave sank down on the bench, put his head between his still-wobbly knees, began gasping for breath.

"You all right?"

"I just need a minute."

"Take as long as you need."

"Everything all right here?" Larry asked, appearing at Dave's side.

Dave raised his head, sweat pouring from his forehead to his thighs as if from a pitcher. He looked as if he was about to pass out.

"Get him some water," Larry barked at Jeff.

In the next second, Dave was on his feet and staggering toward the bathroom. The violent sound of his repeated retching soon filled the gym, competing with the rock music blaring from the speakers.

"What the hell do you think you're doing?" Larry demanded of Jeff.

"He wanted a killer workout. I was just giving it to him."

"You were giving it to him, all right. What was that all about?"

"You heard him—he insisted he could handle it."

"You're the one who's supposed to be the judge of that. Shit. Listen to him in there. We'll be lucky if he doesn't sue our asses."

"He's not going to sue."

"He's in there puking his guts out." Larry began pacing back and forth in frustration. "What are you smirking about?"

"I'm not smirking."

"Look. I can't deal with any more of your bullshit."

"I'm not smirking," Jeff repeated, trying to stop his smile from spreading. Serves the bastard right, he was thinking. With any luck, he'd have a heart attack and die before the day was through.

"You're sarcastic with clients," Larry was saying. "You call in sick when you're obviously as healthy as a horse, you almost kill a guy because . . . what? You don't like doctors?"

"I can explain."

"Don't bother. You're finished here."

"What?"

"You heard me. You're fired. Now get out of here. I'll send you a check for whatever it is I owe you. But I don't want to see you around here ever again."

"Come on, Larry. You don't think you're overreacting?"

"Just get out of here."

Shit, Jeff thought, standing for a minute in silence before walking toward the door.

"Bye, Jeff," Melissa whispered. "Call me sometime."

As Jeff turned back, he saw Dave come out of the bathroom. The doctor raised his hand slowly into the air and waved with his fingers. "Bye-bye," he mouthed silently, then blew Jeff a kiss.

TWENTY-THREE

TOM WAS COUNTING DOWN the minutes until closing time when he saw Carter talking to a man near the front door of the store. The man was young, which wasn't unusual in a place like the Gap, and wearing a suit and tie, which was. Tom pegged him as a wannabe-can't be—wannabe be young, hip, with-it, cool; can't be any of the above. The last thing Tom wanted was to get roped into a late-day makeover. He tried to disappear behind a floating rack of sleeveless summer dresses, but Carter's eye proved too quick.

"That's him," he heard Carter say, directing the man to where Tom was crouching.

"Can I help you with something?" Tom asked, surfacing reluctantly and glaring at the young man, whose dishwater-blond hair was noticeably thinning on top. Wannabe-can't-be-no-chance-in-hell, Tom thought.

"Tom Whitman?" the man asked.

Tom's body stiffened. Since when had a potential customer called him by his name? "Yeah?"

The man pulled a large manila envelope out of his brown suit jacket. "For you," he said, then turned and walked away.

"What the hell is this?" Tom called after him.

The man quickly disappeared out the store's front entrance.

"Who was that?" Carter asked, approaching cautiously.

Tom tore open the envelope, his eyes perusing its contents, flitting from one sentence to the next, unable to settle on any one phrase in particular.

"Is that a restraining order?" Carter asked, leaning in closer.

"That stupid bitch."

"Your wife took out a restraining order against you?"

"She's gonna be so sorry."

"According to this," Carter said, adjusting his glasses as he pressed even tighter into Tom's side, "you're not allowed within three hundred yards of Elaine Whitman, her parents, or her children."

"*My* children," Tom corrected.

"Yeah, well, whosever they are, you can't go within three hundred yards of them."

"The hell I can't."

"If you do, you get arrested."

"That stupid cow."

"Hey, hey. Keep it down," Carter cautioned, glancing warily around the still-crowded store. Several shoppers had stopped their browsing and were hovering nearby. "You don't want the customers thinking you're referring to any of them."

Tom crumpled the letter in his fist, then threw it angrily to the floor. "She's not going to get away with this."

Immediately Carter scooped the paper up and began smoothing out the creases with his fingers. "Throwing things away doesn't make them *go* away," he advised Tom, returning the letter to his hands. "You have to be smart about this. You have to think everything through very carefully."

Tom reached into his back pocket for his cell phone, called Jeff at work. "What are you still doing here, jerk-off?" he asked Carter angrily.

Carter took several steps back. "Just trying to help," he said, managing to sound wounded and superior at the same time.

"You want to help somebody? Help her." Tom pointed to a teenage girl struggling with an armful of blouses. Carter immediately rushed to her rescue.

"Elite Fitness," a young woman's voice announced in Tom's ear.

"Put Jeff on. It's an emergency."

"I'm afraid Jeff doesn't work here anymore."

"What? What are you talking about?" Tom demanded. Had the whole world gone crazy? What was going on?

"Jeff no longer works here," the voice repeated.

"You mean he's not working *today*?"

"I mean he's no longer working at Elite Fitness."

"Since when?"

"Since a few hours ago."

"He quit?"

"I'm afraid you'd have to ask him about that."

"Well, I'm afraid you don't know fuck-all, do you?" Tom snapped, instantly severing their connection. "Shit!" Wouldn't you know it? Just when he really needed to talk to Jeff, Jeff was conveniently unavailable. He punched in the numbers for Jeff's cell, was transferred immediately to voice mail. He left a short message—"Where the hell are you?"—before trying Jeff's apartment. That call was answered on the third ring.

"Hello?" Kristin asked on the other end of the line.

"I need to speak to Jeff," Tom announced without preamble.

"Tom?"

"Is Jeff around?"

"He's at work."

"Exactly what work would that be?"

"What are you talking about?" Kristin asked.

"Apparently Jeff no longer works at Elite Fitness."

"Don't be silly. Of course he does."

"I just called there. They said otherwise."

"I don't understand," Kristin said again.

"Welcome to the club." He hung up before Kristin could say anything else.

"SOMETHING WRONG?" WILL asked as Kristin came out of the bedroom, her long blond hair cascading past her shoulders, her makeup artfully applied, a pair of black stilettos dangling from her left hand, the buttons of her leopard-print blouse undone, her breasts spilling out of her black push-up bra.

"I think Jeff's been fired," she said, leaning forward to slip on her shoes.

Will said nothing.

"You don't seem too surprised."

Will hesitated, trying to decide the best way to tell Kristin that Jeff hadn't gone to work this morning.

"I know Jeff wasn't at work this morning," she said, as if reading his thoughts. "He came home when he realized he'd forgotten his wallet." She related the details of their conversation.

"He told you he was with Tom?" Will repeated when she was through.

A pause. "You don't believe him?"

"Do you?"

Another pause. "I don't know." She shrugged, the shrug causing her breasts to lift up and down. "Obviously his boss didn't believe him." Then, absently fluffing her hair, "You're the philosopher. Tell me, Will, why do men lie? And don't say 'Because they can.'"

Will wished she'd do up her blouse so he could concentrate. Was she being deliberately provocative, he couldn't help but wonder, displaying her body to him in such a seemingly casual, offhand way? Or was she honestly unaware of the effect such a display might have on him? Was he as sexless, as inconsequential, to her—to all women—as a piece of furniture? "I guess men lie for the same reasons women do," he said finally.

"Are we talking about any woman in particular?"

"I don't know. Are we?"

There was a moment's silence.

"Where'd you go after you found out Jeff wasn't at work?" Kristin asked.

"Nowhere special."

"You've been gone all day."

"Just wandering around," Will said.

"That's a lot of wandering."

"There's a lot to see."

"I take it you didn't see Jeff."

Will shook his head.

"So where do you think he is? We know he's not with Tom now."

"I don't know."

"Do you think he's with Suzy?" Kristin asked plainly.

Another silence, longer than all the others.

"Is that what *you* think?" Will asked, throwing the question back at her. Clearly they'd both been giving this possibility a great deal of thought. Even more clearly, they'd reached the same conclusion.

Kristin brought the two halves of her blouse together, began buttoning it from the bottom up. "I don't know what to think anymore," she said, tucking it inside her short, tight skirt and grabbing her purse from the floor.

"How would you feel about it if it were true?"

"I don't know. How would *you* feel?"

Will shrugged, shook his head.

"Well, I don't have time to worry about it now. I have to get to work. You gonna stop by the Wild Zone later?"

"You want me to?"

"Always."

"Then I'll be there."

"Good." Kristin leaned forward, her breasts spilling toward Will as she kissed him softly on the cheek. "See you later, alligator."

He smiled in spite of himself. "In a while, crocodile."

"SO," DAVE SAID as he stepped into the front foyer of his home at approximately half past six that evening. "It looks as if your boyfriend got himself fired."

Suzy fought to keep her face a blank screen. It was important not to betray any emotion, to keep from revealing any potentially harmful information. It was important she stay calm and focused, that she not overreact. Whatever her reply, her voice had to remain steady, her hands still. While a certain amount of curiosity would be tolerated, even expected, she couldn't appear too eager. She had to tread carefully. One wrong inflection could spell disaster. "What are you talking about?" she asked over the loud pounding of her heart. Could he hear it? she wondered. Could he see it beating wildly in her chest?

"Jeff Rydell," Dave said, lobbing the name at her as if it were a football he expected her to catch and run with.

Suzy pushed her features into an expression of confusion. She shrugged, as if the name meant so little it didn't bear repeating.

"The guy in the car on Sunday, looking for Miracle Mile," Dave elaborated, studying her face for the slightest flicker of recognition. "The one holding the map."

"I don't remember."

"'Course you do. The good-looking one in the passenger seat. Heavy on muscles, short on brains. How could you not remember him?"

"I wasn't really paying attention. . . ."

"No," Dave said, pushing past her into the living room. "You were just trying to be helpful."

Suzy followed after him, her mind rushing off in four different directions at once, as if she were being drawn and quartered. Why was he talking about Jeff, and how did he know his name? Had he followed her this morning? Had he seen the two of them at the coffee shop? Had he watched them enter the motel room together? What did he mean when he said her boyfriend had been fired? What was he talking about? How much did he know? "Would you like a drink before dinner?" she asked.

"That would be nice." He sat down on the cream-colored sofa, crossed one leg over the other, undid his tie, and waited to be served. "Vodka, rocks."

Suzy hurried into their square eat-in kitchen, painted the sunny yellows and deep blues of Provence. She threw a handful of ice cubes in a glass, then retrieved the vodka from the freezer and poured her husband a tall drink, trying to control the telltale trembling of her hands. Stay calm, she told herself as she practiced holding out the drink in front of her, as if offering it to Dave, then repeated the gesture several times in an effort to bring her shaking fingers under control. Show no fear, she told herself, taking a series of deep breaths before returning to the living room.

"Aren't you going to ask me how I know he got fired?" Dave said as she approached. He held out his hand.

Suzy quickly handed him his drink, said nothing.

"I know because I was there."

"I don't understand," Suzy said truthfully. What was Dave talking about?

"Remember he told us he was a personal trainer, that he worked at Elite Fitness on Northwest Fortieth over in Wynwood?"

"I don't remember," Suzy lied. Did he believe her? He always claimed to know when she wasn't being truthful.

"Well, anyway," Dave continued, patting the cushion beside him, silently directing her to sit down, "I got to thinking. The guy had some pretty impressive-looking biceps. And I'm not getting any younger. Maybe I should start working out, get myself in better shape. Can't afford to get too complacent."

Suzy sank into the deep, down-filled seat, glancing at the lamp on the cloverleaf table next to her, its dented shade a cruel reminder of how Dave dealt with liars. "What are you talking about? You look terrific."

He put his arm around her, drew her close, kissed her hard on her cheek. "Well, thank you, sweetheart. A man always appreciates a vote of confidence from his beautiful wife." He took a sip of his drink. "Especially one who mixes drinks as good as this one. You been taking lessons from your friend?"

"What?"

"That bartender from the Wild Zone. What was her name again?"

"Kristin," Suzy whispered, feeling her pulse quicken. He was playing with her, the way a cat taunts its prey before moving in for the kill.

"Kristin. Right. You speak to her this week?"

"No."

"No? How come? I thought you two had become such good friends."

"Not really."

"That's good." He took another sip of his drink, leaned back against the cushion, closed his eyes.

"So, aren't you going to finish your story?" Suzy asked in spite of herself.

Dave opened his eyes. "Not much left to tell. I called Elite Fitness, made an appointment for a private session, and went over there this afternoon."

"You went over there?"

"Is that a problem?"

"No, of course not. I'm just surprised you'd go all the way over to Wynwood when there are a million gyms right around here."

"It wasn't that far. Although I certainly won't be going there again."

"What happened?"

Dave shrugged. "Turns out our Jeff isn't much of a trainer, and his boss was smart enough to realize it."

"You were there when he fired him?"

"It's like I'm always telling you, sweetheart. Bad things happen to people who get on my bad side."

Suzy felt a shiver travel from the base of her spine to the top of her neck. She shuddered.

"What's the matter, babe?" he asked. "You cold?"

"I'm fine."

"You're not upset he got fired, are you?"

"Why would I be upset?"

"Good." He reached over and patted her knees. "Now, what's for dinner? All that exercise seems to have given me quite an appetite."

TWENTY-FOUR

THE SUN WAS STILL shining when Jeff got out of the taxi at exactly ten minutes to nine that evening, although it was that peculiar kind of light—intense and yet strangely flat—that belongs to neither day nor night. A borrowed light, Jeff was thinking as he paid the cabbie and crossed the empty street toward the lobby of the oddly named Bayshore Motel—odd because there was neither bay nor shore anywhere in sight. Buffalo was like that, he thought, looking back over his shoulder at the departing taxi. Nothing here had ever made any sense. At least for him.

So what was he doing back here?

He barely remembered boarding the plane, let alone buying the ticket.

A sudden image, like a jagged bolt of lightning, streaked across his line of vision. He saw Dave's face twisted with exertion, Larry's face contorted with anger, his own face flush with disbelief at his abrupt dismissal. And then the good doctor's twisted smile as he waved his victorious good-bye. The best man had won, those fluttering fingers had told Jeff in no uncertain terms. He'd been out-manipulated and outplayed, seduced and then cruelly abandoned, beaten at his own game, Jeff thought, not for the first time, not even for the tenth time, as his fists clenched at his sides.

He saw himself bounding down the stairs from the gym to the street, fleeing the normally comforting smell of freshly baked bread that now threatened to suffocate him, and running full-out until he found himself, sweating and out of breath, back in front of the nearby travel agency with its enticing handwritten offers of discount holidays to far-off, exotic locales. He saw his face pressed up against the glass, like a child in front of a Macy's window at Christmas, as the woman behind the glass beckoned him inside, offering him coffee and a smile crowded with too many teeth. He heard his voice informing her that he suddenly found himself with time on his hands and the irresistible urge to travel. An assortment of colorful brochures had immediately materialized, as if by magic, as the woman's voice droned seductively on about the beauties of Barcelona, the wonders of ancient Greece. And then another voice, this one small and unsteady, a child's voice really, quivering with the threat of tears—not his voice, surely not his voice—interrupting her to say that his mother was dying and was there any way she could get him on the first available plane to Buffalo? And the woman's upper lip falling like a curtain over all those teeth as the smile died on her face and her hand reached for his, lingering perhaps a beat too long. Of course, she'd whispered. Anything she could do to help . . .

"Just get me on that plane," he'd said.

What had he been thinking?

Clearly he hadn't been, Jeff decided now, pulling open the heavy glass door to the entrance of the empty motel lobby and bursting into the too warm, stale-smelling space with such force it caused the sleepy-looking clerk behind the reception desk to take a step back.

"Can I help you?" the young man asked, tugging at the collar of his white shirt with one hand while reaching for the panic button under the counter with the other. He was very tall and almost alarmingly thin, although his voice was surprisingly deep. His skin was freckled with the remains of teenage acne and his reddish-brown hair refused to lie the way it had been combed, preferring to branch out in several different directions at once, so that he managed to look both bored and surprised at the same time.

"I need a room," Jeff heard himself say, his eyes casually absorbing the uninteresting watercolor of a bunch of sailboats that occupied much of the pale blue wall behind the registration desk.

The young man shrugged, his hand relaxing over the buzzer. "How long you staying?"

"Just for one night."

"Air-conditioning's not working."

"I thought it felt a little warm."

"I can give you a break on the price," the young man offered unprompted. "Sixty bucks instead of eighty-five. How's that?"

"Very thoughtful."

The young man's lips curled into a tentative smile, as if he wasn't sure whether or not he was being toyed with. "If you stay an extra night, I gotta charge you full price."

"I won't be staying."

"Where you from?"

"Miami."

"Always wanted to go to Miami. I hear the women are really something."

Jeff nodded, staring into the memory of Suzy's sea-blue eyes. It felt like weeks since he'd seen her, touched her. Could it really have been just this morning that he'd held her in his arms?

"So what brings you up this way?" the boy was asking.

"My mother's dying," Jeff said simply.

The young man took a step back, as if her impending death might be contagious. "Yeah? Sorry to hear that."

Jeff shrugged. "What can you do?"

"Not much, I guess. So how do you want to take care of this?"

For an instant Jeff thought they were still talking about his mother. "I don't understand. . . ."

"MasterCard, Visa, American Express?" the clerk prompted.

Jeff pulled his wallet out of his back pocket, removed his credit card, pushed it across the counter. The motion reminded him of Kristin pushing drinks along the bar of the Wild Zone. He checked his watch. It was nine o'clock. I should call her, he thought. She'd probably be wondering where he was.

Or maybe not.

Kristin had always been remarkably sanguine about his comings and goings. It was one of the things he liked best about her. Still, he thought he probably should have called her to tell her of his plans. Although how could he have told her anything when he hadn't known—still didn't know—what those plans were? Plans, by their very nature, implied a certain level of conscious thought, and he'd been operating on nothing but adrenaline for the past week. How else to explain the events of the last several days?

How else to explain what the hell he was doing here?

He'd always hated this bloody city, he thought, swiveling back toward the street, barely recognizing the seemingly deserted neighborhood, even though the house he'd grown up in was less than a mile away. Was that why he'd directed the taxi here and not to a more comfortable downtown hotel? "The corner of Branch and Charles," he'd instructed the dark-skinned cabbie, not even sure whether the motel he remembered from his childhood would still be standing and only half-surprised to see that it was, although the name had been changed. Not for the first time, he suspected.

The rest of the city looked pretty much the same, he'd decided on the drive in from the airport. Swallowing his growing sense of dread as the taxi bypassed the downtown core, Jeff had watched the seemingly random series of abandoned and derelict warehouses in the surrounding slums gradually give way to a succession of neat, working-class suburban homes. He didn't look too closely, aware of the incipient decay lurking just out of sight—a collapsing eaves trough here, some crumbling front steps there, the damage of last winter's lake-effect snow bubbling like oil beneath each smooth, painted surface. The city even smelled the same, Jeff had noted, a slight breeze blowing the grit and grime of the streets through the cab's open rear window. Jeff felt it sink into his pores like tiny pebbles. Rationally he knew he was being overly sensitive, that the city of his unhappy youth smelled no different than any other midsize American city: an uneasy combination of nature and industry, earth and concrete, decay and renewal, success and failure. Mostly failure, he thought now, standing in the stifling, nautically themed lobby, reluctant to take a breath.

"You want one keycard or two?" the clerk asked, handing Jeff back his credit card.

"One is fine."

"One it is." The young man lifted the plastic keycard above his head as if it were a trophy. "This way."

Jeff followed him out of the lobby, reflexively assessing the boy's flaccid frame, absently drawing up a series of exercises that would add bulk to the scrawny arms that hung lifelessly at his sides. As was often the case with men who were self-conscious about their height, the boy's posture was horrible, his head hunched between his shoulder blades and held in, turtle-like, as if he was already bracing himself for a doorway that was too short to comfortably walk through. "I'm sure I can find the room on my own," Jeff said, wondering if it was a good idea for the boy to leave the front desk unattended.

"Got nothing better to do."

He sounds just like Tom, Jeff thought, shielding his eyes from the preternaturally bright light of the evening sun as he followed the young man along the side of the one-story structure. For the second time that day he felt the uncomfortable sensation of someone shining a flashlight directly in his face.

"You don't have any luggage?" the boy asked.

Not even a toothbrush, Jeff thought. "I travel light."

"That's the best way," the clerk agreed, as if he knew.

Probably never been out of Buffalo in his life, Jeff mused, again thinking of Tom. The first trip Tom had ever taken out of Buffalo had been to Miami. Next stop, Afghanistan.

They stopped in front of a door that was painted navy blue and embossed with a brass number 9 in the shape of a fish. "Here we are," the young man said, slipping the keycard into its slot and then having to do it three more times when the door failed to open. "They get temperamental sometimes," he explained, finally pushing it open and flipping on the inside light to reveal a king-size bed whose blue and silver bedspread was a pattern of quilted waves. "Thought you might appreciate some extra room to thrash around. I'm a pretty restless sleeper myself," he said, handing Jeff the keycard. "Especially in this heat. You want me to open the window? It's kind of stuffy in here."

"It's fine," Jeff said, although in truth, it was oppressive. Still, he was anxious to be alone. He needed to lie down, to think things through, decide his next move.

"There's a drugstore two blocks down, if you need a toothbrush or some deodorant," the clerk offered, leaning against the doorway and transferring his weight from one foot to the other, "and there's a McDonald's around the corner, if you get hungry."

"Maybe later," Jeff said, feeling his stomach cramp at the thought of food.

"Name's Rick. If you need anything–"

"I won't. Thank you."

Jeff stepped inside the room, kicking the door closed with the heel of his right foot, watching Rick's puzzled face quickly disappear from view. Had he been expecting a tip? Jeff wondered. Or maybe he'd been hoping for an invitation to come inside. Maybe that's why he'd been so accommodating, personally accompanying Jeff to his room, giving him a discount he hadn't asked for and a king-size bed he didn't need.

Or maybe the kid was just lonely.

Jeff sat down on the end of the bed, his hands sinking into the blue and silver waves of the bedspread, his tired face reflected in the large, shell-framed mirror on the opposite wall. A rectangular TV sat on the right side of the low dresser, its blank screen reflecting the turbulent green waters of a roiling sea depicted in a painting that hung above the headboard. What am I doing here? Jeff wondered again, falling backward across the bed.

He checked his watch, saw that it was almost nine fifteen. No point in going to the hospital now, he decided. Visiting hours were no doubt over, and besides, he had no energy to confront his mother now. Even in her weakened condition, he'd be no match for her. He wasn't even sure what hospital she was in, he realized with a start. He'd assumed it was Mercy, which was about ten blocks from there, but maybe she was somewhere else. He'd have to call Ellie, find out.

Although not now. Now he was too exhausted. He'd call his sister first thing in the morning, he decided, pulling his cell phone out of his pocket and checking for messages, laughing when he heard Tom's indignant voice demanding to know where the hell he was. Damned if I know, Jeff thought, dropping the phone to his side.

He closed his eyes, feeling the weight of the stale air fall across his body like a heavy blanket and listening to the fan of the broken-down air-conditioning unit whirring impotently from the far end of the room.

Seconds later, he was asleep.

He dreamed he was walking along the wooden pier of a busy marina, a variety of expensive boats bobbing up and down in the nearby ocean, women in tiny bikinis laughing and raising tall glasses of champagne as their husbands threw heavy anchors overboard and their ships set sail in the wind. Above him, an army helicopter circled noisily, so that at first he didn't hear her calling out his name. But then suddenly there she was, standing in the shadow of a high mast: his mother, looking young and lovely, although even from a distance of fifty feet he could make out a hint of reproach in her eyes, as if he'd already done something to disappoint her. "Jeff," she called excitedly, waving him toward her. "Hurry up. Over here."

And then he was running toward her, except that no matter how close he got, there was always one more boat to get past, one more sail to circumvent, and then another, and another. And suddenly the helicopter that had been hovering above was lowering itself to the pier and his mother was skipping toward it, lifting her skirt above her knees, preparing to climb inside. "Mom," he called out, but she refused to look at him. Just then a marching band of pimply-faced teenage boys appeared, their brass horns and woodwinds blasting out a raucous version of "The Star-Spangled Banner" as his mother took her seat beside the pilot, laughing uproariously as the helicopter lifted off into the sky.

"Mom, wait!"

His mother stared down at him reproachfully. "You look just like your father," she said.

And suddenly the helicopter began spinning around in a series of increasingly small circles, and his mother's laughter changed into screams of panic. The national anthem grew louder, rising toward the sky, as the helicopter began careening wildly out of control. Jeff watched helplessly as it crashed against the side of a fast-moving cloud and plummeted into the sea.

He sat up with a gasp, fresh beads of perspiration breaking out across his forehead. Beside him "The Star-Spangled Banner" continued its insistent tune. "Jesus," he muttered, the word as much a prayer as an exhortation, as his hand groped through the waves of the bedspread for his cell phone. What the hell was that all about? he wondered, the dream breaking up like a bad signal as he flipped open the phone. "Hello," he said groggily, what remained of his dream evaporating with the sound of his voice.

"Jeff?"

Was he still dreaming?

"Jeff?" the voice asked again.

"Suzy?" He shook his head in an effort to clear it.

"Are you all right? Dave told me what happened at the gym. I've wanted to call all night. I feel so terrible."

"Don't. I'm fine."

"You don't sound fine."

"I must have dozed off. What time is it?"

"Around ten. I can't talk long. Dave just fell asleep. Are you sure you're okay?"

"I'm sure."

"Maybe if I talk to your boss, explain what happened . . ."

"No. It's all right."

"It's not all right. You lost your job."

"It doesn't matter."

"Of course it matters. Damn it. It's all my fault."

"None of this is your fault," Jeff said.

"Oh, God. I'm so sorry. You must hate me."

"Hate you?" Jeff asked incredulously. Then, before he could stop himself, before he knew the words were even forming, "I love you."

Silence.

"Suzy?"

"I love you, too," she said.

Another silence, a heartbeat longer than the first.

"What do we do now?" she asked him.

"You have to leave him."

Suzy took a deep breath, released it slowly, almost purposefully. "I know."

"Right now," Jeff instructed. "While he's asleep. Do you hear me, Suzy? Just get in your car and go straight to the Wild Zone. I'll call Kristin, tell her what's going on, get her to take care of you until I get back. . . ."

"What do you mean? Where are you?"

He almost laughed. "I'm in Buffalo," he said, convinced now he must be dreaming. "I don't know how it happened. One minute I was standing in front of this travel agency, and the next I was in a cab heading for the airport."

If Suzy was surprised, she didn't let on. "I'm glad."

"You are?"

"It was the right thing to do. I'm sure it meant a lot to your mother."

"I haven't seen her yet," Jeff admitted. "I was planning to go first thing in the morning."

He felt her nodding her head as she absorbed this latest bit of information. "It's probably better if I wait till morning, too," she said.

"What? No. Listen to me, Suzy. You need to get out now. I'll be back tomorrow afternoon."

A sudden intake of breath, then, "I'm sorry," Suzy announced curtly. "There's no one here by that name."

"What?"

"No, I'm afraid you have the wrong number."

And then another voice, a man's voice, as clear and as menacing as if he was sitting right beside Jeff. "Who are you talking to, Suzy?" the man asked just before the line went dead in Jeff's hand.

"Suzy?" Jeff said, jumping to his feet. "Suzy? Are you there? Can you hear me? Shit," he cried helplessly, pacing back and forth in front of the bed. "Don't you touch her, you miserable son of a bitch. Don't you touch her. I swear, if you lay a hand on her, I'll kill you." He sank back down on the bed, burying his head in his open palms. "I'll kill you," he repeated over and over again. "I swear I'll kill you."

TWENTY-FIVE

HE DECIDED TO CALL the police.

"AT&T, 411 nationwide," came the recorded message when Jeff punched in the number for information minutes later. "For what city and state?"

"Coral Gables, Florida."

"For what listing?"

"The police."

"I'm sorry," the recorded message said, somehow managing to sound appropriately contrite. "I didn't get that. For what listing?"

"Never mind," Jeff muttered, snapping his cell phone shut in exasperation. Assuming he'd been able to reach the proper authorities, just what had he been planning to say? "Hello, officer? I think you'd better send a car out to one twenty-one Tallahassee Drive right away;

I'm concerned my girlfriend's husband might be beating the crap out of her"? Yeah, that would go over well.

Although he didn't necessarily have to go into specifics. He didn't have to give the police his name or the reasons for his suspicions. He could just be a concerned citizen calling to report a domestic disturbance. Except what if there'd been no such disturbance? What if Dave had chosen to accept his wife's story of a wrong number without question or fuss? By alerting the police, by sending out a patrol car to investigate, Jeff would only be confirming Dave's suspicions and sealing Suzy's fate.

In any event, he doubted the police would be very quick to act on the word of an anonymous caller. They'd want details. At the very least, they'd demand to know who was calling, and when Jeff refused to tell them, when he refused to provide any explanations whatsoever, it was unlikely they'd pursue the matter further. They couldn't very well go chasing down every vague, unsupported complaint that came their way.

So calling the police was out.

Still, he just couldn't sit here and do nothing.

"Kristin," he decided, pressing in her number on speed dial and listening as the phone rang three times before her voice mail picked it up.

"This is Kristin," her voice purred seductively. "Tell me what you want, and I'll see what I can do."

"Damn it," Jeff said, clicking off without leaving a message. What was the point? He glanced at his watch. Of course she wasn't answering her phone. It was ten o'clock. She'd be at work. "What the hell is their number?" he wondered out loud, searching his memory for the digits he usually knew by heart and finally having to call information again when they failed to materialize. "South Beach, Miami, Florida," he told the familiar recorded voice. "The Wild Zone."

"I'm sorry. I didn't get that," the voice said, as Jeff had been expecting. "For what listing?"

"Shit."

"I'm sorry. Could you repeat that?"

"No, I fucking can't," Jeff hollered.

A real person suddenly replaced the recorded voice. "What was that name again?" the woman asked.

"The Wild Zone," Jeff repeated, feeling his fingers clench and trying to block out the unwanted image of Dave's fist connecting with Suzy's jaw. "Can you hurry, please? It's really very important."

"Is that a business?"

"It's a bar in South Beach."

Yeah, right. Very important, Jeff could almost feel the woman thinking. "Here it is," she said after several more seconds.

The recording suddenly returned with the correct number and the offer to connect Jeff directly for a small additional charge. Seconds later, Jeff listened as the phone rang once, twice, three times, four. . . ."

"Wild Zone," a man bellowed over a combination of loud voices and louder music.

"Put Kristin on the line," Jeff said, hearing Elvis in the background, belting out "Suspicious Minds."

"She's busy right now. Can I give her a message?"

"I need to talk to her. It's an emergency."

"What kind of emergency?"

"Just put her on the goddamn line."

And then nothing. Were it not for Elvis wailing away—*We can't go on together*—Jeff might have thought he'd been disconnected. What was taking Kristin so long?

"Hello?" she asked in the next instant.

"Kristin . . ."

"Jeff?"

"I need you to do something for me."

"Are you all right? Have you been in an accident?"

"I'm fine."

"Joe said it was an emergency."

"It is."

"I don't understand. Where are you?"

"I'm in Buffalo."

"What?"

"It's a long story."

"Did your mother die?"

"No. Have you heard from Suzy?"

"What?"

"Suzy Bigelow. Have you heard from her?"

"Why would I hear from her?"

"Because I told her you'd take her to the apartment, hide her from her husband. . . ."

"I don't understand."

"That emergency just about over?" Jeff heard a man call out. "You got a bar full of thirsty customers."

"When were you talking to Suzy?" Kristin whispered into the receiver. "I thought you just said you were in Buffalo."

"I am. Look, it's complicated. I'll explain everything as soon as I get back. In the meantime, if Suzy shows up at the bar, just get Will to take her to the apartment, and don't tell anyone where she is. Okay?"

A second's silence, then, "Do you want me to come out there?"

"No. It's okay. I'll be back tomorrow."

"You sure you're all right?"

"I'm fine."

"Okay. See you tomorrow," Kristin said before hanging up.

"Shit," Jeff spat, dropping the phone on the bed. He could still hear the confusion in Kristin's voice but knew it wouldn't be there for long. She was a smart girl. She'd have his relationship with Suzy figured out in a matter of minutes. Would she be upset or would she simply take it in stride, accepting these unexpected developments the way she did with most things in life she couldn't control? "Shit," he said again, trying to understand what was happening to him. Could he really have fallen in love? And was that what love was—this overwhelming feeling of helplessness? After pacing back and forth for several minutes, Jeff stuffed his phone back inside his pocket and headed out the door.

TEN MINUTES LATER, he found himself standing in a small line at the all-night drugstore around the corner from the motel, waiting to pay for a bag of disposable razor blades, a toothbrush, some toothpaste, and a package containing three pairs of white Jockey shorts, the only color they carried. He shifted his weight from one foot to the other, trying to keep his balance, his mind spinning, replaying the day's events over and over again, like a deejay spinning records at a busy Miami nightclub: Suzy on the phone first thing that morning, Suzy across from him in the diner, Suzy in his arms at the motel, Suzy on the phone just moments ago, Suzy in his head, his brain, his heart.

Had he really told her he loved her?

Had he meant it?

I love you, he heard himself say.

"How much did you say that was?" an elderly white woman at the head of the line was demanding of the young black man behind the cash register. "I think you've made a mistake. That can't be right. Check again."

"Five dollars and thirteen cents," the cashier repeated with a roll of his eyes at those waiting.

I love you, too, Suzy whispered in Jeff's ear.

"I thought the deodorant was supposed to be on special."

"It is. Two dollars and eighty-nine cents. That's the special price."

"I'm sorry. That can't be right."

I'm sorry. There's no one here by that name.

"It's normally three twenty-nine. Two eighty-nine on special."

"What's so special about that?"

"I don't know. I don't use it."

"Check again. I'm sure you've got it wrong," the woman insisted.

I'm afraid you have the wrong number.

The young man pulled a colorful flyer out from behind the counter and opened it to the second page. "I don't have it wrong. See. It's right here." He pointed to the appropriate picture. "Special price: two eighty-nine. Now, you want it or don't you?"

"What choice do I have?" the woman muttered, shaking her head as she slowly counted out the exact change, then grabbed the plastic bag containing her several purchases from the young man's hands.

What do we do now?

You have to leave him.

"Pack of Marlboros," the next customer said before the woman had vacated her place in line. In response the woman gave him a dirty look and shuffled from the store. "Pack of Marlboros," the man said again, pushing a ten-dollar bill across the counter.

It's probably better if I wait till morning, too.

Listen to me, Suzy. You have to leave right now.

"Can I help you?"

Who are you talking to, Suzy?

"Can I help you? Excuse me, sir. Can I help you?" the cashier was asking.

"Sorry," Jeff said, snapping back into the present and realizing he was next in line.

"Twenty-three dollars and eighteen cents," the young man said as he finished ringing up the various items, his shoulders stiffening as if bracing for an argument.

Jeff handed him thirty dollars and waited as he bagged the assorted sundries and counted out the change. "Thank you."

"Have a good night."

Jeff stepped outside, glancing up and down the street. On the corner, the Marlboro man had stopped under a streetlamp to light up. In the distance, the old woman with the disputed deodorant was proceeding at a snail's pace, the plastic bag in her hand slapping against her side as she walked, her shoulders slumped forward as if she were fighting a strong wind. He thought of running to catch up to her, offering to give her a hand, but she'd probably think he was trying to steal from her and start screaming.

An old memory suddenly sprinted across his line of vision: he and Tom coming home one night from a party, both having drunk far too much, a middle-aged woman approaching, clutching her purse to her chest as she crossed the street to avoid them. "She thinks we're after her money," Jeff had said, and laughed.

"Or her body," Tom had said, laughing louder.

And suddenly Tom was racing across the street and pushing the woman to the ground as he wrenched the bag from her hands, and what choice had Jeff had but to chase after him? He couldn't very well stop to help the bleeding woman to her feet. She'd only have started screaming, accused him of being an accomplice. And so he'd fled the scene, not looking back. "Should have raped her," Tom had said, almost wistfully. "Bet she would have enjoyed it." He'd offered to split the forty-two dollars he'd found in the woman's wallet but Jeff had refused, watching as Tom tossed the purse into the nearest trash can.

He'd spent the next few days scanning the papers for any mention of the robbery, even checking the obituaries to see if a woman had died after being accosted, but there'd been nothing.

It's a wonder Tom and I didn't get our asses tossed in jail on any number of occasions, Jeff was thinking as he headed back to the motel. Except instead of turning left, he suddenly turned right, then crossed the street and continued purposefully down the block, turning left at the first intersection, and then making another left two blocks after that, as if being pulled along by a magnet. He didn't have to check the street signs. He'd have known the way blindfolded.

FIFTEEN MINUTES LATER, tired and perspiring heavily, he found himself on Huron Street, standing in front of a gray two-story house with white shutters and a blood-red front door. His father's house. Two doors away, in the white house with the black front door, had lived his stepmother's closest friend, Kathy, the one who had seduced him when he was barely fourteen years old. "You're a very bad boy," he could hear her coo in his ear. "Your stepmother is right about you." And then, when they were lying naked in her queen-size bed and she was directing him where to put his hands and how to use his tongue, listening to the strange noises she made and the husky sound of her voice as she whispered, "Tell me you love me," and clawed at his back with her long fingernails. And he'd complied, telling her he loved her over and over again, maybe even meaning it, he thought now, who knows? And then one day, two years after the start of their affair, he'd come home from school to find a large FOR SALE sign in the middle of her front lawn, and several months later, that sign had been replaced by another one that said SOLD, and the following month the moving van had arrived and she was gone, moved to Ann Arbor with her husband and two young daughters for her husband's new job.

Jeff never saw her again.

And he'd never said "I love you" to any woman again.

Until tonight.

What's the matter with you? he thought now, feeling Kathy's wicked laugh trembling through his body as his eyes left the upstairs bedroom window of her former house to flit up the narrow, flower-lined concrete walkway of his father's home. What was he doing here? Was he really thinking of proceeding up that walkway, of climbing the steps to the small front porch, of knocking on that red front door? Had he lost his mind altogether? What was the matter with him?

Well, well. The prodigal son returns, he could almost hear his father say as Jeff forced one foot in front of the other. Hell, he thought. It had cost him a lot of money to come to Buffalo, money he could ill afford now that he was out of a job. He'd made the trip at his sister's behest, come to see the mother who'd abandoned him as a small boy. Why not pay a visit to the father who'd abandoned him emotionally at around the same time?

Two for the price of one; kill two birds with one stone, Jeff thought ruefully, looking toward the living room window. He pictured his father and stepmother inside, his father buried behind a book, his stepmother immersed in her sewing. How will they react when they see me? he wondered as he lifted his hand and knocked on the door.

The noise echoed down the quiet tree-lined street, conjuring up years of indifference and neglect. Jeff felt the years swirl like leaves around his head.

No one answered his knock, although Jeff thought he heard someone moving around inside. Just turn around and go back to the motel, he told himself, even as he was lifting his hand to knock again, the knocking assuming greater urgency as his fist slammed repeatedly against the heavy wooden door.

Reluctant footsteps approached. "What's the matter?" a woman's voice snarled from inside. "You forget your keys at your girlfriend's?" The door opened. His stepmother stood on the other side, her expression modulating from anger to surprise to dismay and then to outright horror. "Oh, my God," she said, collapsing against the side of the door as if Jeff had surprised her with a sucker punch. "My son . . . ," she cried out.

Jeff was about to reach for her, to take her in his grateful arms, hug her to his chest, tell her all was forgiven, that there was still time to make things right between them.

"Oh, God. What's happened?" his stepmother demanded. "Was there an accident? Is he all right?"

It took Jeff a few seconds to digest that the son she was referring to was not him but Will. Of course, he thought, his arms withdrawing, his body stiffening as it turned to ice. "There's nothing wrong with Will," he told her, his voice flat. "He's fine, having the time of his life, in fact."

His stepmother pulled herself up to her full height, cool blue eyes narrowing. She was almost five feet ten inches tall, even in the ratty pink slippers she was wearing. An imposing presence no matter how casually she was dressed, Jeff thought, noting that her raven hair was streaked with gray at the temples, giving her a vaguely skunk-like appearance, not helped by her narrow face and almost nonexistent upper lip. Not the most generous of assessments, Jeff knew, aware she'd been considered something of a beauty in her prime, but then, what the hell? His moment of generosity had passed. "I don't understand. Why are you here?" she asked, tugging the sides of her pale green terry-cloth housecoat tight around her.

"My mother's dying," Jeff said simply. "Ellie says she only has a few days left."

"I'm sorry to hear that," his stepmother said, managing to sound as if she meant it. "Did you want to come in? I'm afraid your father's not here. . . ."

Jeff's lips curled into a smile as he recalled her greeting from the other side of the door. *What's the matter? You forget your keys at your girlfriend's?* "Nice to see some things never change."

"You look just like him, you know. It's really quite uncanny."

"So I've been told." Jeff bristled and turned away. "You ever hear from Kathy?" he heard himself ask, his eyes returning to the house two doors down.

"Kathy? You mean Kathy Chapin? Why on earth would you ask about her?"

"Just curious."

"We lost touch years ago. Why?" she asked again.

"No reason."

They stared at each other in silence for several seconds. "Why don't you come inside?" she suggested again. "I could put on a pot of coffee. Who knows–your father might just surprise us and come home early."

"Not much chance of that." Jeff retreated down the front steps, wondering if his stepmother's newfound compassion was the result of genuine concern or if she was simply tired of being alone.

"Tell Will to phone his mother every now and then," she called after him.

"I'll do that," Jeff said without looking back.

TWENTY-SIX

WHAT A STRANGE DAY this has turned out to be, Kristin was thinking as she stripped off the last of her clothes and pulled the covers from her bed. It had started with one phone call and ended with another, a series of lies uneasily filling the space in between. Was Jeff really in Buffalo, as he'd claimed, or was this yet another falsehood? He'd been so adamant about not going home to see his mother. What had happened to change his mind?

Kristin crawled between the cool white sheets, quickly flipping from her right side to her left, replaying their earlier conversation in her head. "I'll explain everything as soon as I get back," he'd said.

Explain what exactly?

And that cryptic message regarding Suzy. *If Suzy shows up at the bar, just get Will to take her to the apartment, and don't tell anyone where she is.* What was that all about? Had Suzy contacted him yet again? Had something happened to make Jeff fear for her immediate safety? Whatever it was, Kristin decided, settling onto her back and staring up at the ceiling, Suzy hadn't come by the bar. Nor had she called. So what was really going on? And should she call Suzy, demand to know exactly what was happening? She didn't like being kept in the dark. She didn't like not knowing where things stood.

One thing she knew for sure: Jeff had won his bet. He and Suzy were now lovers; of that she was certain. She'd known it was a done deal the moment *69 had informed her it was Suzy who'd called their apartment at six thirty yesterday morning.

Something else she knew: Jeff might have won his bet, but he'd lost his heart.

More like his mind, Kristin decided with a laugh, thinking it was unlike her to be so melodramatic. She flipped back onto her right side, brought her knees to her chest, unable to find a comfortable position.

So how did she really feel about this latest development? Was she upset or hurt? Was she afraid of being abandoned? She sighed, long and deep. The truth was that she'd known almost from the minute she and Jeff had said hello that it was only a matter of time before he said good-bye. Even as she was moving in, she'd felt him starting to mentally move out, and she'd been okay with that. She understood the instinct for self-preservation that made him keep her—keep all women—at an emotional arm's length, just as she understood instinctively that no matter how good she was to him or how much freedom she allowed him, eventually he'd grow restless and seek out new challenges, and that sooner or later, he'd find someone to replace her. Especially if that someone played her cards right, if she was vaguely mysterious, made him work hard to get her attention while simultaneously appealing to his masculine ego by making him feel needed.

Kristin had never been especially mysterious or challenging. She'd certainly never been very good at making men feel needed.

Amazing the power of the damsel in distress, she thought now, knowing intuitively that it was the men with the most tarnished self-images who made the best knights in shining armor. But smart as she was, she'd never considered the possibility Jeff might actually fall in love.

Or that his feelings might be reciprocated.

This was something she hadn't considered.

Is it possible? Kristin wondered, her eyes opening wide, penetrating the surrounding darkness.

Where exactly would that leave her?

She heard footsteps in the hall outside her door, the creak of the bathroom door as Will opened and closed it after him. Seconds later, she heard the flush of the toilet and the sound of water running in the sink. She imagined Will, his hair falling into the half-closed eyes of his tired, puzzled face, as he washed his hands and brushed his teeth. When she'd told him of Jeff's phone call—the fact that he'd gone to Buffalo, his instructions regarding Suzy—he'd simply shrugged and ordered another beer. He'd said nothing, although she'd noted his eyes were glued to the bar's front door all night, as if he was waiting for Suzy to walk through. She wondered how he really felt about his brother and Suzy. Kristin suspected he was as confused by what was happening as she was.

Whatever was going on inside him, he wasn't sharing any of those feelings with her. Will had feigned sleep in the car on the drive back from the bar and collapsed on the sofa bed fully clothed as soon as they'd entered the apartment. When she'd asked him if he felt like some hot chocolate or a piece of the apple pie she'd picked up at Publix that afternoon, he hadn't even bothered to grunt out a reply, although she could tell by the stiff arc of his shoulders that he wasn't asleep.

She doubted that either of them would get much sleep tonight.

Seconds later, Kristin heard the bathroom door open, and she lay there, waiting for the sound of Will's retreating footsteps. But it never came. She sat up in bed. "Will?" she called through the closed bedroom door.

Nothing.

"Will," she called again, gathering her sheets around her as the bedroom door slowly opened.

"Did I wake you?" he asked from the hallway.

"No."

"Having trouble sleeping?"

"Having trouble *falling* asleep," she corrected him.

"Me, too."

"Do you want some hot chocolate?" she asked, as she'd asked earlier.

"No."

"Are you okay?"

"Yeah. You?"

"Yeah. Just can't sleep. Too many thoughts."

"What kind of thoughts?"

"I don't know. They're all pretty vague," she lied.

"Maybe you're just not used to sleeping alone," Will said.

"Maybe."

A moment's silence, then, "Can I come in a minute?"

"Sure. Just give me a second to put something on." Kristin reached for the pink silk robe that lay at the foot of the bed and quickly wrapped it around her. "Okay. You can come in now."

Will pushed open the bedroom door and took several tentative steps inside the room. "It's freezing in here," he remarked, hugging his arms to his sides.

"Jeff likes it pretty cold when he sleeps." Kristin noted that Will was still wearing the blue button-down shirt and khaki slacks he'd had on earlier, although his feet were bare.

"What about what *you* like?" he asked.

"I guess I've gotten used to it."

Will moved cautiously into the room, his eyes still not adjusted to the dark. "Uh-oh. I just stepped on something." He bent down, scooped up several items of discarded clothing. Kristin's black push-up bra dangled limply from his right hand. "Sorry. I think I may have killed it."

Kristin laughed. "That's all right. I don't need it anyway. One of the benefits of having plastic breasts." She patted the space beside her on the bed. "Come sit down."

"Should I turn on a light?"

"If you want."

"I don't, really."

"Good. I washed my face. Definitely not a pretty sight."

"You're crazy. I already told you I think you look better without makeup." He perched at the edge of the bed.

Kristin felt the bed sag to accommodate him. She saw his eyes reach through the darkness toward hers. "Thank you. You're very sweet."

"It's the truth. And I'm not sweet."

"I think you are."

"Maybe in comparison to Jeff. . . ."

They were silent for several seconds.

"You want to talk about it?" Kristin asked.

"About what?"

"About what's happening with Jeff and Suzy."

"What's happening with Jeff and Suzy?" Will repeated, turning the statement into a question.

"I'm not sure."

"Yes, you are."

"Yes, I am," Kristin agreed.

"You think they're sleeping together," Will stated.

"Yes."

"You weren't sure this afternoon."

"I'm sure now," she told him.

"Why? What's changed?"

"Jeff."

"I don't understand. Did he tell you they were sleeping together?"

"No."

"So, how—"

"I just know."

"Female intuition?"

"It was his voice," Kristin said after a brief pause.

"His voice?" Will repeated.

"On the phone. The way he said Suzy's name. It was just . . . different."

"Different?"

"They're sleeping together, Will," Kristin said.

Will leaned forward, rested his elbows on his knees, his chin in the palms of his hands. "Yeah," he agreed.

"Try not to take it personally," she advised him after another moment's pause. "I don't."

Will swiveled his head toward her. "How can you not take it personally? Your boyfriend is sleeping with another woman."

"It's really no big deal."

"I *really* don't believe you."

This time it was Kristin who shrugged. "Fine. Don't believe me."

"I think he's crazy," Will said. "To cheat on someone like you."

"He's Jeff," Kristin said. He's a man, she thought.

"I'd never do something like that."

"No?"

"Not if I had somebody like you."

"You don't know me very well, Will."

"I think I do."

"What do you know?"

"I know what I see."

"And just what is it you see when you look at me?" Kristin asked, suddenly needing to know. "Beyond the fake boobs and the dyed blond hair and the false eyelashes? Tell me what you see." She saw Will's eyes travel across the planes of her face.

"I see a woman with a beautiful soul," Will said.

"You see my soul?" Kristin tried to laugh, but the laugh caught in her throat and her eyes stung with tears.

"I've upset you." Will's fingers fluttered toward her face, stopping when they got close. "I'm sorry."

Kristin covered her mouth with her hand. "I think that's probably the sweetest thing anybody's ever said to me."

"Sweet," Will repeated, his hand dropping into his lap. "That word again."

"Nothing wrong with being sweet, Will."

"Except I'm not."

"And I don't have a beautiful soul."

"I think you do."

"Then like I said, you don't know me very well."

"I know all I have to know," Will insisted.

"No," Kristin said, taking his right hand in hers and lifting it to her breasts. "I'm a human Barbie doll, Will. Plastic from the toes up."

"No," he said, his fingers trembling.

"They're fake, Will. I'm fake."

"I can feel your heart pounding. Don't tell me that isn't real."

She shook her head. "It isn't important," she said.

"You don't believe that."

Kristin loosened her silk robe, took Will's hand, moved it across her bare breasts. "You want to know what I feel when you touch me here?" she asked, guiding his fingers from one nipple to the other. "Nothing," she answered before he could respond. "I don't feel anything. You know why? Because all the nerves were damaged by the surgery. So my breasts look great—hell, they look fantastic—but I don't feel a whole lot. Don't get me wrong," she added quickly. "I'm not complaining. It's fine by me. I consider it more than a fair trade. I learned a long time ago that feelings are way overrated."

"You don't feel anything when I touch you?" Will asked, his hand now moving on its own, gently massaging first one breast, then the other.

"Not really," Kristin said, trying to ignore the slight stirring between her legs.

"How about here?" Will leaned forward to kiss the side of her neck.

Kristin heard a moan escape her lips as Will's tongue brushed against her ear.

"Or here?" His lips touched down tenderly on hers.

"Remind me to get my lips done," she said hoarsely.

"Don't you dare do anything to these lips. They're beautiful. You're beautiful."

"I'm not," she insisted.

"Tell me you don't feel anything now," he said, pushing her robe away from her shoulders, his mouth replacing his hands on her breasts.

"I don't feel anything," she whispered, unconvincing even to her own ears, as she arched her back to accommodate his lips.

"What about now?" His fingers traced a line from her belly button to her pubis, disappearing between her legs.

Kristin groaned, a mixture of both pleasure and recognition. Despite her best efforts, she found herself comparing Will's tentative advances to his brother's more assured touch. And soon, an unwanted image began tugging at her brain. In her mind's eye, she saw Jeff with Suzy, felt his deft hands on her bruised flesh, his expert tongue seeking out the folds of her most tender places even as she felt Will's tongue teasing at her own. No, she thought, shaking her head from side to side in an effort to rid her mind of such images, the thought taking shape and acquiring sound, becoming a word. "No," she said as she felt Will fumbling with his zipper. "No," she said louder as she pushed him away. "No," she said, crying as she gathered her robe around her and sobbed into the palms of her hands. "I can't," she said. "I'm sorry. I just can't."

"It's okay," she heard Will say, his voice small, as unsteady as her own. "I'm the one who should be apologizing to you."

"No. I'm the one who—"

"You didn't do anything."

"I tried to seduce you," she admitted.

"Why do you think I came in here?" he asked.

They laughed, although the laugh was one of shared recognition rather than of joy. "I just kept picturing the two of them together," she said, pushing her hair away from her face, digging her long fingernails into her scalp, as if trying to physically remove all such images.

"My brother's an idiot," Will said, pushing himself to his feet.

"Agreed."

"Guess we have that in common, at least."

"You're not an idiot, Will."

"And I'm not my brother," Will acknowledged sadly.

You're better than he is, Kristin was about to say. But before she could form the words, Will was gone.

HE WALKED INTO the kitchen, made himself a cup of instant coffee. What the hell? He wouldn't be getting any sleep tonight anyway. Will sucked the aromatic steam into his nostrils as his fingers wrapped around the cheap ceramic mug, a pink flamingo emblazoned on its side, its handle the crooked leg of the ungainly, yet beautiful, bird. WELCOME TO MIAMI was scrawled in bold black cursive lettering across the bottom.

Welcome to the Wild Zone, Will thought.

Proceed at your own risk.

Which I did, he thought with a shake of his head. And was shot down in flames.

Will took a sip of coffee, felt it burn the tip of his tongue. Even that did nothing to diminish the taste of Kristin on his lips. He took another sip, letting it scald the entire cavity of his mouth. Served him right for being such a jerk, he thought, for thinking he could be a stand-in for his brother. His older, *better* brother, he thought bitterly. "What's the matter with me?" he asked out loud.

What's the matter with you? his father had demanded when he'd been suspended from Princeton after the pathetic episode with Amy.

What's the matter with you? his mother had echoed. *Who do you think you are, acting like that—your brother?*

No chance of that, Will thought now, returning to the living room and grabbing the TV's remote control from the ottoman as he sank down on the sofa. Kristin's rejection had proven to him once and for all that he was no substitute for the real thing.

The Chosen One, he scoffed, recalling Jeff and Tom's derisive nickname for him as a child.

Except if he was truly the chosen one, why were women always choosing someone else?

Someone like Jeff.

He flipped through the channels until he came to a movie starring Clint Eastwood, one of those great old spaghetti westerns where Clint, the Man with No Name, prowled the barren terrain wearing a Mexican serape and a withering squint, not saying much, just shooting anything that got in his way. Will turned the volume down so that the sound of gunfire wouldn't bother Kristin. No point in disturbing her any more than he had already. Seconds later he watched as Clint raised his gun into the air, smirking with satisfaction as he pointed it directly at his enemy's head and calmly pulled the trigger.

He thought of Tom's gun, wondered idly where Kristin had hidden it. He wondered what it would be like to shoot another human being. He fell asleep to the sound of bullets whizzing past his head.

TWENTY-SEVEN

JEFF WOKE UP TO the sound of screaming outside his window.

"Quiet!" a woman yelled immediately. "Joey, stop hitting your sister!"

"She hit me first!"

"Did not. He's lying."

"Both of you, stop it. Be quiet. People are still sleeping. Now get in the car."

The sound of car doors opening and slamming shut. Jeff propped himself up on one elbow and glanced at the clock radio beside his bed, noting that it was barely seven a.m. He sat up, pushing the bedsheets to the floor to join the quilted bedspread he'd kicked off sometime during the night and catching sight of his reflection in the shell-framed mirror over the dresser. I look awful, he thought, wiping the sweat from his bare chest. The heat of the approaching day was already combining with the leftover stuffiness of the night. It was going to be a real scorcher, he thought, climbing out of bed and heading for the bathroom.

He ran the shower, was disappointed to discover that the water pressure was flagging at best, dripping from the showerhead in an uninspired stream. Apparently the motel's nautical theme didn't extend to the plumbing, Jeff thought, trying to work some lather out of the thin, round bar of white soap. He positioned himself directly under the showerhead, letting the tepid water drip down his face and into his ears. In the distance, "The Star-Spangled Banner" began to play.

It took Jeff a few seconds to realize it was the sound of his ringtone. Shit, he thought, grabbing a thin white towel and wrapping it around his torso as he raced back into the main room, scrambling to recover his phone from the pocket of his black jeans. "Suzy?" he shouted into the receiver, even before the phone was fully opened.

But the call had already been transferred to voice mail. "Damn it," he said, slapping his wet thigh with the palm of his hand, silently berating himself for not having taken the phone with him into the bathroom.

"You have one new message," his voice mail informed him seconds later. "To listen to your message, press one-one."

Jeff pressed in the numbers, waited for the sound of Suzy's voice. "Jeff, it's Ellie," his sister said instead. "Please call me as soon as you can."

"Shit." Jeff threw the phone onto the bed, ran his hand through his wet hair. His stepmother had probably called Ellie to tell her of his surprising late-night visit. *You mean he didn't call you to tell you he was in town?* he could almost hear her say as he reached for the phone, his hand freezing in midair. He'd be seeing his sister soon enough, he decided. He'd explain everything then.

Half an hour later he was sitting in McDonald's, sipping on his second cup of coffee and chewing unenthusiastically on an Egg McMuffin, wondering again what he was doing in Buffalo and repeatedly checking his phone for messages he knew weren't there. He pushed aside his tray, then crumpled his paper napkin into a ball and let it drop from his fingers to the table, where he watched it unfold like a parachute and float to the floor. He bent over, scooped it up, then smoothed it out, wondering how much more time he could waste before going to the hospital to see his mother. She's dying, for God's sake, he told himself. What was he so afraid of? How much more damage could she possibly do?

He glanced toward the window, saw a booth full of teenage girls eating French fries and giggling. One of the girls—curly brown hair, pink button lips, green and white checkered skirt hitched up around her thighs—kept looking his way. He watched as she extricated one of the fries from its red cardboard package and lifted it provocatively to her mouth, pushing it slowly between her lips. If Tom were here, he'd probably bet Jeff on how long it would take him to get his hand up that silly girl's skirt. Does your mother know what you're up to? Jeff wondered, staring at the girl until she blushed a deep, embarrassed crimson and turned away. He finished the last of his coffee and pushed himself to his feet. Ultimately, he thought, and almost laughed, it all came down to mothers.

It was after eight o'clock by the time he reached Mercy. The hospital had been constructed in 1911 and looked every one of its almost one hundred years. True, a glass and marble wing had been added to the mustard-yellow brick main building since Jeff had last seen it, but the cream-colored marble was already scarred with graffiti, and the glass was stained with soot and neglect. It looked as tired as he felt, Jeff thought, pushing his feet up the half-dozen front steps as if his legs were encased in cement.

"Can you tell me what room Diane Rydell is in?" Jeff asked the receptionist at the information desk in the middle of the front lobby.

"Room 314," the woman said without looking up. "Third floor, east wing. Turn right when you get off the elevator." Without raising her head, she pointed toward a bank of elevators next to a small gift shop down the hall.

"Thank you." Jeff wondered if he should buy his mother some flowers or maybe a magazine and was glad the gift shop was still closed so he didn't have to decide. He hadn't bought her anything since he was a child, he remembered, picturing the bottle of perfume he'd purchased from the drugstore for her birthday one year. He'd saved up his allowance for months to buy the pretty star-shaped bottle, only to watch his mother sniff at it disdainfully, then push it aside. "His father probably helped him pick it out," he'd heard her complain to one of her friends over the phone later that night. "Smells like one of his whores."

"Okay, don't do this," he muttered into the collar of his black shirt. Not now, he continued silently. He hadn't come all this way to reopen old wounds. There was nothing either of them could do about the past. It was what it was, and the good thing about the past was that it was over. Yes, his mother had made mistakes. Plenty of them. And maybe it had taken her all her life to realize how wrong she'd been, that it had been cruel and selfish to abandon him, but she realized it now, and she was truly sorry for everything she'd done. *Please forgive me,* he heard her beg, her dying eyes filling with tears of regret. *I love you. I've always loved you.*

What would he do? Jeff wondered, proceeding cautiously down the hall as if navigating a dense fog. Would he be able to say it back?

Would he be able to take her frail hand in his and look into those pleading eyes and lie to her, tell her that yes, despite everything, he loved her, too? Could he do that?

And would it really be a lie?

Jeff found himself holding his breath, as if trying to block out the unpleasant combination of hospital odors, the smell of antiseptic vying for control over the smell of the sick, he thought, as he stepped into a waiting elevator and pressed the button for the third floor. Before the doors could shut, four more people suddenly hurried inside, including a young man whose name tag on his white coat identified him as Dr. Wang. He looks barely out of his teens, Jeff thought, remembering that when he was a little boy, he'd had dreams of becoming a doctor. Maybe with a little encouragement . . . Or maybe not, he decided, remembering he'd also had dreams of becoming a fireman and an acrobat. He released the air in his lungs as the elevator opened onto the third floor, and he stepped out, turning right as he'd been directed and proceeding down the hall until he came to room 314.

He stopped in front of the closed door, trying to gather his thoughts as he looked up and down the empty hall. I should have called Ellie, he was thinking, made arrangements to meet her here. Then they could have gone in together. He wouldn't have had to face his mother alone.

"Don't be stupid," he whispered under his breath. She's dying, for God's sake. She can't hurt you anymore.

He took a deep breath, releasing it slowly as he pushed open the door, trying to arrange his features into an impassive mask as he stepped inside the room. "She doesn't look anything like you remember," he recalled Ellie telling him during an earlier phone conversation. "You can hardly recognize her anymore. She's lost so much weight, and her skin is almost transparent."

Jeff braced himself for what he was about to see, concentrating on a square of vinyl flooring as he tried mustering his strength. Only after several seconds and a few more deep breaths was he able to raise his eyes from the floor.

The bed was empty.

Jeff stood there for a minute, not moving, not sure what to do.

Of course, there'd been a mistake. Either the woman at the front desk had given him the wrong room number, or he'd pushed open the wrong door. But even as he was returning to the hall to check on the room number, even as he was hurrying down the corridor to the nurses' station, even as he was asking the pretty, dark-skinned nurse to tell him where he could find Diane Rydell, even as he was pondering the highly improbable possibility that Ellie might have registered their mother under another name or taken her to another hospital, he knew that the information he'd been given was correct, that no mistake had been made.

"I'm so sorry," the nurse was telling him. "Mrs. Rydell passed this morning."

Passed? Jeff thought. What do you mean, she *passed*? Passed *what*? "What are you saying?" Jeff demanded impatiently, taking an involuntary step back as the true meaning of the euphemism sank in. "You're saying she died?"

"At around five thirty this morning," the nurse elaborated, a look of concern flashing through her deep brown eyes. "I'm sorry. You are . . . ?"

"Jeff Rydell."

"You're related?"

"I'm her son," Jeff said quietly.

"I'm sorry. I didn't realize she had a son," the nurse said.

"I live in Florida," Jeff told her. "I flew in last night."

"I've met your sister, of course."

"Ellie. Is she here?" Jeff's eyes shot down the long corridor.

"She was here earlier. I believe she went home to make some arrangements."

Jeff suddenly felt his knees buckle, and he grabbed for the counter to keep from falling down.

"Oh, dear," the nurse said, running around to the front of the station. "Are you all right? Sandra, get me a cup of water. Right now. Here you go," she said seconds later as she directed Jeff to the nearest chair and lifted a paper cup filled with water to his lips. "Just sip on this. Slowly. How's that? Are you all right?"

Jeff nodded.

"I guess it's always a shock," the nurse was saying. "No matter how old our parents get or how sick they are. We still don't expect them to die."

So that's why Ellie had called him this morning. Not because his stepmother had called her, but because their mother had died. Ellie didn't even know he was in Buffalo. He jumped to his feet. He had to call her.

"Whoa, steady," the nurse said, her hand on his elbow, guiding him back to his chair. "I think you should just sit here for a while. Why don't you let me call your sister, tell her you're here."

It was more statement than request, and Jeff felt himself nod his agreement. From his seat against the wall in the hospital corridor, he heard the nurse talking to his sister. "Yes, of course I'm sure. He's right here in front of me. He seems pretty shaken up," he thought he heard her say. "Yes, I'll keep him here until you get here."

And then his mind went blank. Conscious thoughts were replaced by a series of pictures, as if he were watching a television with the sound turned off. He saw himself as a young boy, walking happily beside his mother, his hand tucked securely inside hers as they went from store to store in a large discount mall. That image was quickly supplanted by another—his mother tenderly combing his hair. And then another—his mother kissing the scrape on his knee after he fell off his new bicycle. One picture after another, cascading like discarded photographs across his line of vision: his mother, young and healthy, laughing and vibrant, loving and attentive.

And then more pictures, tumbling like cards from a well-worn deck: his mother pacing beside the phone and sobbing into her pillow, her hands shooing him away when he tried to comfort her; his mother's swollen eyes and twisted, angry mouth, refusing the breakfast he'd brought to her bed; his mother, sad and defeated, crying and deflated, impatient and indifferent.

His mother packing his suitcase and sending him away.

"It's just that he reminds me so much of his father," Jeff heard her say, as if someone had suddenly turned on the sound of the imaginary TV. "I swear they have the same damn face."

No, stop it. I'm not my father.

The volume getting louder. "And I can't help it, but every time I look at him, I just want to strangle him. I know it's irrational. I know it's not his fault. But I just can't stand looking at him."

No. Please stop.

"I just need some time to myself, to figure out what's best for me."

What about what's best for me?

"What about Ellie?" Jeff heard his younger self ask instead. "Is she going to Daddy's?"

"No," his mother replied flatly. "Ellie stays with me."

"Jeff," a voice was saying now. "Jeff? Are you all right?"

The TV set in Jeff's head went suddenly blank.

"Jeff?" the voice said again. Gentle fingers touched his hand.

"Ellie," Jeff said, his sister's face coming into focus in front of him. She was crouching in front of him, her face older and fuller than he remembered it, her hair a less flattering shade of blond, her gray-green eyes ringed with red. She was wearing a light blue sleeveless blouse and Jeff noted the freckled flesh that hung loose on the undersides of her arms.

"You should do something about that," he said absently. There were all sorts of exercises he could recommend.

"Do something about what?"

"What?" he asked, raising his eyes back to her face.

"Are you okay?"

"Yeah."

"You don't seem okay."

"Just tired."

"When did you get here?" Ellie asked.

"Last night."

"Last night! Why didn't you call me?"

"It was late," Jeff lied. In truth, he didn't know why he hadn't called her. "Maybe I wanted to surprise you."

"Maybe you just weren't sure you'd go through with it."

Jeff didn't have to ask Ellie what she was referring to. "Maybe."

"You want some coffee?"

"Already had plenty."

"Me, too. Maybe we could just go somewhere and sit down." Her knees cracked as she pushed herself out of her crouching position.

A few minutes later, they found themselves in their mother's empty room, Ellie perched on the side of the freshly made hospital bed, Jeff standing at the window, looking out at the street below. "So, what happened exactly?" Jeff asked.

"Her heart just gave out, I guess."

"What do the doctors say?"

"Not much. I mean, what *can* they say? It wasn't exactly a surprise. The cancer had pretty much taken over. She'd been in and out of consciousness for the last few days. Her heart was getting weaker by the minute. When I was here yesterday, her skin had taken on that horrible gray pallor. I knew she wouldn't last much longer."

And suddenly Jeff was laughing, loud and long.

"Jeff? What is it? What's going on?"

"The bitch just couldn't wait, could she?" he said.

"What?"

"She couldn't wait one fucking more day."

"What are you talking about?"

"A few fucking hours," Jeff said.

"You think she did this deliberately? That she died on purpose before you could get here?"

Jeff threw his head back and laughed even louder than before. "I wouldn't put it past her."

"You're talking crazy."

"She just couldn't pass up the chance to screw with me one more time."

"That's not true. You know it isn't. She'd been asking for you for weeks. She wanted to see you so badly. She kept hoping you'd come."

"Then why didn't she wait? Tell me that."

"She didn't have a choice, Jeff."

"Of course she had a choice. She always had a choice. Like when she chose to give me up, when she chose to keep you, when she chose to forget I even existed. . . ."

"She never forgot about you, Jeff."

"She knew that sooner or later, I'd show up. She just couldn't be bothered waiting. I wasn't worth the effort."

"That's not true."

"So she abandoned me all over again. The final slap in the face. This time from the grave. Way to go, Mother. I've got to hand it to you. Nobody does it better. You're still the champ." Jeff sensed his sister approaching from behind, felt her hands on the sides of his arms. He flinched and pulled away. "Where is she anyway?"

"They took her to the funeral parlor. We can go there, if you'd like. You can see her, say good-bye."

"Thanks, but I think I'll pass." He laughed again.

"What?"

"The nurse at the station said she'd *passed*. Like she'd passed her driving test or something."

"It's just an expression, Jeff. I guess she thought it was gentler than saying she was dead."

"Hey, dead is dead, no matter how you say it. So, what happens now?"

"We go home, finalize the funeral arrangements. I was thinking of Friday. I don't see any point in dragging it out any longer than that, do you? She didn't have many friends. . . ."

"I'm shocked," Jeff said, his voice a sneer. "And no, by all means, the sooner we put her in the ground, the better."

"You'll stay at my house," Ellie said. "Kirsten, too, if she's coming."

This time Jeff didn't bother to correct her. Kirsten, Kristin—what difference did it make? "She isn't."

"Just as well. This way the kids will have you all to themselves for a few days."

"They won't even know who I am," Jeff said.

"Then it's high time you did something about that."

Jeff swiveled around to face his sister. He saw the sadness in her eyes and understood for the first time that the mother she'd lost was a different woman entirely from the mother he'd never really known. "Okay," he said.

Ellie's face flushed pink with relief. Tears of gratitude filled her eyes. "Good. I'll call Bob, tell him we're on our way home."

"Why don't I just meet you there? I have to go back to the motel, pack my suitcase. . . ."

"You brought a suitcase?"

"You know me."

"I'd like to," she said.

"You go on, finish making whatever arrangements are necessary," he told her. "I'll go back to the motel, take a shower, pack up my things, and be at your house in an hour."

"You promise?"

"I promise."

"I love you," Ellie said, her voice breaking.

Jeff took his sister in his arms and hugged her while she cried.

An hour later, he was sitting in the airport lounge, his head lowered into his chest, images of Suzy filling his brain, when "The Star-Spangled Banner" began to play. He reached into his pocket, pulled out his phone, and checked his caller ID, hoping it was Suzy but knowing it was Ellie, calling to see what was keeping him.

He thought of answering it, but then, what could he say? That he'd had a change of heart? That he'd been lying all along? Surely Ellie had suspected as much. She could have insisted on accompanying him to the motel. She could have refused to let him out of her sight, knowing there was a good chance he would turn and run. Instead, she'd chosen the easy way out. Her mother's daughter after all.

Saying "I love you" had been her way of saying good-bye.

Jeff stared at the phone until the anthem stopped playing, then returned it to his pocket. He settled comfortably back in his seat, closing his eyes as he lowered his head to his chest, and went back to dreaming about Suzy.

TWENTY-EIGHT

TOM OPENED HIS EYES to the darkness of the late afternoon. Not that it was dark outside. It wasn't. But with the living room drapes pulled tightly shut, it might as well have been the middle of the night. He laid his head back against the floral pillows of the sofa, kicking off his sneakers and stretching his legs out to their full length, ultimately bringing them to rest on top of the wood and glass coffee table in front of him. His right foot—wearing the same navy blue sock he'd been wearing for two days now—knocked against a bottle he'd forgotten was there, sending it crashing to the floor. The smell of spilled beer immediately filled his nostrils. It combined with the sickly sweet odor of marijuana and the discarded cigarette butts that lined the floor, marking his territory like a bunch of tiny pebbles. "What the hell are you doing?" he scolded himself in Lainey's voice. "This place is a pigsty, for God's sake. Clean it up."

Tom laughed. "I'm just getting started, bitch," he shouted at the dark room, this time the voice his own. "Wait till you see the bedroom." He laughed again, his eyes lifting toward the ceiling as he lit another joint, his mind returning to last night. What a night that had been!

He grabbed for the half-drunk bottle of beer in his lap and finished it off in one prolonged gulp. How many did that make? he wondered, trying to add up the number of beers he'd had since this morning. Make that since last night, he amended, since he hadn't slept in at least twenty-four hours and he'd started drinking at around seven p.m.—not counting the two beers he'd had on the way home from work. He dropped the empty bottle to the floor, took a deep drag off the joint, and reached for the phone on the small table next to the sofa, his hand slapping against the lamp and almost knocking it over. Tom turned his head lazily to one side, watching the lamp wobble precariously before righting itself, then he rested the phone on his chest and punched in the number he still remembered from last night. Yes, sir, he thought. Last night was some night.

"Venus Milo's Escort Service," a soft voice purred into his ear. "This is Chloe. How can I help you?"

Tom curled his arms around the receiver, feeling himself grow hard at the memory of the girl the escort service had sent over the previous night. "Hi, you," the curly-haired cutie had said in greeting, stepping inside the small foyer and quickly removing the flimsy sweater covering her enormous implants. "I'm Ginny. I understand you like to party."

"I'd like to order a girl," Tom told Chloe now.

"You'd like to hire an escort?" Chloe corrected him gently.

"Yeah. Maybe Asian, for a change." Tom remembered hearing that Asian girls were usually more submissive than Americans. "Is that a problem?"

"No problem at all. When were you thinking of?"

"I'm thinking of right now."

"Right now," Chloe repeated. "Where are you located?"

"Morningside."

"Okay, that's easy enough. Let me see if I have anything. Can I put you on hold for a minute?"

"Not for too long," Tom cautioned, picturing Ginny naked and squirming underneath him.

"Okay, I think I might have somebody for you," Chloe said, coming back on the line approximately a minute later. "Her name is Ling. She's originally from Taiwan, and she can be at your place in about forty minutes. How does that sound?"

"Sounds good."

"That will be three hundred dollars an hour, and you understand we are an escort service only. Anything you negotiate with Ling beyond that is strictly between the two of you."

"Oh, I understand all right."

"Good. I'll just need your name and credit card number."

"Tom Whitman," he said, fishing into his jeans for his credit card, about to rattle off the numbers on his card when Chloe stopped him.

"I'm sorry," she said, the softness in her voice instantly hardening, turning to steel. "Tom Whitman, you said?"

"That's right. Is there a problem?"

"I'm afraid we won't be able to fulfill your request at this time, Mr. Whitman. I suggest you take your business elsewhere. Or better yet, get professional help."

"What do you think I'm trying to fucking do here?"

"Good-bye, Mr. Whitman," Chloe said before hanging up.

"Wait a minute! What are you– What the hell . . . ? Shit!" Tom jumped to his feet, mashing the cigarette butts beneath his toes and almost tripping over the recently discarded beer bottle. "Did you just fire me, bitch?" What the hell was going on? First that little prick Carter at work, telling him his services were no longer required, that smug look on his stupid face when he'd told Tom a number of customers and even a coworker had been complaining about his attitude, then handed Tom his severance check without even giving Tom a chance to explain or defend himself. Not that he would have, in any event. "I've given you every chance to improve yourself," Carter had said.

Was it any wonder Tom had taken a swipe at him, missing his nose but succeeding in knocking his glasses to the floor and then stepping on them for good measure, before being escorted, none too gently either–he should file a complaint with the human rights commission–off the premises by a security guard? And now this glorified cocksucker from the escort service informing him she wouldn't be able to fulfill his request, that he should take his business elsewhere, that he should get professional help!

It was that bitch Ginny's fault. Ginny with the big tits and the mouthful of expensive veneers. He should have knocked them out of her stupid mouth, he thought, his right hand forming a fist and grinding the joint he'd been dangling between his fingers into scraggly greenish-brown dust, letting the loose pieces of marijuana fall to the carpet like dirty snow. She'd obviously run crying to the powers that be. Goddamn amateur. He'd paid her, hadn't he? And still she'd complained about everything. Didn't like being tied up; refused to take it up the ass; wasn't "into pain." Damn cunt–he should have blown her bloody head off.

Now what? Tom thought, heading for the kitchen and searching through the cupboards for where Lainey kept the phone book, opening one drawer after another in his search. It was just like Lainey to hide it from him. He emptied one drawer of paper napkins and another filled with placemats and once neatly folded tablecloths. Cutlery was thrown to the floor, plates shattered. It was only after every cabinet had been emptied and Tom stood ankle-deep in detritus that he stopped. Standing in the middle of the kitchen, sweat drenching his stained white T-shirt, perspiration dripping from his hair into his mouth, panting with exertion, he remembered he'd taken the phone book into the living room the night before, that he'd used it to look up Venus Milo's Escort Service. He laughed. Of all the damn escort services in the book, he'd picked that one. And why? Because he'd thought the name sounded classy. Wasn't Venus Milo some famous work of art, a statue of a woman whose main claim to fame was that she was missing both her arms? Shit, he thought now, returning to the living room. A naked woman was a naked woman. And without arms, how classy could she be?

He got down on his hands and knees and crawled through the filth on the living room floor, the palms of his hands growing wet and sticky with spilt beer and the assortment of chips and dip he'd consumed for breakfast. He stumbled onto the phone book just as he was about to give up, spotting its moist, dog-eared corner sticking out from behind the drapes, as if it had been trying to escape the debauchery. "Get out of there, you miserable piece of shit," he commanded, dragging the heavy book into his lap as one hand reached for the lamp, pulling it off the table and setting it down on the floor beside him.

He recoiled from the sight that greeted him when he turned it on. "Shit," he exclaimed, then laughed triumphantly. "What a dump!" Lainey would throw a fit when she saw the mess he'd made.

"What have you done?" he could already hear her yelling. "My God, what have you done?"

"Just a little redecorating," Tom yelled at the surrounding silence. "Something I should have done years ago." He opened the phone book to the yellow pages at the back, quickly locating the pages marked ESCORT.

There were at least a dozen such pages, some with full-page ads, of listings for various escort services. I shouldn't have too much trouble finding one to suit my needs, Tom thought, assessing his situation. Word couldn't have gotten around this fast. Surely he wouldn't be blackballed by all of them.

EXECUTIVE CHOICE,
MIAMI ESCORT SERVICE.
OPEN 24 HOURS. OUTCALLS ONLY.

And then in smaller, although bolder, letters: **DINNER & BUSINESS COMPANIONS, CONFIDENTIALITY ASSURED, HIGHLY DISCREET, BEAUTIFUL LADIES.**

And then finally: *All Major Credit Cards Accepted,* followed by a phone number, a website address, and an e-mail address.

The next dozen pages were variations of the same: Cachet Ladies, one listing promised. Party girls, another proclaimed. There was a listing for Bodylicious and another for Ooh-la-la. One service specialized in college students, its full-color half-page ad complete with headshots of smiling, nubile teenagers. "That one looks good," Tom said, reaching for the phone, then stopping, flipping to the next page, noting a host of ads offering agreeable Japanese, Chinese, Korean, Filipina, Indian, Singaporean, and Thai female companions. Not that I'd know a Korean from a Japanese, he thought. Not that he cared one way or the other as long as they were as agreeable as the ads promised.

There was a photograph of one Asian lovely peeking out shyly from behind a pleated ivory fan, another of a woman gazing provocatively over the top of a pair of jeweled designer sunglasses, yet another of a smiling, dark-haired girl with a green apple in her hand.

What was that all about? Tom wondered, dismissing the last one. Who wants to fuck a girl holding an apple? An apple a day, he thought, his eyes falling on a full-page ad for a service calling itself Déjà Vu Escorts. What the hell did that mean? That you'd seen them all before?

He turned the page. There was a "Beauty at Sixty"—"You gotta be kidding me," Tom scoffed—and a "Fabulous Lady at Fifty" (another scoff) followed by Captivating Mature Companions (who the hell wanted maturity?) as well as Black & White Maid Services and Bound and Gagged (both of which he thought might be worth investigating another time), Kitchen Depot (what, did they clean up afterward?) and Your Older Slower Better Escort. "Who needs old and slow?" Tom asked out loud. There were ads for Cuban girls, Russian girls, and even "Home-grown Beauties." There was a listing for a Miss Vicki, a Mistress Letitia, and one for a Ms. Carla de Sade. There was a listing for Holly Golightly, one for Thelma and Louise, and one for, simply, Mark. "Sorry, pal. Not in this lifetime." In the end, Tom opted for Last Minute Escorts.

"This is Tanya," a tantalizingly low voice announced over the phone seconds later. "How can I be of service?"

Tom tried to think of something witty to say, but all he could think of was "You can get your ass over here and suck my dick," so instead he said, "I'd like a girl. As soon as possible."

"Certainly," Tanya said. "Do you have any particular preference?"

"You have any girls from Afghanistan?" Tom surprised himself by asking.

"Afghanistan?" Tanya repeated, her voice rising at least half an octave. "You mean, like, Arabs?"

"I guess."

"I'm afraid not," Tanya said. "We *do* have a wide variety of Asian women," she offered, as if Asians and Arabs were easy substitutes for one another.

"You have anyone from Singapore?" Tom had heard about how strict they were in Singapore, where they threw you in jail for jaywalking and doled out hundreds of lashes for just spitting on the street. Shit, hadn't they almost executed some poor American kid for scribbling harmless graffiti on a wall? You had to figure their women would be pretty submissive.

"I believe we do." The sound of keys tapping on a computer. "I can offer you a lovely young lady named Cinnamon. She's twenty-five, five feet two inches tall, and has a twenty-two-inch waist."

"Bust size?"

"Double D."

"Natural?"

"Is that a joke?" Tanya asked.

"Okay. Fine. She sounds great."

"I'll need your name and credit card."

Tom was about to fish into his pocket for his card when he stopped, not wishing for a repeat of what had happened with Chloe. "Can you hold on a minute?"

"Sure."

This was gonna be good, he thought, reaching into his other pocket but coming up empty-handed. "Damn." Where had he put it? "Can you give me another second?"

"Take your time."

Tom raced up the stairs, past the empty bedrooms of his children, and into the maelstrom that was the master bedroom. The *master* bedroom, he repeated silently, turning on the overhead light and pulling at the crumpled white sheets of his bed, trying to ignore the large bloodstain in the middle. Stupid bitch had bled all over his nice white sheets, and *she* had the nerve to complain. He should sue that stupid Venus Milo, he thought, locating his red and black checkered shirt on the floor by the foot of the bed and finding what he was looking for in the shirt's front pocket.

He was chuckling as he returned to the phone in the living room. "Okay, Tanya baby. I'm back. You ready?"

"Name?" Tanya asked in return.

"Carter," Tom said, suppressing a chuckle. "Carter Sorenson." He recited the numbers off the front of the credit card he'd stolen from Carter's wallet a few days earlier. The imbecile hadn't even realized it was missing, or if he had, he still hadn't reported it to the credit card company. Tom knew this because after Carter fired him, he'd gone to Macy's and charged several shirts and a new pair of boots to Carter's account. Then he'd gone to the grocery store and bought half a dozen cartons of cigarettes and an equal number of cases of beer.

Clothes he shouldn't be wearing, cigarettes he shouldn't be smoking, beer he shouldn't be drinking, shady ladies he shouldn't be frequenting–that Carter is quite the dude, Tom thought, and laughed out loud. "Shame on you, Carter baby."

"I'm sorry. Did you say something?" Tanya asked.

"Is there a problem?" Tom asked in return, holding his breath. Was the word out? Was what had happened with Ginny already making the rounds of the escort services of greater Miami? Had she reported him to the police? Had Carter?

"No problem at all," Tanya said, quickly explaining the terms of the contract and ascertaining Tom's exact address. "Cinnamon can be there in half an hour."

"Great."

"Thank you for your business, and please call us again."

"Will do." Tom hung up the phone, then laughed again. "Or Will *don't,* as the case may be." He pictured Jeff's younger brother, the look on his face when Tom had pointed out the obvious truth about Jeff's whereabouts, the way Will had tucked his tail between his legs and run when confronted with the cold, hard fact that Jeff was getting it on with little brother's girl. "Hah!" Tom exclaimed triumphantly, wondering where the hell Jeff was now, why he hadn't heard from him.

He'd tried to call him after his dismissal, but Jeff hadn't picked up his cell. Nor had he returned the message he'd left him. No doubt Jeff was holed up somewhere with the Pomegranate, fucking both their brains out, Tom thought, lighting another cigarette as he headed back upstairs. Might as well take a shower, he decided, noting more blood on the white towels by the sink. "Great," he muttered, grabbing a couple of clean towels from the linen closet. The bitch had made one hell of a mess.

He stared into the mirror over the bathroom sink, looking past his own reflection to see Ginny walking through the front door into the foyer, round face, curly blond hair, bright red lips. He watched her discard her sweater to reveal those huge, balloon-like breasts. He remembered thinking she could give Kristin a run for her money as he directed her up the stairs to his room, his hands already sneaking underneath her short skirt. "A hundred for a hand job, one fifty for a blow job," she'd recited, as if reading from a menu, "two hundred if you want to come in my mouth. Three hundred for a straight fuck, five if you want to do anything fancy. I don't do golden showers and I don't do Greek."

"You got something against Greeks?" Tom joked.

"I like Greeks. I'm just not into pain," Ginny said.

"How about I tie you up?"

"No handcuffs," she said. "Nothing I can't get out of easily."

"How much?"

"Five hundred."

"Okay."

"In cash. In advance."

Tom shrugged, pulled five crisp one-hundred-dollar bills out of his back pocket. He'd been stealing a little bit of cash from his co-workers' purses for months now. Twenty dollars here, another twenty there. Fifty from that twat Angela just the other day. Taking them to the bank, converting them into nice new hundreds. Five'll get you ten that Angela's the one whose complaints got me fired, he bet himself, watching as Ginny took off the rest of her clothes. She had a good body, he thought. Not as great as Kristin's, but a hell of a lot better than Lainey's. That stupid bitch, he thought, securing Ginny's wrists to the bedposts with pillowcases and then climbing on top of her.

"Hey, easy there," Ginny cautioned him as Tom pushed his way inside her, his hands kneading her breasts as if they were made of clay. "Careful, buddy," she said. "Keep squeezing them like that, they're liable to burst."

"I think you should be quiet now," Tom told her. He'd had enough of her instructions, her lists of don'ts. He continued to pound his way inside her, pretending she was Kristin, then Suzy, then Angela, then Lainey, then that little tease in Afghanistan, every bitch who'd ever said no, every bitch who'd ever complained.

"And I think you should go a little easier."

"I'm not paying you to think." Tom began pounding harder, biting her ear as his fingers scratched at her flesh.

"Okay, stop," Ginny said, her eyes filling with angry tears.

"Sweetheart, I'm just getting started."

"No. I told you, I don't do pain. We're finished here." She struggled to loosen the ties at her wrists, whimpering as she squirmed to get out from under him.

"I say when we're finished," Tom said, really starting to enjoy himself now. What was it with women anyway? They were always leading you on, taking your money, and then leaving you high and dry. He'd been discharged from the army, been fired from his job, was about to be thrown out of his house, all because of some bitch. "Tell me you love me," he directed Ginny.

"What?"

"You want me to go easy, tell me you love me."

"I love you," Ginny responded immediately, her eyes saying the exact opposite.

"Not good enough. You gotta make me believe it."

"I love you," Ginny said again.

"You can do better than that. Again."

"I love you," she shouted.

"I'm just not feeling it, sweetheart. Again."

"No."

"I said, again."

"And I said, no!"

Which was when he lost it. The rest was a blur of fists and fury. Tom couldn't remember the number of times he'd hit her, although he could still see the blood gushing from her nose and the bite marks spreading across her neck and chest. Ginny finally managed to free her hands and staggered toward the bathroom, her nose bleeding profusely as she gathered up her clothes. "Can't say I didn't get my money's worth," he shouted after her as she ran down the stairs and out onto the street.

Tom smiled at his reflection in the bathroom mirror, recalling Jack Nicholson's famous remark about hookers. At least he thought it was Jack Nicholson. Maybe it was Charlie Sheen. "I don't pay them to come over," he'd told an interviewer who'd questioned the actor's occasional preference for call girls. "I pay them to leave."

"That's a good one," he said, chuckling. The doorbell rang. Tom checked his watch. "Well, isn't that nice? My little Cinnamon bun is early. Nice and eager, are you, sweetheart?" he asked, bouncing down the steps and opening the front door.

A young man in a beige suit stood smiling on the other side. "Tom Whitman?"

"Yes."

The man thrust an envelope into his hands. "You've been served," he said before making a hasty retreat.

"Again? Are you fucking kidding me?" Tom called after him. "What the hell is it this time?" He tore open the letter, read it quickly, then threw it to the floor. So the bitch was serving him with divorce papers after all, he thought, slamming the front door shut, then kicking at it with his heel. Several minutes later, he was back in the living room, his two .44 Magnums and his old Glock .23 on the coffee table in front of him. "Don't think I'm gonna let that happen, sweetheart," he said, lifting one of the .44s into his hand and steadying it with the other. "Not in this lifetime, anyway." He pictured Lainey cowering in front of him, her shaking hands trying to cover her face. Then he aimed the gun directly at her head and pulled the trigger.

TWENTY-NINE

SHE WAS WAITING FOR him at the airport.

At first, Jeff didn't see her, so engrossed was he in trying to get ahold of Tom. But Tom's line was busy, even after three attempts. Who the hell is he talking to? Jeff wondered impatiently as he strode purposefully along the moving sidewalk at the busy Miami airport. Aside from Jeff, Tom didn't really have any friends, and now that Lainey had left him . . . Jeff hoped Tom wasn't badgering Lainey, that he knew when to leave bad enough alone. "Excuse me. Coming through," he barked at a plump, middle-aged woman who was hogging the left side, despite instructions in both English and Spanish that said those who chose not to walk should stick to the right. The woman exhaled a notable sigh as she shifted slowly to the other side of the walkway, as if Jeff was inconveniencing her and not the other way around, although her scowl turned to a flirtatious half smile as soon as she saw him. Jeff passed her without expression, hurrying toward the exit.

"Jeff," a voice called after him, stopping him dead in his tracks.

He spun around, his eyes searching through the colorfully dressed crowd. He saw a couple of teenage boys laughing and punching each other on the arms in greeting, a young woman arguing in Spanish with an older, gray-haired man Jeff assumed was her grandfather, and another young woman with blond hair and way too much makeup smiling and waving in his direction. He took a few steps toward her, trying to figure out who she was and what she wanted, when the voice reached him again.

"Jeff." It summoned him from somewhere to his right.

Still he didn't see her. Was he hearing things, imagining the sound of her voice?

"Jeff," she said a third time, this time so close he felt her breath on the side of his face, the touch of her hand on his arm.

"Suzy," he said, not quite believing his eyes as he drew her into his arms. He held her tight, feeling her frail body melt into his. "I can't believe you're here," he said, as if trying to convince himself that what he was seeing was real.

"You told me you were coming back this afternoon. There was only one flight from Buffalo. It wasn't very hard to figure out—"

He kissed her. The kiss was soft and tender. Her mouth tasted of toothpaste and Juicy Fruit gum. Her hair smelled like a bouquet of fresh gardenias. "I'm so glad to see you." He loosened his grip only enough to be able to take her all in. She was wearing a yellow blouse and light green pants. Her hair hung in loose brown waves around her shoulders. "Are you all right?"

"I'm fine," she said, although she didn't look fine, Jeff realized. Something was off. Even though it didn't appear as if there were any new bruises scarring her pale skin, she seemed even more fragile, more frightened than usual. "I did it," she said, her voice a girlish whisper. She glanced over her shoulder, squeezed his fingers. "I left him."

Jeff kissed her again, this time harder, longer. His heart was beating faster than he could ever remember.

"I really did it," she said, laughing now.

"You really did it," he repeated, his mind racing as rapidly as his heart, wondering what the hell he should do now.

"If you don't mind," a woman said, maneuvering past them. "You're right in everybody's way."

"Get a room," a man suggested, brusquely brushing past.

"Good idea." Jeff took Suzy's arm. "Where's your car?"

"I don't have it. Dave took my keys when he left for work, said I wouldn't be needing them." She laughed. "Guess he was right."

Jeff hugged her close to his side as he led her toward the exit marked TAXIS AND LIMOUSINES.

"Where to?" the driver asked as they crawled into the back of the cab.

"Do you know a good motel in the area?" he asked. "Something nice and quiet."

"Nothing's going to be very quiet this close to the airport," the cabbie said.

"Not too busy," Jeff clarified, feeling the weight of Suzy's hand in his.

The driver's eyes narrowed in his rearview mirror. "I have no idea how busy these places get."

"Fine. It doesn't matter. Wherever."

"There's a bunch of motels a few blocks from here. Can't vouch for how nice they are."

"I'm sure they're fine," Jeff said. It was only temporary, he was thinking, until he could solidify the plan that had been taking shape in his mind since he'd boarded the plane from Buffalo and then put that plan into action. With any luck, everything could be settled as early as tonight.

Of course, everything depended on his reaching Tom.

"Did you see your mother?" Suzy was asking.

"No. She died before I had the chance."

Suzy looked stricken. "Oh, Jeff. I'm so sorry."

"No big deal."

"Of course it's a big deal. It must have felt as if she was abandoning you all over again."

Jeff felt his eyes well up with tears as he buried his face in Suzy's soft, flower-scented hair. "It's like you're inside my head," he whispered.

"I hope so," she said. "You're inside mine."

The cabbie cleared his throat as he pulled up to the entrance of the Southern Comfort Motel. "Sorry to interrupt, but . . . how's this place here? Looks like the nicest one around."

"Beats the Bayshore," Jeff told him, fishing in his pocket for some cash.

"Don't know that one," the cabbie said, pocketing the money without offering to make change.

Jeff held tight to Suzy's hand as they exited the cab. Was it his imagination or had she winced when he put his arm around her waist? Approximately ten minutes later, room key in hand, they proceeded along the red-and-beige-carpeted corridor to their room at the very end of the hall.

"Make love to me," she whispered as soon as they were inside.

He didn't have to be asked twice. In the next second, his lips were back on hers, and they were pulling at each other's clothes as they fell toward the queen-size bed. He heard a voice say, "I love you," followed quickly by another voice echoing the first, their voices mingling as their bodies merged.

It wasn't until afterward, lying curled up in each other's arms, that he saw the deep welts on the side of her waist. "What's this?" he asked, gently running his fingers along the angry red lines.

"It's nothing." Suzy recoiled in pain in spite of the tenderness of his touch. "It doesn't matter now."

"It *does* matter. What in God's name did that monster do to you? Tell me," Jeff insisted. "Please, Suzy. Tell me what he did."

She nodded, closed her eyes, took a deep breath. "He heard me talking to you on the phone last night. He was so angry." She brought her hand to her head, rubbed her forehead until it grew red. "He hit me with his belt. He kept hitting me."

"That fucking piece of shit."

"He said it was just a taste of what would happen if I ever spoke to you again."

"I swear I'll break his fucking neck."

"I was up all night, planning my escape, but he stayed home this morning, so I couldn't leave right away. Luckily he had an appointment this afternoon that he couldn't miss. He ordered me not to move a muscle, said I couldn't so much as go to the bathroom until he got back. He took all my cash and my car keys, like I told you, even my ID. But I had a few dollars hidden away, and as soon as he was gone, I grabbed it and took off. I went straight to the airport. To you."

"You did exactly the right thing."

"We have to leave Miami," she said.

"What?"

"We'll go someplace where he'll never find us. New York, maybe. I've always wanted to see New York."

"Suzy . . . ," Jeff began.

"Or L.A., or maybe Chicago."

"Suzy . . ."

"It doesn't even have to be a big city. Maybe somewhere smaller, less obvious. It really doesn't matter where we go, as long as we're together, as long as we get out of Miami before he finds us."

"We can't," Jeff said simply.

"Why not? Why can't we?"

"For starters, I don't have any money."

"We don't need money. You'll find a job. Just as soon as we get settled. And I'll get one, too. You'll see. It'll all work out."

"He'd hire detectives," Jeff said. "And we can't spend the rest of our lives looking over our shoulders, afraid of our own shadows. We can't keep running away. Sooner or later, you know he'll find us."

"You're saying we're trapped." Suzy began to cry. "You're saying it's hopeless."

"It's not hopeless. Not as long as we're together. Not as long as you love me."

"I love you," Suzy said.

"Then everything's going to be okay. I promise."

"But how can you say that? He's going to find us. He's going to kill us both."

"I won't let that happen."

"How can you stop it?"

"Do you trust me?" Jeff asked.

"Yes. Of course I do."

"Then trust me when I tell you that everything's going to be okay. I won't let him hurt you ever again."

"You promise?" Suzy pleaded.

"I promise," Jeff said, kissing her eyes closed and rocking her gently in his arms until he felt her body starting to relax. After several minutes, the steady, rhythmic sound of her breathing told him she'd fallen asleep. Jeff waited a few more minutes until he was sure, then he climbed out of bed, resting Suzy's head gently on the pillow as he removed his cell phone from the pocket of his pants and carried it into the bathroom. He closed the door, punched in Tom's number. It was still busy. "Shit," he muttered. "Call me. It's important," he instructed Tom's voice mail. Then he called Kristin, exhaling a deep breath of relief when she answered the phone. "Good. I was afraid you might have left for work," he said as soon as she said hello.

"I was just walking out the door. Are you still in Buffalo?"

"No, I'm here. In Miami."

"I don't understand. Why aren't you home? Where are you?"

"Room 119 in the Southern Comfort Motel, up by the airport."

"What? Why, for God's sake?"

"I'm with Suzy."

Silence. Then, "What's happening, Jeff?"

Jeff quickly apprised her of the situation, that Suzy had been waiting for him when he'd arrived back in Miami, that Dave had beaten her again, this time with a belt, that he'd brought her to the motel to keep Dave from finding her, that she was so exhausted, she'd fallen asleep. He left out the part about him and Suzy making love, although he suspected Kristin had already drawn her own conclusions, that that was the question she'd really been asking.

"What are you going to do now?"

"I'm not sure," Jeff lied, deciding there was no reason to tell Kristin more than she needed to know. If things didn't work out the way he hoped, the less people involved, the better. "Have you seen Tom?"

"Not for a couple of days. Why?"

"I need to talk to him. His line's busy, and he isn't picking up his messages."

"He'll turn up. What is it they say about bad pennies?"

Jeff ran his hand through his hair in growing frustration. Bad pennies were exactly what he needed right now. "Is my brother there?"

"I haven't seen him all day."

"Shit. I need him to do something for me."

"You can probably reach him on his cell."

"You know the number?"

"I have it somewhere." Kristin located Will's number, then dictated it to Jeff.

"Okay, listen," he said, committing the number to memory. "I might need to reach you later. Can you tell Joe that I'll be calling and not to give me a hard time?"

"Should I be concerned?" Kristin asked.

"No," Jeff answered. "There's nothing to worry about. Everything's going to be fine."

KRISTIN HUNG UP the phone, then just stood there in her kitchen for several minutes, staring into space. She knew something was about to happen, although she wasn't sure what. But she knew Jeff well enough to know when he was planning something and that whatever it was, it was going to happen sooner rather than later, maybe even tonight.

She looked at the scrap of paper in her hand, silently reciting the number of Will's cell. What did Jeff want with his brother, and where had Will been all day? He'd already left the apartment by the time she woke up this morning.

At first she thought Will might have left for good, that he was on a jet back to Buffalo, and wondered idly whether his plane might cross with Jeff's in midair. But a quick check of the apartment revealed his suitcase and clothes were still there, so he was probably just out walking, trying to clear his head, figure things out. She felt guilty about what had happened last night, what had *almost* happened, she amended quickly, then just as quickly brushed such feelings aside. Guilt was a useless emotion, she reminded herself. It accomplished nothing and never did anyone any good. Besides, it was too late for guilt.

It was time to move on.

WILL WAS SITTING on a bench by the ocean, watching the waves rush to the shore, only to be dragged back out, then pushed forward again, over and over again. It's true what they say about the ocean making you realize how small and insignificant you really are, he thought, and then laughed, drawing the anxious glance of the elderly, white-haired gentleman sitting on the other end of the bench.

Will didn't need the ocean to make him feel small. He already understood how insignificant he was.

If Amy or Suzy hadn't already convinced him of it, then certainly Kristin had proven it to him once and for all last night.

What a useless fuckup he'd turned out to be, he thought, feeling the vibration of his cell phone in his shirt pocket. Probably his mother, he thought. One more woman to make him feel like less of a man. He extricated the phone and checked his caller ID. "Hello?" he asked when he failed to recognize the number.

"Will, hi. It's Jeff."

Will said nothing. Had Kristin already told his brother about last night?

"Will? Are you there?"

"I'm here. Where are you?"

"I'm at the Southern Comfort Motel."

"In Buffalo?"

"No. Here. In Miami. Up by the airport. Room 119."

"What the hell are you doing there? I thought you went to see your mom."

"I'm back," Jeff said, not bothering to elaborate. "Listen, I've been trying to reach Tom, but I'm not having any luck, and I can't wait any longer. So I need you to do something for me."

"What's that?" Will was in no mood to do his brother any favors. Jeff had lied to him, stolen his girl—hell, he was probably with her right now. He has some nerve, Will thought, asking me to do anything.

"I need you to go back to the apartment," he heard Jeff say.

"I'm kind of busy."

"I need you to find Tom's gun," Jeff continued as if Will hadn't spoken.

"What?"

"Then I need you to bring it here."

"What?" Will asked again.

"And I need you not to ask any questions."

TOM HAD JUST finished emptying four bullets into the plush pillows of the living room sofa when he heard a timid knock on the front door. "Who is it?" he shouted, bringing his gun into the air and pointing it at the door. If it was another process server, the poor guy was about to get it right between the eyes.

"It's Cinnamon?" a voice called back, as if she wasn't sure. "The agency sent me over?"

"Oh, my little Cinnamon bun," Tom said with a smile, tucking the gun into his belt buckle and tripping over the phone on the floor, then stopping to replace the receiver he hadn't realized was off the hook. "You're late," he said, opening the door and ushering the pretty young Asian woman inside, quickly assessing her long black hair and dark green eyes. She was short, not much over five feet, even in three-inch heels, and her implants were so large she looked in danger of toppling over.

"Sorry. It took me longer to find the place than I thought." Cinnamon surveyed the mess that was the living room, now coated with feathers and stray pieces of upholstery. "Wow," she said, eyes widening. "What happened in here?" She sniffed suspiciously at the air, the smell of gunpowder wafting by on particles of dust.

Tom closed the front door, returning the room to darkness. The phone started ringing. "Can you excuse me for half a minute?" Tom asked with exaggerated politeness, kicking at the debris-covered floor until he relocated the phone, then almost falling over as he bent to scoop it up.

"Who the hell have you been talking to for the last hour?" Jeff demanded before Tom could say hello. "I almost gave up–"

"Jeff, how are you, buddy?" Tom interrupted. He was in no mood to be lectured to.

"Are you drunk?"

"No more than usual." Well, maybe a little more than usual, Tom thought, wondering why Jeff sounded so angry.

"Good. We have plans. I need you to–"

"Uh, this isn't exactly a good time." Tom decided it was just like Jeff to expect him to snap to attention at the sound of his voice. Jeff might be too busy to talk when *you* needed *him*, but it was another story altogether when *he* needed *you*. Then you were expected to just drop everything and follow him wherever the hell he chose to go.

To hell and back, Tom thought bitterly, thinking of Afghanistan.

"Is that a gun?" Cinnamon asked, her voice cracking.

"What?" Even in the dark, Tom could see the terror on Cinnamon's face as she backed toward the door. "This?" He began waving it back and forth. "It's just a toy. I swear. Hey, wait a minute. Don't go."

"Who are you talking to?" Jeff demanded.

"Wait a second. Shit!" he exclaimed as Cinnamon fled the house. "Crap, man. She was hot," he whined into the phone. "You scared her away."

"Tom, listen to me," Jeff told him. "This is important. I need you to focus."

Tom plopped down on the sofa, scratched at his scalp with the barrel of his gun. "Sure. Go ahead. Looks like I'm all yours."

THIRTY

WILL WAS REMEMBERING THE first time he saw Kristin.

It had been almost three weeks since he'd arrived on his brother's doorstep, suitcase in hand, fear filling his heart, wondering how Jeff would react when he saw him. Would he be happy to see him or angry he'd come? Would he take one look at him and send him away? Would he even recognize him after all these years?

And then the door had opened, and there she stood, this blond Amazon in a short black skirt and leopard-print blouse, and she'd smiled this magnificent smile and shaken her long hair from one shoulder to the other, her luminous green eyes moving steadily across his face, casually sizing him up, her smile getting bigger as she took his hand and ushered him inside. "You're Will, aren't you?" she'd said, and his fear had instantly disappeared.

And now here he stood, outside that same door, his heart pulsing with that same fear, as he listened for sounds of her moving around inside. If I had one wish, he was thinking as he pushed open the door and stepped inside, it would be that she's already left for work. He couldn't face her. Not yet. Not after last night's debacle.

"Kristin," he called tentatively, then louder, his confidence building. "Kristin. Are you here?" He checked his watch. Six thirty-five. She was long gone, he realized, sighing audibly as he walked through the living area toward the bedroom. "Kristin?" he called again for good measure. "You here?"

The bedroom was empty, the bed neatly made, any sign of him eliminated. As if last night never happened, Will thought. As if he didn't exist.

He caught a whiff of Kristin's shampoo, and he spun around, half expecting to see her in the doorway, her hair wrapped in a fluffy white towel, her pink silk robe slipping open, affording him a tantalizing glimpse of what lay beneath. He recalled the feel of her in his arms, the welcoming softness of her skin. *No. No. I can't,* he heard her say. *I'm sorry. I just can't.*

"Okay, enough of this," Will said out loud, banishing such thoughts from his brain as he walked toward the nightstand by the side of the bed.

The gun was hidden at the back of the nightstand's top drawer, exactly where Jeff had said it would be. Will was trembling as his hand closed around the barrel, trembling even more when he lifted the small weapon into the air and turned it over in his palm. He'd never been this close to an actual gun before, other than in the movies or on TV, never touched one, certainly never held one in his hand. His mother had been adamant about not allowing even toy guns in the house.

"Ah, but boys will be boys," Will muttered now, transferring the gun from his right hand to his left and then back again. Its weight surprised him. As did the unexpected feeling of power he felt surging through his body. He caught sight of his reflection in the mirror over the dresser and blushed at the look of excitement he recognized on his face. What the hell does Jeff want with a gun? he wondered, although he already knew the answer.

Jeff was going to use the gun to kill Dave.

And he expected Will to be his accomplice.

No, not his accomplice, Will thought, amending his choice of words. As far as Jeff was concerned, his little brother was no more than a delivery boy. Right, that's all I'm good for, he thought. A gofer. An errand boy. One who aids and abets without ever actually having to do any of the dirty work.

A thinker, not a doer.

Will's fingers curled around the handle of the gun, his index finger stretching for the trigger. No wonder Kristin had turned him down. No wonder Suzy had chosen his brother over him. No wonder Amy had looked elsewhere. "You're sensitive," his mother had once told him. "That's a good thing. Women respect that."

Will laughed. Women might respect a sensitive man, he decided, but they slept with his brother.

And now his brother was planning to kill Suzy's husband.

Could he let that happen? Could he play any part in it at all?

Will knew that Jeff was a decorated, highly trained soldier who wouldn't be squeamish about firing a gun. Who knew how many men he'd killed in Afghanistan? And Dave Bigelow was a bastard who probably deserved to die. The world would likely be a better place without him.

And yet, he was still a human being. A respected physician whose talent had undoubtedly helped save many lives. Who was Jeff to decide Dave Bigelow had forfeited his right to live? Was this really his decision to make? Jeff might be angry; he might be misguided; hell, he might even be in love. But was he a murderer? Would he actually be able to kill a man in cold blood?

Especially for a woman he'd known less than a week.

Maybe Jeff just wanted the gun for protection, Will tried telling himself. Dave was one scary guy after all. He'd made threats. He'd even put the moves on Kristin. There was no telling what he was capable of doing, especially if Suzy were to leave him. He might come after Jeff, come after all of them, with a gun of his own. So maybe Jeff was just being cautious.

Who was he kidding? Jeff had never been cautious a day in his life.

And now Jeff was planning to kill Dave in order to be with Suzy.

How had this happened?

What did they know about Suzy anyway? That she was from Fort Myers? That she lived in Coral Gables? That she liked pomegranate martinis?

Was it possible she'd set this whole thing up, playing one brother against the other, one friend against the next, that she'd been using all of them to get what she wanted—to rid herself of an abusive husband once and for all? And once that mission was accomplished and Dave Bigelow was dead, would she disappear in a magical puff of smoke, leaving them behind to deal with the all-too-real fallout? Would she care if Jeff were caught and sent to prison for the rest of his life? Would she even visit? Did she have any feelings for Jeff at all?

Will decided he couldn't let his brother take that chance. Yes, he'd go to the motel, but only to try to talk some sense into Jeff. He'd leave the gun behind. Jeff would be furious at first, Will knew, but sooner or later he'd calm down, eventually maybe even thank him.

Will felt beads of perspiration stringing their way across his forehead, and he marched into the bathroom, balancing the gun on the side of the sink as he splashed cold water on his face. It was then he realized he was no longer alone, that someone else had entered the apartment. "Hello?" he called, hiding the gun in the back of the cabinet under the sink behind a stack of peach-colored towels, then walking into the living room.

Tom was standing in front of the sofa, wearing a stained checkered shirt over torn skinny jeans, his dark hair uncombed and greasy, one arm crossed over the other, a stupid, shit-eating grin on his face. He literally reeked of beer and cigarettes.

Will felt his heart rate quicken. "Your mother never tell you to knock?"

"Your mother never tell you to close the door?" Tom countered.

"Jeff isn't here."

"I know that, dipshit. Who do you think asked me to come over?"

"Jeff asked you to come over?" Why the hell would he do that? Had Jeff not trusted him to come through for him? Did the brother he barely knew know him better than he knew himself?

"Apparently he called you when he couldn't get ahold of me," Tom said, not even trying to mask the drunken smugness in his voice. "It appears you're no longer necessary, little brother. I'm to tell you your services are no longer required."

"What are you talking about?"

"I can handle things from here on out."

"I don't think so."

"Look, I'm not gonna argue with you. This is coming from big brother himself. He doesn't want you involved, told me to tell you you're a philosopher, not a fighter."

A thinker, not a doer, Will thought. Hamlet, not Hercules.

Not even the delivery boy.

"So, if you don't mind, since I was nice enough to drive out here, I'll just grab my gun and be on my way."

"It's not here," Will said, praying the look on his face didn't betray the lie on his lips.

"What are you talking about? Of course it's here."

"It isn't. I already looked."

"Then you didn't look very carefully." Tom pushed past Will into the bedroom. "There's only so many hiding places."

"I'm telling you it's not here," Will reiterated as Tom headed straight for the end table beside the bed as if directed there by radar. He pulled out its top drawer, tossing it on the bedspread and quickly rummaging through it. "Maybe Kristin threw it out," he offered as Tom upended the drawer in frustration.

"She wouldn't do that."

"It was kind of freaking her out, having a gun in the apartment."

"Kristin doesn't freak out," Tom said, turning his attention to the dresser.

"Well, then, maybe she gave it to Lainey," Will improvised, instantly regretting mentioning her name.

"What are you talking about?"

Will took a step back, as if Tom had physically pushed him. "Nothing. I was just–"

"When would she have given it to Lainey?"

"When she was here the other day." Will tried to smile, managed only a sickly little half grin. "Nobody told you?"

"No. Nobody told me. What was she doing here?"

"She came to see Jeff."

"Why would she want to see Jeff?"

"How should I know?"

"You're full of shit," Tom said with an angry shake of his head. "Had me going there for a bit though, asshole." He began emptying the dresser drawers, discarding their contents on the floor. "Damn gun's got to be here somewhere," he insisted, dropping to the floor and peering under the bed.

"It isn't," Will said, relieved Tom seemed to have moved on. "I told you I looked everywhere."

"Shit." Tom staggered back to his feet, returned to the living room.

"So, what now?" Will asked. "Do we call Jeff, tell him there's been a change of plans?"

"Who said anything about a change of plans?" Tom sneered. "Tom never goes anywhere empty-handed."

"Meaning?"

Tom pulled up his shirt, proudly displaying the Glock .23 tucked into his belt buckle. "Got the others waiting in the car, all loaded and ready for action."

"You're one sick fuck."

"I'll take that as a compliment, coming from you."

"Shit. No wonder Lainey left you." The words were out of Will's mouth before he could stop them.

Tom's eyes narrowed. "What'd you say?" He took several steps toward Will. "What'd you fucking say?"

"Forget it."

"The hell I'm gonna forget it. First you make up this shit about Lainey coming to see Jeff. Now you're saying she was right to leave me?"

"I'm just saying you probably scared the shit out of her."

"Damn right I scared the shit out of her. Damn cunt deserved to have the shit scared out of her. And she's not going anywhere, I can promise you that."

"'Cause she's your wife, right?" Will said, trying to keep Tom talking, to keep him from leaving, from delivering those guns to Jeff.

"Till death do us part," Tom said.

"So you've got a right to scare the shit out of her."

"I've got a right to do whatever the hell I want with her."

"Like beat her up if she doesn't listen?"

"If the mood strikes me," Tom agreed.

"So, tell me," Will prodded. "What makes you any different than Dave?"

"What?"

"Why does Dave deserve to die and you don't?"

"What the fuck are you talking about?"

"It seems to me you're cut from the same cloth."

"Speak English, for shit's sake."

"Do you ever listen to yourself?" Will demanded. "Have you ever actually thought something through to its logical conclusion?"

"I'm thinking the logical conclusion right now would be to shoot your ass."

"I'm trying to tell you that you're about to kill a man for thinking exactly the way you do," Will argued, not sure where he was going with this but determined to keep talking. "For trying to keep his wife in line. I would have thought you'd admire someone like that."

Tom looked confused. "This is different."

"How is it different?" Will felt his mouth go dry. He was dizzy and in need of a glass of water. He couldn't keep this up indefinitely. It was only a matter of time before Tom, drunk and stoned and stupid though he was, tired of all this sophomoric sophistry and left the premises. Still, it was crucial to keep him here, keep him away from Jeff. If Will could succeed in keeping them apart, at least for tonight, then maybe he could avert the tragedy he felt certain was coming.

"It's different because it is."

"Because Jeff says so?"

"Because it *is* so."

"You're gonna help my brother kill a man because Jeff has the hots for his wife," Will stated more than asked.

"Sure." Tom shrugged. "Why not?"

"Oh, I don't know. Because it's immoral? Because it's illegal? Because it's stupid, and you're gonna get caught?"

"We're not gonna get caught."

"Spoken like a true convict. Tell me, Tom, what are you getting out of this?"

"What do you mean?"

"Well, clearly, Jeff gets the girl. But what do you get? Is he paying you?"

Tom looked genuinely offended. "Of course not."

"So he gets the girl, and you get satisfaction for a job well done?"

"I guess."

"Provided, of course, you don't end up on death row."

"That's not gonna happen."

"Why? 'Cause you never screwed up before?"

"Jeff doesn't screw up."

"No, but you do. Or are you forgetting about what happened in Afghanistan?"

"What do you know about that?"

"I know you screwed up," Will said, sensing he was once again on dangerous ground but unable to take a step back. "I know Jeff came home with a medal, and you got turfed out on your ass."

"Guess that's just the way it goes," Tom said, his eyes narrowing again, turning mean. "Jeff always comes out smelling like a rose. He always wins. You oughtta know that better than anyone, little brother. He stole Suzy Pomegranate right out from under you. Oh, wait. She was never actually under you, was she? Jeff told me you have a bit of a problem in that department."

"Go to hell." What exactly had Jeff told this cretin? *Jeff isn't exactly Mr. Discreet,* he heard Kristin say.

"What was her name again? The one who got you thrown out of Princeton?"

"Okay, that's enough." Surely his brother hadn't told Tom about Amy.

"Abigail? Annie? Oh, I know. Amy!"

He should have known better than to confide in his brother.

"You can bet Jeff wouldn't have let somebody else walk off with his girl," Tom taunted. "He'd have fucked her front, back, and sideways, and trust me, when Jeff fucks a girl, she stays fucked."

"Like Lainey?" Will said, striking back without thinking.

"What?"

"Did Jeff fuck your wife front, back, and sideways? Did she stay fucked?"

"What are you talking about?"

"I'm talking about Jeff and Lainey," Will shouted, the words pouring from his mouth like water from a busted tap. He wanted to stop them but he couldn't. They just kept coming. "What's the matter, Tom? You had no idea your best friend was screwing your wife?"

"You lying piece of shit."

"You asked what she was doing here the other day. What do you think she was doing here?"

The words hit Tom right between the eyes and he spun around, almost as if he'd been shot, before bursting into tears and collapsing to the floor.

Will stared at the crumpled heap in front of him, knowing this time he'd gone too far. "Go home, Tom," he said, his head pounding. "You look exhausted. Get some sleep. You're right. I'm full of shit. There's nothing going on with Lainey and Jeff. I made it up. I swear. . . ."

But Tom was already clambering to his feet and vaulting toward the door, his gun out and in his hand. “Son of a bitch,” he was crying. “I’ll kill you, you miserable son of a bitch.”

“Tom, put the gun away,” Will yelled after him.

Tom stopped abruptly. Then he turned and pointed the Glock .23 directly at Will’s head. “Stay right where you are, little brother,” he said. “You aren’t invited to this party.”

Then he was gone.

THIRTY-ONE

"WILL, CALM DOWN," KRISTIN was saying. "I can't make out a thing you're saying." She cast a wary glance at her boss, who was monitoring her conversation from down the hall and was noticeably unhappy with all the "emergency" calls she'd been receiving tonight. First, Jeff had phoned with an update–Suzy was still sleeping; everything was under control; he'd managed to get ahold of Tom. Now Will was on the line, babbling incoherently about Tom and Lainey and God only knew what else. "Will," she said again. "You have to slow down, tell me exactly what happened." She listened incredulously as Will repeated the particulars of his altercation with Tom. Shit, she thought, leaning her forehead against the wall, feeling it cool against her skin. Trust men to make everything so bloody complicated. "No. Don't call the police," she whispered, covering her mouth with her hand so that her boss wouldn't hear. "You'll only get Jeff in trouble. I'll call him and tell him what happened. He knows how to handle Tom. No. Stay where you are. Don't do anything. Please, let me deal with this. Okay? Promise me you'll stay put."

Kristin hung up the phone, then turned to smile sweetly at her boss. "Just one more call, Joe. Then I'm done." She stopped short of promising, leaving the broken promises to the men of this world. Men like Will, who promised he'd stay put when they both knew he wouldn't. Men like Jeff, who promised everything was under control when it was anything but. Men like Norman, who'd promised she'd like the taste of his huge, unwieldy tongue inside her small, vulnerable mouth. Men like Ron, who'd told her she'd enjoy it as he tore away her virginity. So much for promises, Kristin thought, pulling a crumpled business card out of her bra and checking the number. Good thing she hadn't thrown it away, she decided as she stabbed at the numbers with her long burgundy fingernails.

The phone was picked up in the middle of the first ring. "This is Dr. Bigelow," the voice barked, impatient already.

"Dave?" Kristin asked, surprised by the quiver in her voice. Can I really do this? she was thinking.

"Who is this?"

"It's Kristin, the bartender from the Wild Zone."

"Is my wife there?" Dave asked without further preamble, clearly not in the mood for games.

"No." Kristin took a deep breath, steadying herself against the wall with the palm of her hand. "But I know where she is."

Silence.

"She's at the Southern Comfort Motel, up by the airport," Kristin continued unprompted, her voice gaining strength as the words tumbled from her mouth. "Room 119."

. . .

WILL STOOD IN the middle of the living room, not moving, Kristin's heartfelt pleas ringing in his ear. *Stay where you are. Don't do anything. Promise me you'll stay put.*

Except how could he just stay in the apartment and do nothing? His careless lies had put a match to Tom's notoriously short fuse, and now Tom was on his way to the motel, not to help Jeff with his plan but to carry out a murderous plan of his own. So how could he just stay there and do nothing?

Again Will thought of notifying the police, but Kristin had warned him that calling them would only get Jeff in more trouble, and she was probably right, as she was right about most things. His brother was in enough trouble, thanks to him. He thought of phoning Jeff to warn him about Tom, but how could he ever explain the awful things he'd said, the lies he'd told? No, it was better to let Kristin deal with everything.

Still, he couldn't just stand there. He couldn't let his brother pay—yet again—for his thoughtless acts. For once in his life, he had to stop thinking and *do something.*

"I'm sorry, Kristin," Will said as he ran into the bathroom to retrieve Tom's .22. Stuffing it into the pocket of his khaki pants, he fled the apartment, taking the outside steps to the courtyard two at a time.

Five minutes later, he was in a cab, heading for the Southern Comfort Motel.

"SUZY, HONEY," JEFF whispered, leaning forward on the bed to kiss her cheek. He hated to disturb her. She'd been sleeping so peacefully.

Suzy opened her eyes, as blue as the Intracoastal Waterway. "Hi, you," she said.

"Sorry to wake you."

"That's okay. What time is it?"

"After seven."

"Oh, my God." She pushed herself into a sitting position. "I can't believe I passed out like that."

"You've been through a lot. You were exhausted."

"I guess. Has anything happened?"

"No. Nothing. Everything's fine. You hungry?"

Suzy laughed. "Starved."

"Good," Jeff said. "There's something I need you to do."

TOM WAS STUCK in traffic only minutes away from the airport. "Let's get a move on, people," he shouted out his open window, the hot, humid air slapping against his face in reply. "What the hell . . . ?" He opened the car door and stepped onto the pavement, trying to see around the huge eighteen-wheeler directly in front of him. How had he gotten stuck behind this damn truck anyway? More important, how long was he going to be here? Time is a-wasting, he thought. He was already late, having spent far too long arguing with Will. Jeff wasn't going to be happy.

Shit, Tom decided with a laugh. Jeff wasn't going to be happy no matter what.

Maybe he wouldn't go. Let Jeff deal with everything all by his lonesome. Make him understand what it felt like to be betrayed, make him realize how much he needed Tom, how much he'd always needed him. "I'm not the fuckup in this equation," Tom growled, catching sight of the flashing lights of an ambulance up ahead.

Looks like a pretty bad accident, he thought, hoping whoever had caused it had died in the crash. He returned to his car, lit another cigarette, and turned the radio up to its full volume, listening to some country singer whining in an impossibly high register about her cheating boyfriend, all the while picturing Lainey having sex with his best friend. "That lying bitch," he cursed. Telling him she'd never understood why women found Jeff so attractive, that she'd never found him particularly appealing herself. While all the time she'd been screwing him behind his back. Tom slammed his fist against the steering wheel, wondering how long their affair had been going on, how long his best friend had been laughing at him behind his back. "Let's move it, motherfuckers."

As if scared into action, the long line of cars and trucks began to move, gradually picking up speed as they drove past two badly mangled cars at the side of the road, a uniformed police officer taking statements from several of the people involved. "Learn to drive, assholes," Tom called out when he was safely out of hearing range.

He transferred into the right lane, took the first exit, then spent the next ten minutes driving around in circles, trying to locate the Southern Comfort Motel. "Couldn't stay at a Holiday Inn," he muttered. "Had to stay at some stupid little place nobody's ever heard of."

You should get one of those GPS thingies, like I have, Lainey had once suggested. *I use mine all the time.*

"Of course you use it," Tom said now. "You couldn't find your ass with both hands."

Although she'd known how to find Jeff easily enough.

"Where the hell are you?" Tom shouted as, overhead, a plane flew in low for a landing. And then he saw it, the glow of a neon sign halfway down the next block, to his left. SOUTHERN COMFORT MOTEL, the sign announced, a smaller sign flashing VACANCY directly below.

"No, thank you," Tom said, glancing lovingly at the guns on the seat beside him as he guided his car into the left lane. "I already have a room."

JEFF WAS SITTING in the brown upholstered chair across from the bed when he heard a car pull up outside the door. "Finally," he said, releasing the air in his lungs and wondering how long he'd been holding his breath. What the hell had taken Tom so long to get here? He walked to the door, catching sight of his reflection in the bathroom mirror. He looked scared, he realized, wondering—not for the first time—whether he could actually go through with his plan. Could he really gun down a man in cold blood?

More important, could he get away with it?

Yes, to both questions, Jeff assured himself. And now that Tom was finally here, everything could proceed according to plan.

Jeff pulled open the door. "About time you got here," he said.

He didn't even feel the punch until he was on the floor, didn't know what hit him until he saw Dave's fist coming at him again. "Where is she, you son of a bitch?" Dave was hollering, his knees straddling Jeff's chest. "Suzy, get out here, unless you want to see your boyfriend beaten to a bloody pulp."

"She's not here," Jeff sputtered, trying to regain his equilibrium. What the hell had happened? Where was Tom?

"The hell she isn't. Suzy, I'm warning you. Don't make me come looking for you."

"I'm telling you," Jeff cried. "She isn't here."

"You're lying."

Jeff couldn't remember the last time he'd been sucker-punched, and he fought to clear his head as the room gradually came back into focus, although it continued to spin. It isn't supposed to be going down like this, he was thinking. What the hell was happening?

Dragging Jeff by the throat, Dave lifted the bedspread and peered under the bed. "Where the hell is she?"

"I have no idea."

"You might want to rethink that answer." Dave hit him again, this time a powerful blow to the stomach that left Jeff gasping for air. "Now where is she? And please don't tell me you don't know. I'm a doctor, remember? I know just where to make it hurt." He dug his fingers between two of Jeff's ribs to illustrate his point.

"She left. About half an hour ago."

"Where'd she go?"

"I don't know." Jeff screamed in pain as Dave Bigelow's fingers dug deeper into his flesh. "She said she couldn't go through with it, said she was going back home."

"How convenient," Dave said. "Why is it I don't believe you?" Once again, his clenched fist connected with Jeff's jaw. "Now I'm going to count to three," he continued, as behind him the motel door swung quietly open, "and then I'm going to start breaking every bone in your body."

Jeff's head was spinning as he felt his jawbone shatter. His vision blurred; unconsciousness threatened. Where the hell is Tom? he wondered as darkness began filling the room a slow step at a time, the shadow moving ever closer.

"One . . . two . . ."

A shot rang out.

Dave's back arched, his shoulders stiffening, his eyes widening in a combination of shock and disbelief, then clouding over, freezing in place as he lurched forward, then crumpled like a rag doll on top of Jeff.

"Three," a voice said from the shadows.

It took all Jeff's strength to push Dave off his chest. He knew Dave was dead even before he saw the blood seeping into the front of his shirt, creating a widening circle around his heart. Jeff's eyes shot toward the figure standing in the doorway as he leaned his back against the bed and fought to catch his breath. "Tom! Jesus. What happened? Where the hell have you been?"

"You complaining?" Tom kicked the door closed behind him with the heel of his black leather boot.

"Shit, man, no way."

"Where's Suzy?"

"I sent her out for something to eat, told her to take her time, that I had a few things to take care of and I'd meet her back here in a couple of hours. I wanted her to have an alibi. She has no idea what's going down."

"Ever the gentleman."

Jeff thought he detected a note of sarcasm in Tom's voice but dismissed it as just a ringing in his ears.

"So what happens now?" Tom asked.

Jeff took several deep breaths before responding. It hurt to talk. His head was pounding, his jaw throbbing. He needed to think things through very carefully. The original plan had been to lure Dave to the motel by telling him that Suzy was there, something Kristin had pulled off with her usual skill and aplomb. Except instead of Suzy, Dave would find Jeff and Tom waiting when he arrived. They'd then force him to drive to the Everglades, where they'd shoot him and dump his body in some alligator-riddled swamp. But Dave had shown up early and Tom late, which had thrown everything off-kilter. "Everything's changed," Jeff said out loud, each word sending fresh spasms through his jaw.

"Meaning?"

"Well, for starters, we no longer have to dispose of Dave's body."

"How do you figure?"

"It was obviously self-defense."

"You didn't kill the prick," Tom reminded Jeff. "I did."

"It's still a legitimate defense. You killed him to save me."

"Except the bastard doesn't have a gun," Tom said, frisking Dave to make sure. "Police are gonna say I used undue force."

"You've been watching too much television," Jeff said, the words sliding from his drooping mouth.

"Don't have a TV anymore, remember? I shot it."

"But you have more than one gun," Jeff reminded him, "and none of them is registered. Who's to prove one of those guns didn't belong to Dave? That he didn't come here to kill me?"

Tom sneered. It was just like Jeff to make everything all about him. Jeff's problem had been taken care of after all, felled by a bullet from Tom's .23. And now Tom was expected to deal with the repercussions while Jeff rode off into the sunset with the girl of his dreams.

No way, Tom thought. Not this time.

"Besides," Jeff was saying, "I'm sure someone heard that gun go off. We can't just go sneaking out of here with a body. Odds are people are watching, that somebody's already called the police."

Tom digested this latest bit of information, thinking Jeff was probably correct. The police were very likely on their way. Which didn't leave him much time to finish what he'd come here to do. "So, once again, you come out a winner. The once and future champion."

"Is something wrong?" Jeff asked.

"What could possibly be wrong?"

"We should call the police." Jeff reached for the phone, deciding to ignore the nasty undertone in Tom's voice. "Tell them what happened before they get here. It'll show we have nothing to hide."

"I don't know about that. I'd say you've been hiding quite a bit."

"What's that supposed to mean?" Jeff was growing impatient. What was the matter with Tom? Yes, he'd probably saved his life by showing up when he had, but his tardiness was what had put Jeff's life at risk in the first place. And now that he needed time to put his thoughts in order, to prepare his story for the police, now that everything was about to fall into place, Tom was being difficult for no reason. Clearly he was drunk. Quite possibly he was in shock. "Look. Why don't you sit down?" Jeff said, ignoring his own pain. "You just killed a man. That's never easy."

"Easier than you think," Tom replied cryptically.

"I'm gonna get you a glass of water. Then I'm going to call the police."

"You're not calling anybody." Tom raised his gun, pointed it at Jeff's head.

"What the hell are you doing?"

"What does it look like I'm doing?"

"Okay, I've had just about enough of this–"

"When have you ever had enough?" Tom demanded. "Of anything?"

"What are you talking about?"

"I'm talking about the fact it's not enough you're fucking Kristin and Suzy, and probably half the state of Florida, you gotta go after Lainey, too?"

"What? Are you crazy? You think I'm fucking your wife?"

"You're denying it?"

"Of course I'm denying it. You're my best friend. For God's sake, Tom, think about what you're saying. You know I wouldn't–"

"I know she was at your place."

Jeff frantically searched his memory for the last time Lainey had been at his apartment. "She wasn't . . . Wait a minute. Okay. Yeah. Kristin told me Lainey dropped by the other day. She wanted me to talk to you, but I wasn't home. I didn't even see her. Ask Kristin if you don't believe me. Or Will. He was there. He'll tell you."

"He already did."

"Okay, then—"

"Told me all about you and Lainey."

"What are you talking about?" Jeff asked again.

There was a loud banging on the door. "Jeff . . . Tom . . . ," Will called from the other side. "Please let me in."

"Thank God," Jeff said with relief. "There's obviously been a giant misunderstanding. . . ." He was moving to the door when he felt a sharp pain tear through his chest, followed almost immediately by another. "What the . . . ?" he started to say as a third bullet from Tom's gun burrowed deep into his flesh, spinning him around and lifting him off the floor with a dancer's languid grace. A fourth bullet sent him sprawling facedown across the bed, his mouth and nose disappearing into the folds of its rumpled white sheets. Suzy's scent immediately enveloped him, as if she were taking him in her arms.

"I love you," he heard her whisper in his ear, her words silencing all other sounds.

"I love you, too," he told her.

Jeff felt her lips soft and tender against his own.

Then he felt nothing at all.

WILL WAS STANDING outside the motel door when Tom opened it and beckoned him inside.

The first thing he saw was Dave lying facedown on the floor in a dark pool of his own blood.

The second thing he saw was Jeff stretched out across the unmade bed, his face half-buried in the sheets.

The third thing he saw was Tom, now standing in the middle of the room, a self-satisfied smirk on his stupid face, a gun at the end of his outstretched hand. "Look what you did, little brother," Tom said as police sirens swirled around them.

Will's eyes filled with bitter tears. His body swayed, his knees buckled.

"Okay. Drop your weapons," he heard a voice cry out behind him, only then becoming aware of the raised .22 in his hand. "Police. Drop your weapons," the voice repeated. "Now." The sound of car doors slamming, of rifles being readied, of footsteps edging closer.

Will's finger twitched over the trigger, his whole body aching to pull it. Could he do it? he wondered, thinking that no jury in the world would convict him for shooting the man who'd murdered his brother. Although he was guilty of a crime far bigger than that, he acknowledged silently, his shoulders slumping forward in defeat. *Look what you did, little brother,* he heard Tom repeat.

Tom was right.

It was because of him that Jeff was dead.

Will dropped the gun to the floor, raised both hands in the air in abject surrender.

"Now isn't that a surprise?" Tom said, laughing as he raised his own gun and fired the remaining bullet into Will's chest.

He was still laughing when the sound of rifle fire filled the room.

THIRTY-TWO

THE MIAMI AIRPORT WAS as busy as she'd ever seen it.

"God, where's everybody going?" Kristin asked.

"They can't all be going to Buffalo," Will said, a slow smile creeping onto his lips.

Kristin put her hand carefully through the crook of his arm, helping him maneuver his way through the crowd toward the proper gate. It's good to see Will smile again, she was thinking, however tentatively. It had been a long time since she'd seen even a flicker of a grin register on his sweet face. "How are you managing?" she asked. "Am I walking too fast?"

"No, you're fine."

Even so, she slowed her pace, listening for the soft shuffle of Will's left foot as it dragged behind his right, the result of police bullets to his knee and thigh. The bullet from Tom's gun had missed his heart by inches, knocking him to the floor and ironically saving his life when the police opened fire. Tom hadn't been so lucky. He'd died instantly in the hail of rifle shots that followed.

Will had spent the better part of four weeks in the hospital, enduring several painful operations, followed by almost two months in a convalescent home. He'd lost weight, maybe ten pounds, and his skin was still very pale, almost translucent, although the faintest of blushes had returned to his cheeks in the last week. His mother had visited often, even staying with Kristin on several occasions. His father had managed the trip down only once, too busy with his new girlfriend and the baby they were expecting early next spring. "Looks like I might be getting a little brother of my own soon," Will had confided during one of Kristin's last visits.

"I wish you were coming with me," he said now.

"I can't," Kristin said. "You know I can't."

They stopped walking.

"Why not?" Will asked, as he'd asked at least a dozen times already this morning. "There's nothing keeping you here."

"I know."

"Then come with me."

"I can't."

"My mother will be so disappointed not to see you get off that plane."

"Your mother will be thrilled. She thinks I'm a bad influence."

"Nonsense. She loves you."

Kristin resumed walking, leaving Will no choice but to follow. "She *tolerates* me," she corrected.

"And what is love if not just a higher degree of tolerance?" Will asked.

Kristin laughed, loud and long. "Careful," she warned him. "The philosopher in you is starting to show."

"Oh, no, not him again."

"We can't help being who we are, Will."

"Now who's the philosopher?"

Kristin smiled, stopped walking. "I'm going to miss you." Her hand reached up to stroke his cheek.

"You don't have to. Come with me," Will said again, grabbing her hand with his own, placing it directly over his heart. "We could start fresh. We don't have to stay in Buffalo. I don't have to go back to Princeton. I can finish my dissertation anywhere."

Kristin turned away, her eyes filling with tears. "I can't," she said again.

"Because of Jeff?"

Kristin felt her body deflate at the sound of Jeff's name, like a tire punctured by a nail. She was losing air, she thought, struggling to remain upright. It hurt to breathe. "Maybe. I don't know." Even after almost three months, it was hard to accept that Jeff was really dead. That was never supposed to have happened. Kristin shook her head, her long ponytail slapping at the sides of her neck.

"I like your hair like that," Will told her, trying to prolong their good-bye, still hoping he could find the magical combination of words that would make her change her mind and come with him. *So what would you clowns wish for if a genie offered to grant you one wish?* he heard his brother ask that fateful night in the Wild Zone. The night that had set everything in motion.

"Will?"

"Hmm? Sorry. Did you say something?"

"I said, I'm thinking of having my implants removed. Do you think I'd look all right?"

"I think you'll look great no matter what you do."

"You're so sweet."

"I'm not," Will said.

"Yeah, you are."

They approached the long lineup for security.

"Is all the hardware in your body going to set off a bunch of bells and whistles when you go through the X-rays?" Kristin asked, only half in jest.

"Probably. Maybe they won't let me leave," Will said almost hopefully. Then, "I don't have to go, you know."

"We've been through this."

"I know."

"You have to go, Will. You don't belong here."

"Do you?"

She shrugged.

"You'll call me if there are any problems?" he asked.

"There won't be."

"The police could have more questions. . . ."

"They won't."

"They won't," Will repeated.

The police investigation had concluded that Dave Bigelow had found out about his wife's affair with Jeff and had gone to the Southern Comfort Motel to confront him, and that Tom, high on dope and drunk on beer, had shown up soon after, shooting to death both Dave and Jeff. Their report further stated that Tom Whitman was already well known to the police and that he was prone to random and unprovoked acts of violence. This scenario was given further credence by the statements of Tom's estranged wife, his former boss, and a girl from an escort service whom he'd recently assaulted. Suzy Bigelow had been brought in for questioning and quickly cleared of any involvement in her husband's death.

"Have you heard from Suzy at all?" Will asked now.

Again Kristin shook her head. "She kind of dropped off the radar after the funerals."

"I guess Dave's death left her pretty well-off."

"I guess."

"Do you think she ever really loved Jeff?"

"I think she did," Kristin acknowledged sadly. "At least a little."

"May I see your ticket and boarding pass, please?" a uniformed guard demanded.

"Looks like this is where I get off," Kristin said as Will showed his ticket and boarding pass to the stern-looking woman, who examined both closely.

"There's nothing I can say . . . ?"

Kristin leaned forward and kissed Will gently on the lips. "Have a good life, Will," she said. "Be happy."

"Sir, I'm afraid I have to ask you to move along," the guard urged.

Kristin pulled back, stepped out of the way. Reluctantly Will moved forward, pushed along by those behind him. "It's not too late to change your mind," he called back, stopping abruptly, deciding to give it one last try.

Will saw her standing off to the side, leaning against a pillar. He saw the final shake of her blond hair, the blinding flash of her smile as she waved good-bye. Then he watched her disappear into the crowd.

THE SKY HAD turned cloudy by the time Kristin pulled her car to a stop in front of 121 Tallahassee Drive. The sixties music blasting from the stereo immediately fell silent.

Kristin looked toward the front door of the tan bungalow with the white slate roof and smiled. Suzy was sitting on the front steps, her tanned feet bare, her toenails painted bright pink, her sandals resting on the step beside her. Soft waves of brown hair cascaded past her shoulders, framing a face that was blissfully free of bruises. A few yards in front of her, leaning up against the prominent SOLD sign in the middle of the front lawn, was her overnight bag.

"Hey, you," Kristin said tenderly, opening the car door and climbing out as Suzy jumped to her feet.

"How'd it go?" Suzy asked, slipping quickly into her sandals.

"Pretty much like we expected."

"I'm sorry I couldn't be there with you."

"It's better that you weren't."

"Did he ask about me?"

Kristin nodded. "I lied, said you'd pretty much dropped off the face of the earth after the funerals." She reached for Suzy's overnight case, prepared to hoist it over her shoulder. "My God. This weighs a ton. What have you got in here?"

"Dave's ashes," Suzy said matter-of-factly.

"What?" The bag dropped from Kristin's hand.

"Careful. You'll break them." Suzy laughed. "And I want everything to be perfect when I feed the bastard to the alligators."

"I don't think there *are* any alligators in San Francisco."

"We'll make a slight detour," Suzy said. "Would you mind? I've been dreaming about this moment for years."

"Everglades, here we come," Kristin said, picking up the bag again and tossing it in the backseat of the car.

"How old's this car anyway?" Suzy asked, climbing into the passenger seat and once again removing her shoes. "Remind Dave to buy you a new one." She laughed again, the laugh dying in her throat when she saw the look of reproach on Kristin's face. "Sorry. I guess that wasn't very funny."

"Oh, God, Suzy," Kristin moaned. "How did everything get so screwed up?"

"Things happen," Suzy said. "Things you don't expect. Things you can't always plan for."

"The only one who was supposed to get hurt was Dave. Will wasn't supposed to get shot. Tom and Jeff weren't supposed to die."

"It's amazing, isn't it?" Suzy agreed. "You think you have everything all worked out, and then something happens, somebody says something that isn't in the original script, and it changes everything."

"Three people end up dead."

"*We're* alive. I'm finally free of that monster." Suzy took Kristin's hand in hers, brought it to her lips.

Kristin glanced quickly out the side window. "We shouldn't. Not here."

"It's okay," Suzy said. "Nobody can hurt us anymore."

"I'll never let anyone hurt you ever again," Kristin said, studying Suzy's lovely face, the blue eyes she'd first looked into as a frightened young girl of sixteen. *I can't find my wallet,* she'd said to Suzy, baiting her, during one of their early encounters. *You have something to do with that?*

Suzy is right, Kristin was thinking as she pulled the car away from the curb. Things happened that you didn't expect, that you couldn't always plan for. Who could have predicted that two lonely girls, living in a group home under the indifferent auspices of Child Services, would not only fall in love but forge a bond stronger than any relationship either would ever have again, that their love would survive separation and distance, husbands and lovers, disappointment and disillusionment, time and circumstances?

That they'd found each other again was a miracle in itself. Suzy had just moved to Coral Gables with her abusive husband. On a whim, feeling desperate and lonely, she'd looked Kristin up on the Internet and discovered she was working in South Beach at a bar called the Wild Zone. One afternoon when Dave was at the hospital, she'd stopped by, not sure Kristin would even remember who she was.

They'd recognized each other immediately, the years disappearing like fading old photographs as they brought each other up to speed, confiding the intimate, occasionally heartbreaking details of their lives since they were last together. Kristin told Suzy about Jeff; Suzy told Kristin about Dave. It wasn't very long before they came up with a plan to use one to get rid of the other.

Dave's attacks were getting worse, increasing in both frequency and ferocity. They couldn't afford to wait too long.

And then suddenly, everything had fallen into place. Will had turned up on Jeff's doorstep, bringing with him unpleasant memories, enhancing long-standing rivalries and creating new ones. Old grudges resurfaced; new alliances were forged.

Time for Suzy to make her entrance.

It had taken just a few choice words to get the ball rolling.

Then Lainey had walked out on Tom, leaving him even angrier than usual, and Ellie had called Jeff with the news of their mother's imminent death, rendering him vulnerable and confused. After that it was a question of knowing when to advance and when to fall back, of knowing what buttons to push and what strings to pull, how hard to provoke and how lightly to tread. A lethal combination of cunning and spontaneity, of feminine wiles and male willfulness, of opportunity and the luck of the draw.

Both women had played their parts beautifully. And while it had been difficult, sometimes almost impossible, for them to stay away from one another once their plan had been set in motion, they'd agreed to keep their contact to a minimum until the deed was done.

Of course, neither could have predicted the speed with which everything had progressed, how fast the stately waltz had degenerated into a spastic jive, how quickly the slow merry-go-round began spinning out of control, morphing into a wild and deadly roller-coaster ride.

And no one could have foreseen that Jeff might actually fall in love.

Kristin shivered with the memory of those agonizing moments when she feared his feelings for Suzy might actually be reciprocated, that Suzy might be falling for Jeff as hard and unexpectedly as he'd fallen for her. And maybe she *had* fallen in love with him, Kristin thought now. At least a little, as she'd said earlier to Will.

Just as Kristin had fallen at least a little in love with Will.

"You cold?" Suzy asked now, reaching out to stroke Kristin's arm.

"No, I'm fine."

And she was. Dave Bigelow was dead. The money from the sale of his house and luxury automobiles would go a long way to ensuring a comfortable future for his widow. Will was on his way back to Buffalo. Kristin had quit her job at the Wild Zone. In a matter of minutes she and Suzy would be on the highway, and after a slight detour to give Dave the send-off he well deserved, they'd be heading across the country for their new life in San Francisco.

Suzy tugged gently on Kristin's ponytail. "I love you," she said. "So much."

Kristin smiled, feeling the smile spread from the top of her head to the bottom of her feet before it settled in comfortably around her heart. "I love you, too."

This is how it ends.

POCKET
BOOKS

Joy Fielding

Still Life

Beautiful, happily married, and the owner of a successful interior design business, Casey Marshall couldn't be more content with her life. Until a car slams into her at fifty miles an hour, breaking nearly every bone in her body – and plunging her into a coma.

Lying in her hospital bed, Casey realizes that although she is unable to see or communicate, she can hear everything. As the visitors gather at her bedside, she is horrified to discover that her friends aren't necessarily the people she thought them to be – and that her accident might not have been an accident at all.

As she struggles to break free from her living death, Casey determines to find out and somehow expose the truth. Whatever it takes.

ISBN: 978-1-84739-362-3
PRICE £6.99

POCKET
BOOKS

Joy Fielding

Charley's Web

A beautiful single mother who writes a controversial column for the Palm Beach Post, Charley Webb has spent years building an emotional wall against scathing critics, snooty neighbours and her disapproving family. But when she receives a letter from Jill Rohmer, a young woman on death row for the murders of three small children, her wall slowly begins to crumble.

Jill wants Charley to write her biography so that she can share the many hidden truths that failed to surface during her trial – including the existence of a mysterious man she calls Jack. But when Charley delves into the background of this deeply troubled woman, she starts receiving anonymous letters threatening her son and daughter. Jill is safely locked away – so does this mean the elusive Jack is still out there?

As Charley races against time to save her family, she begins to understand the value of her seemingly intrusive friends and relatives. For this network of flawed but loving people might be her only hope of getting out alive.

ISBN: 978-1-84739-046-2
PRICE £6.99

POCKET
BOOKS

Joy Fielding

Heartstopper

Welcome to Torrance, Florida. Population: 4,160. A safe place where residents leave their doors unlocked and allow their children to run freely. It's here that English teacher Sandy Crosbie and her teenage children have found a refuge, following the painful and very public breakdown of her marriage.

But that was before the disappearance of popular, pretty Liana Martin. And suddenly it seems that everyone has something to hide in this seemingly quiet town with shocking depths of scandal, sex and brutality churning beneath its surface.

As Sheriff John Weber digs up more questions than answers in a dead-end investigation and the body count rises to three, one truth emerges: it's the prettiest girls who are being targeted, the heartstoppers. And Sandy Crosbie must do everything in her power to help protect her family and unmask a ruthless killer before it's too late . . .

ISBN: 978-1-84739-045-5
PRICE £6.99